Geo. Wm. Parker

# TESS OF THE
STORM COUNTRY

SHE TOSSED HER FACE UP TO THE SUN.

# TESS OF THE STORM COUNTRY

GRACE MILLER WHITE

ILLUSTRATIONS BY
HOWARD CHANDLER CHRISTY

NEW YORK
GROSSET & DUNLAP
PUBLISHERS

Copyright, 1909, by
W. J. WATT & COMPANY

WITH
LOVE AND GRATITUDE
I DEDICATE THIS BOOK TO
MY FATHER

# TESS OF THE
STORM COUNTRY

# TESS OF THE STORM COUNTRY

## CHAPTER I

ONE September afternoon, not many years ago, three men sat on the banks of Cayuga Lake cleaning the fish they had caught in their nets the previous night. When they glanced up from their work, and looked beyond the southern borders of the lake, they could see, rising from the mantle of forestry, the towers and spires of Cornell University in Ithaca City. An observer would have noticed a sullen look of hatred pass unconsciously over their faces as their eyes lighted on the distant buildings, for the citizens of Ithaca were the enemies of these squatter fishermen and thought that their presence on the outskirts of the town besmirched its fair fame. Not only did the summer cottages of the townfolk that bordered the lake, look down disdainfully upon their neighbors, the humble shanties of the squatter fishermen, but their owners did all they could to drive the fishermen out of the land. None of the squatters were allowed to have the title of the property upon which their huts stood, yet they clung with death-like tenacity to their homes, holding them through the rights of the squatter-law, which conceded them the use of the land when once they raised a hut upon it. Sterner and sterner the authorities of Ithaca had made the game laws until the fishermen, to get the food upon which they lived, dared only draw their nets by night. In the winter whilst the summer residents were to be found again in the city, Nature herself made harder the lot of these squatters, by sealing the lake with thick ice, but they faced the bitter cold and frozen surroundings with stolid indifference.

A grim silence had reigned during which the three men had worked with feverish haste, driven on by the vicissitudes of their unwholesome lives. Moving his crooked legs upon the hot sand and closing a red lid over one white blind eye, Ben Letts spoke viciously.

"Tess air that cussed," said he, "that she keeps on saying fishes can feel when they gets cut. She air worse than that too."

"And she do say," put in Jake Brewer, grasping a large pickerel and thrusting his blade into its quivering body after removing the scales, "that it hurts her insides to see the critters wriggle under the knife. She air that bad too."

Ben Letts scratched his head tentatively.

"She ain't had no bringin' up," he resumed, again plying the sharp-bladed knife to his scaly victims, "and they do say as how when she air in a tantrum she'll scratch her dad's face, jumpin' on his back like a cat. Orn air a fool, I say."

"So says I too," agreed Brewer; "no wonder his shoulders air humped. But you never hears as much as a grunt from him. He knows he ain't never give her no bringin's up, that's why."

"Some folks has give their kids bringin's up," interposed Ben Letts with a glance at the third man, who was industriously cleaning fish and had not yet spoken.

"And they hain't turned out no better than Tessibel will."

At this the industrious one turned.

"I spose ye be a hittin' at my poor Myry, Ben," he muttered. "I spose ye be, but God'll some time let me kill the man, and then ye won't be hittin' at her no more, 'cause there won't be nothin' to hit at. It air dum hard to keep a girl from the wrong way, love her all ye will."

For an instant Ben Letts dropped his head.

"We always wondered who he was, but more wonder has been goin' on why ye ain't made no offer to find the fellow."

"Ain't had no time," said the desperate cleaner of fish; "had to get bread and beans, to say nothin' of bacon."

"But why didn't ye send the brat to the workhouse?" asked Jake.

"Satisfied" Longman, as he was called, shook his head.

"I was satisfied to let it stay," was all he answered.

"My old mammy says," offered Ben Letts, "as how yer son Ezy asked Tessibel Skinner to marry him and as how she slicked him in the face with a dirty dishrag."

He slowly closed the scarlet lids over his crossed eyes, suspending the pickerel in his hand the while.

"Tess ain't had no mother," remonstrated Longman, after a long silence, pausing a moment in his bloody work and allowing his eyes to rest upon the magnificent buildings of the University, rearing above the town, "and Myry says that them what has ought to be satisfied."

Just then a shadow fell upon the shore of the lake near the fishermen.

"There air Tess now," muttered Letts and his two companions eyed a figure clad in rags, with flying copper-colored hair and bare dirty feet, which dropped down beside Longman without asking whether or no.

"Cleanin' fish?" she queried.

"Can't ye see?" growled Ben.

"'Course I can," she answered; "just wondered if ye knowed yerselves."

"Where be yer dad?" queried Longman, smiling as he caught up two long fish, depositing one beside him where it flopped helplessly about upon the hot sand.

"Gone to Ithacy," replied Tessibel, and without change of expression or color caught the floundering fish in her dirty fingers.

"I air a hittin' the little devil on the head with a stone," said she, and with a pointed rock she expertly tapped the fish three times behind the beady eyes and threw him down again motionless.

"Suppose seein' the fish wrigglin' gives Tessibel mollygrubs in her belly," grinned Jake Brewer, but Ben Letts broke in.

"How be yer toad to-day, Tessibel?"

This he said with a malevolent smile, as he took from his pocket a huge hunk of tobacco and munched a generous mouthful therefrom.

"Pretty well," answered Tess pertly, and measuring the blue water with her eye, she sent a flat stone skipping across it. Then with darkening face she wheeled about upon the heavy squatter.

"But air it any of yer business how my toad air, Ben Letts?"

"Naw," laughed Ben, nudging Jake in the ribs with his bare elbow, "only I thought as how he might be dead." Then he whispered to Brewer, "Wait till I get at him."

"Dead — dead, who said as how he air dead? Ye ain't been a rubberin' in his hole, have ye, Ben Letts?"

Ben only laughed in reply.

"Ye have, Ben Letts, ye have, damn ye," screamed the girl now glowering above the fishermen with eyes changing to the deep copper of her hair. "Take that, and that, and that."

She had snatched the long fish from his fingers, and with swift swirls slapped it thrice into the fisherman's face. Turning she flashed away, her long shadows giving out the smaller ones of the tatters that hung about her.

"I'll be goldarned," gasped Letts, "and I'll be goldarned twice if I don't get even with her some of these here days. The devil's built his nest in her alright, and if hell fire don't get her, it'll be 'cause she air burned up by her own cussed wickedness."

He rubbed his face frantically with the soiled sleeve of his shirt, spitting out the scales and blood that had lodged between his dark-colored teeth.

"Ye're always a tormentin' her, Ben," said Longman; "now if ye was only satisfied to let her alone, I air a thinkin' that she wouldn't bother ye. Tess air a good girl, for Myry says as how she can hush the brat when he air a howlin' like a nigger."

"She'll cast a spell over him, that's what she will," muttered Ben Letts. "Her ma could take off warts afore she was knee high to a grasshopper, and so can Tess. Once she whispered ten off from Minister Graves' hand under his very eyes when he was a laughin' at the idee."

"Wish they'd lit on his nose," broke out Jake Brewer, darkly, "he wouldn't be makin' it so hard for us down here. He gets his bread on Sunday if any man does. But they do say as how, when he sees Tess a comin' along, he scoots like a jack-rabbit."

"Sposin' the Dominie don't laugh now, sposin' he don't," put in Longman with a chuckle, "he air lost the ten warts, ain't he? Tess ain't the worst in this here county."

"She can keep the bread-risin' from comin' up," objected Brewer; "she did it with us one day last winter. She scooted by our hut and down dropped the yeast. Wouldn't as much as let her step her foot in my kitchen bakin' day. Air we goin' out again to-night, fellers?"

"Yep," answered Ben Letts. "Sposin' Orn'll go, too. He air in town but he'll get back, Orn will. There ain't no man on the shores of this here lake that can pull a net with a steady hand like Orn Skinner. Pity he has such a gal."

Letts gave another wipe at the scales which still clung to his neck and his eyes glittered evilly as he looked in the direction the girl had taken. He turned when Longman touched his arm. For years it had been the custom of the fishermen to allow the subject of netting to remain undiscussed. They plied their trade, spent a term in prison if detected, and returned to again take up their occupation of catching and selling fish. Ben Letts knew he was venturing upon dangerous ground.

"Broad daylight," he growled, catching the expression upon his companion's face, " and there ain't no one in sight that'll tell."

" Better be satisfied to keep yer mouth shut, Ben Letts," cautioned Longman, " nettin' air bad for the man what gets caught."

" Got any bait out there? " he finished, pointing lakeward to a bobbing box anchored a distance from the shore.

" Not a damn bit," replied Jake Brewer, " don't need it now. Keep the bait cars a floatin' to blind the eyes of some guy that might be a rubberin'. They don't know a minnie from a whale, those city coves don't."

" Ain't that Orn's boat comin' under the shadders of the trees? " queried Longman, rising to his feet and wiping his long jack-knife on his blue-jeans breeches. " Yep, it air him," he added, getting a closer look at the approaching flat-bottomed boat in which sat a big round-shouldered individual working vigorously away at the oars. Orn Skinner was called the " Giant Fisherman," because even in his bare feet he was seven inches above every other man in the settlement. Two enormous humps stood side by side on his shoulders, and a grizzled head lifted and sank with each sweep of the oars. Glancing around to direct his course, Skinner saw the men waiting for him in front of Jake Brewer's hut. With a sharp turn he swung the boat shoreward and a few vigorous strokes sent it grating upon the sand. Jumping out he dragged the boat to a safe mooring, from where the waves could not beat it back into the lake.

## CHAPTER II

IN the beginning, it is said, God made the heavens and the earth. He made the seas and all that in them is, with the myriads of fish, the toads, the snakes and afterward man. Then to grace His handiwork, He created the heart of a woman — the loving, suffering, unteachable heart of Eve.

The first tinge of thinking sorrow comes into a woman's heart at the age of fifteen, and this was the beginning of Tessibel's sorrow, as she lifted her feet over the hot sands and sped onward. Tessibel was what most people would call a careless, worthless jade. She shamefully neglected her father, but covered the fact to him by the wild, willful worship which she bestowed upon him. If he uttered a word of disapprobation she would fling herself, like a cat, upon his crooked shoulders and bend back his head until the red of her lips met his — the pathos in her red-brown eyes quieting his qualms as to the dirt he had to go through to get into bed.

In the mornings, either in summer or winter, he was obliged to tumble the ragged girl from the roped cot he had made for her (when at last she had reached an age too old to sleep with him), and force her, grumbling the while, to eat the bacon and fish he had prepared. But he seemed happy through it all, for the brown-eyed girl brought back to his mind the slip of a fishermaid who had died when Tessibel was born. True, there was more copper in the girl's hair and eyes than there had been in the mother's — more of the bright burnishing like that of a polished old-fashioned kettle hanging over the spigot in a tidy housewife's kitchen. But Tessibel's one room was never tidy nor had she a kettle. In one iron frying pan she cooked the fish and bacon, while a small tin pail held the water for the tea. These were the only cooking utensils of the hut.

Tess could climb to the top of the highest pine tree in the forest yonder; she could squirm through the underbrush with the agility of a rabbit. She loved every crawling, hateful thing, such as all honest people despised, and she once fought with the son of an uphill farmer for robbing a bird's nest, making him give up the eggs and restoring them herself to the top of a pine tree in the fodder lot of Minister Graves.

According to the ideas of all who knew her, save her father and Myra Longman, Tessibel was full of eccentric traits; for who but Tess would feel the "mollygrubs," as Ben Letts had said, at the wriggling of the agonized perch and pickerel, as they flopped painfully upon the sands; or who but Tess would mind the squeaking of the mother-bird calling for her own. It was something of this "mollygrub" feeling that hastened her dirt-caked feet, as she rounded the mud cellar near her father's hut, and sped back of the weeping willow tree hanging in green fringes over the cabin. She dropped quickly upon her knees before a large log, which in some former time the flood-waters had dashed to its place.

Tessibel ran her red, bare arm into the hole in the end of the log. Then she sat up and gazed around.

"He air gone," she said aloud, "he air gone. Ben

Letts has took him, damn his dirty hide. He ain't no more good than —"

Something caused her to close her lips. A large high-warted toad sprang into her dirty lap and slipped to the ground through the rent in her skirt. Tenderly she took the reptile in her fingers, for she loved this warted monster who seemed by the turn of his head to reciprocate in some way the devotion the girl showered upon him. She lifted him close to her face, and intently searched his poppy eyes.

"I said, damn his hide, Frederick," she said in a low tone, "'cause I thought he took ye. And ye ain't done nothin' to him, have ye? Ye was just out huntin' flies, wasn't ye, Frederick? Don't never stay long or ye'll git hit with a spear. Ezry Longman don't like ye nuther, 'cause I kisses ye, and 'cause, on my birthday, I hit his mug with a dishrag when he was tryin' to kiss me fifteen times, and was askin' me to marry him. I'd rather kiss —"

Her sentence remained unfinished. She looked up to see a tall boy leaning upon a rake, a boy with pale gray eyes, and an evil face. His short hair looked as as if it had passed through the fingers of a prison barber. His blue-jean breeches were held up by a rope fastened in the button holes with small iron nails, and the blue blouse which had been clean that morning was now drenched with perspiration.

"Ain't ye got nothin' better to do than to be kissin' a toad," he expostulated, without waiting for the girl to greet him, although she had risen to her feet, holding fast to her reptile treasure.

"Ain't nothin' to you, air it, what I does as long as Daddy don't care?" she retorted, and sullenly counted one, two, three, four, five, six, seven, eight long weeping willow leaves which had died that day and had fallen to the ground. She gathered each leaf between her great bare toe and its next-door neighbor, deftly throwing them aside as she counted.

"I care," stolidly said the boy coming nearer, "and ye air a goin' to throw that toad away, does ye see? Ma says as how ye could be made into a woman if ye hadn't got batty with birds and things. She says as how when ye sing to the brat that yer voice sounds like an angel's, and that's why the kid sleeps. He air a cryin' all the time to have ye sing to him."

Tess hadn't expected this. She did love the tiny unwelcome child of Myra Longman, a child without a father, or a place in the world. Tess loved the babe because there was an expression in its eyes that she had once seen in a wounded baby bird's . . . a pitiful unborn expression which would go with the brat to its grave.

She stooped down and placed the toad again in his hole, shoving him deep down into his cavity, for the sun was going down and Frederick would sleep as long as there were no flies about.

The boy spoke again.

"Mammy says as how if ye don't stop runnin' wild ye'll be worse than Myry with another —"

Suddenly the clenched fist of the girl flew up and struck the fisherman with a swiftness and force that took him from his feet. Tessibel was standing over him rigidly.

"I hates ye, I hates ye, I'd ruther marry — yep, I'd ruther marry my toad or a man as ugly as him than you, Ezry Longman, does yer hear, does yer hear?"

The lumbering body raised itself from the ground. The squint eyes were almost closed, only a glint of the gray ring that surrounded the pupil showing between the lids.

"Ye think that ye can hide from me what ye be a doin'," burst out Ezra. "Why did ye name that toad after the student of Minister Graves? Just 'cause he wears nice clothes and don't do no honest rakin' of hay, nor catchin' a fish only by trollin'. Ye loves that feller, that's what ye does."

Bewilderment leapt alive in the girl's brown eyes. The shade deepened almost to black as the thought the boy had planted in the sensitive mind took root and grew. Then the dirty young face flooded with crimson which tinted the rounded neck and colored the low forehead, and Tess dropped down beside the log and covered her face with her hands. The fisherman was so surprised that he uttered not a word while the wild storm broke over the girl's heart, dying away in a smothered moan.

Without a glance at the boy, she lifted herself slowly from the earth and walking, erect and tall, into her father's hut, closed the door with a bang. She slipped the leather fastening into its place and dazedly adjusted the iron peg in the opening to hold it. Tessibel's heart had manifested its hitherto unknown burden and the woman lived amid the dirt and squalor of the fisherman's cabin.

Tessibel's peremptory leaving and the hauteur in her face were so foreign to her that Ezra Longman did not dare follow. He leaned upon his rake looking after her, his gray eyes gathered into an incomprehensive squint. Had Tess again cuffed his ears, he would have been secretly delighted; but this manner, so unlike her, seemed to take her as far above him as that flock of black crows yonder, flying to the forest to find shelter for the night.

"Tessibel," he called helplessly, under his breath, but Tessibel did not hear. He limped away not knowing that she had passed as effectually out of his life as if she had not dwelt in the rickety cabin on his right.

## CHAPTER III

BEN LETTS rose to his feet after cleaning his jack-knife in the water and took the same path around the mud cellar which Tessibel had taken. The cabin door was closed — Tess nowhere in sight. Ben had intended — Ben didn't know just what his intentions were. He stopped short when his eyes fell upon Frederick's log. It took a long time for a thought to be born in the dense brain of the fisherman, but one was there, for the cross eyes opened and the red tongue licked greedily at the thick chops like that of a wolf when he comes upon prey for which he does not have to fight. Letts looked sneakily at the hut window where hung the remnants of a ragged curtain — all was quiet. He quickly ran his long arm into the opening of the log and with a snap of his teeth drew out the high-backed toad.

Holding the reptile in his hand, he slunk behind the willow tree and stood an instant in abstract hesitation. Suddenly his fiendish face became flooded with the exultation of a plan fully matured. He let the toad fall to the ground, needing both hands to draw the blade of his jackknife. Frederick hopped vigorously along in the direction of his log, but Ben, gorged with the instincts of an inquisitor, snatched him up as he was about to escape. After divesting Frederick of all the ornaments which nature had given him, the man allowed him to hop about, grinning, as he watched the rapid leaps of the toad. Frederick had forgotten the path to his log, he could only turn around and around as if he had been born to radiate in a circle. Ben could have watched this tumbling toad all night, so great was his joy at the sight, but it was getting dark and soon the call would come for the fishermen to gather for the netting and he would be expected to go.

Taking the toad gingerly up from the earth, he returned it to the hole in the log, and with but a hasty glance at the dirty curtain which hung limp and ugly at the cabin window, sneaked away.

After leaving Ezra Longman, Tessibel stood in the cabin for one single moment with the terrible thought which the boy had planted there, burning in her brain. She had but a few times seen the minister's son who lived in the big house on the hill and not even to herself had she mentioned that he was her ideal of manhood — he was as far above her as the learned minister was above her own squatter father. Her heart seemed to almost stop beating as she sprang headlong into "Daddy's bed" and covered herself with the ragged blanket.

Only when she heard her father pounding at the door did she lift her head. She jumped swiftly from the bed to let him in. No thought of supper for him had entered her mind. He looked his hunger as he noted the absence of a fire, and spoke rather mournfully, but Tess cut him short. The lithe young form bounded squarely upon the bible-back of the fisherman. She drew back his shaggy head, her bright wide eyes shining into Skinner's and a low voice deepened by the first arousal of womanly emotion which had ever come knowingly into the young life, was murmuring to him.

"I loves ye, Daddy, I do. What does ye care for supper when I loves ye like this. Daddy, I could — just bite ye hard, that I could, I love ye so."

"Get off my back, Tess," ordered Skinner, trying to loosen her fingers from his hair. "I air tired, Brat, and there be nettin' to-night. Ye air goin' to Mis' Longman's till we get back."

"Won't get off till ye kisses me square on the bill, Daddy," replied the girl softly, "square where I does my eatin's." And square on "the bill" the girl got the caress — and then eagerly hastened to fry the inevitable fish.

"I air coming after ye to Longman's when the nettin's over," broke in Orn Skinner presently, his mouth full of bread and fish, "and ye'd best duck yer head in the lake, Tess, afore ye go. Yer face has a week's dirt caked on it."

Tessibel allowed her red lips to spread wide in a loving smile.

"Ye air a dum good Daddy, ye air, and I loves ye, if my face be dirty."

She rose quickly and came to his side.

"Daddy," she began, twisting his big head so her eyes met his, "Can't I go nettin' to-night? I air a good helper, ain't I, Daddy?"

Orn Skinner dreaded the wheedling tone in Tessibel's voice and the pleading in the eyes so like her mother's. He dropped his gaze upon his plate and slowly shook his head.

"Nope, Tess, ye air goin' to Longman's. Don't . . . now there be a kiss . . . sit down and eat . . . that air a good brat."

The last ejaculation was brought forth by Tess herself. She had turned back to her place at the table and had complacently begun to eat the crisp, brown fish.

"And ye ain't to stay on the ragged rocks, nuther, Tess," cautioned Skinner, rising from the table. "Ye be a good Tess. Scoot along now."

The fisherman moved lumberingly to the water's edge, pushing his boat into the lake, and stepped in. Thrusting his powerful head down between his shoulders, he pulled lazily away at the oars until he lost sight of the shore on which stood the small silent figure in the fast gathering gloom.

Tess did not fancy netting nights. She always feared that something might happen to her father. But she knew, too, that they could not live, even meagerly, through the long winter unless the nets were used. So this night after she had received many kisses, "square on the bill," she watched her father's bent shoulders, rising and falling with the motion of the oars as long as she could see him, and turning, scudded through the underbrush which grew in profusion near the forest — up to the rugged rocks toward the Longmans' hut. She slid down beside a large stone as she heard the lapping of oars below her on the lake, and knew that "Satisfied" Longman and his son Ezra were going to join the others at Jake Brewer's shanty.

She was alone under the heavens, alone with the eagles and sleepy twittering birds — she could think of what had been forced upon her that day. She bitterly regretted the tears shed before Ezra, and she must never, never again look at the student Graves. She felt that to see his face, even from a distance, would cause her to drop dead before him. Every muscle tingled and her eyes burned with unshed tears. She had never dared to speak even to his sister, the pretty Teola Graves, who fluttered about with pink ribbons among her curls and wore high heels on her shoes.

Suddenly Tess opened her lips and sent ringing over the lake in glorious tones of pathos, the hymn she loved best,

> " Rescue the perishin',
> Care for the dyin'."

Tessibel knew what it meant to almost perish from the cold. She had felt the cruel blasts of the winter winds upon her chilblained feet, for she had never known the luxury of shoes. She had also seen the dying and understood what it meant to turn a longing face toward heaven, with a burning desire to know what was beyond.

Such a voice as Tessibel's had never been heard upon Cayuga lake. Ben Letts said it put him in mind of listening to the wild cry of a lost soul, while Myra Longman could hear only the songs of angels in the exquisite tones which fell, pure and sweet, from the red lips. Tess knew nothing of breath power, nothing of trained trilling tones, but nature had given her both and like the birds of the air she used them.

The girl had not moved from beside the stone near which she had fallen. The night was so strange, so different from any night Tessibel had ever known.

Her whole idea of life had been altered that day by the word of a fisherman, and the woman's heart grew larger and larger, until the squatter girl felt that it was going to burst. Something crawled over her bare foot and brought her to her senses. Leaning over she drew to her lap a long, slimy lizard, which she held caressingly in her fingers. She lifted him high up and looked at him through the moonlight.

"Green," she said slowly, "ain't he a dandy. But I don't dare carry him even a little way for fear he'll lose his house. I bet he has a pile of green babies."

Dropping the lizard beside the rock, she sped away.

Just before reaching the Longman cabin, she raised her voice and sang again,

> "Rescue the perishin',
> Care for the dyin'."

Some one opened the door and she bounded in.

"Glad ye come, Tessibel," said Mrs. Longman, a small wizened old woman. "The brat air sick to-day. He does nothin' but squall so that my head air a bustin' the hours through. Give him to Tessibel, Myry."

"After she air rested a spell," replied Myra, who resembled her mother, but was smaller and thinner. "He seems to have a pain, Tess."

"Mebbe he has," responded Tessibel, "give him to me."

The wee boy stopped his tears immediately. His back grew limp and his fists opened out as Tessibel began to sing. This time the song was, "Did ye ever go into an Irishman's shanty?"

The child fell asleep and Tessibel laid him gently in the box prepared for him. Bed room was scarce in the huts of the fishermen and the small members of the family slept on rope beds, let down from the ceiling. But Myra's child, still too tender and always sick, slept in a box which his grandfather, "Satisfied" Longman, had made for him as soon as he was born.

"It air a seemly night for the men to fish," commented Myra when Tessibel had seated herself again. "I air always a hopin' that nothin' will happen to none of them."

"The hull bunch air cute," assured Tessibel, "and Daddy can row faster than any man on this here lake."

"But when them game men gets after 'em with the permit to shoot, that's what I fears," complained Mrs. Longman — and she sighed.

The fisherwoman's life she had led had been harder than most women bore, for Ezra was going a crooked path, while Myra, well — the brat slept in the cradle. Both girls saw her glance toward it and read her thoughts.

Myra's face deepened in color, Tessibel hummed a tune.

"'Taint no use to try to bring up children anywheres decent," the woman broke in sharply, after a silent moment. "God! but to see one's own —"

"Ma," Myra's voice was pleading, "it air over and ye said —"

"I knows I did, and so did yer Daddy. But I ain't thinkin' only of ye to-night, Myra, look at the mess that Ezry's a makin' of things, and just 'cause ye won't marry him, Tessibel."

# TESS OF THE STORM COUNTRY

"I ain't never goin' to marry no one," said Tess sullenly; "goin' to stay with Daddy."

"Yer Daddy won't live allers," interposed Mrs. Longman, "and what's more, yer better off with a man what will look after ye as Ezy will. Be ye a thinkin' of it at all, Tessibel?"

The girl shook her head.

"Nope, 'taint no use; don't like Ezy anyway."

"Ezry ain't the worst boy in the world," defended the mother; "if the right woman gets him, Tess, he'll make her a good man. Ye couldn't think of tryin' him, could ye?"

Tessibel shook her head again. She shuddered perceptibly, and Myra thought she realized the feeling in the girl's heart.

"Don't bother her, ma, don't bother—"

"If ye'd a bothered a little yerself, Myra," broke in the woman pettishly, "we might all been better off. It ain't 'cause of the brat, air it, Tessibel?"

She shot a glance at the infant's box.

"Why 'cause of the brat," asked Tessibel sharply, "why 'cause of the brat?"

"He air a come-be-chance, ye know—"

"That ain't no fault of his'n, air it," demanded Tessibel. "Nope, 'tain't nothin' to do with the brat. I loves him, I does, come-be-chance or no. It don't make no difference to me."

Myra pressed Tessibel's bare toe with hers in loving fellowship.

"Ye allers was a funny gal, Tessibel," ruminated Mrs. Longman. "Now Ezy says that yer takin' a likin' to such things as toads, lizards and snakes, shows as how ye needs some one to help ye. God'll make **ye a** happy mother if ye'll keep yer nose low in the air, and not think too much of yer betters."

Ezra, then, had told his mother of the student. A frown deepened on the girl's brow. She hated Ezra Longman with an inward fury for what he had said that day.

"Ye might have a come-be-chance, yerself, Tessibel," warned Mrs. Longman as she went to bed, clambering up the long ladder to the loft, leaving the girls alone.

## CHAPTER IV

OUTSIDE the Longman hut the wind had quickened its pace up the dark lake, but inside there was no sound save the small snore of the infant.

"Don't hurt you and me bein' friends, does it, Myry," broke in Tessibel impetuously, "'cause I can't love Ezry?"

"Nope, I wouldn't love him nuther. Ma don't know all that's to know and I wouldn't a married the brat's pa if I could," and she shivered, for she knew that she had lied to Tess.

This was the first time Myra had mentioned her trouble, that is, in just that confidential manner. Tessibel came closer. Had it not been a mystery since the coming of the brat, who had been responsible for his tiny life?

"It air some un what ye knows, too, Tessibel," Myra said, shifting her eyes from her companion's face to the box where the infant lay, but Tess did not ask the name. Suddenly Myra leaned over and whispered something in the other girl's ear, and Tessibel started as if she had been stung by an adder.

"Nope . . . it ain't him," she cried, starting up, "he air bad but not so bad as that."

"It were him," replied Myra, "and he beat me that night on the ragged rocks and that air what broke my arm. Ye remember?"

Tessibel nodded. She had heard a secret that not even Myra's mother knew — she felt intuitively that Myra intended her to keep silent. She did not dare to speak again, fearing the woman above was not asleep. But Myra, with less fear, resumed,

"'Taint no hopin' the brat will live, and if he does he'll get his eatin's alright. What brats don't? But, Tessibel, I telled ye this to keep ye away from the ragged rocks for there air no tellin' what will happen to ye. And yer that pretty —"

Tessibel stared blankly.

"Pretty! pretty!" she gasped, stumbling over the words, "ye say pretty. Me — pretty, Myra Longman?"

"As if ye didn't know it," scoffed Myra, "but yer face air allers so dum dirty that ye can't see nothin' but yer eyes, and yer matty old hair — it air a shame to live like ye do.""

Tessibel sat up. This was her first ambitious moment. Never had lips said such things to her, and she had always known Myra Longman. Rising from the chair she disappeared into the outer room, and Myra could hear the splashing of water and the shuffling of feet as Tessibel stood first on one and then the other, washing her dirty face. She mopped the long red hair in and out of the wash-basin, and Myra was not prepared for the vision which Tessibel made in her new state of cleanliness. The impetus of being good-looking by an effort of her own had blackened the copper colored eyes. The long fringed lashes dripped with pearls of water while the skin had reddened from the vigorous rubbing, but it was very, very clean.

"I wants yer comb, Myry Longman," said Tessibel slowly shaking herself like a big dog.

Myra hesitated.

"Ye got too much dirt in your hair yet," said she, "but if ye'll take care of yer mop, I'll be givin' ye a comb to yourself."

Tess did not deny the accusation of her filth. She took the comb and drew it through the wet locks. Myra was regarding her critically. Tessibel — was beautiful. In the last year Ezra's sister had seen the change coming. The complexion had whitened under the perpetual dirt and the long eyes had gathered an expression of knowledge, while their color changed from light to dark with passing emotions.

Myra bent her brows as she examined Tessibel closer. The skin was clean and shone with the glossiness of much soap. The low brow was covered with small wet ringlets, which turned and twisted here and there in luxurious confusion. Over the shoulders, hidden by a soiled calico blouse, the copper colored mass hung in dripping flame-like waves.

"You air pretty," said Myra slowly, "but ye air so dum dirty no one can ever see it. Why ain't you washed up like that every day?"

"Never knowed how before. Didn't see nothin' to keep clean in my face."

As Tessibel spoke she stood before the glass looking at her own image — spying upon the prettiness which Myra said was there.

"This hair air like red snakes," she gasped passionately. "Just like the snakes that eats the little birds in the spring. In the sun their backs air red like this — and this — and this."

She was angrily tearing at the beautiful tightly curled ringlets with but one thought dominating her brain. Students never liked red haired girls with eyes which looked like copper.

"Don't," ordered Myra, catching the rough hands as they pulled at the profusion of redness. "Don't, ye air tearin' it out by the roots, and it looks like — like the sun when it air goin' down in one ball of fire. It air beautiful."

Beautiful! beautiful! Tessibel caught her breath and looked at Myra with a yellowish glint, born of a new emotion in her eyes. Was the brat's mother making fun of her? All her short life had this been Tessibel's portion. Ben Letts had followed her along the ragged rocks over which her bare feet flew with the swiftness of eagle's wings and when he found she could not be induced to stop he would shout in defiance,

"Brick top, red head," and such names that went deep into the sensitive little heart. When she reached home she would tear at the curls and cut them fiercely with the knife which her father used to skin his fish and large eels. Yet nature would send more and more of the burnished gold to adorn Tessibel's head, and not until to-night had she ever heard one word in praise of it.

The reformation had begun. Tessibel went again to the soap and water and Myra looking through the crack of the door, saw Tess dragging madly at her hair, sopping it first in the pan and then in the deep bucket which Ezra used to give the pig their swill. Once Myra saw the mass of gold disappear into the pail, and when Tessibel came again to view she was sputtering, coughing, and blowing the cold water from her nose and mouth.

"Won't be much left if ye keeps on at yer hair that way," called Myra grimly, "but the soap air good for cleanin' it. There air other days and nights, too," she went on sarcastically, "and it air almost midnight. Yer Daddy'll be here soon. Wonder if the game warden air out to-night?"

As if in answer to her question they heard the dipping of oars and a little later a boat was dragged to its moorings on the shore. "Satisfied" Longman entered with his son and Ben Letts.

"Daddy were tired and didn't come for me?" asked Tessibel.

"Your Daddy didn't come child," replied the elder Longman, whilst Ben Letts stood with his squint eyes lowered. He had an exquisite feeling within him, longing for the sight of the girl after she had heard their news.

"I air goin' home to Daddy — I ain't afeared to go home alone," she said stoutly and defiantly, for Ben Letts made a move to accompany her. "I ain't afeared of the night things, nor nothin' that crawls nor flies. Ye knows I ain't afeared, Myra."

"Ye ain't goin' home to-night, Tessibel," said Longman, "for yer father ain't there."

At first Tessibel didn't comprehend. She thought of the care which was taken to keep the fish fresh for the market. Daddy was putting the pickerel and numerous eels in the blind fish cars until they could be cleaned. She looked into "Satisfied" Longman's face.

"Air he a carin' for the fish?"

Longman shook his head in the negative.

"Where air he then?"

Tessibel's voice was sharp and penetrating. It awoke Mrs. Longman upstairs and the infant in the box beside the rope cot.

"He air gone to prison," put in Ezra opening and shutting his eyes, and licking his thick lips with his red tongue. "He air where ye won't see him to scratch his face when ye goes into a tantrum. He air in prison."

The bronze eyes widened and lengthened till the very fear in them startled her companions. The tall, slight figure with its weight of rags, swayed to the hut floor — the clean shining face gathered into a painful pucker, while the two fists which had fought many a hard battle, clenched until the nails entered the calloused skin under each finger. Not one word came from the tightened white lips. The dumb agony was worse than a child's frantic scream of fear. Somehow, Ben's mind went back to the toad, when it also had borne its misery dumbly.

"Satisfied" Longman, stooping down, grasped the girl and stood her on her feet. No one had ever seen Tess like this. Ben leered, the sides of his fat cheeks protruding in the joyful emotion he felt at Tessibel's suffering.

"He killed the gamekeeper," he grinned, leaning back against the wall. "He air where ye won't hurt him now."

The tortured Tess could bear no more. She had striven to be brave when she thought of "Daddy" in the small cell which she had heard many times vividly described. She had thought vaguely of months, perhaps a whole year without him, but Ben's words made her father a murderer, and murderers went away sometimes never to return. Her Daddy! — and Ezra had said that she could never scratch his face again. She hurt Daddy? Did every one in the settlement think that? She sank down beside Myra's father and winding her arms about his legs implored him to say that it was only Ben's and Ezra's fun.

"It air fun, only fun, Satisfied, ain't it," she pleaded, "for Daddy, poor old Daddy, never killed no man."

"We all says as how it were a mistake," replied Longman. "Ben says the gun went off in yer Daddy's hands and the warden dropped, and the other gamekeeper took yer Daddy away at the point of his pistol. I were at the north reel and couldn't save him nohow."

Tessibel understood. It was all plain now. She loosened her arms and painfully raised herself. The shock had hurt her flesh, and made her sore and lame. She started dazedly toward the door, "Satisfied" trying to stop her flight, but the strong young body, mad with grief and newly found despair, slipped through the friendly fingers, and the night, Tessibel's night, gathered her into its arms, till she was lost in the long shadows of the pine forest.

## CHAPTER V

A NIGHT owl hooted in Tessibel's ear as she ran. A bat whirled into her face — then took himself off. Over the shadowy rocks which cut and bruised her feet, Tessibel flew.

Daddy was home in the shanty; he was in his bed tired from hauling his nets. She remembered Ezra had grinned at her as with one hasty look she had fixed his face in her mind. He had lied to her. Daddy was in the hut, and if he were up waiting for her — there passed through Tessibel's small mind the thought of how joyfully she would hop to the bowed shoulders, and she longed for the kisses she knew would be hers. She halted before the dark hut and waited. Insects whizzed about her ears as though they little feared her. The long branches of the weeping willow dragged themselves across the tin roof with a ghostly sound. This was Tessibel's night of heart experiences — her first day and her first night. Oh! to go back to yesterday, with the hidden fear of the student sleeping soundly in her breast and a Daddy, a dear stooping old Daddy. She slipped open the shanty door, lighted a candle and looked around. The frying pan lay bottom up on the floor where she had dropped it. The tea pail was on the table; a cut loaf of bread lay beside it, covered with a host of small red ants. All this was familiar to Tess. She kicked the pan from her path with her bare foot, and sat down on the three legged stool which her father used at his meals. Portions of fish and plenty of bones were spread about upon the floor, but the littered shanty did not distress her newly found notions of cleanliness.

Daddy might go away to the black place where they had taken the Canadian Indian, who had killed his squaw. Tess remembered hearing how he had been carried to prison, twelve men had found him guilty of the crime and at last — Tessibel started up with a groan — the Canadian Indian had been carried to the place where the rope was.

Daddy Skinner and the Canadian Indian. Tess dared think no longer. She caught a glimpse of herself in the cracked mirror which Skinner used when he plied the pinchers to his beard — and her wild eyed bronzeness caused her to give a startled ejaculation. Daddy was gone; and Frederick the toad, was her all. The thought of the reptile she loved brought her quickly to her feet. Frederick should sleep in the shanty while Daddy was away. Tessibel halted apprehensively in the open doorway.

From the shore willows, hoot owls pierced the inky night with their sonorous cries — while in throaty discord, a million marsh frogs bellowed farewell to summer. The lake shores caught the unceasing waves in eternal laps, the rhythm soothing the ears of the squatter girl as her unfathomable gaze pierced the midnight gloom. But the weight of sorrow and longing on the strong nature, untried by emotion, strangled the rising fear, and Tessibel advanced a step to the pebbly path. Once outside in the darkness, she lifted her voice and repeated as of yore,

"Rescue the perishin'
Care for the dyin'."

Never before had the words roused her as now — Daddy Skinner needed that refrain.

She darted around the corner of the mud cellar, and shoving her hand into the familiar hole in the log, Tessibel drew Frederick quickly out. She dropped him into her blouse and retraced her steps to the shanty. She could never be lonely and quite without hope if Frederick were with her. Hadn't she loved him for four long months, and daily fed him his portion of flies? She took him from her bosom, where many times he had sunk into toad dream-land, and without looking at him, placed him on the floor.

"It air a bad night for us, Frederick," she said out loud, "it air. But you'll not sleep in the log to-night, but in Daddy's bed. And I'll just pretend ye air Daddy, and when ye croak with the daylight ye can have all the flies lightin' on the sugar, and then we air goin' after Daddy and bring him home to the shanty, Frederick."

Tessibel turned her head and glanced at Frederick. Generally when she spoke he would give an answering grunt. She gazed at him but dared not venture closer. Had she lost her mind like Jake Brewer's sister, when they brought home the body of her drowned husband? Tessibel lighted another candle and then the third — the match burned low between her fingers as she touched it to the fourth. Once more she looked upon the horrid sight — terror striving and struggling for some outlet in her torn young soul. Frederick blinked a pair of beady eyes, filmed with death, — he moved a mutilated body with painful jerks, but there was nothing to show the girl that he felt her presence. The silent awful pulsating of the toad manifested its dumb suffering. A candle flickered as she sought to solve the problem. The night wind flapped the dirty curtain and Tessibel turned her head slowly toward it. A bird's cry from somewhere in the weeping willow, came in through the window. With silent intensity, she dragged her body slowly across the floor toward the flattened reptile — above him she squatted — the gorgeous hair sweeping the filth strewn floor. Tess could mark the places where the beloved warts had been — she knew how many there were even to the tiny ones. With the halting precision of the ignorant, she had counted them singly every day. But the severest heart wrench of all was to come to Tess. The great squat hind legs, which had been her pride, when Frederick jumped through her rounded arms — curled to make a hoop — were gone, and the movements of Frederick's body left a tiny trail of dark blood upon the shanty floor. She couldn't touch that dying thing. In her vehement desire to relieve him of his pain, she burst into song which went upward and outward, ringing over the lake, returning again, only to be sent further and further into the heavens.

"Rescue the perishin'
Care for the dyin'."

This was all Tessibel knew of the hymn — over and over she sang it, fearfully watching the toad move grotesquely in the candlelight. Time after time the blinking eyes closed and flew open — again and again

Tessibel sent her importunate prayer into the heart of the Great Unknown.

Frederick gave a great deep sob, his fat sides lifted and fell twice, and as the petitionate lips of the girl sent the song once more into the night, he flopped over on his back, straightened out the little wounded stumps, and died.

Daddy Skinner, the Canadian Indian, and Frederick! Tess couldn't separate the three — the prayerful mood died with the toad. She opened her lips and uttered two great piercing shrieks, which sounded and resounded through the rafters of the shanty, out into the darkness and up to the ragged rocks. It was the cry of a wounded human thing, amounting to but little in the great whirling universe. The dying of the scream brought words from her lips.

"Daddy Skinner, Daddy Skinner."

Then twice in equally shrill longing, resounded the name of her dead friend.

"Frederick, aw, aw Frederick!"

Both cries followed the prayer, echoing their agony out through the window — the flapping curtain with its tatters offering no impediment for its outgoing.

Suddenly Tessibel staggered to her feet, for back to her through the window, from somewhere near the mud cellar, came an answering voice, deep-toned and vibrant —

"What? What?"

Frederick, the student, stood in the door of the dirty shanty, looking upon an unkempt, copper-eyed girl, and a great squat, dead, wartless toad.

## CHAPTER VI

"YOU called me?"

A silence.

"You called me?"

The student repeated the words twice, so satisfied was he that his name had been called out in tones of great insistence.

Tessibel was deaf to his words. His presence had filled her completely. Leaning against the post of Daddy's bed, she glued her eyes upon the student's face, the fringed lids sprung to their fullest capacity. The extreme fascination in her gaze held the boy spellbound — then the eyelids quivered and it was over.

Frederick glanced hurriedly about the room, the untidiness of it all striking his sensitiveness. He noted the pungent smell of fried fish mixed with inferior grease, the ant-covered bread, the confusion of ragged bed-clothes, and lastly of all, the other Frederick. Tessibel gasped as the newcomer looked longest upon her dead. She thought she saw him shiver as he stepped back a little.

This brought her grief vividly back to her. The pain, as acute and sharp as the knife which had ended the life of Frederick, entered her already riven soul. The instant before a mingled sensation of shame and embarrassment had swept over her because of the appearance of the hut, and her own bare legs and feet; but the helpless dead sent even that from her.

"He air gone," she said chokingly, coming forward with a totter.

Disgust rested paramount upon the student's face. Surprise followed this as Tessibel threw herself in limp unconcern beside the other Frederick and gathered the stiffened toad into her arms. She rocked to and fro as a mother might who had suddenly discovered that the great White Mystery had robbed her of her child. Tessibel's maternal instinct was being strongly developed in her agony of the hour, and the identity of Frederick the student, was lost in Frederick, the toad, her one little friend, to whom she had told all her sorrows, and had been ruthlessly torn from her. Already she could feel the short front legs growing stiff, and the throat which had so often grunted for its supper, was falling into a curve. The great mutilated back which had lifted and then receded with every breath was still, and Frederick lay like the lump of clay that he was, in the arms of his foster mother. Tessibel's child by adoption would never again gather into his slit of a mouth the flies which favored the sugar. Then Tess, still clasping her dead friend, lifted her head. A stranger had intruded upon her grief. She gathered her bruised, sore feet under the short, ragged girl's skirt, and lifted a woman's soulful face toward the student.

"What do ye want?" she asked sullenly.

"You called me?"

"It were him I wanted," she said hysterically, hugging her little dead burden.

"The toad?"

"Yep, he were all I had,— him and Daddy, and — Daddy Skinner air gone too."

Then Tessibel forgot the student, and the forlorn red head with its burden of curls lay relaxed upon the lifeless Frederick, while the child-woman wept in abject loneliness.

Impetuously the second Frederick stepped forward, the movement closing the door with a bang, and causing the candles to lift their smothered flames and flicker smokily. The wind shrieked through the broken window and the cracks between the shanty boards. A storm played with the water, casting its grayness into white capped rollers which beat upon the shore like the restless spirits of an ocean. Still the girl wept on,— wept for Frederick, for Daddy, and once a shuddering thought went through her mind of the Canadian Indian.

"He killed the gamekeeper, Ezy says,— Daddy Skinner," she whimpered.

Suddenly she sat up, her small round face puckered into such lines of pain that the student turned his head away, feeling dangerously near tears. He had always been taught, by his father and by his mother who feared contagion, that of all people in the world, the squatters must be most avoided; they had no hearts; they killed men and broke the laws simply for their own gain. But here was a girl magnetically drawing him toward her. Dirty? Yes, and barefooted, wild-eyed and untaught, but suffering — and such suffering! Frederick Graves, like his father, would teach the Gospel of Christ, of peace and goodwill to all mankind,— but the deep burnishing of the beautiful hair as it swept the floor in red curls had much to do with Frederick's sympathy, for man-like, he looked upon Eve in her beauty and pitied.

"Your father is Orn Skinner, who shot the gamekeeper to-night?" he asked presently.

Tess nodded, still looking fearfully into his face.

"He was disobeying the law," replied Frederick gravely.

Again she nodded, for Tess had no spirit to thwart an argument at that moment.

"People who disobey the law," went on the student in his youthful righteousness, "take their life in their hands, and other people's too. Don't you think that the woman left without her husband, the gamekeeper's wife, is weeping for him?"

It was a new thought for Tess, but she would not harbor it. It didn't seem quite just to Daddy. She drew down the red lips at the corners, and helplessly clung closer and closer to the toad.

"What are you going to do?" asked the student. "You lived here with your father, but you can't stay here alone."

"It air my home," she said distrustfully, "and I stays here and hangs to this here shanty till Daddy comes back. Aw, he air comin' back, ain't he? He won't go to that place —?"

She closed her lips, fearing to utter the thought.

Frederick shook his head.

"Poor child," he said, with a fatherly air. "It i a dangerous position."

If the case had been placed before Frederick Graves to decide, yesterday he would have hanged Orn Skinner for the murder of the gamekeeper. But to-night — well, to-night his ideas of men and . . . of women, too, had changed.

"But he didn't mean it," went on Tess, casting back

the unruly hair which shrouded her face in its new state of cleanliness. "He wouldn't have hurt a fly, Daddy Skinner wouldn't."

A whistle from the outside, heard plainly through the beating of the wind, caused Frederick to fling open the door.

"Yes, father," he said loudly, "I'm here. I missed you on the way. Come in a moment if you will."

Tessibel gathered herself more closely into a small human ball than ever. She had feared the minister since the time she had talked off his warts with the wizard words she had learned from a hag living on the ragged rocks.

"What's this," demanded the Dominie, looking sternly at her, and she dropped her eyes in confusion.

"It's Orn Skinner's girl," replied his son. "Skinner is the man who shot Stebbins to-night. You heard Deacon Hall talking about it at the cottage."

This explanation was superfluous, for the minister well knew the girl and her father.

"It's a nice mess your father's got himself into," he said harshly.

Tessibel lifted her head.

"He didn't mean to do it, sir," she replied, not daring to rise, because of her bare, long legs.

"Didn't, eh?" roared Graves in his wrath, placing his hand on his son's shoulder. "He was right glad to have the chance to use his gun, or why did he take it with him?"

Tessibel raised her eyes to the rafters, and her face flooded with color. The rifle was gone — Daddy Skinner had taken it with him. She was too young to argue with such a man and only wiped her face with her sleeve and sobbed.

"God will see that justice is done, my girl. Your father will hang, do you hear?" shouted Graves. "Hang by the neck till he's dead, and this shanty will be burned with all its filth!"

Frederick clutched his father's arm, his face changing from red to white as he watched Tessibel. She had clambered to her feet, ridiculously tangled in the rags of her dress. The dead Frederick was forgotten, falling with a great thud upon the floor. Her face was so mobile, so glassily white that if the hand of death had smitten her, she could not have looked ghastlier.

Standing before them, the tears drying over the hot blood which rushed in torrents afresh from her heart to her face, Tessibel learned her first lesson in suppressed emotion. She took two steps backward and wound her hands behind the post of Daddy's old-fashioned bed.

Truly it was Tessibel's first day and first night!

"He air to be hanged dead?" she asked, the painful shiftiness of her eyes settling questioningly upon the minister's face. "Aw, he air good, Daddy Skinner air, gooder than ye be, with ye cross and ye crown that ye sing about. Gooder than all ye whole church, if his gun did kill the gamekeeper. We has our rights to live, to eat bread and beans, like ye have, hain't we? If Daddy Skinner air hung, then Tessibel hangs too."

Here the tired young face drooped a little.

"Ye'll hang him will ye? Well! ye won't — cause — cause —"

Her red head flashed back upon the uncovered shoulders — the wild eyes lifted a moment to the rocking rafters in the roof.

"If ye lives in the sky, Jesus, that cares for the dyin', take Daddy Skinner and Tessibel —"

Her eyes dropped to the pan on the floor, against which the stiff body of the toad lay, and she ended,— "And Frederick."

It was a prayer,— a rough prayer, from untaught lips, but through the action which followed, it instantly lost its dignity. Tessibel forgot her lesson — forgot all save the taunting face of the minister. She gave her familiar leap in the air and came down with a cry upon the Dominie's chest.

"Ye'll kill him, will ye? Then I — I air goin' to kill ye," and deep into the face of the minister sunk the ten little toad-tainted fingers.

Frederick loosened her by extreme effort from his father's body and thrust the gasping preacher outside the door. The student placed his hand upon the panting girl's shoulder.

"You're wrong," he said gravely, "Your prayer was good and God heard. There is in the sky a suffering Christ and His cross — and by your prayers you may save your father, and also save — poor little Tessibel Skinner." Then glancing about the filthy room he added, "and cleanliness is next to godliness."

She opened the door proudly — his words had taught her a newer dignity.

"This air my shanty," she said. "I air sorry I hitted yer Daddy's face, cause — cause he air yer Daddy. Scoot now!"

## CHAPTER VII

FOR one short moment after the going of Frederick, Tessibel stood, gapingly, looking out into the darkness. The student had gone and with him her horror of the minister. The steps died away and dazedly she closed the door. She remembered the day she had talked the warts off from Graves' hand — remembered how he had said to her that she was possessed of the devil. Just what that meant the child didn't know, but the darkening frown on the minister's face plainly told her that it was nothing pleasant — since then she had scurried away when the Dominie had appeared.

This was the first time she had heard the student's voice, for he had spent most of his summers away from home, and the fisherman's child had had little chance to see him. He had said that the cross and crown would save her daddy — had said to pray to the God of whom she knew so little, and his words had given birth to a great faith within her.

Tessibel's fingers were stained with Frederick's blood and shudderingly she looked at them in the candle light. Frederick lay where she had dropped him, his fat white belly sunken and misshapened. The very stillness of him made the girl round him in a circle, watching him with an intentness which showed her superstitious fear of the stiffening dead. Then her great love for him overwhelmed her and she darted like a bird toward her friend.

"I were afraid of ye, Frederick," she groaned softly, "but I ain't no more. Ye wouldn't hurt the kid what loves ye so, would ye, if ye air dead."

She turned the great body over and sobbed. Again the words of the student softened her grief, and through Frederick Graves, for the sake of her loved ones, she accepted his mysterious far-away God and His sacrificed Son.

With loving hands she tumbled the toad into a soiled rag and placed him in the corner. There was nothing left for her to do save to rescue Daddy Skinner from the black cap, and she must see him before the rising of the sun. Mother Moll, the settlement witch, would tell her if Daddy Skinner were in danger.

She opened the door and stood for a moment before stepping into the abating storm. Her eyes fell upon a giant pine tree at the edge of the forest, far beyond her father's hut. It was silhouetted against a light streak in the southern sky, its long arms extending straight into the air. The branches of the tree had always made a fantastic figure in Tessibel's eyes. It took the form of a venerable old man and it had been one of her vivid imaginings, since she could remember, that some time the man shaped against the skies would step down in the flesh. Tess had grown to love him in sunshine and in rain — to watch him in silent, mystified longing as he bent toward her day after day. In the nodding head and swaying arms, Tessibel suddenly established Frederick's deity. As a man from the east worships his sun god through a wooden image, so Tessibel directed a prayer to this moving figure in the pine tree. Her pain-drawn lips parted slightly as she stood for a short space of time watching him.

"If ye be a God," she breathed, "help me see my Daddy."

She said this with bowed head, for grief and the student's admonition had made a path for reverence through her soul.

Then she closed the cabin door and started toward the shore. Pushing a flat boat into the lake, which was still turbulent from the storm, she deftly rounded the long fishing dock, rowing to the bobbing little fish car which held Daddy's eels. She pulled out the nail, and holding up the top of the car, ran her hand quickly about inside. Drawing out four huge eels, she threw them into the bottom of the boat, closed the trap door and rowed away toward the shore.

Inside the shanty, she placed the fish upon the wooden table and stood for an instant regarding them. One long eel drew itself into tense half circles, turning over and over until as he neared the edge of the table Tessibel caught him. Longer the girl's eyes rested upon this one. Suddenly she snatched him up — slipping him, wriggling, tail-end first into the water pail, still holding fast to the pointed head.

"God made ye beautiful," she crooned, "ye can stay there and let me pet ye. I air got to have somethin' to love."

Turning back to the table, she contemplated the remaining fish for thirty seconds or so in indecision. Had her own desire ruled, she would have put them all back into the lake — she would not have killed them; but to-night — to-night it was for Daddy's sake — he was more to her than all of nature's creatures. With expert fingers, she sent the life from the twisting eels, and gathering them into a small bag, Tessibel slung them over her arm and broke off into the dark forest, the twigs cracking under her small bare feet as she went. Here and there the curls of red hair would catch in the branches, and the girl would tear them loose, leaving a blazed trail of copper threads marking her path.

Up to the ragged rocks she went, through the gorges and brooks until she came in sight of a small dark hut set deeply in the opposite bank of a ravine, through which water was flowing. To reach the hut the child scaled the deep gorge and clambered up the other side.

The shanty was dark and Tessibel stood long looking intently at it. Over the top, which was covered with tar paper, scraped the branches of a large tree — the wind was dashing a dead vine mournfully against a broken window. Although on friendly terms with Mother Moll, Tess had always stood in awe of her, but the squatter girl had infinite confidence in the future events foretold by the witch. To-night she must see the woman — must ask her news of Daddy Skinner from the fortune pot. The dead fish hanging upon the slender arm were to propitiate the witch's anger for being dragged from her bed in the night.

Tess stepped shivering to the door and knocked. Receiving no answer, she sent another pealing sound through the howling wind, for she knew Mother Moll was there.

Suddenly a voice came from within.

"What in the devil's name do ye want here, at this time of the darkness?"

"It air Tess, Ma Moll. I wants yer fortune pot."

"Go home and come agin to-morry."

"Won't," Tess sent back defiantly, " air goin' to see

ye to-night. I air goin' to give ye somethin' for yer luck pot."

A scramble, a hurrying sound from within, and the door was dragged open. Tess stepped into the dark room,— the whizzing of insects overhead coming dimly to her through the rocking of the shanty. One broadwinged clammy night bat whirled close to her, but was gone before she could put up her hand.

"It air a bad night that brought the brat out to me, so it air," growled the hag, "be it the headless man from Hayte's place what air been hauntin' ye, or the Indian squaw with her burnt brat?"

She was feeling about for a match as she croaked out her words. Tess did not answer, but waited until Mother Moll lighted a candle and then dropped her load upon the floor.

"They air for the luck-pot, I says, Ma Moll," said she, opening the bag, and displaying the eels, "I comes to know what air in it for me."

"Air they dead eels what you found on the shore," asked the hag suspiciously, "Maybe them ain't fresh ones."

"I killed them myself but a time ago," responded Tess. "It hurts them to lug them livin' out of the water, but they fills your pot for many a mess."

It was a tempting wage for the hag. She blew the dying grate embers into a blaze over which she hung a small iron pot. The bats had ceased the infernal flapping of their grotesque wings, and were clinging trembling to the rafters above. Tess could mark them through the shadows, as one by one she slowly counted them.

Ma Moll was crooning over the kettle. She was a woman older than any one even dared guess. With a cackling laugh she always answered questions as to her age with the assertion that she was "nigh on to two hundred and a deal more than that," and no one could contradict her, for she was old when Orn Skinner was a small boy.

Tess, taking her eyes from the hanging bats, allowed them to rest upon the hag. The small dwarfed figure was not so tall as her own and the rounded shoulders, drawn down by great age, held a head grizzled and shriveled. A few tufts of gray hair hung over the ragged wrapper-like garment which covered the thin body. Great bunches stood out on the bare feet, while the long fingers stirring the liquid in the pot, were knuckled high on each hand.

"Air it the headless man what I spoke of," Moll asked again peering into the pot, "no — it ain't that . . . it air somethin' worse than that."

"Worse than that," echoed Tess coming forward, and sinking down upon her knees beside the hag.

"It air worse than the squaw and her burnt brat . . . Aye, worse —"

"Worse — than — what?" faltered Tess, with a sob in her throat.

"It air the shadder of a rope —"

Here the hag moved closer to the bubbling kettle while the red-brown head pushed nearer and nearer.

"And there air a loop in the end," went on Mother Moll.

Tessibel caught her breath. It was the black place — the rope of the Canadian Indian. The awfulness —

the loneliness of her despair made her whimper brokenly behind a tattered sleeve. The hag was muttering her incantations and did not heed the girl.

"The rope air a long 'un and a stout 'un," Ma Moll's voice had raised to a shrill cry as she described the instrument of death. Tessibel's head was now close to the hag's. Her wild terror-stricken eyes following the stick as it stirred the contents of the pot.

"Air the loop around a neck, and air there humps under the head what's a hangin'?"

She quivered as she spoke. The thin body of the hag crept nearer to the child — the gray straggling locks mingling with the copper curls, and the youthful shoulders of the fishermaid contrasting strongly with those of the bent old woman.

The hag was searching for the humps — her wild old eyes glaring into the seething mess. A trembling bat loosened its hold upon the rafters above and blinded by the light of the candle, thrashed its zig-zag course about the shanty, banging first the window, then the door, and causing both watchers to lift their heads. They saw him as he fell fluttering to the floor, lifting his body pantingly up and down.

Again they gazed into the pot, and as one thin hand held the whirling stick the hag's bony finger pointed mysteriously to the shadow marking the future.

"Be there humps," persisted Tess, "big round humps standin' out as how the hills stand by the lake?"

The hag replied in a hoarse whisper:

"There be no humps, but there air a dead man."

So thoroughly did Tess believe in the witch's words that she sank back with a cry, upon her wet red feet.

"It ain't daddy," she breathed slowly, hardly daring to utter the name.

"There be no humps," repeated Ma Moll. "There air a storm and a dead man, but his face ain't a showin'. There air another dead one on the shore. He ain't the same kind of one, he air—"

"A gamekeeper," filled in Tess.

The witch wobbled her head in assent, as Tessibel leaned over to follow the long finger defining the shadow.

"There air a shanty," Mother Moll went on, "a child alone, and dead things layin' about and there air a—a—"

The two heads were now bent directly over the pot. Tess caught her breath in a sob. Was Daddy Skinner coming back to the shanty? The dragon blood sputtered, boiling higher and higher, over the heat of the fire, as the witch dug it upward from the bottom of the kettle.

"A prison cell and a man," ended Moll.

"Be there humps?" gasped Tess.

An acquiescent nod came from the gray-grizzled head. Tessibel wound her fingers about the arm-bone of the hag.

"Air there a cross with a Christ hangin' on it?"

The witch looked deeper into the dark mixture, her eyes squinting to narrow slits, and Tess continued:

"A hangin' Christ that air hurt, and be there thorns a-diggin' in Him?"

Deeper and deeper into the sizzling pot stared the faded blue eyes of the hag, the dark wide-spread ones of the girl following every movement of Ma Moll's hand.

"Aye, there air a cross for ye, brat, to carry on yer back —"

"Air there no Christ a bearin' one for Daddy?"

Suddenly the door burst open, and the raging wind flickered out the candle. It had been so sudden that Tess screamed, and the witch muttered a curse. The rain tore its way through the small dirty room; the bats loosened their hold upon the wooden rafters and circled the darkness, first into the open, then into the room — against and away from Tessibel's face, until the girl broke into wild weeping.

Ma Moll had failed to find the cross. The wind forcing the door bespoke evil for Daddy. Without the student's Christ how could she save him?

"Go home, brat," ordered the hag. "Go home, there air a cross with a Christ hangin' to it, and there were a dead man without humps."

Out into the rain the sound of the hag's words ringing in her ears, the whizzing bats for the first time filling her with a strange mysterious fear, Tessibel went. She turned into the dark forest of which she was not afraid, and crossing the gorges again, sought the upper hill which led to the tracks.

## CHAPTER VIII

ELIAS GRAVES was pastor of one of the largest churches in Ithaca. His family consisted of his wife, his son Frederick, and his daughter Teola, a girl of sixteen, and little Babe, the spoiled pet of the family. Besides a beautiful town rectory, he owned the lake farm and held the title to the small piece of property upon which Orn Skinner squatted. That the hut and its filth injured his own magnificent cottage no one denied.

It was true he only spent ten or twelve weeks of the summer in the lake house, but every man desired his own. For several years there had been a continual fight between the pastor and the fisherman — Orn Skinner answering the minister with the squatter law of the state which gave him the use of the few feet of ground upon which his shanty stood.

Still the Dominie insisted that some day he would rid his summer home of the pest and the time had come.

After leaving Tessibel he walked up the long lane leaning on the arm of his son, sputtering against his enemies.

"The very idea of that malicious brat jumping upon me as she did. She ought to have a sound whipping."

Frederick shivered slightly. His heart was full of sympathy for the primitive girl who had so devotedly loved her toad.

"We would be rid of the whole family if we could get

that girl away," went on his father, " then I could file a request to take what belongs to me. Hall said only to-night that he would like to see all the squatters gone. We've decided to make a move."

Frederick tried to make a small complaint, but the minister commanded him to silence.

" Get rid of them I will, do you hear? " he shouted, " they have no moral right there whatever the law says. Get rid of them, I will."

When the Dominie reiterated strongly his whole family remained silent, and this time Frederick dared pass no remark. He wondered if it were not for just such people as the Skinners that the Christ had suffered. He felt an incentive rising in his heart to seek guidance from the Book, for although Frederick Graves greatly reverenced his father he would not give up his own opinions without a struggle.

" I've got this Skinner just where I want him after all these years," hurled forth the minister, as they passed the pear orchard, and then added:

" But I don't understand how you came to be in the hut."

" I heard the girl crying," replied Frederick curtly.

" I missed you when we left Hall's," explained the Dominie. " Charlie called me back to ask about the plans for the new church, and if I had not whistled just when I did, you might have been in that hut still, I suppose."

Frederick found himself wishing that his father had not whistled, his mind going back to the girl in the shanty, whom he had left with her living grief — and her dead.

He saw his sister, Teola, standing on the broad porch

waiting for them. The girl scented something unusual in the angry tones of her father's voice. She followed Frederick alone into the library which looked out upon Tessibel's hut.

"What's the matter?"

Frederick shrugged his shoulders impatiently.

"Nothing much."

The brother and sister had grown into a confidential friendship during the past two years. Teola's face dropped as she heard Frederick's halting answer.

"I know better," she retorted decidedly. "You have been having words with father."

"No, not words," replied the boy, "but you see father thinks that no one can have any ideas but himself. It sort of makes me tired, for sometimes I know when a thing is right or wrong."

"What was the matter?" insisted Teola once more.

"The Skinners," replied Frederick slowly.

"You mean the squatters?"

"Yes."

"Aren't they alright where they are?" hesitated Teola.

"Skinner killed the gamekeeper to-night, and the girl is alone in the shanty. Father doesn't seem to realize that they have souls to be saved as well as the rest of the world."

Teola thought an instant before answering.

"They are so dirty," she said at last.

"That's true," Frederick reflected, "but nevertheless they are human."

"Were you in the hut?"

"Yes, with father."

"Whew! What did he say?"

The question was answered by loud words from the minister talking to his wife in the dining room.

"I tell you," said his voice, ringing out so that the two listeners could hear, "those squatters have got to go. I'm not the only one who thinks that way. If they had the instincts of decency I wouldn't say a word, but they haven't. I say it's time to make a move."

"You know," continued the minister, "that their hut is in direct line with our view. There's no buying them off . . . I've tried that. Now that Skinner is arrested it won't be hard to frighten the girl away, for she can't stay there alone."

"I'm not so sure," mused Mrs. Graves; "those people are not easily frightened."

"She's afraid of me," shouted the Dominie, "and she will be more so before I get through with her and her father. If Skinner is hanged, she shan't stay there."

Later there was a long discussion between the father and son upon the rights of squatters, which ended in Frederick's going to bed before it was half finished more disgusted and unhappy than he had ever been before. He looked out upon the lake. The wind was still rolling the water into white crested waves, and his eyes could scarcely outline the small hut under the willow tree. Into the boy's life something had come — a new something he could not explain, while out of it another something as hard to define had gone forever.

Two jack rabbits perched on the tracks above the fodder lot of Minister Graves lifted their long ears and listened. Human steps at this time of night were out of the ordinary. The dog at Kennedy's farm beyond the tracks heard them, too, and bayed loudly. Then as they grew more distinct he bounded toward the fence, capering madly about, to scent the intruder. It was but a forlorn little figure, but Pete, the brindle bull, lifting his voice in a pleased howl, crouched close to the fence as a small hand came through to pet him.

"It air only Tess," said a voice in which tears had gathered. "Ye air glad to see Tess, ain't ye? . . . Tess air glad to see ye, too . . . Frederick and Daddy air gone and I must be goin'."

Tessibel placed her face down near the big dog and he shoved out his long red tongue, touching her with delight. The girl hugged the large head with an admonishing appeal that Pete must go back to his kennel — and stepped again to the track — that long, black winding road which she must travel before reaching her destination.

It was raining again, the water falling in steady drops upon the bare head. Frequently the girl wiped the water from her face with a torn calico skirt. Once she sat down and gathered her feet under her wet dress to stop their stinging pain — and here alone under the dark sky, Tessibel offered up her first balanced prayer, for had not Frederick said that God would save Daddy Skinner.

"He do say," and she lifted her eyes upward with a simultaneous wipe at her face, "that there air a God who'll help my Daddy . . . I wants to find my Daddy . . . for a minute . . . a little minute . . . be it pleasin' to ye, Goddy?"

Tessibel always put "dy" to Dad to make it more effective — and it was with the same sweet, serious voice, with which she would have pleaded with her own father,

that she made familiar with the majesty of heaven.
She could make no distinction between Daddy Skinner
and Jehovah. Both to her were the reigning powers
of the earth. Daddy she had always known, but the
other — Frederick had said it was good to pray. She
rose stumbling, and at three o'clock in the morning
entered the city of Ithaca, walking up State street
drabbled and thoroughly wet. She knew the streets that
led to the city jail, for many a time when selling greens
and berries had she gone steathily to the gray stone
building and examined the barred windows.

She crossed Dewitt park, and passed by the churches
which surrounded the jail. Around and around the ivy-
covered stone structure wandered the rain-soaked, barefooted girl. She could not distinguish one ray of light
at first in any of the windows. . . . Suddenly she
stopped and took a long breath. Up near the roof line a
faint light flickered . . . some one was moving to
and fro. Tessibel could distinguish a rounded shadow
on the ceiling of the cell, and tears choked her, as she
saw cast upon the wall the shadowy outline of a large
humpbacked form. It was Daddy — Daddy Skinner,
and Tessibel backed from the building, straining her
eyes to get a better view of him. Now the image was
in sight, again it disappeared — Daddy was walking
up and down, but he did not come near enough to the
window for her to see his face.

Seven times she counted Daddy's rounded shadow on
the wall, and seven times it faded. The eighth — a
grizzled head cast its outline distinctly across the bars.

"Daddy — aw — Daddy Skinner."

It was only a loving name breathed by a troubled
child, but it was caught in its upward flight by the

father's ear above. Tess saw the pictured humps pause, and as she whispered the name again, Daddy Skinner came to the iron lattice. She could discern her father plainly through the rain and held her arms up toward him.

"It air lonely in the shanty, in the . . . shanty . . . without ye, Daddy," she breathed, "and Tessibel . . . air sorry . . . for all her badness. Come home, Daddy . . . dear, good Daddy . . and Tess —"

She stopped, for a sight strange and unusual fell upon her. Daddy Skinner was looking down, clinging to the bars mightily, his under lip shaking, his dark teeth chattering together — the grizzled head making a sharp picture of misery in the barred window. Emotion in her father was new to Tess. A little frightened cry fell from her lips and she clutched hurriedly at the thick creeping ivy which clung to the old gray stone building.

"I air comin', Daddy Skinner," she cried. "I air comin'."

She followed the main body of the ivy on its upward growth, slipping and sliding on the wet creeper as she made her perilous ascent. Daddy Skinner was near the roof and it took Tessibel many torturing minutes to reach him. He knew she was coming by the continual dragging at the ivy, but he dared not speak, for the guard walked outside his door in the hall, and the sound of a voice would bring danger to Tess. Once he strained his face to the bars — saw her climbing frantically, and the sight made him dizzy. He could only wait — wait the interminable time until the red-brown head appeared and the wide eyes stared into his. Skinner quietly drew his child to the stone sill,

and placed his fingers over her lips to enjoin silence.
Tess understood and even drew softer breaths, holding
tightly to the beloved hands.

"I comed for kisses on the bill, Daddy," she breathed.

"Tess . . . air lonely without ye."

The livid, shaking lips met the quivering mouth
through the iron rods. A long, long kiss, such as Tess
had wanted quieted her suffering a little. It was the
same old Daddy whom she was going to save by
praying. She had asked to see him only a minute, and
the student's God had granted her prayer.

She whispered again, shivering and shaking with the
cold.

"Did ye kill the gamekeeper, Daddy?"

The gray head shook the answer, "no."

"If ye did ye didn't mean to, did ye?"

The two negative replies made Tessibel's heart bound.
It would be easier for God to help him if he had not
committed a crime, and for no instant did she doubt
his word. She kissed him again passionately, clinging
to his lips with all the young growing emotion in her
body.

The squatter clung desperately to the body of his
child. He could not let her go, fearing she would fall
to the hard stones below, but he knew that she stood in
danger of being discovered and dared not detain her.

"Kin ye get down again?" he whispered.

"Yep, Daddy Skinner, and ye ain't goin' to hang,
'cause some one what can, air goin' to help ye."

"Who air he?"

"God . . . up there!" and Tessibel motioned
with her hand toward the dark sky. "He says as how
He helps folks like us . . . that a cross was beared

for us . . . and I says to Him to-night, and I says every day till ye come back to the shanty . . . that He lets ye free, Daddy. . . . I asks the sheriff to-morrow if I can come afternoons to see ye. And, Daddy, I holds the shanty till ye come home."

He kissed her small pinched face again and again — and took his arms away. Tess slipped down the creeper and when she reached the ground called softly:

"I air here, Daddy Skinner."

She saw him pressing against the bars, his lips shaking and his eyes closely shut as if he were stumblingly offering a prayer for the child of his fisherman soul.

## CHAPTER IX

THE fraternities of Cornell University gave home and social comforts to students, rich and popular enough to be invited to join them. Each fraternity had its own spacious house, with its staff of servants, where the members lived during the college year.

Every first-year man had the ambition to join one, which if he attained assured him a luxurious home during the four years he spent in Ithaca.

One evening, three weeks after Tessibel's secret visit to her father in the city jail, twenty fraternities were preparing all the practical jokes which boyish minds could concoct, with which to initiate their new candidates to full membership. Five new men were to join the " Cranium " fraternity. The house of this society stood high upon the eastern hill above the lake and overlooked the forest-mantled town. The first story of the building contained the smoking, dining, billiard and two drawing rooms. Above were sleeping chambers and private studies for the students, and annexed to the house proper was a small stone structure built purposely for the initiation of the new members.

On this night all interest was centered upon the annex where Frederick Graves, Dan Jordan, Billy Dillon, Oscar Brown and Jimmy Preston were to be taken through the " stunts."

In the afternoon the five young men had been locked

in one of the student's rooms, and told that they would receive their dinner during the proceedings that evening. The gravity which had settled upon the upper classmen frightened the three smaller candidates, for Billy, Oscar and Jimmy were miniatures in size compared to Dan Jordan and Frederick Graves.

"Do you think they are going to hurt us," asked Billy Dillon, turning to the two larger students. "I don't want to be hurt — I like the thought of being a fraternity man, but I don't want to go through any business that will injure me."

"Neither do I," put in Oscar Brown. "I promised my mother —"

"It won't be well with you fellows if those chaps downstairs hear you talking that way," cautioned Jordan, "besides the initiation is only fun, and any of us are willing to stand jokes."

After a three-hour wait, a group of sophomores, and the freshmen's tormentors — appeared upon the scene and ordered the candidates to follow them into the dreaded annex. In this "torture chamber" the older members, juniors and seniors, seated on benches placed around the wall, were waiting gravely the arrival of their victims.

The honors of the occasion had been given into the hands of the sophomores, and as they trailed in followed by the quaking applicants, a hush fell over the expectant members of the society.

The five freshmen were ordered to stand in a row, and Richard Hall, the spokesman of the second-year class, came forward, holding up one hand in mock reverence.

"Gentlemen," he began, "I first christen you all in the name of the 'Cranium' Fraternity. I give you,

Dillon, the name of 'Swipes.' You, Brown, shall be dubbed 'Shorts'— here he hesitated an instant, perusing a slip of paper which lay on the table beside him — Preston, you may add another 'S' to make a trio — your name shall be 'Spuddy.'"

Hall allowed his eyes to gaze reflectively upon Dan Jordan.

"To a big fellow like you, Jordan," he resumed, "I give 'Captain.'" His voice dropped as if he had either overlooked or forgotten Frederick, and the young fellow waited expectantly.

Suddenly Hall flashed him a glance, then dropped his eyes with twitching lips.

"'Parson' is good enough for you, Graves."

Sweeping the five candidates with his searching gaze, he took up the speech again —

"If at any time your fraternity brothers desire to call you by your new names and you refuse to answer, you shall receive the punishment which goes with disobedience."

"Gentlemen," he said again, dismissing the last subject with a wave of his hand, "it gives us great pleasure to receive you into this fraternity, but before we can give you full membership it is necessary for us to go through a few more formalities."

Hall's eye fell in hesitation upon the ponderous form of Dan Jordan.

"You will all no doubt soon see the value of prompt obedience," his voice rang out, and a smile touched each corner of his lips, but faded instantly.

The three little freshmen moved uneasily — Hall, with a touch of irony in his tones, directed the rest of his instructions to them.

"We have decided," resumed the speaker, "to initiate you fellows all at one time."

Oscar Brown sighed in relief. "Misery loves company," and if the society had any indignities to bestow, he would not be alone.

"We have found it necessary in times past," Hall took up again with a tragic tone in his voice, "to use discipline upon such occasions as this, and if by chance an incoming member becomes obstreperous, we employ a friend to help us — he holds an honored position in our fraternity . . . Mr. Manchester, introduce 'Mazuka.'"

The sophomore thus adjured, stepped nimbly to the corner, and lifting from a hook a long vicious-looking carpet beater, brought it toward Hall.

"Handle him with reverence," shouted the spokesman, taking it carefully in his hands and turning it over with a benign smile. "Many a time has 'Mazuka' done good service for this frat! You will understand," the freshmen heard him say, "that an indecorous smile on any of your faces will immediately call for three strokes from 'Mazuka,'" and he waved the carpet beater threateningly, "and for disobedience you will get five. We will now proceed to business. 'Captain' Jordan and 'Parson' Graves, please step forward . . . Blindfold the eyes of those two, Frank," Hall ended, addressing one of his classmates near him.

He turned to a group of his companions — and after whispering with them, came back saying aloud — "that's a good one to begin with."

Directing his eyes upon Jordan, he said:

"Down upon the floor and scramble like an egg, Captain."

A titter came from Billy Dillon.

"Duck that fresh chicken for laughing," shouted Hall, "and give him three strokes of the 'Mazuka.'"

A sophomore brought a pail of cold water, and two other students, grasping the little fellow, immersed his curly head in it. They then stood him on his feet and laid the carpet beater three times across his back. Billy almost wished he had not chosen the fraternity life, but the others were suffering with him, which made it easier than if he had been alone.

Meanwhile Dan Jordan was industriously trying to imitate a cooking egg.

"Scramble, Captain, scramble," cried a sophomore, prodding Jordan with a stick.

"Cook the 'Parson,' too," shouted some one, and Frederick was ordered to follow the movements of his friend.

A faint flush mounted to the broad brow of the minister's son and he hesitated.

"Bring the 'Mazuka,'" commanded Hall, and the eager sophomore rushed up with the persuader.

"Scramble, you," he roared, waving the carpet beater dangerously near Frederick's head, and down beside his strapping friend dropped the dignified Frederick — two more long legs, and two more heavy arms were wiggling over the floor.

"Those eggs are burning, give them some grease," suggested a senior from his seat near the wall.

An agile, willing sophomore snatched a bucket of water and emptied its contents over the two floundering giants. As the icy bath submerged the freshmen, Dan

Jordan, sputtering and gasping, bounded to his feet.

"Five strokes of the 'Mazuka' for the 'Captain,'" shouted the delighted Manchester waving the carpet beater, "he got up without permission."

Three students held Jordan fast and the little sophomore, dancing with glee, belabored the huge half "scrambled egg," each blow resounding through the room.

"There! I guess that will hold him a while," chuckled the chastiser, putting the carpet beater under his arm, his face reflecting the pleasure of well-performed duty.

Frederick, wet and looking very bored, was still flopping about the floor, and after passing a few more remarks about rotten eggs and undignified positions, the sophomores allowed him to stand up.

"Now put the wet booby in the corner," ordered Hall, and Frederick was accordingly led away.

Oscar Brown and Jimmy Preston, a little pale after witnessing Dan Jordan's punishment, were then told to come forward. Both trembled perceptibly as they were blindfolded by a sophomore and commanded to lie upon their backs upon the floor.

"You fellows are going to get that dinner we promised you now," he said, stooping over the frightened prostrate students, and giving the bandages a last tightening pull; "the first course consists of something you are sure to like, and we guarantee them to be absolutely fresh. Bring the supper in, for these kids are hungry!"

Some one brought a dish and the two boys could plainly hear the rattle of the cover as it came off.

"Open your mouths," came the next command.

Oscar Brown timidly opened his lips and waited, but Jimmy Preston, thinking the joke had gone far enough, obstinately refused to open his lips.

Bang! came the carpet beater over the side of his leg, and his mouth flew open like a trapdoor.

"That's just a little reminder for you to do as you are told, Spuddy," the wielder of the "Mazuka" laughed.

"Here's the dinner, boys," cried Hall, "and I bet you can't imagine what we've brought you. . . . Do you know what that is, 'Shorts'?"

Brown shivered, for something snake-like and cold was drawn across his cheek.

"It's an angle worm," continued the speaker, "and you're going to eat it. . . . Don't be afraid, 'Spuddy,' you needn't wiggle, you are going to have one, too," he added the last part of the sentence, seeing a shudder pass over the form of the other blindfolded boy.

"Keep your mouths wide open," shouted a senior.

Simultaneously the two boys felt the promised but undesirable dinner drop into their mouths. With a groan Oscar Brown rolled over on his side and allowed his portion to fall slowly out. But Jimmy Preston, amid howls of joy from the onlookers, jumped to his feet and tore the bandage from his eyes.

"No fraternity for me," he yelled. "I've never heard of such a dirty trick. If you fellows—"

His disgusted gaze fell upon the plate held by a sophomore convulsed with laughter. Jimmy rubbed his eyes, blinked, and looked again — blank astonishment taking the place of his anger. In the dish were only a few strings of cold cooked macaroni.

"Golly! What a fool I am," and Jimmy glanced about upon the grinning faces with a sheepish air.

"That's what you are alright," said Manchester, trying to be serious and securing a better grip upon the carpet beater. "Who said you could take that bandage off. That will cost you five strokes of the 'Mazuka.' . . . Here, fellows, hold him on his stomach over that chair, so that I can get in some of my fine strokes. . . . One . . . two . . . three . . . four . . . five . . ."

Jimmy was jerked to his feet, the injured expression upon his sorrowful face plainly showing Manchester that his strokes had been telling ones.

"There! We're through with you for to-night, 'Spuddy,' old boy," said Manchester, proudly feeling his biceps. "Go sit down . . . if you can," and Jimmy limped away with a muttered "thank heaven."

During a conference in undertones, amid giggling and snickering, Richard unfolded a new plan. Then he said in a loud voice,

"One of you fellows see if the surgeon is here yet. And hurry back."

Billy Dillon who had remained in trembling silence during the proceedings, received his bandage without a complaint, although his face was ashy pale, and his knees shook beneath him as Hall approached.

What did they want a doctor for? They surely wouldn't do — anything bad enough to need a surgeon. Thoughts like these went racing through his frightened mind, the sophomore leading him in terrifying darkness to a chair near by. Silence fell upon the room, and all that Billy could hear was his own excited breathing, made louder by the explosive beats of his heart.

"Swipes," he heard Hall say, "we've decided that we can't stand that pretty face of yours around, but as we like you and don't want to send you away, we will change the expression on it. A gash on each of those rosy cheeks will alter your whole appearance, so much, that not one of your lady friends will ever recognize you again. In after days, when you grow to be a man, you will thank us for this. Frank, tell Dr. Wallace to come in."

A pause . . . and Billy heard the door open and close, and someone coming toward him, the person smelling strongly of drugs.

"Is this the unfortunate young man," asked a strange, but not altogether unfamiliar voice.

"Yes," Billy heard Hall answer in heartbroken tones, "and please, doctor, do the best you can for him."

"Oh, we'll fix him alright in just about a minute," responded the strange voice. "Mr. Hall, will you please hold his arms, for when patients are excited they sometimes forget themselves, and . . . now . . . my instruments, please."

Billy's arms were held tightly behind him, and for a moment he heard nothing — then came to his ears the sound of a box being unclasped and — horror of horrors — the rattle of surgical instruments.

Would they dare cut his face? Why his father would —

Billy felt the cold blade of the knife touch his flesh, and hot blood run down to his chin.

Upon this he became possessed by the strength of a giant. Jerking his hands loose he struck out with all his might, his fist hitting something with the force of a kicking donkey. There was a sound of some one falling and a roar of laughter went up from the students as Billy was grasped by what seemed a thousand hands. The bandage was snatched from his eyes and he looked upon a sorry sight. Manchester, the expert wielder of the Mazuka, had failed as a surgeon. He lay a few feet away amid pieces of broken ice, which he had pretended was a surgical knife — his coat bespatted with hot milk which represented poor Billy's blood, and his left hand clasped tightly over a swollen eye.

"What hit me?" gasped the fictitious Dr. Wallace.

"What hit Manchester, fellows?" one of the seniors managed to howl out to the convulsed fraternity members.

"I believe that rascally freshman did it," exclaimed Manchester excitedly, "bring me the 'Mazuka,' and I'll put a bunch on him that never will come off."

"Gee Whiz! Look at his eye," some one called out.

This brought Manchester to a standstill.

"What's the matter with it," he groaned, putting his hand again to his face, "is it gone?"

The lids were puffed shut, and were rapidly darkening. Richard Hall, laughing uproariously, held a pocket mirror for the young sophomore to peep into. After a moment's contemplation of his bruised face, Manchester came forth in a hoarse whisper,

"That freshman's got to die — If I only . . . had an ax," and his one eye gazed wildly around in search of a weapon.

"Come, come, Teddy Manchester," soothed a tall senior, "we'll arrange with the freshman alright. Don't work yourself into unnecessary excitement."

"And he shall use all his spending money for your tobacco, Teddy, for the entire year," cajoled Hall, "and black your boots and brush your clothes, into the bargain, and besides you will get a chance to get even at the Freshmen's Banquet," he whispered.

"Gentlemen," he concluded, turning with a winning smile upon the assembled society, "we have five new members in the 'Cranium' Fraternity."

## CHAPTER X

MINISTER GRAVES' city home, the Rectory, was a magnificent house, covered with a thick growth of ivy; one bay window ornamenting it on the west, another looking on the street.

The first evening in November, the family was seated about the table, the minister reading the evening paper. "Babe" was arguing with her mother that all little girls should be allowed to roller skate upon the pavement; that "there wasn't a bit of danger in it."

Frederick was silently eating his dinner — Teola following his example. Suddenly the minister ejaculated:

"Ah, that's good."

"What's good, father?" inquired Mrs. Graves.

"Skinner is brought to trial to-morrow. The paper says there isn't the slightest hope for him to escape. And listen to this:

"'Of all the happenings in the annals of the Ithaca courts the following is the most extraordinary. Orn Skinner, the squatter, who is to be tried this week for the murder of Emery Stebbins, the game warden, is the father of a girl some fifteen years old. The day after his incarceration the girl presented herself at the office of the sheriff, asking permission to see her father. The sheriff thought wiser not and refused the request. But the night before last the girl was discovered ascending, like a squirrel, the thick growth of ivy that covers the stone structure of the jail. For nearly a month she has been tramping the Lehigh Valley railroad tracks after dark, reaching the jail at midnight, and holding converse with her father on the stone sill of his cell window, two stories above the ground. The girl was closely questioned but refused to answer, probably fearing the consequences of visiting a prisoner without the consent of the sheriff. Skinner has been removed to an inner cell, the authorities fearing some plan of escape. The girl is very pretty, with long red hair, and brown eyes, and those who have seen her say that she is like a frightened rabbit, refusing to talk with any, save a few of her kind."

The Dominie grunted, as he finished reading.

"I should think they would remove him to an inner cell," said he. "Such goings on! The girl ought to have a taste of the rawhide."

"Maybe she loves her father and wanted to see him," ventured Babe, who had no reverence for paternal opinions.

"Love, love," retorted the Dominie, "all the love those people have in their lives you could put in a nutshell."

"Her father's trial comes up to-morrow — I wonder if they will allow the girl to attend."

This was from Frederick — he had not seen Tessibel since the night he had told her how to help her father. His face gathered a crimson shade as he remembered that he had promised her that he, too, would pray for her Daddy. The sympathy he had felt in his heart, throbbed again as he thought of her lonely grief — and the dead toad. He would keep his promise to Tess —

pray that something might come into her life if somebody went out.

"Mother," said Teola, changing the subject abruptly, "why can't we have a toffy pull. I want one so badly."

"It's such a messy thing," sighed Mrs. Graves, looking about upon the tidy home, "and not one of you young people can keep your sticky hands from the curtains and furniture. But I suppose, if you will have it, nothing I can say will alter it. But remember this: I won't have those boys and girls tramping through my house and mussing up everything."

As they rose from the table Teola followed her brother into the hall.

"Frederick, if I arrange the toffy pull, do you suppose Mr. Jordan would come?"

She dropped her eyes — the blood curling to the edge of the tiny ringlets that clung to her forehead. Her brother gave a low laugh.

"He would be only too pleased, Sis, and he is a capital chap. He's a great favorite at the frat with all the boys. Shall I invite him?"

"Yes . . . for day after to-morrow evening. Will that suit you?"

"Let me see," reflected Frederick, "we are having a meeting at the fraternity, but we might come down afterward, unless we are kept too late."

"Don't let them keep you," pleaded Teola, flashing her brilliant eyes into Frederick's face, "you and Mr. Jordan have influence enough to get away, even if you are freshmen."

The student stooped and kissed his sister fondly.

"I'll arrange it to suit you, Sister . . . I want to go to the Skinner trial to-morrow. I suppose father will go, too?"

"Everybody will be there," rejoined Teola. "I wonder if his daughter will be permitted to see him after she has been discovered breaking the law."

This time it was Frederick who flushed — it suddenly dawned upon him that he was going to the court simply to see the squatter girl again. He explained his embarrassment by exclaiming:

"Poor little soul! She is the loneliest child in the world. I wish we could do something for her!"

"Father wouldn't let us," put in Teola in dismay; "then, too, I don't know what we could do for a squatter."

"Neither do I, that's the problem," finished Frederick, and after he was gone Teola mused long with Dan Jordan in her mind.

At the break of the first day of the Skinner trial, smoke could be seen curling up from the chimney of Tessibel's hut. A candle stood in the window, flickering its smoky flame toward the light streaks in the east. From the lighthouse to the ragged rocks the lake was covered with the ice and snow of an early winter. Beyond, the little waves curled up and washed over the frozen masses, adhering here and there, making an icy fringe along the edge. Flocks of wild ducks fluttered close to the lake surface, filling the morning air with discordant quacking.

Tessibel had not forgotten that her father was to be brought that day before his accusers,— she had made elaborate preparations for the reception of her dear one, when he should be free to return to her. She would stay in the shanty during the trial — and pray.

Daddy was playing a part in a most agonizing drama — he and the student and herself were the principals — while a few others, their enemies, made the background. . . . When the curtain fell Tessibel would bring " Daddy " home to the hut — and it was for this that she was preparing.

The bed had been dragged from the wall, and the squatter girl was sweeping out the dust of ages which settled again upon the coats and among the webby meshes of the net now dry and shrunken from disuse. One leg was missing from the stove, but three red bricks shoved under the side did the work of the broken part; the ancient frying pan with patches of grease upon it suspended itself from a newly driven nail in the wall.

Tess had learned many things since her father's imprisonment — had learned that a girl of fifteen couldn't run barefooted in the open with impunity. She had found a pair of Daddy's old cast-off boots, tied rags about her feet, and clambered into them.

How like a woman she felt with covered legs! True, the water gushed in through the holes that Daddy had cut in the soles on the rocks, but the tops were whole — and Tess looked upon them with pride.

When the daylight flooded the cabin Tess blew out the candle and viewed her work with delight. How pleased Daddy would be — after this she would be a model housekeeper. He should sleep in the morning until she had prepared his breakfast, and her fingers would fly in the summer, gathering the berries and fruit to make more money so that he should not run risks with the netting!

That first day of waiting seemed interminably long, but Tess spent it happily, for ever vividly into her mind came the words of Frederick the student — that God would hear, and answer.

Day by day her faith in the efficacy of her petitions had grown upon her. In spite of the fact that she had been caught by Daddy's enemies in her nightly scrambles up the ivy at the jail, God had answered in letting her see her father so many times at the end of her midnight walks.

Three men of squatter's row staggered through the storm up the Lehigh Valley tracks. They passed the line of huts, making an occasional comment upon the inhabitants of some lighted shanty.

It was the evening of the second of November, the first day of Orn Skinner's trial. The squatters had turned out in great numbers to see how the humped prisoner looked before his condemnation, for all believed that the fisherman would hang. It would be establishing a new precedent if Skinner were acquitted — and Ithaca never established new precedents with squatters.

So mused the men as they sullenly toiled toward home, each satisfied in his heart that, if Skinner went the way of others from the row, it would be but another act of revenge upon the part of the townspeople, for had not one and every witness save Elias Graves testified that day to the good character of the accused man?

The headlight of a locomotive sent them to the side track.

"Orn's face were yaller'n saffron, wern't it, when Minister Graves said as how he were a cussed pap of a cusseder gal," said Ezy Longman to Jake Brewer and Ben Letts.

"He were that mad," agreed Letts, "that the humps on his back just riz up and down — he were that mad, he were."

"But it were screechin' funny when the jedge made the parson speak out what Tess done," laughed Jake Brewer.

"You bet," assented Ezry Longman. "But why weren't she there to-day?"

"Don't know," answered Jake. "She were home, I guess. She 'lows as how her Daddy comes home to-morry . . . I 'lows as how he don't."

"I 'lows it, too," grunted Ben Letts.

They walked on in silence for some time, the wind crooning its endless tune through the telegraph wires. As they passed Kennedy's, Pete, the brindle bull-dog, howled in rage at not being able to attack the squatters. The dog snapped viciously at all strangers — and more than this would he have done if he had had an opportunity to reach Ben Letts and Ezra Longman. These men had spared neither stones nor sticks, in times past, to arouse the dog's ire; and Pete never forgot an enemy.

At the end of the lane, the candle in Skinner's window flickered them an invitation to stop. Tessibel answered their knock and embarrassedly offered each a chair as the door closed behind them.

"It ain't ended?" she faltered with a hasty glance at the three stolid faces, the post of Daddy's bed supporting the supple young form.

"To-morry," replied Jake Brewer.

Ben Letts moved uneasily in his chair. It was the first time he had ventured into the presence of Tessibel since he had put Frederick to death.

"He air comin' home, then?"

There was a question in the pleading voice as her eyes fell first upon one and then another.

"Nope," grinned Ezry, "he air to be took away."

Tessibel shrank back further and further, every muscle tired in its agony of burden-bearing. The rotten post squeaked loudly, bending beneath her weight, and over her in lightning rapidity swept the shadow of the rope, snatching her father from her — and God. The student had not limited the power of the cross; but Tess had discovered its limitations in Ezra Longman's statement — limitations that made her quiver with pain, as she pictured the evil thing which darkly menaced her loved one.

"He air a damn liar," burst forth Jake Brewer, "the jedge ain't said no words what Ezy says he has."

Tessibel heard and understood. The splendid, buoyant youth gathered instantly together, faith in the eternal promise of God sweeping over her once more. She might have known that Daddy was safe. Every long day had been filled with petitions, hurled at the feet of the Almighty: Tess, in her ignorance, had juggled with the sacred name of Jehovah, expecting the fulfillment of her prayers just as a boy, filled with ecstatic faith, expects his ball to come back to him after he has tossed it into the air. So would Daddy Skinner come to her, snatched from the shadow of an ignominious death, through some miracle of God's goodness.

"It air over to-morry?" she stammered, holding no grudge against Ezra Longman for his untimely joke.

"Yep."

"Then he air comin' home to-morry night?" she said almost in a whisper.

Ben Letts, looking at Ezra, closed one red lid, letting it fall slowly over the blurred blind eye. Neither he nor the boy spoke.

Letts brought his squint gaze back to Tess.

"He air comin' home to-morry night?" she repeated questioningly, raising her voice a little with an insistent glance at each fisherman. This time Tess read denial in their faces, but smiled radiantly. What did they know about it? What did fishermen understand of the student's God . . . of the faith that would bring Daddy home to her in spite of the twelve grim men, and all her father's enemies in Ithaca. Hadn't she consigned the beloved hump-backed father to Him who held the worlds in the hollow of His hand.

Ben Letts still gazed steadily at Tess, the red eyelids opening wider and wider. She had never been so beautiful before. During the past two months the girl had grown into a woman, into a soulful creature whom the squatter Ben ardently desired for his wife. Ah, he would see to that!

He shoved his great legs up and down before him, tumbling these things over in his mind. The taming of such a girl would be his vicious delight. The first thing to do would be to ply the scissors to the red curls. Ben could see that the hair was clean, each curl clinging lovingly to its mate, yet living apart — so different from the matted locks of the Tess he had always known.

"Yer Daddy got good and mad to-day," remarked Jake Brewer abruptly, the deadly silence grating upon his nerves.

"What about?" said Tess sharply.

"Dominie Graves were in the witness-box, and said as how yer pap were a wicked daddy of a wickeder gal, and the jedge made him tell as how ye was so cussed, and yer daddy's humps riz up like a cat's back wet with cold tea."

Tess waited expectantly.

"And the Dominie said as how ye twiggled yer fingers to yer nose at him," continued Jake. "Did ye?"

The pale face went to a deep crimson — she remembered the day well. The Dominie had caught her stealing berries and like all the weaker ones in a strife Tess had used her tongue bitterly — and had twiggled her fingers.

The squatters went away, leaving Tessibel with a new feeling of shame. Ben Letts went with reluctance — he dared not remain. After Skinner had gone the way of all squatters who incurred the penalties of the law, he, Ben Letts, would have the girl for weal or woe.

## CHAPTER XI

THE last day of Skinner's trial found Tessibel taking her lonely way toward town. She was going for Daddy Skinner — to bring him home to a shanty which she thought was clean, although the ragged curtain still flapped its tatters over a dirty window and the cobwebs hung listlessly from Daddy Skinner's unused net. But Tess had done her best, and her heart sang with delightful expectancy as she neared the dangerous open trestle which spanned the Hoghole gorge.

When she turned into town, her mind was at work with the thought of how she would bring Daddy triumphantly through the row of squatter huts, lead him even through the streets of Ithaca. Her vivid imagination played with the scene: Frederick the student would see her; he would know that together they had saved the dearest life ever given into the hands of a jury.

Up the snow-covered street, through Dewitt park, and into the little lane she tramped. Here Tessibel halted. The court-room was so crowded that an overflow of men stood in the street with overcoats tightly buttoned, stood listening for the words that would satisfy their demands: Orn Skinner must die. A demonstration of joy ringing from the court made the child shiver — then smile. Not even the wicked jeering of Daddy's enemies could shake her faith in the student's word. Twelve jurors sat in their chairs, but a useless set of men, for a unanimous ban of death had been pronounced upon the fisherman before any one of the jury had taken the oath. Some of the evidence did not reach their ears for they were thinking of other things — the man of two humps was as far away from their homes or their hopes, as the rope that would end him.

During the trial the prisoner had remained silent in his chair, with a stolidity that aroused no sympathy for him. Not once was he seen to lift his eyes to the judge; and but once, when Tess was being maligned by Dominie Graves, did the bible-back rise and fall as if the heart beneath were beating wildly. Skinner had not been allowed to testify in his own defense, and, knowing the futility of it, he had not insisted upon speaking.

His attorney made a few feeble remarks which, because of the speaker's indifference and his disbelief in his client, fell without effect. The prosecuting attorney took but ten minutes to sum up the case, telling the jury that they knew their duty too well for him to attempt to instruct them. "But," said he, "I will add one word of your own convictions. These people have infested our beautiful city, sapping its life like a great pest. The law is nothing to them — human life less. There is one thing, gentlemen of the jury, of which they stand in awe, and it is in your hands to give them one more lesson. That one thing they fear is — the rope."

He sat down amid a dense silence. The judge spoke shortly and the twelve jurors filed out past the stooping prisoner, who seemed to care so little that he did not look upon them as they went.

Twenty minutes elapsed and the court officer announced in stentorian tones that the verdict had been reached. Solemnly the twelve men seated themselves whilst an expectant flutter passed over the room.

Then a voice droned:

"Prisoner, rise."

The lumbering form painfully raised its two humps.

"Prisoner, look upon the jury; jury, look upon the prisoner."

The grizzled head settled itself back between the two pulsing humps; the steady eyes under the shaggy brows looking out for the first time in two days upon the row of men who hated him — all popular citizens of Ithaca.

"Foreman, of the jury, have you found the prisoner innocent or guilty?"

A pause, a hush; then a deliberate:

"Guilty of murder in the first degree."

A little higher rose the bible-back of the fisherman, lower sunk the large head between the deformed shoulders, like the receding head of a turtle, hiding itself under its shell when an enemy draws near. Skinner still stood with hypnotized eyes fastened on the jury; one thought in his mind — Tess.

"Orn Skinner," began the judge, "is there any reason why the sentence of this court should not be pronounced upon you in accordance with the law?"

The fisherman turned his piercing eyes upon the judge, but attempted not to speak.

"Orn Skinner —"

The judge was interrupted, there was a disturbing commotion in the back of the court-room. He lifted his gavel for silence, his gaze falling upon a dripping, shivering, red-haired girl, who raised to his face a pair of copper-colored eyes in which shone a soul, the magnitude of which the judge could not fathom with all his dignity.

"Orn Skinner," he finished, turning again to the fisherman, "twelve men have found you guilty of murder in the first degree. The court, then, passes its sentence upon you: you are to hang by the neck until you are — dead."

The ponderous form of the doomed man straightened as though unafraid, whilst the commotion increased — Tess was madly tearing her way through detaining hands. Once free, she started up the aisle, the most ridiculous little figure ever seen in Ithaca. The red hair was in curls to the girl's hips — the young form covered with but a calico blouse confined about the waist by a piece of hemp rope. Four huge thorns held together the edges of a rent down the center of the skirt, which came just above the knees, Daddy Skinner's cowhide boots lifting themselves under the hem.

Every one save him whom she loved was unseen by Tess, and everything unheard save the terrible sentence of death.

The pain-puckered wrinkles settled out of the wan little face; a smile brightened the brown eyes and dimpled the tender twitching mouth, altering the woful expression — for what was the mandate of an earthly judge compared to the majestic promise of Heaven? the student had said — but her smiling eyes fell for a moment on those of Frederick Graves. The boy partly rose but sank back again, white to the ears, a picture of mental suffering. Here through the silence came a shock to the citizens of Ithaca. Sweet as a spring bird carolling its love song rose Tessibel's beautiful voice:

" Rescue the perishin'
Care for the dyin'."

On and on up the aisle toward Daddy Skinner, forgetting or not knowing that she was desecrating the dignity of the honorable judge upon the bench, Tessibel clattered. Still no hand stayed her progress. Daddy Skinner was standing outside the railing, close to his attorney, guarded by a deputy. His fierce eyes turned at the sound of her voice, and the sight of his beloved snapped them shut like a vise.

The old beard, now shaggy and unkempt, trembled, whilst a parched tongue licked over the lips.

The long arms of the humpback slowly rose, and Tessibel sang herself into the throbbing bosom of her father.

The prisoner's great horny hand descended upon the curly head and for a moment the fingers of the girl tried to pry the wrinkled eyelids open. Her singing ceased, and she spoke — no great orator ever had a more intense audience.

" It air — it air Tess, Daddy Skinner, did ye think that her — had forgot — and Goddy?"

Everyone in the room heard the musical voice.

" The jedge didn't know," Tess went on, " that God promised that ye was to come home with Tessibel." And then, loosening herself from the trembling fingers, Tess leaned toward the judge, a wealth of hair falling over each shoulder.

" Did ye, kind, good man?"

His Honor, fascinated by the sight, bent toward her to make sure of her words.

"I air Daddy's brat," she urged with a smile, "and Goddy in the sky said as how Daddy Skinner would come home with Tessibel . . . He air to go with me, ain't he?"

Her voice, raised in sudden entreaty, the long eyes filled with an anguished anxiety, sent a pang of pity unknown before through the heart of the judge.

The audience rose as one man — only a swish and another dead silence.

"Ye air to come, Daddy Skinner," and without waiting for any further consent she took her father's hand and drew him slowly through the aisle up which she had so lately sung her way.

A man stepped into her path from among the spectators. Tess glanced up, and saw before her the lowering face of Dominie Graves. From every other soul in that room she had been given the bible-backed prisoner, for the majesty of human law had been forgotten in the appeal to the higher one.

"Stop," shouted the pastor, determined to see the sentence of the court carried out. He had placed himself directly in the squatter-girl's path, and, turning toward the jury, flashed indignant eyes upon them.

"Have you all gone mad?" he demanded. "Are you going to allow a murderer to escape from your hands?"

For one instant the condemned giant and the man of God scanned each other's faces with intensity. There was dumb pleading in the one gaze, and hard supremacy in the other. A spasmodic tremor ran over the spectators — Tess had struck a note of tragedy in the affair which had been overlooked by the thoughtless throng.

The judge, startled, spoke confusedly,

"Of course, of course," said he, "such a thing as this—"

"Would make our city the laughing-stock of the state," put in Graves, his interruption of the judge passing unheeded. "Skinner, you know you can't leave this court with that girl—"

Here a small boy broke in:

"She's the girl that twiggled her fingers at the minister."

Dominie Graves hushed the speaker with a wave of his hand, and went on:

"You have committed a murder, Skinner, and have been condemned to die by hanging."

His voice was low and vibrant.

"And there's no escape for you, Skinner," he finished.

As his voice died away, Ithaca received another impetus to curiosity and interest. A tall man in the back row rose and came forward.

"Mr. Graves," said the stranger solemnly, "you say that this man is to hang for murder. I say that he shall be given another chance for his life, and that he shall not hang if I can prevent it."

Deforrest Young, the noted professor of law from the University, was looking at Graves. A frown gathered on the broad brow of the minister, and every one gasped as the professor took Tessibel's hands in his.

"My child," and he bent lower that she might hear, for her bowed head was the only evidence of her grief, "Your prayers have accomplished more than you think. Keep on praying and pray hard, and the next time you come here you shall take home — your Daddy Skinner."

## CHAPTER XII

TWENTY young people had gathered for the toffy pull at Minister Graves'. Tess was the topic of conversation; every one was eager to talk of the unheard-of action in the court-room that day.

"My mother says," chimed in a pretty girl, "that when that Skinner girl walked up through the court room, she sounded like a horse trotting along."

"She had on a pair of man's boots, that's why," said another, "but she has a beautiful voice, hasn't she?"

This question was directed to Frederick Graves.

"Yes," he assented, flushing to his high-forehead line.

"And besides a beautiful voice," broke in Richard Hall, "she has a mighty pretty face — and such hair! If she hadn't been crying and had so many people around her, I should have spoken to her. She's worth consoling!"

A sharp pang of jealousy shot through Frederick's heart. That another should make lighter the burdens of the squatter girl filled him with unrest. A pleading face flashed across his vision and Tessibel's voice rang anew in his ears. He was living over again the moments spent in the cabin, and his heart thrilled at the memory of the momentary glance sent to him over the heads of the spectators in the crowded court-room.

Teola entered the drawing-room, turning the conversation from Tess to the pleasure of the evening.

"Will some one help me pull the toffy?" said she.

Her eyes were upon Dan Jordan — he rose quickly to his feet and followed the girl smilingly to the kitchen.

"I wanted you to help me get it ready," Teola said, coloring.

"I'm glad you chose me," replied Dan.

"I didn't ask you, did I?" The beautiful head hung low over the brown mixture in the kettle.

"Your eyes did," laughed Dan. "Didn't you notice that none of the other boys got up when you spoke." His glance filled with merriment as he went on: "I think, too, that I should have been a little — jealous if anyone else had — helped you."

"And your hands are so strong," murmured Teola.

"You only wanted my hands," queried the boy, trying to catch a glimpse of her face. "I wish you had wanted me for some other —"

Teola stood with the long wooden spoon twirling in her fingers.

"I did want you for yourself, Dan —"

And then she stopped and nothing could be heard but the click, click, click, of the toffy as it snapped to and fro in the huge fingers of the student.

"I'm mighty glad that I chose Cornell for my college," broke in the boy presently. "I thought first of going to Yale. . . . And you're pleased, too, Teola, that I came to Ithaca? Aren't you?"

"Very glad," came the low voice distinctly.

"And I've never been so ambitious in all my life as I have since I've been here, and known you, and I was wondering to-day if — if —"

Frederick's voice broke off the words; his big form loomed in the doorway before Dan could finish his sentence.

"Haven't you kids finished that toffy? Better let me help, too."

There was a noticeable tremor in Teola's voice as she replied:

"We've finished, Frederick, and you can carry the butter and those plates."

"I've something important to tell you, Teola," whispered Dan.

The girl did not answer, but the student knew that she would listen to him in some future time.

The drawing-room was festooned with evergreens and winter ferns, wound here and there with streamers of various-colored ribbons. Two large lamps, one in the window, and the other on a table near the dining-room door, sent forth their light through red shades. Glass dishes filled with apples and golden oranges decorated the top of the piano and surrounded the lamps.

When Dan and Teola left the kitchen, both flushed with the first emotions of their youthful hearts, there came to them gurgles of girlish laughter, intermingled now and then with the loud voice of some merry, happy boy.

After two hours of strenuous toffy-pulling the tired young revellers sat down to plates heaped with goodies.

Just at this juncture a ring of the door-bell pealed through the house. A silence fell over the company and a sound of altercation came to them distinctly. Suddenly the drawing-room door burst violently open and a spectacle, in strange contrast to the cheery scene about them, flashed upon the eyes of the young people. A red-haired girl, unkempt and dripping, wild anxiety portrayed upon her face, stood in the doorway. There was not the slightest embarrassment in her glance as her peculiar eyes traveled the lines of boys and girls, sitting round the wall. When at last they fell on Frederick, she took an impetuous step toward him, a brilliant smile lighting the wan face. Stupefaction rested upon the student as he recognized Tessibel Skinner.

"It air time — to pray," said she, looking straight at him, as he slowly rose from his chair. "Daddy Skinner air to be took away — unless yer God stops the rope."

Every word was distinct — unless God would stay the rope. The words repeated themselves over in the boy's brain and his face deepened in color. It was the beautiful faith of the wild, untaught young girl with the hot blood rushing in her veins that called forth the flush. His heart sickened with his own lack of confidence in God. He was to preach of a crucified Saviour, but no such faith and hope as this of Tessibel Skinner's would aid him. He was even now ashamed of the girl in cowhide boots and torn, thin skirt.

As these thoughts floated past him, he saw the young squatter wither under a giggle from a girl in the corner.

"Look at her feet," were the words that changed Tessibel's frankness to embarrassment, her eager pathos to wofulness.

Tessibel shrank close to the door, for the first time realizing how out of place she was.

"I were — I were — a fool to come, but — but —"

The earnestness of the vibrant voice, the proud, appealing young face moved Frederick to pity and self-reproach.

"It was right — you should have come," said he, gently taking her hands, "and no one dare question your privilege to ask a prayer for your father."

Still retaining her fingers in his, he turned, explaining:

"This is Miss Skinner whose father is suffering now from a stroke of the law. We, who have fathers and mothers whom we love, must wish her well."

Tessibel sank down, down, among her boots and rags, his words reducing her to tears. Teola came to her brother's side. She had never before been actually in the presence of a squatter, for, when they had brought fish and berries to the back door, her mother had always ordered the children to the front of the house; but now, filled with sympathy she stooped down and placed her hand upon Tessibel's head. The touch was so gentle that the fishermaid lifted her eyes to see who sorrowed with her.

The squatter covered the white fingers with tears and kisses. Then she struggled to her feet, the nails in Daddy's boots scraping the polished floor, making long white marks. To Tessibel there were no other persons in the room save Frederick and his beautiful sister. She made a queer upward movement with her head, wiping the tears away with the tattered sleeve.

"I was afeared ye'd forget Daddy Skinner," she murmured. "The big man from the hill said like you did. And I says it air prayin' time and I comed."

She had forgotten the tears of a few minutes before, forgotten that twenty pairs of searching youthful eyes watched her every movement and mentally criticized her, from the masses of long hair to the rock-torn boots on her feet. She only remembered the student — that he was smiling into her eyes, and that his sister, too, Teola Graves, had sympathized with her.

With a radiant, grateful smile, she turned to go, the door opening under her eager grasp. It was here that Dan Jordan spoke:

"Won't Miss Skinner have some coffee?"

Tessibel looked at him with an incredulous glance. He, too, had come forward and stood with his kindly gray eyes fixed upon her face.

"Yes, yes, of course," hurriedly put in Teola, "pardon me — I forgot. . . . You shall have my cup. . . . Here, Tessibel! I may call you that, mayn't I? Please drink some of mine."

Teola held the cup invitingly to the shivering lips, and Tessibel swallowed it down in one gulp.

"I air goin' now," she said desperately, wiping away coffee drops that lingered upon her face, "and ye ain't goin' to forget?"

This last was to Frederick, and he shook his head emphatically. He would not forget again; he would make the girl's father a special medium to establish a line of faith between the God he professed to love and himself — the quality of which should be no less than the one that Tessibel had cultivated during her weary weeks of waiting.

No thought entered anyone's mind of asking the girl if she were afraid of the dark night — she seemed so much a part of the darkness, of the falling snow and thrashing trees, that she was allowed to depart without a question. As he stood on the Rectory steps, the clicking of the big boots came to Frederick long after the slender form had disappeared from sight.

After that the party broke up, for the merriment had died in Tessibel's grief. An impression had been made upon the thoughtless boys and girls, and a shadow rested on each face as they bade " good-night " to their young hostess.

" She's the prettiest girl I ever saw," confided Teola to Frederick afterward; " her eyes are the color of a marigold."

In her heart Teola was glad that she had gone to the squatter in sympathy, for, upon leaving, Dan Jordan had whispered words that had burned deep into her soul:

" You are an angel, Teola *dear*, and I — love — you."

For one instant the tall student had bent his head, laying his lips upon hers — and had gone without another word.

## CHAPTER XIII

THE last day of the trial was so different from that of Tessibel's dreams! Again she must cross the dark Hoghole trestle alone on her way to the hut. But the singing in her heart when she left the Rectory took away the pain of her loneliness. Frederick Graves had said that she had done right in coming to him and asking prayers for "Daddy Skinner." Her faith in the student carried her above the material things of the earth, more than her absolute faith in God, for like women, Tessibel lived and had faith through the man of her choice.

It was nearly midnight when she passed Kennedy's wheat field in which capered Pete, the brindle bulldog. She called to him softly, pronouncing his name twice in loving resonance, which brought a low, pleased howl from the coarse throat of the dog. But the exhausted squatter-girl did not wait to touch the long, red tongue as Pete thrust his nose through the fence. She passed quickly down the lane to her father's hut. Turning the corner of the mud cellar, she saw dimly a man's form leaning against the shanty door. Her eyes were accustomed to marking correctly through the darkness, and it took Tess but a moment to ascertain that the lounging figure was Ben Letts.

In an instant, the first real fear she had ever felt swept over her and she drew back into the shadows. As a child she had fled from this man because he tantalized her; as a woman she dreaded him more than any reptile that came from the earth.

The man, hearing footsteps, raised his head; the silence continuing, he dropped it again, thinking he had been mistaken, and resumed his former position of waiting.

Tessibel wondered if she should go bravely forward — insist that the shanty was hers, and that he should go away. The mud cellar was between her and the waiting man, and as she peered closer to see if Ben were still there one brilliant tangle of hair fell over her shoulder. Ben Letts caught the movement and Tessibel knew it.

Alert as a young deer, she turned and fled back up the lane. Daddy's boots impeded her speed and one after the other she kicked them off. She could hear the man running after her, shouting his rage into her tingling ears. He was gaining upon the girl and commanded her to stop.

"If I get my claws on ye once," he growled; "it'll be bad for ye."

Tessibel heard and flew faster. There was no one to help her and her only salvation lay in her own two sturdy little legs and bruised feet. She reached the tracks but did not dare run the ties — she might trip in the darkness, and nothing could save her from her enemy. Her eyes, strained with convulsive fright, lifted one moment to the sky, and her glance fell directly upon the giant pine whose branches formed the image of her fantastic God. Her lips fell apart with a gasp — she fancied her Deity sent her an assurance of aid.

"Goddy — Goddy," was her petition, "for the love of yer Christ . . . and the student."

Suddenly out upon the air rang the voice of one of Tessibel's friends. The brindle bulldog from Kennedy's farm had heard the unequal race. With short tail raised, his fat neck bristling with stubby hair, he started for the tracks, as Tess did for the fence when she heard his growl. As the girl came on and on, the dog bounded along the ground toward her. Tess opened her lips and spoke sharply — and a pleased bark came in response.

God had heard and answered her. One wild leap in the air, and the sound of tearing clothes as her already tattered skirt came in contact with the barbed wire — and Tess was crouching down in the safe-keeping of the brindle bull. The dog whirled frantically around, licking her face. Fear weakened her tongue — she could not speak — only little spasmodic sobs burst from the parted lips. She caught the huge dog to her breast and waited.

Ben Letts was on the tracks; she could hear his big chest heaving with fast-coming breath. He halted on the other side of the fence.

Pete scented an enemy and straightened out his strong muscles like whip cords, a hoarse growl coming from between his jaws.

Ben leaned over the fence with an oath.

"Ye'd better come away from him," he grunted threateningly. "Ye air thinking the brute can save ye — but I'll put a bullet through his pate."

Tessibel knew that the man had no rifle with him; and by the time he could get one she and the dog would be far away. Her mind worked fast under the pressure.

"What do you want, Ben Letts?" she demanded.

"I just wanted to talk to yer," wheedled the man. "Come over the fence, will ye?"

"Ye can talk to me here," sullenly replied Tess. "I don't want to hear none of yer dum gab."

"It air somethin' nice — it air candy," feigned Ben. Then the tones hardened in the coarse voice, and he ended:

"Ye can't stay always with the brute."

"To-night I can, and in the day I ain't afeared — I don't want no candy."

The brindle bulldog lifted his head again and sent a low snarl in the direction of the fisherman — Ben in his rage had come too close to the fence. The animal's warning sent him back. Months before, Pete had buried his teeth in the man's hand and Ben would bear the marks to his grave.

"Ye go home, Ben Letts," insisted Tess. "Ye ain't no business here. Go home to yer mammy."

"I'm a-goin' to stay, just the same," rejoined Ben, sitting down upon the tracks.

Tessibel wound her arms around the dog's neck, banking the red curls under her cheek for a pillow. It was good to rest with her friend. Between the fence wires she could see the branches of the pine tree, its shadowy arms creating odd figures across the light streaks in the sky. What a wonderful being the student's God was! He had listened to the cry of a squatter and had saved her.

"Yer daddy ain't a-comin' home," Ben Letts broke in upon her meditations.

"He air," retorted Tess. "He air the nextest time I go for him."

"It air a lie," insisted the fisherman, " ye comes with me to the minister and I'll make yer an hones' woman. Ye'll have to cut that mop and settle down like a woman should. Do ye hear? . . . Tessibel, I says an hones' woman!"

Tessibel shifted her head from Pete's neck and sat up.

"Ye says as how — ye and — me — will go to the minister?"

"Yep."

"And we air to be — married . . . eh?"

"Yep."

"How about — the — brat — and — and — and Satisfied's girl?"

Myra's secret had slipped from her. Ben's silence invited her to proceed.

"Yer brat air sick to his grave, he air," said she mournfully, a tear settling in her voice, making its sweetness rough, "and Myry air a-dyin' of a broken heart. . . . If yer wants to make an hones' woman, make her one, that air what I says, I does. And ye broke her arm on the ragged rocks! Ye did! And then yer comes — and talks about bein' hones'," the musical voice rose to a cry. "Ye can't make a woman hones' for ye ain't hones' yerself."

Without a sound Ben rose from the tracks, reached for a stone and whirled it through the fence at Tessibel. The stone missed her, but struck the dog. Trembling with rage, Pete lifted his great body with a low, vicious growl.

Tessibel sprang from the ground, whilst another stone hurtled through the air, catching her curls in its flight.

Then she lifted the lower wire of the barbed fence. Pete crouched, and wiggled his flattened body through. Ben hadn't expected this — he turned and ran. The skurrying legs of the dog carried him quickly on after the fisherman. While Ben, screeching like a great night owl, hooted out his fear of the maddened dog, and yelled for Tess to call him off.

The girl did not speak, only waited, waited until a louder cry from the hunted man assured her that Pete had gripped him. Tessibel scarcely dared breathe; her friend, God's earthly instrument, sent to save her, and her mortal enemy were in deadly combat.

Ben's cries had ceased, but the listening girl could hear the two bodies as they turned over and over beyond on the tracks — and rolled into the ditch. Her feet were nearly frozen but she gathered them under her skirt and dumbly waited.

Then came no sound — there was nothing but a deathly silence in the dim shadows near the land.

Would she ever see either Ben or the dog again? There was no danger that Pete would —

"Ben," she called loudly, leaning over the fence. No answer came from the deep trench by the railroad bed.

"Pete, Pete, come to Tessibel, come to Tessibel."

Out of the blackness came the dog, his head hanging low, the angry sparkle in his eyes quenched.

Tess raised the wire once more for Pete's body to wriggle under. The girl shouted anxiously for Ben but no answer came to her call.

Crouching beside Pete, Tessibel reasoned out a way of escape: if she took the brindle bulldog to the hut with her, she would be safe from Ben were he lurking about,

She propped the lower wire of the fence high with a stick so that Pete could reach Kennedy's barn on the hill again when she sent him home. Together the girl and the bristling Pete slid silently to the railroad tracks, Tessibel holding tightly to the dog's collar. Some fifty feet beyond he twisted his heavy neck, set forth his huge jaw, and refused to move.

Beside the track was a long dark object — it was undeniably, unquestionably quiet. Tess tugged at the dog's collar and dragged him resisting from the spot.

Down the lane ran the squatter and the dog with no pause save to pick up the cowhide boots from the side of the path, where Tess had cast them in the mad race. She clasped the head of Pete as she opened the hut door.

"Ye can come in, too, Pete," she whispered, lifting the ugly head, "and go home in the morning."

Tessibel locked the door, but did not light a candle. Slipping her wet clothes to the floor, she crawled into Daddy's bed, and with the forgetfulness of youth sank into a sleep.

## CHAPTER XIV

THE next morning after her encounter with Ben Letts, Tess sat up in bed, wondering what had happened. Then she remembered. One slant ray of sun breaking through the dirty curtain showed that the day was far advanced. She jumped out of bed, opened the door and allowed Pete to scamper away.

After kindling a fire and frying a fish, she sat down to eat.

Suddenly a knock on the door startled her. Ben might return even after his lesson of the night before. Without unclasping the lock, she called out:

"Who air it?"

"It air me, Tessibel. Open the door.— It air Myry!"

Tess flung open the door with a smile. She drew back, seeing Myra's seamed face, white and drawn.

"Ye be sick, Myry?"

"Nope!"

"Air it the brat, then?"

"Nope, it air Ben Letts. He were hurt by the Brindle Bull at Kennedy's Farm. Ezy and 'Satisfied' found him near dead on the tracks and took him home."

Tess stood waiting, wide-eyed, without a word.

"He wouldn't say nothin' about it," complained Myry; "just says that he air goin' to get even with some one."

"Have ye seen him?" stammered Tess.

"Yep, this mornin' in his shanty. He were cut bad. They got the horse doctor to sew him up. He air sick, Ben air!"

"And the brat," demanded Tess, changing the subject purposely.

"Sick the hours through," replied Myra bitterly. "He hes got the pitifullest cry that breaks my heart all the time. But he ain't so sick as his pappy."

"Ben Letts ain't a-goin' to die, air he?"

Tessibel's woful expression caused Myra to shake her head emphatically, her thin lips twitching, then tightening under the nervous strain.

"Nope, he ain't, but he air goin' to be sick a long time. He air the brat's pa, and I want to do somethin' for him."

"What?"

"He air wantin' to see ye, Tessibel. Will ye go to him?"

"Nope," Tess burst forth spontaneously.

Myra looked at her curiously.

"He ain't amountin' to much," she ventured, "but he air a pappy — that air somethin', ain't it?"

"Yep," mused Tessibel. "A daddy air more than a mammy."

So had Tessibel and Myra been brought up to believe. The squatter women fawned at the feet of their brutal husbands, as a beaten dog cringes to its master. That Ben Letts had broken Myra's arm on the ragged rocks, and yet the girl wanted to aid him, showed Tess the superiority of the male sex, and Myra loved the squint-eyed fisherman, she evidenced it in every action.

The lips of the younger squatter were sealed about the trail which she herself had laid in the midnight tragedy. But through the tender young heart flashed the hope that the experience with the dog would cause Ben Letts to turn his face toward the wretched, shrunken creature, who had suffered so much through him. She contemplated Myra an instant.

"Do ye want me to see him?" she asked, rising.

"Yep," replied Myra, the dull eyes filled with a momentary sparkle. "He hes somethin' to say to ye, and I did say as how ye would come."

"Air he alone?" questioned Tess.

"Nope, his mammy air with him — we'll go now — eh?"

Slipping on Daddy's boots was Tessibel's assent, and they started through the underbrush in silence.

"The brat ain't goin' to die, air he?" asked Tess presently.

It had been several days since she had seen Myra's little son. The troubles of Daddy Skinner had taken up every moment of her time.

"Mebbe," grunted Myra unemotionally; "he howls like a sick pup from mornin' till night."

"I air a goin' home with ye, Myry," assured Tessibel; "he won't yap when I sings to him."

The lake had risen over the strip of beach, its waters freezing against the rocks. This forced the girls to take the path through the wood to the hill beyond. Until they came in sight of Ben Letts' cabin, they said no more.

At their knock Ben's mother softly opened the door. Her shaggy gray hair had not been combed and her fierce old eyes glowed with agony unsoftened by tears.

"Ben air too sick to get up," she explained awkwardly, presenting each girl a chair, "I said as how ye couldn't come, Tessibel, but Ben said Myry were to bring ye."

From the back room came the sound of belabored breathing and a hoarse voice called for Tessibel. The squatter girl rose to her feet, her color changing from red to white. The thought of the fisherman with his dog-bitten face was repulsive to her.

"Ye be goin' in with me to see him, ain't ye, Myry?" The brown eyes entreated that she should not be sent to Ben Letts alone.

Myra Longman shook her head. She knew that the brat's pa did not want to see her, and again she shook her head as Tessibel waited.

"He air been askin' all the mornin' for ye, Tess," urged Mrs. Letts, "Ben ain't no likin' for Myry, Ben ain't!"

A dull red flush crimsoned Myra Longman's face. She watched Tess enviously as the girl tiptoed through the doorway and disappeared.

Ben Letts was stretched out on the rope cot, his massive head and thick neck swathed in bandages. Two huge hands, with patches of plaster here and there lay outside the red Indian blanket. The swollen upper lid was tightly pressed over his blind eye, the squint one slowly opening at Tessibel's entrance.

She looked down upon the bandaged face but for a moment; neither of them spoke.

"I see ye comes," Ben broke in at last.

"Yep, I's here . . . What do ye want?"

A drop of salt water oozed from the weak eye; Ben moved his head as if in pain.

"Sop up the tear with the rag, will ye, Tess?" he grunted. "It air burnin' like hell fire."

Tessibel took the soiled cloth in her fingers, and not too lightly did as Ben bade her.

"Ye didn't tell Myry how I comed sick, did ye?" asked Ben, settling his head back upon the pillow.

Tess gave a negative gesture.

"Er no one else?"

"Nope!"

"Ye be a pert girl, Tessibel, and I were a cuss for trying to scare ye — but the brindle bull has got to die."

"Nope, he ain't got to die," frowned Tess.

"When I gets up he eats what I gives him," assured Ben. "He has to die, I says, I does . . . But ye be a pert gal, Tess."

Ben moved his head to bring the girl within the vision of his one eye.

"What be ye wantin' with me?" Tess muttered. "I wants to go home."

She saw another tear roll down the plastered cheek, and repeated her operation with the rag.

"What do ye want?" she demanded again.

"To tell ye thet I air a goin' to make an hones' woman of ye. I's a goin' to marry ye. I knows I's a pappy, but the brat'll die, and he'll be forgot like yer daddy will!"

Tess instantly froze into a white, tense little form. She did not follow the fisherman's glance as he motioned her to take up the cloth.

"I's a tellin' yer mammy to wipe yer old eye," she said pettishly. "I ain't got no notion of bein' an hones' woman . . . I hates yer like I hates Ezry Longman."

She wheeled to go out, but the man stayed her with a grunt.

"I's to be sick for a long time," exclaimed he, "and mammy will step to the grave most any day . . . I wants pert fingers to put the plasters on my cuts."

Here he groaned and fought for the cloth, the salt tears scorching the rents in the skin as they rolled hot from the red eye and soaked into the plasters. The squatter girl mechanically wiped away the tears, turning again.

"Myry air pert," she said, halting in the door. "She air more than that — her fingers air lovin' ones. These," and she held up her two brown hands, "would be hurtin' ye, cause I hates ye so."

Tessibel and Myra walked away from Ben's hut in silence, up the ragged rocks to the Longman shanty.

"Ben were askin' to marry yer, Tess, weren't he?" demanded Myra as they approached the door.

Tess nodded.

"Were he sayin' as how ye could take care of him?"

"Yep."

"Be ye goin' to?" The intense longing and misery in her voice made Tess gasp:

"Nope, he air too mean a cuss to live. If he air the brat's pa, let the brat's ma take care of him. The brat air a good little devil."

Mrs. Longman was moving about in the loft overhead when the two girls entered the shanty.

Tess went to the wooden box and looked down upon the small, pinched face of the sleeping infant. The babe had worn out his little lungs, screeching in his pain, the small faded eyes rolling backward as he slept.

The young mother came quietly to the side of her squatter friend.

"If the brat dies," she began in a low, tense tone, "be ye goin' to marry Ben Letts?"

"Nope, I ain't never goin' to marry nobody!"

"Yep, ye will, when ye gets done bein' a baby!"

Tess drew her eyes from the dozing infant and glanced at Myra.

"I wants a Bible," said she deliberately.

"What for?"

"To read out of!"

"Can ye read?"

"Nope, not much, but I can spell out words, and write a bit. And the Bible says as how, if ye seeks, ye'll find what ye seeks."

The shining eyes were sending a truthful message into the heart of the young mother.

"That ain't nothin' to do with Ben Letts," muttered Myra.

"Yep, it air," insisted Tess. "It says what ye seeks ye find. Ain't ye seekin' Ben Letts?"

"I knows where he air already," sullenly replied Myra.

"But ye can seek his lovin's, can't ye? . . . I's a seekin' Daddy — and somethin' else."

"What?"

"To be readin' and writin' like — like the minister's gal does. I air a-seekin' it every day!"

"How?"

Tess flushed. She could not tell Myra of the long bearded God in the pine tree, nor of the stumbling prayers she had repeated night after night. Myra understood that she could sing, so Tess said laconically:

"I sings for it sometimes, and that air a seekin'."

Myra grunted.

"I can't sing," and she frowned.

The babe whined in the cradle and Tessibel took him up. The glorious voice hushed the child to sleep, Myra Longman bitterly scanning the beautiful face. There were only two years between her and Tessibel, and her own poor, ghastly wrinkled face looked years older. If she were only pretty, Ben might love her. Tess had the splendid vigor of healthy youth — Myra, the worn-out complexion of a bad digestion. Beans and bacon had made the one beautiful — and destroyed the other.

Suddenly Myra leaned over with a new expression in her eyes.

"Tessibel, I tries to seek Ben Letts and his lovin's for me and the brat."

Tessibel placed the small boy in the box, then she and Myra obeyed Mrs. Longman's fretful demand that they draw up and eat.

## CHAPTER XV

THAT evening Minister Graves came blustering in after his family were seated at the table. What was this ridiculous thing that he had heard? His home disgraced, his position ruined, his children ostracized. He glanced at Teola and Frederick. His wife, fastening Babe's napkin under the child's chin, remonstrated.

"Why, father, what's the trouble?"

"I was making a clerical call on Mrs. Robman to-day," fumed the Dominie, "and that girl of hers, and a saucy one she is, too, burst into the room, and, mother, what tale do you think she told — before us?"

Frederick glanced at his sister, but Teola's eyes were upon her empty plate. Mrs. Graves shook her head.

"That that Skinner girl came here last night and in all her rags and filth drank coffee from our daughter's cup! Madame, did you ever imagine that such a disgrace could fall upon you?"

Mrs. Graves looked helplessly from her husband's distorted face to her son and daughter.

"She came into your home," went on the minister, "and was asked to take refreshments from your cups. Mrs. Robman said that she disliked to think that such degraded guests were allowed in your home. . . . Do you understand what that means, Mrs. Graves?"

"Let Frederick explain, father," pleaded the trembling wife; " he was going to speak and you stopped him. What and how did it happen?"

"The girl came to the Rectory to ask prayers for her father," said Frederick, an expression darkening his eyes which his mother dreaded.

"Prayers . . . prayers!" roared the minister, "Prayers for a squatter and a murderer! . . . And drinking coffee from your cups. Such a disgrace can never be lifted from this house."

"What hurt did she do?" irreverently asked Babe. Frederick was thankful for the child's frank question.

"Hurt? Harm, you mean. If she should just hurt a person that could be mended. Harm was what she did!"

"What harm?" persisted Babe.

"Madam, you see your children are all growing up like heathens. There arn't any of the parents whose sons and daughters were here last night, who won't think a long time before they allow them to come again. You understand, don't you, that that squatter covered with germs of all kinds drank from your daughter's cup."

Mrs. Graves started preceptibly. She was noted for a fear of germs.

"Teola, your mouth must be scoured with peroxide . . . Oh, if some one would only tell me how it all happened!"

Frederick rose from his chair and impulsively laid his hand on his mother's shoulder. To Teola he looked so tall and strong, so capable of explaining, that she rose, too.

"I will tell you mother," said the student. "The

girl was in distress. In some way she had been led to believe that prayers, effective prayers, could bring about any desired result. She simply came to ask us to pray for her father."

Teola was by his side now, reassuringly pressing his arm.

"And where would she go," she broke in suddenly, "if not to a minister's home?"

The pastor's whole family, at least the members that had been submissive — for Babe had always challenged her father's commands — was rising against him. His wife, instead of taking her willful children to task, was weeping; his son and daughter stood beside her refuting every word he said. He brought down his hand with a bang, his eyes narrowing into a slit.

"You will every one do as I say," he cried. "Frederick, you are to stay away from classes for two days, your professors knowing that you have disobeyed your father. If your fellow students ask you why you are absent, you must tell them what I have said. And, you, Teola —"

Frederick stopped the rush of words.

"If I stay away from college two days," he said in a low tone, so deliberate that every word burned into the mother's brain, "I shall never go back again. I am no longer a child and I won't be punished. And what is more, I shall leave your home forever. You may take your choice, father, but not until I make another statement. The girl from the lake asked me to pray for her. That is my intention, and I shall do more if possible. I shall use every bit of influence I have to aid her father to escape hanging . . . Also, if you punish Teola, you will never see me again."

Mrs. Graves had risen from her chair. She walked straight to her son — placed her hand upon him.

"Frederick, you wouldn't leave your mother?"

The strong arm pressed about the wearied little form reassuringly.

"And you can bet, papa Graves," put in Babe, "that I'll go with mamma any old day, that's what I will."

Teola stood irresolutely, looking first at Frederick, then at her father. She went toward the minister and almost whispered,

"Father, let me speak! The girl came without having been invited by anyone, and she did not stay five minutes. She was drenched through, and cold . . . I gave her my cup of coffee, and she stated her errand and went away."

The minister rose, leaving his supper untouched, put on his overcoat, not one remonstrating word coming from his family, and went out.

Pastor Graves made his way up the town through the main street to Bates' drug-store, his hunger having died in his anger and amazement.

He was positive that he could have brought his children to terms, had not their mother taken sides with them. His thoughts went back to the early days of his married life when nothing had disturbed their peace; the children obeyed, and Mrs. Graves thought her husband's word the essence of all law.

He turned into the drug-store in the middle of the block. Here met, nearly every evening, the head ones of his flock for a little while to talk over religion and politics. Outsiders called it the "Amen Corner" of Ithaca.

"Ah," exclaimed the druggist, "you're early, Graves. Must have had your supper at the going down of the sun."

Graves coughed his embarrassment and sat down.

"Feeling sick, Elias?"

The druggist opened the door for a child to pass out.

"No, not ill, only disgusted with the world in general."

"Skinner's girl coming to the court went against your notions, eh?"

"And every one else's with any sense," snapped Graves.

"Professor Young stopped in here to-day on his way up the hill," resumed Bates, "he had been over to the jail, talking to Skinner, and he says that the man will be murdered if the state hangs him."

"That's all Young knows about it," growled the minister. "You and I know these people, Bates, better then Young does, and Skinner's word isn't worth the powder to blow it up with."

Bates took his accustomary position on the bookkeeper's stool and spread his long hands out on his knees.

"Well, the professor says," he went on, "that Skinner can prove that he didn't use the gun."

"How can he prove it?" asked Graves sharply, "only by the oaths of men with no more veracity than he has. I wouldn't believe one of those squatters if he used the sacred oath twenty times over."

"Maybe the next jury will think differently," argued the druggist.

"Bigger fools they then," interrupted Graves. "I don't know what the town is coming to if the fishermen can shoot down our officials without even remonstrance. I'll tell you what, Bates, there'll be a city war over Skinner. Let Young take up the cudgel, and I'll see what the church can do. There's power in the pulpit, I can tell you that."

Bates agreed to this.

"If the citizens of this city," continued the minister, encouraged by the evident acquiescence of the druggist, "should take this matter up as a body, ten men like Young couldn't bring about Skinner's acquittal."

"I'm not so sure," muttered Bates.

"I'm sure," insisted Graves strenuously, "very sure, for, if to a man every one is ready to do his duty, what kind of a jury could they have? Like yesterday's — conviction, swift and sure."

"But" objected the druggist, "a juror who takes his oath in a murder case, must know little or nothing of it. Men would not be accepted if for a week or month they had listened to combative sermons against the prisoner. And you certainly wouldn't have a juror perjure himself, would you, Graves?"

"The district attorney is no fool," replied the minister, softening his argument under the shocked expression of Bates; "he knows when the state is to be benefited by the outcome of a trial. He can leave off certain questions; it has been done."

"I know it," interrupted Bates. "But — it seems hardly fair."

Just then the door opened, and Silas Jones, the richest man in the town, took his seat with the other two "Ameners." The fascinating subject of the day, the unusualness of the squatter trial and the girl with the singing voice, continued to be the topic of conversation. Minister Graves' family, in standing out against him in a matter so near his heart, only strengthened his desire to see the end as he wished it to be — the sentence of yesterday executed against the fisherman without another trial.

"Young lost his senses to-day, don't you think so, Silas?" he asked.

"Well," drawled Jones, "if Skinner didn't commit willful murder, I'd hate to see him hang. It wouldn't do any harm as I see to give him another chance."

"You'll change your mind in church next Sunday," commented the parson. "I'm going to show every man his duty clear and plain."

He brought down his hand upon his knee with an egotistical slap.

"All folks don't think the same way you do, Dominie," persisted Jones. "Now then, Bill Hopkins of the toggery shop, he don't believe in women speakin' in meetin'."

The minister distinctly remembered this. More than once had he taken the delinquent Bill Hopkins to task for taking his letter to another church, but Bill could not be induced to return, because the creed had not been followed by its members, nor enforced by the shepherd of the flock.

Hopkins was the best-read man in the whole county, and his voice went far when he spoke, but for over a year his place among the "Ameners" had been vacant — also his pew in Graves' church. The Dominie needed such men as Bill in his congregation if he would win his fight against the squatters. These thoughts were prominent in his mind when the door admitted a great gust of wind — and the famous Bill Hopkins. The parson caught his breath. Bill spoke a genial good-evening, shook hands around, and bought a small bottle of witch-hazel, some camphor, and was about to leave, when Graves ejaculated:

"Sit down, Bill."

Bill sat down, took his hat from his bald head, and placed his fingers complacently around a smooth white wart on his cranium, and waited.

He looked questioningly at the rich man, and the druggist with the wide-spread hands. The church subject had been thrashed out long ago — the women of the congregation gaining the day in spite of the august presence of some of the deacons, who openly declared that the female portion of the church was unbecomingly usurping the authority of the men. Because of this flagrant disobedience of the church's creed, Bill Hopkins had taken his name from the roll, and was known to have said that he would not be led by a shepherd who could not order his flock. To-night he smacked his lips for the coming argument while the minister, glad to have him among them again, felt his hopes rise higher.

Bates flattened his hands with delight, noticing a smile that drew down the corners of Jones' lips. Long ago the pleasant religious argument of Ithaca's "Amen" corner had become a thing of the past, because of the absence of Bill Hopkins. He had been the zest of the crowd.

The Dominie, forgetting his grievance of the supper table, straightened himself for the combat. He had suddenly conceived a plan whereby he could gain a friend to aid him in the coming squatter fight. Bill Hopkins still waited with a quizzical expression in his shaggy-browed eyes.

"Strange happenings in town for a few days past," said Graves.

"The Skinner case?" asked Bill, rubbing gently the smooth white wart.

"Yes," assented the minister. "What do you think of it all, Bill?"

"The girl's a brick," commented Hopkins — and sank into silence.

"The girl's not being tried for murder," rebuked the mnister sharply.

"But she played her part with feelin' and power," was the drawling reply.

The clergyman saw a flitting expression of triumph in the druggist's face.

"She'd make a capital actress," ruminated Graves.

He glanced at the rich man to see if he coincided with him, but that gentleman was looking into the street.

"We all act in this world," excused Bill; "even you ministers use methods that you have found in elocution to bring your beliefs to bear upon your congregations."

Graves did not relish being classed with the squatter's child, but he made no comment upon it. He changed his tactics.

"Bill," said he, "have you altered your ideas about the church?"

"What ideas?"

"Well, about women having the privilege of speaking in meetings."

Bill shook his head, and Graves resumed:

"Well, I'm changing my mind . . . I'm going to stop this nonsense."

The rich man sat up and the druggist, scenting a religious rumpus, drew his stool nearer. Bill coughed loudly.

"Those women," continued Graves, "have had their own way too long . . . I shall put a stop to it immediately."

Bill Hopkins wondered what was coming. It behooved him to wait and see; so he settled back with his head bowed and his piercing eyes directed steadily upon the pastor. A dark flush mounted to the minister's face. He had expected that such condescension to an ex-member would be received with enthusiasm. As no other of the "Ameners" offered a word, Graves continued:

"Next thing that we know, the women will be coming into the church with uncovered heads. I wonder I've stood it so long."

Still Bill did not speak. He could remember that when the dispute had been at its height these had not been the sentiments of Pastor Graves. In fact, when a delegation had gone to the parsonage to demand obedience to the constitution of the church, the Dominie had replied that the ladies had come out victorious in the matter, and that it was an old-fashioned idea to forbid the women to speak or pray in public if they so wished; and the crest-fallen delegates had gone away from the rectory, and Bill Hopkins, with several others, from the church.

Seeing that not one of the respectable "Ameners" was going to help him, the Dominie sputtered out his wrath in another direction.

"If Young had kept his hands off that Skinner business, there wouldn't have been the slightest chance of the fisherman winning out."

"Ah! here's where the shoe pinches," thought Hopkins; "the parson needs help to wrest Skinner's squatter rights from him."

But he did not voice his thoughts.

"I guess that's right, Dominie," were his spoken words. "Skinner didn't have many friends in the court until that girl came in. She certainly did make a change in the ideas of most people in this town."

"Fools! to let a child like that break up the dignity of a court-room." Graves settled back angrily in his chair. He had lost in the game he was about to play with Bill Hopkins — lost before the game had begun.

"Skinner can thank his kid for his life, nevertheless," interjected Jones, "for another jury will never convict him."

"Think not?" queried the druggist.

Bates' question remained unanswered, for Dominie Graves turned the subject again.

"Bill, if I come out strong in the church and give you your own way in the disputed question, then you must do something for me. I'll speak to you later about it."

"Pretty far along in the day," was Bill's answer, "but as you please, Dominie. I don't know what you want, but most of your friends will stick by you if the church is run on its old plan and according to the creed and the Bible.

When Minister Graves walked home he felt that in spite of family differences he had scored a point in getting from Hopkins a tacit consent to come back into his congregation.

## CHAPTER XVI

WHEN the family gathered about the table the next morning in the rectory, the Dominie told his wife solemnly that he wished to talk with her after the children had gone to school. Breakfast over, he broached the subject of the women talking in prayer meeting, Mrs. Graves listening eagerly. As the pastor's wife she had done the best in her power; but her power had been weak, and the stronger ones in the congregation had ridden over her convictions and teachings.

There was Augusta Hall, the beautiful wife of one of the deacons who had demanded that she be allowed to voice her sentiments in public; and other women had followed her lead, although it had been absolutely against the tenets of the church.

This woman was in Mrs. Graves' mind, when the Dominie brought down his hand upon the table, saying he had decided to stop once and for all the nonsense in his church, which was keeping the best of his members away.

Mrs. Graves breathed Mrs. Hall's name meekly to her husband.

"She can leave the church," growled Graves. "In my mind it's almost sacrilegious for women to dare to go so far that some of the best of its members will leave a well-regulated church. Maria, you must talk to Mrs. Hall and bring her to reason."

"If you can't succeed," replied Mrs. Graves, "how do you expect me to? You're her pastor."

"I will go and talk to her first, then you follow close upon my heels, Maria, and between us both, we will get Bill Hopkins and Carey back among us. If they come the rest will."

Late in the afternoon Mrs. Graves put on her bonnet, and, with a sigh, tied the strings under her withered chin. In the very moment when the congregation had at last become reconciled to the privileges extended to its female members, another church war was to be fought. But the little woman dared not refuse her husband's command, so she climbed the long hill toward the south and timidly rang the bell marked "Hall."

Her husband would have been there and gone, for the afternoon was well toward its close.

As the servant ushered her in, Mrs. Graves heard loud voices coming from the drawing-room, and instantly recognized one of them as the clergyman's.

"It's all very well, Mrs. Hall," he was saying, "for the women to work if they can do it without showing too much authority, but, my dear lady, I have been studying into this matter and it is positively against the Scriptural injunction for women to speak in church."

"Where did you read that?" asked Mrs. Hall, handing the Dominie a Bible, which he did not take in his half-extended fingers.

"I know, and you know where it is without looking," said he sharply. "There is a command from Paul that all women should keep silent in the church in the presence of men."

"Paul was an old bachelor," irreverently answered Mrs. Hall. "What did he know about women and their needs?"

"He received the commandments from God," replied the pastor gravely.

"Not that one, and what's more, I am going to talk all I want to, and if there is a man who does not want to hear, let him go away until he either changes his mind or desires to take things as they are. . . . Why! the women have been speaking in our church for over a year."

At this juncture, Mrs. Graves walked in, pale and weary. She dropped weakly into a chair.

"Your husband has just informed me," snapped Mrs. Hall, her beautiful face flushing as she spoke, "that we are not to speak any more at the church meetings. Do you approve of that, Mrs. Graves? I'm sure —"

"Like all dutiful and obedient wives," came the sharp interruption from the minister, without giving his sorry-looking spouse a chance to speak, "my wife thinks as I do. Mrs. Hall, allow me to entreat you to follow the dictates of your conscience, and obey your husband always."

"My husband gives me my own way," answered Mrs. Hall with a toss of her head.

"There he is wrong, but I shall leave you to talk things over with my wife. On Sunday I shall make it the theme of my sermon and I hope before Wednesday, my dear Mrs. Hall, that you and some others will look upon the matter in a different light."

The Dominie wended his way toward the business quarter of the city and turned into the Gas Company's office. Inquiring for Mr. Hall, he was ushered into a private room marked " President," and heartily greeted one of the deacons of his church.

" Anything wrong? " asked Hall, noticing the expression upon his pastor's face.

" No, only I called about a new rule which we're going to pass Wednesday evening, and you can help us if you will."

The president looked up inquiringly.

" The women must no longer speak at the prayer meeting."

Mr. Hall half rose from his chair as these words fell from the clergyman's lips, but he sank mutely back.

" It has become necessary to enforce the laws of the church," explained Graves, " and I have taken up this matter with some of the members — also with your wife."

Mr. Hall dropped his eyes upon his left hand with the fingers of which he was bending back those of his right.

" And what did she say? "

" I think it will be necessary for you to talk with her, Hall; surely you have enough influence over her to make her see that it is absolutely necessary that women should cease their —"

" I thought, Dominie," broke in the deacon, " that we had long outgrown such notions. You had better let matters go on as they are."

The minister shook his head emphatically, and looked searchingly at his parishioner.

" Fact is, Mr. Hall, you know that it is not a personal thing with me, but for the good of the church. Hopkins has left and Carey only comes when he feels like it. Several others stay away without a place to worship, simply because the ladies will have their way. I have no trouble with my wife and no man would if he were to demand obedience as God says that he should. I shall preach upon it Sunday."

"Don't make it too strong," ventured Hall, thinking of his beautiful wife.

As far as he was concerned it made no difference whether women were silent or not, whether they wore hats to church or came in with bare heads. He was happy in his home life, and was not willing to bring about discord by arguments that meant nothing to him. When the church matter had come up before, he had acquiesced without a word, had watched the fight as it progressed, and when it ended had settled back to enjoy peace — a happy official of Ithaca's gas company.

He looked out under his brows at the clergyman, as he fingered the paper-cutter on his desk. He took it up mechanically and read the inscription on the handle: "From me to you."

His wife had given it to him, and Hall mentally wondered if the woman who could think of, and would dare to use, such a unique expression would be frightened by a word from him.

Without asking Augusta, the husband knew that his wife would be the first woman to rise to speak next Wednesday evening. This much he intimated to Graves. An expression of sarcasm flitted over the clergyman's countenance, but it quickly vanished — Graves was trying to add to his strong friends that day. He only remarked that he hoped it would be settled amicably. The president ventured another shot:

"Dominie, there's a complete turn in the affairs of Skinner; he says that he did not commit the murder — that he positively did not pick up the gun from the shore. Simply because he owned the gun is no proof that he used it. Young says —"

"Young had better attend to his campus business," interrupted Graves. "He will have all he can do. There's no doubt in my mind that Skinner is guilty. I should have thought that his conviction was proof of that."

"But he didn't have a chance to prove his innocence," replied Hall. "He has such a good reputation among his own people that Young is going to take up subscriptions for another trial."

Elias turned sharply upon the gas official.

"Few people who understand the matter will give money to save the life of a squatter. That's another thing I'm going to preach upon next Sunday. The very manner in which they live would prove what bad citizens they are."

"We can't hang a man," argued Hall, "because he doesn't live in accordance with our stilted notions. Professor Young says that the girl is a genius — that she has a beautiful voice. I promised that if he took up — a contribution for the family that I would send him a check."

Elias Graves rose hastily to his feet, forgetting to put out his hand as he went out. He now hated Tessibel Skinner with a deep religious hatred, and it would be war between him and her for the life of the imprisoned squatter.

President Hall, with a smile upon his face, closed the door of his private office after his pastor had departed.

"It's evident why Graves wants the women turned down," mused he; "he thinks that he will draw about him again such men as Hopkins and Carey and that they will help him in removing Skinner from his land. I won't help persecute the poor devil — Gad, but that daughter of his did turn things upside down. I wonder what Augusta will say to me when I go home?"

It was a keen, cold and blizzardly Sunday morning when the bells of the different churches rang out upon the air. Ithaca was astir and her citizens anxious to worship. For one-half hour the streets teemed with well-dressed people, then became as silent as if the town were uninhabited. Minister Graves took his place in the pulpit and scanned the pews which were filled to overflowing. Not only had his members come, one and all, but people from other congregations were standing at the back of the railing, eager to hear the mighty effort which would be given forth from the clergyman's eloquent tongue. Elias Graves took his text from Genesis —"And thy desire shall be to thy husband, and he shall rule over thee."

The minister leaned far over his flock, as he finished this impressive text.

His eyes fell upon Deacon Hall's pew, then upon his own in which sat his wife with Babe near her. Frederick was between Teola and the little girl, and they were all earnestly watching their father — something was going to happen, but they did not know what. The deep voice broke out into a prayer, followed by a soulful anthem from the choir.

Minister Graves rose with dignity, and began his sermon.

"It is my intention," said he, "to divide my sermon this morning directly in two, because my subjects are so entirely different. Before the expiration of it, you will see the force of my argument and will, I hope, profit by it."

He continued by saying, a house divided against itself would surely fall, that even a stone structure built upon sand would slip into the sea.

"Brethren, the sea of which I speak is a sea of discontent and disobedience. From my reading text you will see that God commanded that woman should be obedient, that she should obey her husband to the letter — to the letter, brethren."

There was a decided rustle of silken petticoats in the church.

"It was the disobedience of our first mother," spoke the clergyman, "that threw Adam into ill-repute with his Creator, and also Adam's love for her that drove him from the Garden of Eden. Brethren, God is good to mankind, ever ready to listen to his appeals. If Adam had only believed in the greatness as well as the goodness of God, he would have spurned the woman who had dared to so flagrantly disobey, instead of following her from the garden.

"Adam had more than one rib," went on the minister, "and how readily and kindly would God have disposed of the first sinning Eve and under the pleasant sleep of the man, Adam, extracted another rib out of which he would have constructed another and yet more beautiful woman. Some of us are finding it impossible to keep order in our families, and until we do, we cannot expect to live to the glory of God."

A loud hacking cough came from Deacon Hall's pew

and many heads were turned toward it. This disconcerted the clergyman for a moment, but he picked up the threads of his sermon and resumed:

"If every man in this little city would rely upon the goodness of God to supply him with another Eve, when the woman joined to him in holy matrimony disobeys His law, it would be a simple matter to re-establish order in his household. Just as happiness was given to Lot after the turning to salt of his wife."

The minister paused — the silence was so deathly that it appalled him. He allowed his eyes to fall upon the memorial window with a man's face upon it. The words underneath the figure passed before him dimly. Then he remembered that he was preaching a sermon. Was he not the chosen shepherd of the flock? Was he not the one man called by God to show these people the righteous paths in which to walk? Should his voice be silenced because others did not believe as he did? And was he not showing them the light through the Scriptures? With these thoughts in his mind and renewed energy in his voice he spoke again:

"I should be the last man in the world to raise a false alarm, neither do I desire to enter homes and bring discord there. But I read from a passage under my hand, 'If thy right hand offend thee cut it off.'

"From the words of the Scriptures I have proven to you that a household must be ruled by the husband and by him alone. And that it is the duty of every wife to obey her husband as long as she shall live.

"I shall ask the women of this congregation not to rise next Wednesday evening in the prayer meeting, either to pray or testify. The privilege has been withdrawn as one perniciously against the tenets of the church. For Paul says in first Timothy, 'I suffer not a woman to teach nor to usurp authority over the man, but to be in silence;' also I give you Paul's further command, 'Let the deacons be the husband of one wife, ruling their children and their own houses well.'"

He ran over the last few words quickly for the louder rustle of silk could be heard. The minister changed his subject and gave them another text which said that the wicked people of the earth should be cut down. Was the minister going to sanction the killing of wives who refused to obey their husbands? Had he lost his mind? But his voice rang out upon the congregation upon a subject in which they had recently become so interested.

"There is on our city," said the clergyman, "a terrible blot. The wicked ones of Jerusalem could not equal them in wickedness.

"The plans of God in keeping peace among his people are to be carried out to-day, with as much vigor as they were three thousand years ago. I need not give you the details of a murder committed a short time ago within the limits of our city. The very fact that the murderer has the chance of another trial after his conviction demonstrates that something must be done, and quickly. If the secular law is not able to wipe out such a blot then the church must help. It is my idea, brethren, that the weeds of the earth must be cut down, and by weeds I mean bad men. If a petition is handed you to sign asking time for Orn Skinner, I ask you one and all not to place your names upon it."

The clergyman suddenly stopped, closing his Bible. "Papa would cut off Tessibel's father's head if he could, wouldn't he, Frederick," whispered Babe.

Frederick gave the child a reproving glance and the little girl sank back after explaining that if Skinner were hung "papa" would have the land which ought to be his.

But as his father was speaking again the student turned his serious face toward the pulpit.

"Brethren," finished the pastor impressively, "before I close I would adjure every one of you to take the reins of his household into his own hands," and then looking straight at Deacon Hall, he concluded:

"And if you have never had the reins, then I command you to take them this day and rule your homes as God would have you. 'Let us pray.'"

Augusta Hall made but one remark on her way home from church.

"Wednesday evening, I am going to show Dominie Graves that he can't rule every woman in Ithaca, and I want you to go with me, dearie."

## CHAPTER XVII

ORN SKINNER was to be taken to prison the Monday after the famous sermon preached by Dominie Graves. Professor Young had gained permission for Tessibel to spend fifteen minutes with Skinner before his departure. There was something about the fishermaid that touched his heart. Her ignorance, her devotion to her father, and the loveliness of the anxious young face haunted the professor during his working hours, and at night, when he could not sleep, he created plans for her future and her father's release. He persuaded himself continually that Tessibel was not the motive for clearing the fisherman of the murder charge, it was the love of justice — justice to the squatter and his lovely child. Often the lawyer had set his jaw when he thought of Minister Graves and the evident malice shown by the parson against the fisherman.

That Monday afternoon he met Tessibel as she came into the jail-yard, much the same Tessibel he had seen in the court-room.

Professor Young took the girl's hand in his and led her into the small waiting room of the stone prison. He desired to be alone with her for a few minutes that he might satisfy himself as to her history, which since her dramatic entrance into the court-room had been so distorted.

"You have no mother, I understand, my dear," he began.

"Nope," and Tessibel shifted one boot along the seam in the red carpet.

"Do you remember her?"

"Nope; don't remember none but Daddy."

"Have you ever been to school?"

Tessibel shook her head, displaying her teeth in a smile which quickly faded.

"Squatter's brats don't never go to school," she muttered.

She edged away from the professor, raising her eyes pleadingly to his. The man read the desire the girl dared not put into words, but without heeding her glance he proceeded to question her.

"Would you like to go to school?"

"Nope, all I want air Daddy home in the shanty. That air enough for me."

She suddenly turned her face away toward the door that led to the upper cells.

"But if I assure you," urged Professor Young, "that your father will positively get another trial, which is all that can be done at present, would you then like to study?"

A definite shake of her head and another quick glance was Tessibel's answer.

"I wants to read the Bible," she said, presently turning toward the professor; "it air a dum hard book to read, I hear."

Professor Young tugged at the corners of his mustache to keep down a smile.

"It would be easy for you to read any book if you went to school," he told her. "How old are you?"

"Comin' sixteen."

"And cannot read — it's a pity! And wouldn't you like to learn to sing?"

Young was desirous of touching a responsive strain in the girl.

"Dum sight rather see Daddy — that's what I came here for! Ain't ye going to let me see him?"

Professor Young rose with a sigh. Like the rest of her race, she did not know gratitude. He had worked diligently, preparing an appeal for a new trial which would bring acquittal to her humpbacked father, and he was interested in her own welfare, but her thankless words checked his inquiry. The professor did not realize what love meant to Tessibel, for every desire within her paled into insignificance beside her passionate devotion to Daddy Skinner.

Tess followed him silently up the long winding stairs, her heart thumping in anticipation. The deputy's search of her clothing brought a flush to her face, but without a word she allowed him to draw off the great boots and quietly watched him as he turned them upside down, receiving them back gravely. Her longing to see Daddy Skinner, to be in his arms, to hug the grizzled head, overshadowed even this indignity. So long had it been since Tess had nestled in the shaggy chin hair, that her heart was sore and wildly impatient. Faith in Frederick's God had been forgotten — no other thought occupied her mind save that they were going to take away her beloved — the only one left to her. She deigned not a glance at Professor Young after the deputy had gone, and measured the oilcloth-covered floor restlessly with the stamp, stamp, stamp of the big boots.

Professor Young's presence was no more to her than the small insects which scurried from the edge of the floor covering into the light and then back into their hiding places, afraid of the human giants which loomed up before them. What did she care for reading, writing and such things. She wanted to be with Daddy Skinner — wanted him home in the shanty, as of old.

She kept her eyes riveted upon the open door. Suddenly she leaned forward, for the ominous clanging of irons came to her ears. She thought of the night she had been found scaling the ivy to Daddy's cell — how long she had waited in the darkness for only a little word about him. They had given her none, and her vivid imagination brought back the anguish of that lonely walk through the storm to the hut.

Approaching footsteps made her alert, and in the paling of the sweet face Professor Young divined the tumult going on in the tender, uneducated heart.

"Child," exclaimed he, "don't make your father's going away harder for him!"

"Shut up," muttered Tess, just as the huge shackled prisoner appeared at the door.

Every muscle in the strong young body stiffened. Tess had not seen her father since the trial. Intensity narrowed the eyes, the drooping white lids covering the lights in the brown iris, the small hands clutched convulsively. Daddy Skinner — her Daddy — was standing before her, his blue-gray eyes piercing her very soul from under the long shaggy brows. She bounded toward him, and two creatures of primeval passion met in one long embrace. It was the passion of an aboriginal father for his child, of a primitive girl watching her loved one separate from her through the portals of death. Tess had lifted herself deftly to the bible back, and lowered her head to the grizzled face, the man's large mouth covering the twitching lips of the girl. The shrouding red hair hid the squatter faces from the professor, and he turned his eyes away. He could not look upon them without distressing emotion. The strange maid was an enigma to him and he found himself wishing that he might guide her future. When Young glanced again, the fisherman had seated himself and had slipped Tessibel from his shoulders, gathering her closely into his great embrace — for she was the brawn of his brawn and the bone of his bone.

Under the squatter's huge red arm, the fisher girl had wedged her head tightly, the low brows were taut with pain, the bronze eyes defiantly closed. Tess was as firmly fixed in her position as the iron chains that encased her "Daddy's" ankles. She had come to stay with Daddy Skinner, to go with him where he went, in spite of the great man from the hill, in spite of the majesty of the law — even in spite of Daddy himself.

The deputy warden with open watch stood over the prisoner with observing eye. The fifteen minutes allowed the girl were gone, and he slowly touched the humpback on the shoulder.

"Time's up, Skinner," said he. "Sorry, but it's the law, you know."

Skinner tried to draw the curly head from under his arm but the muscles in the girl's body only tightened, the white lips grew more rigid.

"It air time fer me to go, Tess," murmured the squatter in her ear.

"I air — I — I air a goin' with ye."

The words were scarcely more than the flutter of a breath. The deputy warden stepped forward a little, then back to his place by the door; the professor rose but sank again to his chair; the bible-back of the fisherman pulsated as if a separate heart was beating in each great hump. Tess was as immovable as if nature had aided her to grow into her position. Skinner again tried to loosen the bare red arms.

"Ye can't go to prison with me, Tess," he said coaxingly; "set up like a good brat . . . Daddy'll kiss ye good-bye."

"I air goin'," she insisted. "It air like a dead man's yard without ye in the shanty. . . . I can wash dishes. I can do a hull lot if ye'll take me with ye, Daddy Skinner."

Not one whit less rigid was the slender body, the closed lids only pressed tighter together.

The deputy grunted impatiently.

"Come, Kid," said he gruffly; "it's the law ye're tamperin' with. Do you hear? Let the prisoner go."

Professor Young felt his throat tighten. The pitiful sight of the girl, the ragged skirt, the terrible unkemptness of the small body, almost brought a shout from his lips. It was a new sensation to the learned man, a stinging, rebellious, pitying sensation, a feeling tha' he wanted to shake the girl from her father's arms, an' then care tenderly for her. One great boot had falle: from Tessibel's many times frozen foot. The little toe marked and cut by frost, limply hanging independe *. of its fellows, made Young wince.

Suddenly Tessibel sat up and wound her arms m(r : tightly about the big humpbacked body.

"I can't go back to the shanty without ye, Daddy,' she whimpered, "and they said — as how ye was comin' — home to stay. . . . And I ain't goin' -- da i i (d if I air."

Young turned his head again toward the window. He could not banish the wish that Tess would listen to him.

The deputy placed his hand firmly upon the prisoner's arm, the fisherman himself trying in vain to loosen the girl's fingers from the shaggy beard.

"I — I — air to go with Daddy — I air — I air!"

Tessibel brought out the words snappingly, but Skinner, with the aid of the deputy, opened the clenched hands. Tessibel gave way; she was unable to stop the awful impending danger that hung over her — absolute separation from Daddy Skinner.

"Daddy, Daddy," she gasped, sitting up straight: "man — man, let me go . . . I air dyin' without my Daddy . . . I air alone — all alone!"

The official moved anxiously as she made this appeal to him. She was now standing on her bare feet, but she bounded forward as the bible-back rose and fell, and large tears dragged themselves from the lowered lids of the fisherman's blue-gray eyes. She pantingly caught her father's hand in hers.

"Kisses, Daddy Skinner, kisses on the bill for Tess — before ye go . . . Tess air a bad brat —"

She could not finish the sentence for the squatter had pressed her to him convulsively. Then Skinner dropped the slender, relaxed body into the wooden arm-chair, and, iron-hampered, took up his march behind the deputy. The professor mutely watched the storm, desperate and terrible, break over the squatter girl. Her wild weeping settled into sobs, the sound of which rent and shook the man's emotions. At last he ventured to speak:

"Child, may I be your friend?"

"'Taint no friends I want. It air somethin' to love — to kiss. It air Daddy I want."

The voice came brokenly from the veil of red hair.

Just then the great iron door clanged in the distance behind the prisoner. Tessibel sprang to the open door, straining her ears to catch another sound from the "black place" which had enveloped her father within its menacing shadows.

"He air — gone. . . . Daddy — air — gone!"

The words were spoken slowly, and hurt the watching man almost as if the torture were his own. A shriek rose from the rounded white throat and the girl threw herself bootless upon the floor, and screamed in passionate childish sorrow, the wealth of disheveled hair mantling the dirty jacket, and covering the woful face.

Neither the professor nor Tessibel heard the hurrying footsteps upon the stone floor in the prison corridor, but Tess, still in the frenzy of her new grief, heard her name spoken through a maze:

"Tessibel Skinner!" And then again: "Tessibel Skinner!"

The squatter raised a pale, tear-streaked face to Frederick Graves. She sat up with a painful flush, drawing the bare legs closely under the wet skirt. The student spoke again:

"Tessibel Skinner has forgotten that God rules and is just. Have your prayers proven nothing to you?"

Tessibel gazed scarlet and embarrassed, into Frederick's face, her under lip quivering. The red head sank slowly down, and the exhausted child wept as only a hurt child can weep.

"I were a-goin' with him," she cried between her sobs, "I could have washed dishes in the prison — to be near Daddy. I air such a lonely Tess 'out him in the hut."

The student lifted her gently in his arms and seated her in the wooden chair. With the tenderness of a brother, he placed the great boots once more upon the girl's feet, and Tessibel was ready to start again upon her long tramp through the row of huts to her shanty home.

The tears had ceased to flow, and with bowed head she was hanging upon every word the student uttered. Professor Young went quietly out, unheeded by either girl or boy.

"No one blames you for your grief, child, at being obliged to leave your father," Frederick said huskily. "But are you going to take off the 'Armor of God' and forget all that He has promised you?"

Tessibel blinked ignorantly at the long words, "Armor of God," "Armor of God." It was something she had not heard before — perhaps it meant that the student's Christ would not help her now. It all came back in a flood of light — her utter faithlessness in the prayers of the student, in the pine-tree God who had waved her so many assurances. She had not dared to look into the noble face above her, but when they stepped from the jail into the street, she raised her eyes to Frederick's and murmured:

"I air sorry cause I were so cussed . . . I only wanted to go with Daddy."

"I realize that," replied Frederick, making preparations to walk with her by drawing his coat collar tightly about his neck, "but it was impossible, and, from now until the time he comes back, study your Bible."

# TESS OF THE STORM COUNTRY

Tess halted a moment, looking up steadily into the dark eyes of the tall boy.

"Does the Bible talk of Daddy Skinner?" she entreated; "does it tell as how he air comin' home?"

"Indeed, yes," was the student's answer. "There's nothing the Bible doesn't contain. The Saviour was nailed to the Cross bearing his misery to give you a heavenly harp and crown, Tessibel. If you read Matthew, Mark, Luke and John, you will see it all plainly. You can be happy if you pray and are a good girl while your father is away." Then, desiring to ease the tense-drawn face, he added:

"It will please him if you write him often and tell him about yourself. . . . Come now, it's getting too dark for you to walk those tracks. Child, haven't you a friend in town with whom you can pass the night? It's frightful to tramp that distance alone."

Tess stiffened instantly. Daddy's shanty was in her care, and of what night had she ever been afraid?

"I air a goin' home," she answered almost sullenly; "ain't a dum bit afraid of nothin'."

As Frederick turned to her side, Tess glanced up confusedly.

"Ye can't walk with me through the streets of Ithacy," said she.

"Why not?"

"Cause — well, cause ye can't, that's why!"

Frederick understood, and, gravely lifting his hat, turned in the other direction with the remark that he would see her again soon.

The girl stood for some seconds staring fixedly after him. Then, wiping her face with the sleeve of a ragged jacket, she started off toward the squatters' row.

## CHAPTER XVIII

MANY were the troubling thoughts which possessed the mind of Tess as she strode along. In the fulvid depths of her red-brown eyes there dwelt an expression of misery. As the child took her way through the streets, with none to care whither she went, her face lighted with a sudden determination. Frederick had told her to read, to study, to pray — that these three with faith would save Daddy Skinner from the rope of the Canadian Indian; but the student, like all those having plenty, forgot to enquire how Tess was to read without books, or study without anyone to teach her. True, Tess could pick out a few words which Daddy had taught her, could haltingly count the stars in the heavens at night, and the rain-drops on the shanty window. She could read the names upon the store signs and had often seated herself on the railroad tracks with a bit of newspaper to stammer forth the words she knew.

But it was a Bible she needed — to learn about the student's God and the Christ. Tess was more interested in the cross than the crown, more interested in the nails that had opened the wounds in the Saviour's hands and feet, than in any royal head-covering that might come in some future time to her. There was too much misery in her own life, too much desperate desire for her loved one, to allow the glitter of a promised crown to affect her. She wanted to know of the suffering Christ, to read of how He had promised — Here Tess stopped and tossed back the red hair. What was it she wanted to read about? Ah, yes — not heaven and its glories nor hell and its terrors, but of Daddy Skinner back in the shanty.

The Bible would tell her just how to bring him back, — but where should she get one? At the squatter mission, of course. Tessibel remembered that once she had been coaxed to enter the mission, but the children had laughed at her rags and after that she could not be induced to go again. Then in the bitterness of her heart she had thrown stones and clay from the edges of the track through the open window upon the other children, and had been told by the superintendent never to come near the small church again. But that was four long months ago, and not once since — since the horror of Daddy's going, had she even looked toward the mission.

The dusk fell, slowly striking out the day-shadows from the railroad bed and she halted where the two tracks met. The mission was opposite her. Would she dare ask for a Bible? A rich, warm light flooded through the window and then the old squatter who had kept the place in order for many years came out and closed the door. Tessibel's eyes followed his form through the dim twilight until he disappeared into his shanty.

Her hand clutched convulsively the knob of the mission door; it yielded to her touch, and for the second time in her life Tessibel Skinner was inside the mission room. The small reed organ stood open: a hymn book stretched back with a rubber band caught her eye. A bright bit of red carpet wound its way about the altar.

The squatter did not pause to examine the pictures on the wall nor even an instant before the glowing fire. Her eyes were searching for a Bible — the shade deepening in them as she sidled toward the nearest seat.

She read "H-y-m-n-a-l" on the back of the first book — dropping it she gathered up another.

"H-o-l-y B-i-b-l-e," she spelled.

Thrusting it into her blouse, she bounded out into the night, and raced up the railroad track almost to the Hoghole trestle before she stopped, satisfied that no one had seen her theft.

Then, taking the book from her bosom, she kissed it reverently.

"Them old fools ain't goin' to have every damn Bible in this here town. I air a right like them to this un." Again she kissed it, as she mumbled: "Matthew, Mark, Luke and John."

That night the candle burned longer in the Skinner shanty, and an auburn head bent over an open book. A faltering voice spelled out the sufferings of the Nazarene. Once Tess smiled wanly when reading of how the Saviour had borne all the woes of the world — that any one believing could be saved. Her head nodded over the pages, and almost instantly the rapt face dropped upon the open Bible and Tessibel slept.

A strange dream filled her sleep. A great light flashed suddenly into the sky — Tessibel's sky — and through the brightness of it she could see the cross with the Man upon it; could see the nail prints in the swollen flesh, the thorns pressing into the bowed head. Then as Tessibel dreamed she moved upon the open Bible and groaned with the dream-Christ upon the cross. Directly in front of the crucified Saviour Daddy Skinner was coming toward her with the student.

She started up — a cry of disappointed anguish escaping her lips. The candle had burned out in the grease cup, the wind was rocking the shanty and making the rafters creak dismally. Tess shivered as she tossed her clothes upon the floor, and crept exhausted into Daddy's bed. The last thing she heard was the splashing of her pet eel in the water-pail.

The next morning, on a piece of yellow paper, she scratched Daddy a small note. Frederick's words that her father would be pleased with it filled her with a desire to write. For three hours she struggled with her first letter.

" daddy the ice air a goin out of the lake  ben letts air a gettin well   he air a cuss   i air lonlie yit without ye   i red my bible last nite   i cribbed it frum the mishion   it says as how god air gooder then i thote he wer   cum home  and i reads as how a brite lite was a shinin about the cross  and as how the christ ruz up   here air a story bout a squatter brat it air bout tess   she cride and cride fer her dady   til her eel what she luved herd her and he cride hisself to deth this here mornin he wer belly up in the bucket   i air yer brat dady

" the man on the cross ruz fer the hull world   aint it nise to ruz."

This delicate effusion of love to her father, Tess read over many times. With pardonable pride she folded it carefully and placed it in the Bible where she had read about the cross and dying Christ.

## CHAPTER XIX

ON Wednesday evening Deacon Hall tucked Augusta's pretty hand under his arm with a happy sense of proprietorship. He was proud to stand by his beautiful wife in her fight for church liberty. Hall really believed, as he had told Dominie Graves, that the world had outgrown its foggy notions, and he delighted in hearing Augusta air her ideas in meetings; in watching the rich blood mantling and playing under the transparent skin; and in listening to the modulated tones of the vibrant voice. Augusta was his style of woman. The thought of her force of character made him throw back his shoulders that Wednesday evening as they neared the church door. Few members had gathered for the hour was early. Deacon Hall nodded pleasantly to Bill Hopkins, and a broad smile parted the latter's lips, giving his square face a softer, more genial expression. Bill calmly took his seat on the left side of the room; crossed his legs, placed his fingers about the white wart, and then sat looking thoughtfully out of the window into the lighted street. For the first time in many months Bill Hopkins was in his chair at the weekly prayer meeting. His one idea in being present was to witness the Dominie's success in keeping the women in their places. He had had conscientious scruples about remaining in a church, which, in spite of the fact that its tenets forbade its females to rise and voice either prayers or opinions before the males, countenanced this very abuse.

Bill Hopkins had no objection to women in their places — in fact, he enjoyed the company of a pretty woman — but it was not her place to try and teach him. Hopkins had the overwhelming idea of the physical and moral superiority of men, while, as far as intellectuality was concerned, women were leagues and leagues behind.

Many a warm argument had been held between Bill and the pretty Mrs. Hall, and as this lady came into the chapel she saw the former elder seated in his old chair, the familiar wart shining high and white on the bald pate. She tilted her pretty chin an instant before inclining her head, then to the amazement of those present, she parted from her husband in the middle aisle, marching to the right, her amiable deacon taking the left. Bill Hopkins smiled inwardly as the thought flashed over him that there must have been a secret female conclave among the strong-minded women as well as among the men during the past week. The same idea occurred to the minister's mind as he saw his members separate in the middle aisle.

He drew his brow into a pucker which furrowed the flesh between his brows. Mrs. Graves was seated at the rear of the room to the right, her eyes upon an open book in her hand. She did not raise them as her husband took his chair behind the small pulpit table upon which lay a huge Bible marked by a dangling blue ribbon. The clergyman bent his head a few moments in secret prayer, drew the book toward him, opened it, found his text and placed the marker carefully between the pages. He coughed slightly and with an extra effort raised his eyes to his congregation. This is what he saw:

The middle aisle divided almost every woman from her husband; only here and there had a timid wife with lowered eyes followed her lord and master to the left.

Dominie Graves caught a peculiar gleam in the eye of Augusta Hall and followed the line of her vision which was leveled at Bill Hopkins. There was no enmity in the latter's mien, but Dominie Graves knew that when the elderly deacon toyed with the white wart his nerves were vastly disturbed. For an instant the thought traveled through the clergyman's brain, that if Tessibel Skinner could work with her magic words on the dull protrusion upon Hopkins's glistening head the former deacon would lose his favorite occupation. He looked doubtfully down upon his own hands and remembered the warts which Tessibel had whispered away. Then, trying to drive all thoughts of the fisher girl and her squatter father from his mind, the minister rose to his feet. Frederick Graves had been watching his father intently and as he saw his effort to rise the boy whitened a little and settled back. Just growing into manhood and beginning to think for himself, the lad blushed with shame at the state of affairs that rose before his eyes this night. He threw a sidelong glance at Hopkins and met a dejected expression from the eyes of his mother. She looked so tired, so humiliated, that a bitter rebellious feeling arose in Frederick's heart against his father. Then his mind wandered again from the church to Tessibel Skinner in her shanty home. The quick look she had given him in the court-room had impressed him as nothing else could. He saw again the bright head thrown back in eager appeal and the shining eyes filled with pain. How he wished that his own faith in the Infinite had a touch of the strength which made that of Tessibel stand alone by itself! Little did Frederick realize or know that the intensity of the fishermaid, the wonderful faith and trust she had exhibited in her time of trial and trouble, had come to her from him. Every prayer Tessibel had uttered, every devout wish of her heart for Daddy Skinner, had been vaguely centered about the student. Her love for the Christ of whom she had heard so little was based upon the power of attraction that Frederick Graves held for her.

Twice had he, unobserved, seen Tessibel through the hut window; and the picture of the tired little figure with its drooping prayerful attitude came back with a force that brought a great lump into his throat, invigorating his desire to raise the standard of his own love for God's words and promises.

His father's eloquent voice brought him back to the present and, as his eyes fell upon Hopkins, he saw the nervous fingers twiddling the great white wart and a smile forced itself to his lips.

Then he dragged his truant mind from outside subjects and concentrated his attention upon the pulpit.

"In accordance with the creed of the church," the clergyman was saying, "and of the laws under which our beloved congregation holds together, I speak. It is with love for all I adjure you this night. When I say that the subject of my talk will be upon duty you will not be surprised, for you, one and all, know what I mean. I shall ask the sisters in the church not to rise again to speak. If they desire church work there are the poor, the blind, and always the needy. By needy I mean those desiring the faith of God and yet being unable to grasp it without help. To the dear sisters of the congregation I commend all these." He made no allusion to the division of the men and women nor to the sermon of the past Sunday.

After the hymn he sat down, bowing his handsome dark head quietly, and remaining mute in the dismal silence that followed. Suddenly an elderly woman with a meek face struggled to her feet, glancing toward Augusta Hall for an encouraging smile. Several trimmed hats however loomed up between her and the deacon's wife, so still standing she lowered her eyes and began to pray. Simultaneously with hers a masculine voice broke through the air mingling with the weak petition of the woman. Frederick Graves lifted his head quickly — the trend of war cutting through his mind like a knife. It had evidently been planned before the meeting just how severely the women were to be dealt with, for Frederick noted that his father's eyes did not raise from his reverent position at the unusual happening. As the man's voice grew louder, importunately seeking guidance in this unhappy church affair, the woman closed her lips and fell backward upon the seat, crying weakly. The masculine voice rose higher and clearer and finished the petition with ringing clarity. Another embarrassing silence out of which came scarcely a breath. Augusta Hall caught a glimpse of the piercing blue eyes peering from under the shaggy brows of Bill Hopkins. The deacon was watching her, and Augusta knew that he exulted as one woman after another was driven to her chair by the masculine voice of her shouting opponent.

# TESS OF THE STORM COUNTRY

So far the men held the day. This was demonstrated to Augusta Hall and Bill Hopkins by the undertoned sobs that continually emerged from behind the numerous white handkerchiefs. So dense was the quietude of the painful meeting that Frederick Graves could plainly hear the thumping of his own heart. Suddenly Augusta with a slight cough and a rustle of her fine skirts rose to her feet. She started to speak reverently in a low tone. It was the usual petition that blessing should descend upon the missions, the sewing circle and the children's work — and here her voice wavered a little, for a man's bass voice joined in with her own. It was that of the deacon who carried the offering plate each Sunday morning, opposite her husband. On and on both man and woman shouted their words with strength and rapidity upon their hearers' ears. The Deacon's voice lifted and fell with the power of an orator. Augusta strained forth her tones high and clear. Minute after minute until fifteen had passed was the oratorical word display of each pitted against the other.

Dominie Graves' fingers were twitching nervously beside his well-shaped nose. Bill Hopkins still twiddling his wart had drawn himself to a straighter position, and was listening with all intentness. The pallor of Deacon Hall's face deepened as Augusta talked on and on until all thought of prayer had left her mind, and her words shaped themselves into a discourse. She was holding the floor against the church official, whose brow was now running with the sweat of his embarrassment -— his voice had become fainter and his words fewer and less well chosen. Augusta's voice, on the contrary, rang clearly through the room, a prepared speech upon the aptitude of women and their field of labor. Her husband was watching her intently — and thought how beautiful she looked as the blood mantled to her white forehead, descending and rising as her thoughts took turn after turn. The unfortunate deacon was mumbling forth a few ill-connected sentences. At last with a groan he sank to his seat and placed a handkerchief to his fevered brow. Presently Augusta sat down and there was again an awful silence. No one advanced another petition and Dominie Graves pronounced a halting benediction.

The congregation rose hastily and hurried toward the doors, with no desire for further discussion.

Bill Hopkins leaned back against the outer door and as Mrs. Hall passed him he grasped her hand.

"You had nerve," said he, "I'm not saying it's the right kind . . . but it's nerve just the same, and, well, I do believe that you women have gained the day in this church."

Augusta, leaning on her husband's arm, looked down meekly from a pair of wicked twinkling eyes — she could be a sweet clinging creature if she wished, and this was her special charm to Deacon Hall.

Suddenly she raised her gaze and looked winningly into Bill Hopkin's face.

"I suppose you won't give me the money I asked you for, to aid Skinner," she said slowly.

"I'll send you the check to-morrow morning," and Bill Hopkins' big shoulders disappeared through the open door.

"It frightened me at first," exclaimed Deacon Hall to his wife afterward, "but, as your voice went up and up, I knew my little woman would win, God bless her."

"And we'll win about poor Skinner too," rejoined Augusta. "Every man and woman so far has agreed to help a little, and I don't want you to try to drive the squatters from our lake property."

Here her words were checked by a sudden thought which darkened her eyes — she burst forth with a rich low laugh:

"That'll make two triumphs over my haughty parson."

## CHAPTER XX

A SENSE of embarrassment accompanied Dominie Graves to the breakfast table the next morning after the triumphant victory of Augusta Hall. He made no remark upon the disagreeable episode of the previous night, and ate silently amid the chatter of Babe and the monosyllabic answers of her mother. Teola to break the strain spoke of the sleigh-ride and dance coming off that evening.

"I fear it will be too cold," objected Mrs. Graves, in her fretful, weary voice.

"I can wrap up warmly," argued Teola. "All the girls in town are going and Dan will take care of me. We are going in separate sleighs to Slaterville. I'm going, mother, and that's all there is to it."

"It seems to me that you are growing rather friendly with that young Jordan, Teola," her father said. "He's been here every night for a week, hasn't he?"

Teola muttered sullenly that she wasn't the only girl in town who had callers, and looked pleadingly to Frederick for aid. The young student flashed her a smile.

"Teola will be perfectly safe to-night, father," he exclaimed.

"Are you going?"

"No," answered Frederick, "but sister would be no safer if I were. I have implicit confidence in Dan Jordan and the country roads are perfect . . . By the way, Dan would like to take a class of boys in the Sunday School. I told him to see you about it."

The mollified minister finished his meal without further comment.

The sleigh-ride was a thing of the past. That it had brought disaster to Teola Graves showed in the tired eyes as they rested on the sky, gray with the coming morning. She had stolen silently into the house, reaching her chamber without disturbing either father or mother. At the window she halted. Here and there a star sparkled, dying dim in the advancing sky. Teola's eyes rested upon the street below for several minutes, then dragged her gaze upward and beyond — beyond to the long road that led to the yard of the dead which stretched over the hillside, rearing its monuments among the leafless trees, like sentinels over sleeping soldiers. There was something alluring, something compelling to the pale girl, watching the birth of her first real day of living. The University frowned down upon the graveyard; in its turn the graveyard frowned menacingly upon the town. A snow-bird peeped a "good-morning" to its mate in the Rectory eaves. A bell pealed out twice, striking the air with its sonorous sound reverberating into the hills. And still the girl stood waiting for — she knew not what.

Yesterday girlhood offered Teola Graves happy hours of peaceful meditation — to-day, the new day brought the woman its ceaseless silent agony of regret and remorse, strong forces of which she had known nothing.

If Dan were only glad that she loved him, if he loved her in return. Suddenly tears welled into the dark eyes;

Teola Graves hid her face from the new world of painful joy — and forgot in sleep.

Teola's next hour with her lover was the most embarrassing one of her life. Dan took her hands in silence, and the seriousness of his face bespoke his heart pain.

"Sweetheart, is there anything in all the world that I can say to you to make you love me more — precious, precious little darling!"

"Only say that you do love me, Dan," breathed Teola, " and — and —"

"Don't turn your eyes away from me, sweetheart — love you, Teola? I'll study so hard, dearest, and when I finish college we'll get married, and go away and have a home of our own. Teola, forgive me and have faith in me! Will you, sweet?"

"Yes," murmured the trembling lips — and Teola buried her flushed face upon the broad breast of Dan Jordan and was happy.

Frederick Graves had been made president of the freshman class, a short time after entering the "Cranium" fraternity. He was considered by most of his fellow students a serious, earnest worker and had been taken many times into consultation with the upper classmen concerning plans for the development of the society.

In past years at the end of every January, the freshmen had held a banquet in the opera-house of the city. This event called forth practical jokes of all descriptions upon the first-year men from the sophomores and seniors, giving many anxious and worried moments to the younger students over the outcome of the one important event of the year. It had also been the custom to try to capture the president of the freshman class and hold him in seclusion until after the banquet, thereby making his opening speech impossible. The dread that they should lose their leader became more and more apparent among the banquet holders as the days advanced, and extensive plans had been made to protect Frederick Graves from his class enemies. For one whole month previous he had not been allowed to walk alone about the town, and it had been ordered that he should sleep at the fraternity house instead of at the Rectory, in order that the young president might be guarded against any surprise concocted by the sophomores.

One evening at the Cranium Society several freshmen were seated in the billiard-room.

"It's a great note," muttered Shorty Brown, "that we have to wait on those big lubbers of Sophomores and seniors. I'd as soon die as to run down the hill after their letters."

"You might as well go, Shorts," put in Spuddy Preston; "you'll only get yourself disliked if you don't, and you'll be made to go in the end. The blessing of it all is that they did the same thing in their turn."

He took a slow measure of the distance between himself and the cuspidor, and shot a piece of gum into it.

"It doesn't make it any pleasanter," put in Swipes Dillon. "Just think of me, I haven't had a cent to spend on myself for weeks. Manchester's capacity for smoke is enormous. I wish I had knocked his head clean off his neck."

He looked gloomily out of the window as he muttered this, but instantly brightened as he finished:

"But I can stand almost anything if they don't get hold of Graves. That would spoil our fun altogether."

He unbent the small round body drawn up in a woful-looking ball, sitting up to hear what the others had to say.

"Just let them take him!" growled Shorty Brown. "We will make it warm for those sophs, but they're such sneaks that we can't put a moment's trust in them. Why don't you say something, Captain?"

"Nothing to say, Boy," replied Jordan musingly, "only that we must do all we can to shield Frederick. If they once get him we won't see him until after the banquet. I fear, too, they might hurt him, for he would be sure to put up a fight."

"So would I," boasted Spuddy. "You bet I would."

Swipes broke into a ringing laugh.

"You'd make a nice fighter, Spud," he chuckled; "you're not bigger than a minute with fifty seconds in it. Gosh, I wish something would happen. I'm tired sitting about doing nothing."

His words came to Dan Jordan through a dim maze of tangled thoughts. During all his short, happy life anxiety had never been his companion until now. It strangled his class ardor and made conscientious study impossible. Teola Graves' tearful, pain-stricken face rose constantly before him. His own eyes darkened at the thought. Oh, to go back to the toffy pull — to live over again those last few weeks — how different it all would be, and how repentant he was. He sighed and shook his great shoulders and rose to his feet.

"I wonder where Graves is now," he exclaimed. "I met Armstrong and Howe coming up the hill last night, talking with their heads close together. I noticed that they stopped suddenly when I came upon them."

The blood had crept accusingly into his face as he spoke Frederick's name. Never for one moment in the presence of Teola's brother had he forgotten — how could he ever forget! But he did love Teola Graves madly and wished with all his soul that he were through college. He had hoped that in the excitement of the banquet his remorse would be quieted a little, but his conscience lashed him so constantly with self-reproach that it seemed imperative for him to give up his studies, marry Teola, and take her away.

"Let's all go down town," cried Swipes in a loud tone with a side wink at Spuddy, "and get boiling drunk. If something doesn't happen —"

"Lordy," groaned Spuddy, "Swipes is always wanting something to happen. I bet it will before long. What you wish for you'll get, old horse! Don't forget that."

Spuddy went on tapping the window, staring out into the gloom.

"We'd better go down town and look for Graves and see that he is all right," said Dan. "That will be enough for you kids to do now. It's your evening anyway to guard him."

The four freshmen walked down the hill together. Dan separated from the three at the Ithaca Hotel with the injunction that they should keep their eyes open for the young president, guarding him while the other night watchers were having a play spell.

On the next corner Dan Jordan ran into Frederick with two of his own classmates.

"You fellows can go now," exclaimed Dan to Frederick's companions; "Brown, Preston and Dillon are just up there on the next corner, to protect Graves while you fellows go to supper. How are things going now, Frederick?"

A sinking sensation attacked his heart as he asked this question, and he remembered afterwards that he had expected Frederick to impart ill news to him. The fear had come from his over-burdened conscience.

"Everything is all right, but Teola wants to see you. Could you go down for a little while?"

Dan nodded and turned with a happier heart toward the Rectory, leaving Frederick looking for "Spuddy," "Shorts," and "Swipes."

## CHAPTER XXI

THREE hours afterwards the three little freshmen walked zig-zaggedly, arm in arm, up the long hill toward the University Campus.

Shorts had a shaky grasp of one arm of Dillon, and Spuddy the other. On through the cold night they dragged him, until they reached the broad white carriage way that led to the fraternity house. Here Swipes stumbled, loosening himself from the grasp of his companions.

"Well, ju — just look at him," growled Spuddy in a disgusted tone; "he ought to freeze stiff. Look how his le — legs wab — wabble! They lo — look like four — four —"

"Shut up, Spud," cried Shorts. "He's only got — got two legs. What the mat — matter with you? . . . You're as drunk as he is. Don't let him drop on those stones!"

"I ain't drunk," retorted Preston. "What's the mat — matter with you, yourself? I bet I can ge — get into — that — that fraternity without any of the fe — fellows seeing me!"

"I don't believe you will," returned Shorts in a more sober manner. "Look there, Spud, the whole house is alight. I say — Swipes — Swipes, it's after midnight, and the fraternity is all lighted up."

"I — I — I don't care if it is," grunted Swipes in

a low, thick voice. " I — I want to go to bed. Tha — that's what I want to do."

He sank into a stupor again but the boys dragged him to his feet.

" Do you want Jordan and Graves to see you like this, Swipes? " demanded Shorts stopping in the center of the carriage drive. " If you don't — you take a mighty quick sneak up the back stairs, and —"

The sentence was never finished for the door opened and Dan Jordan's big form loomed up before their dazed eyes.

" Is that you, Shorts? " called Dan.

" Yes."

" Where have you been for the last three hours? "

" Down there," mumbled Shorts in a smothered tone, desiring to hide their plight if possible.

" For the love of all that's good, Shorts," groaned Spuddy, " let me get into the house and change my clothes. . . . There goes Swipes again in the snow. Get up, fool, here's the ' Captain.' "

" To — to the devil with the ' Captain,' " muttered Swipes.

But Dan's next sentence completely awoke the senses of all save Swipes. He only grasped it dimly through the cobwebs of his drunken brain.

" Where's Graves? " demanded Jordan, coming to the top step.

The silence that followed was as grim as the falling snow. Spuddy and Shorts were dragging the limp Swipes up the long steps.

" Graves? . . . We haven't seen him," interjected Shorty Brown, and Dan Jordan answered gravely:

"Then the sophomores have captured him, that's a certainty! He hasn't been here, and he hasn't been to the Rectory."

Shorts, now thoroughly sober, followed the big freshman into the drawing-room, where a dozen or more downcast-looking boys were curled up on divans. Swipes was being urged up the broad oak stairs, Spuddy now and then giving him a severe poke in the ribs. Preston perched the hapless boy against his chamber door with the injunction to get to bed the best he could. Swipes turned helplessly to his room-mate.

"Look here, Spuddy, help a fellow, will you? Just give me my pyjamas."

"Get them yourself!" retorted Preston, shoving Dillon into his bed-chamber. "It's a nice mess we're in with the 'Parson' gone."

With a disgusted kick at Swipes he left him reeling desperately once more. Dillon swayed forward from the center of the room toward the doorway. He had heard as in a dream Spuddy's parting shot about fellows getting drunk and forgetting how to act. Suddenly the floor rose up and hit him on the nose, but the polished boards, so bright that he could see his face in them, fell back politely, leaving Swipes standing, looking helplessly about him. Every piece of furniture, bed, bureau, table and chairs, flew around and around him in the wildest disorder.

His eyes reeled after them, in their flight through the room. Around and around past the bed to the door — once Swipes thought they would fly through. Bracing himself to catch the flying bed, he came up with a bang against the beveled mirror which broke and splintered under his weight. He was lying in the ruins when some one came and put him to bed.

The regret of the little freshman the next morning when the dismal news of the missing president came to him was intensely genuine. They told him that the whole town had been searched, but that Graves had disappeared as completely as if he were no longer on the earth.

When Dan Jordan left Frederick Graves on the corner of Ithaca's main street, the young president began to search for his three class-mates. Shorts and the other two must be somewhere near for Dan had told him so. He turned to the left, walking toward " Jay's " resort, where with his knowledge of the three little freshmen's habits, he would probably find them. It was a nuisance to be followed about and guarded as if he were a criminal, yet he would go through anything rather than be absent from the banquet.

Suddenly he felt a bag thrown over his head and he was dragged completely off his feet. Then with much force he was shoved into a carriage, a heavy hand held over his mouth. He heard a pair of horses whipped into rapid motion. Frederick could not imagine in which direction he was being driven, for the constant turning of corners made it seem to the smothered boy that they were tearing around in a circle.

Suddenly the vehicle came to a sharp standstill. During the ride his ankles and wrists had been tightly corded, and no sooner had the carriage halted than several pairs of hands carried him swiftly up a flight of stairs into a house and along a carpetless hall.

When the cloth was removed from his head, Frederick

was in the presence of two sophomores, Mathew Armstrong and Paul Howe.

"Hard luck," said Armstrong, looking at Frederick with a grin.

"Rather," he replied, glancing about. "But what can't be cured must be endured. If I am to stay here, I hope I am to be fed."

"Not with banquet cake, Freddy," laughed Howe; "you'll have plain bread — until after the banquet. Now just give us your coat and vest, old chap, and your collar and tie."

Frederick's ready obedience made Armstrong exclaim jovially:

"That's the right attitude, isn't it, Howe? No one would think to look at you, Graves, that you were so docile. You knew what you were saying when you said, 'what couldn't be cured must be endured,' and I say, 'all's fair in love and war,' so you stay here until after that grand supper."

Without answering, Frederick turned his eyes gloomily about his prison. The room was almost bare. In one corner was a bed, in another a cot with some blankets upon it. A long window ran nearly to the floor, minus a blind on one side while on the other a green shutter hung by one hinge, making a creaking noise as the wind swung it back and forth. Frederick reasoned that the window faced the street for he could hear crunching footsteps in the hard snow as pedestrians passed.

A wagon rolled squeakingly by and all was quiet.

In the night Frederick endeavored to plan his escape. He believed the house to be within the city limits, but during the long, dark drive he had lost all sense of direction. Through the flickering of the smoky lamp he saw Armstrong with a revolver in his hand, watching him intently. So the darkness passed and the daylight came in at the window, throwing long slant rays upon the dusty floor and lighting the faded paper on the wall.

## CHAPTER XXII

DOMINIE GRAVES had a consultation with Dan Jordan over the disappearance of his son, and then climbed the University hill to Professor Young's office.

"I feel sure that Frederick has not been harmed," said Graves after greeting the professor, but there was question in his voice.

An expression of deep concern spread over Young's face.

"I heartily hope not," responded he, "for I know of no finer young man in the University."

"I think the boy would put up a great fight if he had a chance," resumed the minister, "but with a lot of fellows against him one chap can't do much. I hardly know what to think. There seems to be nothing to do but to await his return. Young Jordan said last night that they had searched every place where it was possible for him to be, but the boy was not to be found. His mother is growing anxious."

"I should think that she would be worried," replied Young. "It's a beastly practise this stealing of the freshman's president, and unworthy of such a college as this. I shall be glad when it is abolished. There is nothing during the year that creates such furore as this banquet."

A file of papers was under Professor Young's hand and as he spoke he toyed absent-mindedly with one of the long official envelopes. Dominie Graves caught a glimpse of some words that made the color rush hot into his face. The envelope contained an appeal for a new trial for Orn Skinner. He coughed slightly and opened a new topic.

"I see you are still interested in Skinner?"

"Yes!"

"Have you succeeded in getting him a new trial?"

"Not yet, but at any hour I expect to hear that the governor will give me an opportunity to defend him. I fully believe that the man is innocent, that he ought to have another chance for his life. As I said in the court-room the squatter trials are but farces. I don't approve of them."

"You're but a stranger in our town," interposed the Dominie. "When you've been here as long as I have, Professor Young, you will see that the strictest measures are necessary with these people. The rope is none too good for that man, Skinner."

"God forbid," ejaculated Young, "that I should live ever to wish away a man's life on any — personal motive."

Tessibel's sweet upturned face, shrouded in red-brown hair rose before him, but it did not obscure the dark flush that swept over the handsome face of the minister. The professor had intimated that he thought personal motives were being used to persecute the squatter. This tried the patience of Elias Graves as he sat gathering an argument to refute the accusation. He had even persuaded himself that it was for the good of the town to remove one after another of the loathsome fishermen either by the rope or imprisonment. Without their men the squatter women also would disappear from the shores.

He rose with a sense of coming evil stealing over him for the man seated opposite was a tower of strength and his own position in the town had been weakened in the late church conflict. The reins of affairs were being swept from his hands. He could not speak out more emphatically than he had against Skinner. On all sides, friends were rising mushroom-like to rescue the fisherman from the hangman's noose.

If he himself could gain a few strong friends he would be able to sweep the squatter from the face of the earth.

As he walked toward the Rectory after leaving Professor Young he set his teeth hard, these thoughts rushing through his mind, and inflaming his desire to rule in Ithaca as he always had. Even his anxiety about Frederick was obscured by the multitudinous plans that one after another were born in his brain. He closed the library door of the Rectory with an annoyed air and dropped into an arm-chair to think.

Professor Young sat long after the departure of Dominie Graves, looking at the bundle of papers in his hand. He had not dared to venture to the Skinner hut, although his heart called constantly for the red-haired girl who was holding the shanty home against her enemies. He knew that Tess was living as best she could, existing on the meager fare allotted to her kind. Young had seen Tessibel but once since her father had been taken to Auburn Prison and his face flushed as he thought that in a few days he would be able to tell her that her "Daddy" had received a stay upon his execution, that he honestly believed the shadowing rope would never seek the beloved head again.

It was only of late that Deforest Young would allow himself to admit that Tessibel Skinner had a stronger hold upon him than he ever thought possible for any woman to obtain, much less a child of such a race. He knew now that his life's interest lay in making a woman of her, a woman such as only Tess could make, with her deep primeval nature and splendid soul. If the girl could but return his love in part, it would place him in a position to help and educate her, but his great growing love gave birth to a fear that he might not be able to awaken in the squatter girl a soul affection for himself. Nevertheless he would spare nothing to elevate her. He expected a hard task to prove Skinner not guilty, and every hour he hoped to receive a letter from the Governor of the state giving him the desired year to gain the necessary evidence in favor of the fisherman.

He was still meditating in this strain when the Governor's letter was handed to him. For almost an hour he sat with his head in his hands, building an imaginary home, which he had never thought would be his, and in still sweeter imaginings he held close to his heart a fair, sweet girl, growing into her heritage of womanhood.

For two whole days Frederick Graves had been held a captive in his unfurnished prison. He knew that forty-eight hours marked the time before the banquet, also that if he could not escape before then he would have to be absent from the class dinner. Only once had Armstrong spoken to him that day and an expression of fine scorn upon the handsome president's face had been the answer. The sophomore was stretched out upon the bed, the revolver still in his hand, and drumming with the fingers of his left hand upon the much soiled wall:

"Graves," he began, "if you think this is any snap for me or that I like my job you're mistaken. I hate to be cooped up here as much as you do."

Frederick might not have been within hearing of the words for all the attention he paid to the speaker. Armstrong sat up straight with a deep far-fetched yawn.

"Come on, Graves," implored he, "let's play cards. It's hanged dismal with nothing to do."

Still Frederick kept his dignified silence. He looked down upon his coatless arms and pondered, then raised his eyes to the long window, but settled them again upon his boots. From the corner of his eye he saw his jailer place the revolver upon the table — it roused him suddenly for he was getting desperate to escape. With lightning-like rapidity he made up his mind to action. Lunging forward he brought his right fist in heavy contact with his companion's nose while the strong left hand swept the revolver under the opposite bed.

Simultaneously with the sound of the falling weapon came the crash of broken glass — Frederick Graves had swept like a young hurricane through the long window. The falling of the heavy body, and running footsteps brought Armstrong hastily to his feet. He dazedly brushed back a lock of hair from his brow, scrambled back under the bed after the gun then rushed to the broken window.

"By gosh, that was brave," ejaculated he.

Three times he fired the pistol into the night — the

signal of trouble to give to his classmates — then sat down and waited disgustedly, nursing his bruised nose.

Frederick landed in the street, stunned for a single instant, but the snow was soft and the moment critical. He gathered himself up, rubbed off the blood that trickled from his fingers, and broke through the street on a run. He found himself in the lower portion of the town not far from the Leigh Valley tracks. To go eastward toward home would attract attention for he was without hat, coat, or vest, and it would probably lead to his recapture. He crossed the inlet bridge, passing a man here and there who stared after him as if he were a shade, which had risen from its grave seeking some kindred soul to haunt.

As Frederick passed the lighted squatter mission, the thought of the warmth within made his teeth chatter. He would have given much to have been able to place his cold hands over the fire which burned brightly in the room. Suddenly he stopped in his rapid flight for liberty for stepping to the tracks directly in front of him was the squatter girl. She had not noticed him and the student knew that she was homeward bound.

"Tessibel Skinner!"

The girl stopped, electrified, and tossed up her head.

"Tessibel Skinner!" called Frederick again.

When the girl recognized him, she came toward him with the awkward, conscious gait of a maid walking before the man she loved. Her eyes took in the half-clothed form of the student with one hasty glance.

"What air the matter?" she asked in an undertone.

Had the student been brought face to face with a dilemma like that of Daddy Skinner? With the instincts of a squatter Tess could think of nothing that would intimidate but the law.

"I have just escaped," replied Frederick, shivering.

Then he was in danger. He needed her as she had needed him, and Tess had no doubt but that he was on his way to her shanty to ask her aid.

"Ye air runnin' from some bloke?" she demanded slyly.

"Yes."

"But ye air cold," said she, "ye can't walk four miles without a coat."

"Where are you going to take me?" Frederick scented a place of safety.

"To my hut," replied the squatter stoically. "Wait! Ye stop here a minute."

She bounded into the road from the railway tracks, leaving Frederick staring helplessly after her. At the door of the mission she halted with the slyness that had been taught her from the cradle, bending her head forward to ascertain if any person were witness of her action. She opened the door and fled like a young deer toward the organ, then, ripping the crimson cloth from the altar, she fled out again into the night, running pantingly toward the student.

"It air for you — put it on," she ordered, proffering him the embroidered spread.

"Where did you —?" hesitated Frederick.

"Put it on, I say. I'll fan it back some time if ye will. Ye can't freeze with that — and there air bacon, fish and bread in the hut."

Her voice was low and vibrant with untried emotions. Something uplifting in the criminal action of the girl so touched Frederick that the nearness of tears called a throb to his throat. Without expostulating he wrapped the brilliant covering about his head, the embroidered ends hanging to his waist. Frederick Graves appreciated for the first time in his short, shielded life the awful temptations that make these squatter people in their cold and misery take what did not belong to them. He followed Tessibel, with no spoken word; on and on, up past the lighted huts, to the gaping gorge under the trestle. Tessibel knew that the student could not traverse it without her help, and she also knew that to touch his hand would be the sweetest of happiness to her. At any other time her soul would have recoiled from such temerity, but the life and welfare of Daddy's deliverer were at stake. She halted abruptly. The night was so dark she could scarcely outline the student as he stood near her.

"Take hold of my hand," she ordered. "It air the trestle. It air a long one and the steps be far apart."

Without a demurring word, Frederick grasped the strong fingers she held out to him. A smile, obscured by the darkness, played about the girl's sensitive mouth. The young body was pulsing with life — with intense gratitude, for was not she, Tessibel Skinner, helping her friend? With halting steps the boy and girl commenced the most perilous part of their journey, Tessibel leading the way. The student stopped in the middle of the long trestle.

"Are we nearly over?" he asked in a low voice. The awful magnificence of the dark night, the rushing water tumbling and roaring over the rocks beneath them, awed him into what was almost timidity.

"Nope; come on, don't stop here," urged Tess. " 'Taint a good place."

At the end of the gap Tess tried to draw her hand away, but it was a feeble motion and she ceased as she noted that Frederick was still clinging to it.

"Let me walk with your hand in mine," he said simply, with no extra pressure of the fingers within his. "It is dark for us both."

During the rest of the journey a silence fell upon them. Kennedy's brindle bull, scenting a friend, capered madly for a word from Tess, but the squatter paid no heed to her dog chum.

She took her hand from Frederick's to unfasten the door and light the candle. While they were walking the tracks, the woman in her had tried to remember in what condition she had left the hut. She looked about hastily. Before lighting another candle she smuggled the frying pan from the floor and picked up the loaf of bread that had fallen behind the stove from the table. While Tessibel lighted the fire, Frederick sat huddled in the wooden rocking-chair, still wrapped in the crimson altar-cloth, and watched the girl, who, as she moved clumsily to and fro, uttered no sound save now and then a characteristic grunt. Instinct told the squatter that she would choke the sensitive throat of the student if she raised the dust by sweeping and she refrained from using a broom, but Frederick wished vaguely that she would gather up the fish bones and crumbs of bread from her path that they might not crunch so audibly under her heavy boots. An open Bible placed on Daddy Skinner's stool attracted his attention in his survey of the room. Through the flickering light he could see the passages Tessibel had marked. He must say something or his brain would burst.

"You have a Bible, I see?"

His words sounded strained and his voice foreign to his own.

"Yep."

"Can you read it?"

"I spells at it," Tess replied in tones a little surly.

"Where did you get it?" asked Frederick presently.

She waited a moment before answering, straightening up from the oven where she had placed the cold bacon left from her breakfast to heat.

"Where did I get what?" she demanded.

"The Bible," replied Frederick.

He had asked about the book in the first place for something to talk of, for the roaring of the wind through the hut's rafters distracted him. He desired to hear the squatter say something — it all seemed so much like a dream that he feared to awaken only to find himself in the empty house with the sophomore's revolver staring at him.

"I cribbed it from the mission," answered the girl, pronouncing her words plainly. She leaned toward him and finished abruptly. "I took it from the place that comed from."

She was pointing toward the warm red altar-cloth bound about Frederick's head. Alas, Tess had needed a Bible and had stolen it: he had needed warm covering and had accepted it. There was no difference between the minister's son and the squatter's daughter. Vicissitude had forced each into a like position, and somehow Frederick lost his sense of right and wrong, for he could not sit in judgment upon either action. Never before in all of his short young life had he really needed anything for personal comfort — but the altar-cloth. Tess saw the struggle going on in his mind; she bent toward him, reasoning:

"I needed the Bible, didn't I? Didn't ye say that to save Daddy Skinner's life I had to have it? Ye needed that red rag what ye got round yer head. There air only one way in this world —" She was moving toward him inch by inch, the soles of the fisherman's boots dragging the bread crumbs and fish bones beneath them. "Ye takes what ye need to save yer life, or the life of yer Daddy. Folks mostly never steals what they ain't needin'."

The message went straight home to Frederick. He could not combat such reasoning. He knew well that he would have frozen but for the timely stealing of the altar-cloth — also, he knew that the Bible was as necessary to Tess as the altar-cloth was to him. He mentally lashed himself into a state of unrest. Why had he not thought of a Bible and given Tess one? It would have been so easy for him to have supplied her small needs!

He was watching the girl through the gloomy haze of the bacon smoke, but spoke no more until Tessibel ordered him to draw up to the table and eat.

"Have a piece of bacon," said she.

Frederick held up his plate, and Tess shoved a generous portion into it. She gave him a tempting brown fish, cut a slice of bread, placing it upon the side of his tin plate, and commenced to eat rapidly from her own.

Neither boy nor girl mentioned sleeping until the hands of the small nickel clock on the shelf in the corner pointed out the hour of eleven. Then Tessibel opened the subject without hesitation or embarrassment.

"It air time fer ye to turn in," said she, banking the embers in the stove for the night.

"I shall sit up," replied Frederick stiffly.

"There air two beds," commented Tess in simple ignorance of all law save necessity. "Mine air under Daddy's — see?"

She dragged the rope cot from under the larger bed — a cloud of dust rising white to the shanty's rafters and settling like a soft mist upon the student.

"I air goin' to sleep here," explained Tess with no mention of the lately exposed dirt. "I only slep' in Daddy's bed cause he wasn't here. . . . Ye go to bed while I gets the sticks fer the mornin'."

Frederick placed his hand on her arm almost timidly. She was so different from any girl he had ever known!

"Please allow me to get the wood for you."

Two rows of white teeth bared themselves in a frank smile.

"I's a squatter," she said, "and squatter women allers gets the wood. Scoot to bed."

When Tessibel came in from the mud cellar, Frederick lay with his face toward the wall, Orn Skinner's soiled blankets wrapped closely about his shoulders. Tessibel placed the leather strap over the staple in the door, and barred up for the night.

## CHAPTER XXIII

FOR almost an hour Tessibel lay thinking deeply, her brain alive with the past rapid happening of events. That the student would ever sleep under her roof was more than she had dreamed. She could hear him breathing evenly; he was asleep with "Daddy's" blankets wrapped tightly about his finely shaped head. Through the dim light Tessibel could follow the outline of the great form stretched out on the roped bed. A feeling of thanksgiving swept over her — she was his protector. She had not thought of asking about his crime. Of course he was fleeing from the law, but he could have done nothing that would lessen her desire to aid him. If he had murdered, then it was necessary that he should; if he had stolen, it was the common lot of all men in need. The one thing to do was to keep him from the clutches of the law. She felt herself getting drowsy, and soon the even breathing of the squatter and the student told that both slept.

Tess would never know what time it happened. Suddenly her eyes flew open and through the light of a lantern she saw Ben Letts leering into her face. The frosty air was blowing in gusts through the window which the squatter Ben had forced open. The horror of the situation came slowly over her. For the instant she forgot the student sleeping in her father's bed, and Ben Letts had not noticed him.

Ben began to speak in low tones:

"If ye wants to live, don't holler . . . Get up!"

Tess crawled out of bed, fully dressed. Frederick slept on, hearing no sound, for the cold room had compelled him nearly to cover his head. Suddenly the presence of the student came into the girl's mind; but she only threw a furtive glance at the sleeping youth.

"What do ye want?" she demanded vaguely.

"First ye air to come with me to the Brindle Bull at Kennedy's — I air got somethin' for him. . . . He air dead in the mornin' by the hand of the girl what loves him."

There was unlimitable sarcasm in the vile, low face as Ben hissed this out.

"And after that?" asked Tess, edging toward the lower part of "Daddy's" bed. There she could reach for the covering over Frederick, and he would save her. The feeling of the night before that she was his protector vanished. He would —

"Never mind after that," growled Ben. "Ye had yer chance at bein' hones' and ye wouldn't take it."

Tessibel slipped her feet into Daddy's boots — she was strangely buoyant and unafraid. It was the woman in her rising to that supreme moment when she should call upon the man she loved, and he would answer. Ben was leaning against the wall, his eyes having sought for no other person in the room.

With the agility of a hare, Tessibel dashed around him toward Frederick, and snatched the blankets from the bed. The workings of Ben's mind were so slow that the form of the student loomed up, before he realized that the minister's son was in Tessibel's cabin.

"Ye air here to save me, Frederick," cried Tess, the

# TESS OF THE STORM COUNTRY 181

light of the lantern sending a ray into the upturned widening eyes.

Letts dropped his under jaw, his body relaxing in fear. He was an arrant coward like the most of his downtrodden race. Then something shifted through his thick brain, and he smiled knowingly.

"So the high and the low air together — eh? The Dominie's son, and the fisherman's brat — the student — and the —"

Before he had finished the sneering words, Frederick had struck him full in the face. Boyish dignity — his father's position — God — everything was forgotten save Tess. He only knew that she was being maligned, and that her holy mission of rescuing him from the frost of a night like this was being turned into evil by a squint-eyed fisherman whom he had never seen before.

Into the man's fat flabby body crashed Frederick's strong fists. Tessibel stood looking on, her head bent forward alertly. One arm was clasped about her neck — excitement sparkling from the flushed face and panting lips. Once the throat sound that came when she was excited rolled forth; otherwise she was silent.

Thrashed from side to side, his ragged coat made worse by the severe shaking Frederick was administering, Ben Letts groaned audibly.

"Have you had enough?" demanded the student, standing over the fisherman.

"Yep, I's a goin' home."

Tess laughed low and wickedly. She loved to see the blood oozing from the mark in the ugly face. Every drop matched those dragged from the hearts of the brat's mother, who had suffered for Ben, and of the poor little miserable child himself, struggling for life in the Longman shanty.

"You'd better go home," ordered Frederick, "and I want to tell you something. If I ever hear you uttering a word about my being in this hut, I'll follow you to the ends of the earth, and flog the life out of you. . . Don't try any of your tricks on me, either."

Frederick shivered as the wind swept cold from the frozen lake to his damp brow. Ben had lifted his lantern and was swaying toward the door.

"I'll go hum," said he, "but I ain't done with ye — some day —"

Frederick bounded forward like a whiplash, but Tess held him back. Ben gave a quick jump and was gone.

"He wasn't worth a-hurtin' any more," Tess commented, lighting a candle. "I know he air the man what killed my other Frederick."

The name slipped out with loving intonation.

Then the boy and the girl turned and faced each other. The shanty rocked in the wind like the cradle of a child. The willow mourned its tale of winter over the roof, scraping the broken tin in hollow groans, shrieking now and then as a gust roared through it.

For fully three minutes after the going of Ben, Tessibel stood looking at the student. He had saved her from Myra's fate, from a hated thing that made her teeth press hard together, and her eyes gather an expression of melting gratitude.

"It were — it were —"

But the halting tongue could not finish. Untutored as she was, Tess had read the message in the student's eyes. Love teaches in one night its dreadful longing and response. Its domineering power brought Fred-

erick Graves nearer to Tess in her rags. It made them
equal, even as all are equal in love — and in death. In
an instant the girl in the fish-tainted tatters was clasped
close to his heart, the bright, beautiful face lifted to his.
Then came the kiss, the making of which blended two
lives indissolubly together. The paleness of death settled over the boy; the strong muscles of his shoulders
stood out beneath the whiteness of his shirt sleeves,
while his fingers pressed the red-brown head closer to
him, his kiss deepening the crimson richness in the
squatter's face. It was the one supreme passionate moment of Tessibel's life. The sound of the whistling
wind left her ears. The cold night blasts driving
through the window were as the faint breezes of a summer's evening. The smoldering candle lifted its flame,
blazing forth a glory that surrounded the student with
a golden halo. Tessibel had experienced her first kiss.
The nature in her demanded that she know the fullness of
it — the pitying fullness which would bring to her that
which it brings to all loving women dominated by the
passion born within them. The blood of her race, her
uneducated primeval race, rose and clamored for its own.
In her untutored youth she could have crushed the lad in
her wild longing for such another kiss.

Pantingly she drew herself from Frederick. Why?
Tess could never tell why! Myra's love for Ben Letts
rushed over her overwhelmingly. . . . The "brat's"
mother knew the sweetness of a kiss, and in it had forgotten the blasting winter winds on the ragged rocks
where Ben Letts had broken her arm.

Frederick, ashy-pale, struggled for control; a con-
sciousness of the ignorance of the girl — and his own
godly profession broke upon him; and he sank upon the

stool with a sob. His face in his hands filled Tessibel's soul with remorse. Delicately, with the touch of a lady born, she rested her hand upon the student's dark head. The small fingers, used to the drudgery of a fisherwoman's life, lifted the damp hair from the high forehead. Her woman's sense of the fitness of things rose keenly to quiet the boy's grief over his indiscretion.

"It were good of ye to remember that Daddy were gone," she whispered. "He gives me kisses on the bill."

All passion had left her tones. Of course, thought the student, she was but a child — but a forlorn beautiful child born without — without what? If he could have known —

The next moment he did know. With abandon, complete and absolute, the hot blood coursing madly from her heart to her face, Tess threw herself upon the shanty floor. Frederick Graves drew her quickly to her feet.

"Tess . . . Tessibel . . . Tess . . . Stand up, Tess!"

The last word came out in a shout. He had her in his arms, and she was clinging to him as ivy clings for life to an old church.

Tessibel made no effort to support herself. She was leaning limply against him with closed eyes.

"It air good to forget — sometimes," she stammered, "I air a forgettin' all but the — student."

As on that memorable day when "Daddy" had been taken to prison in Auburn, and she had planted herself in his arms not to be removed, so Tess hung to Frederick. Ben Letts was forgotten, the suffering child in the Longman shanty whom she loved was forgotten; even Daddy Skinner was forgotten. Tessibel had found her man, and all the experiences of her kind could not help her in her hour of temptation.

"Tessibel, Tess, we can't forget, stand up." The boy's words spread through the dazed brain. Frederick dragged her arms from his neck, forcing her to the stool.

"Tessibel, have you forgotten — the Christ, your father and me?"

Had she forgotten him? Only him she had remembered — only his voice rang through her like the sweetest music. But she was so quiet now that the boy seated himself beside her, drawing her hands into his.

"Tess," he began, intensely, bending to look into the flushed face, "Tess — look at me!"

Slowly the brown eyes dragged their gaze upward until the boy and girl were staring wide-lidded directly at each other.

"Tess, have you ever thought that, some time, we might be more to each other — some time in the future when you have learned and studied much?"

Wonderingly she drew her hands from his, hiding them in the folds of the torn gingham skirt.

"I air a squatter," she got out at last. "You be high — I air low, as Ben Letts said. . . . But, but," she faltered, finishing her sentence brokenly, "But I's yer squatter."

For one bitter moment the Longman child with its old-man face flitted across her vision. She shivered, rose hastily, and went to the stove, scattering the lids from their openings before uttering another word.

Frederick was watching her critically.

"You ought to go to school, Tess," he said presently.

"I has to stay here," she replied beginning to stir

the embers. "If I left the hut alone yer pappy could fire it, and Daddy and me wouldn't have a home. . . . Ain't nice nights like this to be without a roof to cover ye."

Frederick realized this. Had he not been that very night with no place to lay his head, and no kindly hand save hers to give him something to eat? He flushed deeply at the mention of his father, and marveled that the squatter girl had not spoken with any hard feeling in her tone. It was what could be expected — so her voice implied; if she left the shanty alone, the rightful owner could then take back what the law would not allow if the squatters remained.

"Ye be a goin' to stay here to-morry?" asked Tess later by five minutes.

"If I may."

"Be ye goin' to tell me what ye air hidin' for?"

Frederick threw back his head and laughed. He had forgotten to tell her.

"Of course. You see I am the freshman class president. . . . The boys in the upper classes kidnaped me, and kept me prisoner in an unused house at the inlet. . . . I escaped last night, and you brought me here."

The story was so tame — so unlike what Tess had expected to hear that she drew a long, disappointed breath. There had been a vague wish within her heart that she were going to be of infinite benefit to him. It was such a little thing to lose a fine supper. His life had not been in danger as she had supposed.

"You understand, Tess, that it's a disgrace to our class not to have the president there," Frederick burst forth, "even if he is kept away by force. I would rather sacrifice anything than have it happen — only, I do not want to harm your good name, Tessibel."

Tess stared at him blankly.

"Squatter's brats don't have no names. . . . Ye can't do me any harm."

"Oh, yes, I could," insisted Frederick. "What if that scoundrel who was here a little while ago should say that I were here? . . . It would harm us both."

Tess paused in her breakfast preparations long enough to say simply,

"Yer Christ wouldn't let him harm ye, would He?"

The boy swept her with an incredulous glance.

Did she so thoroughly have faith in a miraculous interference in human affairs by divine power? The delicate face was lighted with exquisite coloring which came and went in the morning light like the tints of a sea-shell. The bright trustful eyes were shining into his, every motion of the lovely head and body bespeaking the blind faith in which the squatter girl lived. Frederick found himself wishing impetuously with all his soul that he could command a faith like hers. His own seemed so dead, so unlike a living faith that he sighed as he turned toward her.

"Tessibel," he said honestly, "you are a better girl than I am a boy . . . I am learning many things from you." Then, looking up with a smile after a moment's thought, he finished: "No, I believe with you, that it is impossible for him to harm one of us if we have faith in God."

"So, I can help ye to-morry if ye ain't in Daddy's fix?"

Then Frederick understood that she would have saved him, even if he had been in danger of his life.

"Yes," he replied, "you can aid me. . . . Do you know where my fraternity is?"

Tess shook her head with a troubled expression.

"I can tell you where it is! I want you to go there and ask for Dan Jordan and tell him I am here. You must speak to no one else about me, or they will come and take me away, and I told you I would almost rather die than not be with my class at the banquet."

Tessibel's spirits rose high. She could help him — after all.

"How air ye goin' to get into the place where ye eats without gettin' took again?"

A flashing intelligence leaped into the brown eyes during her question.

"I knows how I can help ye." She lowered her voice and began to describe the escape and the final fulfillment of their plan.

Frederick chuckled when she had finished.

"That's capital. You tell Dan Jordan, then, to-morrow what you have told me. You see the banquet takes place to-morrow night."

"Yep, I tells him, so I will. I goes to town early to-morry and up to your house. . . Come and eat now!"

## CHAPTER XXIV

THE next morning at eight o'clock Tessibel walked eastward up the long hill toward the college. The "Cranium" fellows were yet asleep. The whole house was tired out from looking for their captured president. The underclassmen did not know that Graves had escaped, Frederick's enemies keeping them in ignorance as long as possible.

Tessibel turned into the carriage drive toward the fraternity with a fish-basket upon her arm.

A man cleaning snow from the flight of steps addressed her.

"What do you want here?"

"I want to see Mr. Jordan. . . . He air here, ain't he? I has somethin' for him."

"Give it to me," ordered the janitor, "I'll take it to him."

"Can't! He said as how I wasn't to give it to no one but hisself, and I won't, so there!"

"He ain't up yet."

"Don't care, I'll wait, then . . . Tell him, will ye, that I air a waitin'?"

Dan Jordan wondered as he crawled slowly out of bed what a girl could want of him at that early hour. He met Tess at the front door, and without waiting for him to speak Tessibel said in an undertone.

"I has somethin' to tell ye. . . . I air Tess the squatter's brat, what ye gived the coffee to at the parson's house. I said as how I has somethin' to tell ye!"

"Will you tell me now?" asked Dan kindly. "You see, I can't ask you in here —

"I ain't a comin' in," and lowering her voice with a furtive glance she almost whispered, "I knows — I knows where the minister's son air."

Dan started and looked at her sharply. She could mean no other than Frederick. He placed his fingers on his lips.

"You have fish to sell," he asked, "I will take them all. Go around to the back door and leave them. . . ." Then in a lower tone he ordered, "Meet me in five minutes at the bottom of the hill."

The last of the sentence was breathed rather than spoken. Dan Jordan turned into State Street some minutes afterwards, and he could see the glistening red head of the fishergirl as she swung her empty basket on her arm and jingled the money in her hand which she had received for the fish.

"Tell me quickly where Mr. Graves is," commanded Dan rushing toward her.

"He air in my hut," answered Tess bluntly.

"Did the boys bring him there?"

"Nope, he got away. . . . And I took him there."

She described the plan she and Frederick had formed.

"Ye see by that way ye can get him to the supper, can't ye?"

"Yes," replied Dan delightedly, "and we will never be able to thank you enough for what you have done. Let me assure you that we are very grateful to you."

"Aw, shut up!" Every white tooth showed in the

wide smile, " I ain't done nothin'. He air done more than that for me."

The sweet face lighted by the infinite love for the student hidden in her hut spoke its own secret to Dan Jordan and through his recently acquired knowledge of heart emotions, he stared vaguely at the girl. Would Frederick — no, no — the minister's son was a better lad than he. His eyes filled with tears and a lump came into his throat. He stood watching the figure of Tess moving away, and regarded intently the great boots, the ragged skirt, the beautiful ringlets and the proud young head set so well upon the sloping shoulders. Dan's mind reverted to another girl, no older than the squatter, and with a sigh mournful enough he turned back to the fraternity.

Tess walked down the lane, running as she neared the foot of the hill. She wanted to impart to the student what Dan had told her. With her fingers upon the hut latch she stopped short. Voices came from inside. She dropped her hand — Ben Letts was there or another squatter. Suddenly she opened the door and stood in the entrance. Frederick was seated upon "Daddy's" stool; Professor Young was standing in his fur coat with his back to the stove.

The student's face had blanched to the hue of death; an expression such as Tess had never seen in human eyes rested in his. He was speaking and the girl's ears caught the words.

" I would forfeit my life before I would harm her, believe me!" Two pairs of masculine eyes turned at the opening of the door, and both men were looking into the eager face of Tessibel. The Professor did not come forward to meet her; his manner was stiff and formal. For a moment even the student's last words left her mind, and Daddy Skinner rose before her.

"Ye be here to tell me about Daddy?" she asked.

"You needed me to come more for yourself than to tell you of your father, child!" said Young with accusing eyes upon Frederick.

A sullen expression flitted across Tessibel's lips.

"Ye didn't need to come, if yer a goin' to make the student sorry," she answered haltingly. "Ye has yer own business to mind."

Tess was standing between them, her glance turning first to Frederick, then to the Professor. She didn't fully understand his words, but she knew that Frederick had been hurt by something the lawyer had said. Young began to button his coat. He had thought the girl worth saving, and Frederick had ever been in his mind as the perfection of young manhood. His throat tightened; he looked at Tess and thought of his love for her. It was almost mastering him. Why should he suffer over such a girl, who insulted him even while he was trying to help her?

Frederick stood up wearily. Professor Young ought to realize the situation, to remember that some shelter was necessary for him. Tess was stolidly arranging the table.

"You do not know how I came to be here," said Frederick briefly.

"It is enough that I see you here," replied Young.

In a temper Tess slammed the oven door loudly.

"She found me on the tracks," explained Frederick. "I escaped from the sophomores and she brought me here. I should have frozen to death otherwise — and I did not think that it might harm her."

"It ain't hurt me," cried Tessibel coming forward. "He air the one what helped me get my Daddy Skinner out of trouble. He air my friend!"

The rage of the girl when she wheeled impetuously upon him made the Professor catch his breath. He had been the one who had done all the work, had given her father a new lease of life. He had come now to tell her about the letter, and to hear her say that a lad with no influence whatever had done that which it would have been impossible for him to do, to hear Tess give the credit which should be his to Frederick made Young pass his fingers through his hair nervously, and wonder just what the student had done to gain such praise. His own love for Tess, his great desire, pleaded with him to believe in both the boy and the girl. Tessibel's soulful expression went far in giving back to DeForest Young the hope that had made his days brighter and filled the future with promise.

"May I stay with you to dinner, Miss Tessibel?" he said, shaking his shoulders. "I did not understand . . . In fact I had forgotten about the banquet. I am glad you helped Mr. Graves make his class dinner. . . . May I stay?"

Frederick stepped forward, holding out his hand.

"Thanks," he said brokenly; "I shall never forget this — in you."

The clasping of the two hands and the smile on the lips of the student made Tess broaden her own.

"Yep, jerk off yer coat, and eat," ordered she. "Air ye heard about Daddy?"

"Yes." Young hesitated a moment.

"What is it, Professor?" ejaculated Frederick. "Don't keep her in suspense."

"Daddy ain't a-goin' to hang! . . . He can't!" Her eyes turned to Frederick. "'Cause ye said he couldn't."

The boy flushed to the roots of his hair and glanced at Professor Young. Again she was giving the credit to Graves — credit the lad so little deserved. Frederick felt this, and muttered:

"She doesn't understand yet what you've done, Professor — I'm sorry!"

"They've placed a stay upon your father's execution," explained Young, "that will give us a chance to prove him innocent. . . . I am positive that he didn't kill the gamekeeper. I went to the prison last week."

"Ye seed him?" asked Tess eagerly, striding close to him. He felt the hot breath against his face and a feeling of longing coursed through his veins.

"Yes," was all he said.

"What did he say about me?"

"Everything good! You will have him very soon here with you, Tessibel."

The girl was fatigued with turbulent emotions, lonely and heartsick. The shadow of the rope was gone from Daddy Skinner. Like a relieved child she sank down upon the floor and began to whimper. Both men were silenced by the swaying red head. The bacon sputtered in the frying pan upon the stove, spitting the grease to the lids, where it burned away in tiny yellow flames.

Then Tess raised her head.

"What a bloke I air to cry when Daddy air a-comin'

home. . . . We air a-goin' to eat now," she ended, wiping her eyes.

Before the meal was over Tess was on better terms with Young than she had ever been before. He outlined to the delighted girl his visit to the prison.

"Your father says, child," he related, "that he took the gun from the stern of the boat, and laid it on the shore, near where he was hauling the net. . . . He heard a shot and ran forward and was arrested. He swore to me that he did not fire the gun and I believe him. The fatal step was in his taking the rifle at all, because that was disobeying the law."

"Ye air my friend, too," Tess said beamingly, leaning over and taking the Professor's hand in hers. Before he could stop her, she had raised it to her lips, kissed it several times, and dropping it again, calmly went on eating.

## CHAPTER XXV

AT the "Cranium" Fraternity, Dan Jordan was closeted with three little freshmen. Swipes looked downcast.

"I want to do something to help," he wailed; "I feel as if it were all my fault that the parson is gone. We can't have any fun without him. It's tedious, too, being cooped up here not being able to go anywhere for fear of being taken ourselves."

Dan cleared his throat preparatory to speaking.

"If you fellows won't peach," said he in an eager undertone, "I'll tell you something and you can help."

"What?"

"We'll have Graves if you will all do as I tell you."

"Watch me," cried Swipes, turning a somersault. When he was in the most harrowing position, Brown gave him a swift kick.

"Give him one for me, Shorts," whispered Spuddy, but Swipes was on his feet again, ready to listen.

There was a general hurrah when Jordan in subdued tones had outlined the plan.

"Where are Graves' evening clothes," demanded Dillon; "we must smuggle them into the opera-house some way."

"They'll be there all right," replied Jordan; "they've gone in with the caterer's stuff. You'd better send your own best togs in a barrel or the sophomores will see to it that you won't have them when you want them. . . . Now mind, mum's the word."

The fishermen of squatter's row did not recognize the stranger who slouched along by the side of Tessibel, the night of the freshman banquet. She was on her way to the city with her fish. One after another women poked frowsy heads from the hut windows at the barking of their dogs. But Tess went steadily on, not even heeding her companion who hurried his footsteps to keep close to her.

"Ye sells yer fish for a shillin' a pound," said she after a few minutes' walk.

The man nodded. Once only did he raise his eyes. They were passing a dingy-looking empty house, with a large broken window.

Just then, Ben Letts, accompanied by Ezra Longman, met them. The red head of the squatter girl rose a little higher, the lines growing deeper about the narrowed lids. To the fisherman she deigned no good-morrow, nor had she a thought of them after they had passed.

"He air a new squatter," said Ben laconically, turning to look at the queer pair.

"He air her uncle," added Ezra pompously; "he air here to help her pappy out of his scrape."

Ben did not answer, but stepped to the tracks with another evil backward look at Tess and her squatter friend.


Forty or fifty sophomores loafed about the operahouse watching the caterers buzz to and fro. Tables had been spread inside for several hundred guests, and the president's chair was decorated with roses and winter ferns. Three little freshmen and Dan Jordan, surrounded by many juniors went calmly in to inspect things.

Several underclassmen stood disconsolately inside.

"Be on your guard," whispered Dan, passing them.

The fifty sophomores outside were waiting for something to happen. Graves would be produced — how, they could not tell. The strangeness of the actions of Frederick's fraternity brothers made the affair more unsolvable. Threatening looks were showered upon them as freshman after freshman, guarded by juniors, filed in. Dan Jordan slouched to the door of the opera-house, his eyes falling mechanically upon Tessibel Skinner across the street. He heard her arguing with the man from the café about her fish. Tessibel then crossed to the opera-house.

"Does ye want any fish?" she smiled, showing her white teeth.

"No," replied Jordan. "What have you? . . . Eels?"

"No, nothin' but bullheads and suckers."

Dan looked about, grinning upon the sophomores.

"There's enough of them here already. . . . I want some eels —"

The sophomores pretended not to hear. They were not interested in fishermen, but kept their eyes open for a carriage that would dash in from the main street with the rescued president within it.

"Sling them eels over here," commanded Tessibel, beckoning to the slouching squatter across the way. The man with the basket offered the contents to Dan.

"I'll take what you have, too, girl," said Jordan in a loud voice, "how much do they weigh?"

"Don't know," replied Tess.

"Take them in and get them weighed," said Swipes, innocently coming to Dan's side.

"Hey there, you old guy," chuckled Spuddy; "drag your fish into the opera-house and dump them out. . . . We're going to have some fun. . . . If we can't have our president, eels will have to do."

The squatter disappeared inside the building.

"A pile of fun they'll have without their president," grunted a sophomore.

Tessibel gathered her empty basket upon her arm and amid the smiling looks of the students who stood watching her she walked away with her head high in the air.

But Dan Jordan, with a mighty yell, triumphantly taken up by his classmen, grasped the hat from the squatter's head. The smiling, open face of Frederick Graves was before them. The sophomores never quite puzzled out how the freshman president was in his chair at the banquet, and directly in front of him in the place of honor was a huge dish of eels.


Shaking the snow from her shoulders like a great dog in a storm, Tess knocked softly on the Longman shanty door. Mrs. Longman had gone to the city with Satisfied, and Myra, with the whining brat in her arms, welcomed her.

One whole week had passed since Tess had seen the student — seven long interminable days since — and now she had come to ask Myra Longman some of the mysterious questions about the kiss that Frederick had given her. Myra relinquished the child to her and the little fellow sank to sleep under Tessibel's crooning voice. His regular breathing told her that he slept; she placed him in the box and sat thoughtfully down.

"Air Ben Letts been here lately?" she asked after a pause.

Myra shook her head.

"He ain't got no time for such as the brat and me," she replied bitterly.

Tess waited until Myra had ceased scattering the shanty chairs in her rage.

"Did he say as how he loved ye that night in the storm on the ragged rocks?" she asked presently.

"Yep, he did say it, he did," answered Myra.

"Air he — air he a-knowin'— how to kiss?"

The very word slipping from her lips brought back with a sudden joy that night a week ago, and the never-to-be-forgotten kiss of the student. She could feel again the warm, strong lips pressed to hers — the long muscular arms enfolding her.

Myra scanned her face closely.

"To kiss — yep; but he ain't never kissed the brat."

There was wonderful longing and passion in her tones.

This was a new thought for Tess. The "Pappy" should kiss his brat — but were they one and the same kisses? She remembered the sweetness of that first caress "Daddy" had given her on the stone window ledge of his cell. It was tinged with bittersweet — bitter because Daddy was going away, sweet because she had desired it so fondly. But it had not been like the student's kiss. She was going to ask Myra Longman to solve the first great problem of her life.

"Air the kisses what ye had from Ben Letts —

burnin' ones? Did ye lose the thought of the night and the night things on the ragged rocks? . . . Did ye want 'em again and again — more and more kisses till they scorched yer face like the bread oven in the spring?"

Tess had risen to her feet, had whitened to the small ears covered with the tawny hair. Myra had risen also. Both girls were eying each other with intentness. Tess started to speak again, coming forward a step toward the other squatter.

"Did ye forget the storm, the wavin' trees and all 'cept — Ben Letts?"

"Ye air been to the ragged rocks," moaned Myra, sinking down upon the floor in a heap.

In a twinkling the meaning of Myra's words dawned upon Tessibel.

"I ain't been there with Ben Letts," she replied suddenly. "I ain't got no likin' for the brat's Pa's kisses —"

"But ye hev been to the ragged rocks," insisted Myra, settling back with a sob against the box where the child slept.

"Nope, I ain't; but I had a kiss, and Myra, it were — like the singin' in the heavens what the song tells about — like the feelin' in here," she placed her hand upon her heart, her eyes flashing golden, "when the world air filled with flowers and the birds air a singin'. . . . Were it like that with Ben Letts? Were it?"

"Nope," replied Myra sulkily, "Ben Letts ain't got no singin' kisses."

She rose languidly, tucked the blanket closer about the sleeping child's head.

"Tessibel," she broke forth hoarsely, "for all women

folks there air brats a cryin' for their Pa's to tell 'em yep or nope. And there air men a-walkin' on the ragged rocks with singin' kisses for yer pretty face and tangled hair. There air a brat sleepin' till it's dead in the box." The tired young mother allowed her hungry gaze to fall upon the quiet infant. "Tessibel, yer brat —"

But Tessibel bounded out of the door, over the snow-covered rocks like a deer. She would not lose the sweetness of the kiss in Myra's warning words — that penetrating holy kiss she had treasured for seven long days and nights.

The torturing thoughts that had filled the mind of Professor Young at finding Frederick Graves in the cabin of the fishergirl were new sensations to him. He loved Tessibel, and in her lay his future happiness. Her stolid indifference to his endeavors to aid her through her father had blasted his hopes somewhat. Then again he would feverishly reason that she had been born to overlook all save those whom she desired and for whom she fought. It was like her kind. Excuses for the girl in the aid she had given the student ran willingly through his brain. If Tess had seen the young fellow in the storm, it was but like the tender, loving heart to aid him. It was no proof that Frederick had found a place in her affections. With these thoughts in his mind he had worked for several days, quietly hoping that the girl might seek him.

Tess found him waiting at the shanty door for her one afternoon after returning from town. She smiled a welcome as she recognized her visitor.

"It air about Daddy ye comed," she said, lifting the padlock from the staple.

"Yes, child, I wanted to tell you of some new friends your father has made in Ithaca — strong friends to aid him."

"Friends," echoed Tess wonderingly. "Daddy Skinner had fishermen for his friends — and not people of Ithacy — come in," she added. The fire crackled on the hearth and Tess sat down to listen with open lips.

"I can't explain just how this came about," said Young, "but some of the people who were in the courtroom the day your father was convicted have risen to befriend him."

Professor Young did not add that he himself had urged that money should be raised for a second defense.

"So last night," he went on, "there was a meeting of several prominent men and money has been placed in my hands for another trial for your father."

Tess tried to understand the long words, and blinked knowingly. The import of it was plain. Daddy was coming back — but how soon?

"When air he comin' home, then?" she demanded.

"After another trial. . . . See if you can read this?"

From a long envelope the lawyer took a piece of paper. Tess examined it carefully for some moments, Young eyeing her with a sense of happiness. He would fight for this child as man never before fought for woman. She would love him out of gratitude if for nothing else. He took the paper she was holding out to him.

"Can't read a damn word — can't read writin' anyway. Tell me what it says about Daddy."

"It's a list of names," replied Young, " mostly members —"

" Of Graves' church? " put in Tess eagerly.

Hadn't the student been praying for just this? she thought.

" Yes; they are all desirous to see your father home again with his little daughter."

" Air the minister givin' money for Daddy? " was the anxious demand.

Young shook his head. He felt a sudden swift-coming desire to tell her enough about the minister's family to make her hate them all. Deforest Young realized for the first time that he was jealous of the student, of a tall dark lad of whom in the past he had taken no more notice than of many other students.

He drew a long breath.

" Not exactly the minister," said he, flushing with shame. " Here — let me read the names to you. William Hopkins of the toggery shop, one hundred dollars. Do you know him? "

Tess shook her head in the negative.

" Deacon Hall and his wife Augusta gave one hundred dollars."

" I know her," Tess cried, " and I knows him a little, too. I tooked them berries and fish — they has a cottage below the ragged rocks."

" And there's the druggist, Mr. Bates — he did not put down his name on the list, but he gave fifty dollars."

Tessibel listened to the explanations as Young read on, making it all plain to her as he proceeded.

She was leaning far over toward him, her chin resting on her open palm.

"They be dum good blokes, to give their money to a squatter, ain't they?"

The professor started perceptibly. She did not understand that all had been done under his supervision; he had tried to impress upon her his great desire to help her, but no words of praise fell from her lips for him. He would have willingly given worlds had she said that he was "a dum good bloke."

"They are all sorry for you and your father," he ended lamely.

"It was the student, Graves, what brought Daddy the money," she burst out with a vivid blush.

"No, the student, Graves, had nothing to do with it," was the grim reply.

"He's a-been prayin' since Daddy went away — that air somethin'," Tess said stubbornly.

Professor Young rose — then seated himself again. He had come for something else, something that meant work and satisfaction for him.

"Now that your father is sure to be saved, will you leave this hut?" he asked peremptorily.

"Nope!"

"But it's not fit for you to be here alone, Tessibel. Listen . . . I'll save your father's squatter rights, if you will study in some good school until he returns."

"Aw, cuss! Who air to pay all the money?" Tess got to her feet with effort.

"I will," deliberately answered Young.

"Nope, I air goin' to stay here," snapped Tess. "I can fish and live likes I have been doin' till Daddy comes. I promised him I'd stày. I can read the Bible now," she ejaculated, promptly producing the book from under the blankets of the bed. "I's a-readin it every day. . . . If ye don't believes, ye can listen and see."

She tossed back the curls from her shoulders as she ended emphatically: "I air a goin' to bring Daddy home through this here book — the student says."

Again the terrible jealousy of the handsome student flashed alive in the professor. Tess had opened the Bible to a chapter she had never read before.

"And straightway in the morning," she spelled, "the chief priests — Aw, that ain't no good! Wait till I find about Daddy."

Then suddenly she threw the Bible down upon the floor.

"There air places what says as how Daddy air a comin' home. The student says it air there. I ain't found it yet but I air a-lookin' for it every day. 'Tain't in that place where I just read about them geezers, the priests."

The lawyer stood up. A pain seized him. He would save this ignorant girl in spite of herself, marry her in spite of Frederick Graves. It would be as difficult as scaling the icy mountains, but he would force her to love him more than the whole world.

"You understand," he said shortly, "that these good people have given money toward helping your father come home. It will be some time before the trial will come up, but when it does — I will bring him back to you."

The assurance in his tones brought Tess to his side.

"Ye be a lawyer," she said abruptly, "and the squatters says as how lawyers air liars and tramps, but ye ain't no tramp, and ye ain't no liar, ye ain't — and when

I sells a lot of fish I air bringin' ye the money for what ye air a doin' for Daddy and me. I says once and I says again as how ye air Daddy's friend, and I air glad that the student's meeting-house folks gived ye a little money to help us."

Mist had gathered in her eyes and she slipped her fingers into Professor Young's. She laid her lips upon his hand, covering it with tears and kisses. Opening the shanty doors, she said:

"I likes ye, I likes ye, but how much a squatter's brat likes don't make no difference. Ye go now, for the tracks get dark about five."

"I have my horse at the top of the hill," replied Young, confusedly.

The sensation from the moist lips upon his flesh prompted him for one brief moment to take the girl to him. He was filled with a strange desire to force this rude shanty maid from her surroundings and place her in another life with him.

## CHAPTER XXVI

THAT night, as Tessibel slept and dreamed of Frederick, another girl waited for her lover. Teola Graves watched for the approach of Dan Jordan with strange emotions. When he was with her, his great strength and constant assurances that everything would go rightly with them gave the girl courage and confidence. But in the night-watches, when youthful sleep refused to come, she was afraid — afraid!

She stood just outside the door, upon the veranda, shrinking from the raw winter wind. Relievedly she noticed Dan's tall form, when he swung around the corner.

"You should not stand in the night wind, dear," Dan chided, gently kissing her. "There! now, I have come for a good chat. Teola, do not look so sad — please."

The little drawing-room in the Rectory was partially dark when they seated themselves on the divan.

"I am so unhappy Dan; so different from what I used to be. Then, life was sweet and I was glad to live —"

"But you don't want to be dead now, sweetheart! — Think of it, Teola. When I shall have finished college, I shall be of age. We will go away from Ithaca, and no one will ever know —"

"But we shall know, Dan. If I had only been a good girl!"

Dan was visibly moved.

"Let's make a bargain," said he suddenly. "To-night we won't talk of anything but the pleasantest of things. I have something funny to tell you."

"I have something to tell you, too," breathed Teola.

"Is it pleasant?" demanded the boy, bending and forcing the lowered eyes to his.

Teola shook her head.

"Then we will leave it until to-morrow," he exclaimed. "I'll tell you my news. Shorts, Spuddy and Swipes are in disgrace at the fraternity. If Shorts would keep away from those other two fellows, he might get through college. It was really their fault Frederick was stolen."

"What have they done now?" asked Teola listlessly. She had little interest in the boys of the society, for, nestled close to her heart, was a secret she could not forget. She had a realization that something unusual had fallen upon her of which she was afraid.

"Well, you see," explained Dan, "there is a comic opera playing here. This afternoon, Swipes, Shorts and Spuddy took some of the chorus girls to the house, when the other fellows were away. They might have known the officers would have found it out. Sure enough, they did! The little rascals were all drunk on champagne, and the girls had to be sent to their hotels in carriages. The kids received a great beating, let me tell you. They are all in bed, in the cupola prison rooms, trying to get over big heads."

Teola wanted to smile, to be happy, but the smiles refused to come. Dan turned the subject.

"Haven't they gathered a deal of money for Skinner?"

Teola nodded, and presently responded,

"Yes, and father thinks it is so strange. Mrs. Hall

and Professor Young were at the bottom of the plan. They think the Skinner girl is a great marvel. I, too, think she is beautiful — and so does Frederick."

"She has a lot of courage," mused Dan, thinking of the girl who had rescued the class president from the hands of his enemies. Teola knew nothing of this episode, for Frederick had asked him to be silent upon it.

"Your father does not wish the man liberated?" The question in Dan's voice brought a flush to Teola's pale face.

"No; he thinks the tribe is a menace to the town, and he is sure the man is guilty. They do tell dreadful things of them, and I can't help but believe some of the tales, although I feel sorry for the girl. But her coming to the toffy pull that night made a great deal of trouble for brother and me."

"So I supposed. But I love you, Teola, for the manner in which you treated her."

Teola straightened herself from her lover's arms, and was about to speak. She would tell him, then, tell him her secret — tell all the fears that weighed upon her heart, as if they were loaded with lead. He would comfort, and tell her not to worry — cheer her, until she could smile again and be happy.

Shorts, Swipes and Spuddy had broken the laws of the fraternity. Rather than suffer the disgrace of leaving it, they had elected a severe punishment.

"I'd rather be cut to pieces, boys," Swipes hiccoughed, turning upon the grave seniors, "than let my mother know what a beast I've been. Go ahead and lick!"

Afterward, the three little freshmen slunk to the rooms in the top of the Society house, which were kept ready for young men whom the officers reprimanded. They had been ordered to bed for three days, and were thankful that the punishment had been no worse than it was.

Swipes demanded a cigarette.

"Go to sleep," ordered Shorts. "It was all your fault in the beginning, and you're drunk."

"No such thing! I couldn't haul a whole bunch of girls up here alone, could I, if I'm drunk! Could I, now? I wish there wasn't any such a being in the world as a woman. . . . They bring heaps of trouble on us poor men."

Saying this, Swipes tumbled into bed, and sank into a stupor.

The cry of "Fire!" rang out upon the night air, startling Dan Jordan and Teola Graves. The volunteer fire companies were gathering from all parts of the town, and Dan stepped on to the Rectory veranda as a hose-cart rolled by. In an instant he was back in the drawing-room.

"Sweetheart, sweetheart," said he, with a strangling kiss upon Teola's pale lips, "I am sure it's our fraternity house. I must go, dear. I must, I must!"

He pressed her to him again, bounded through the door and was gone.

"Dan! Dan!" exclaimed Teola. "Dan, come back!" I have something to tell you . . . I'm so — afraid — so afraid!"

Teola stood watching the yellow flames kiss the sky.

The whole campus gleamed under the lurid glare of the fraternity fire; the light in the heavens told her that it was no ordinary conflagration.

Until the day of her death she would not forget that night. She was longing to hear one word from Dan or Frederick. Her world seemed charged with hideous forces hitherto unfelt. Teola sickened, and waited. If Dan would only come back!

The very moment after he had fallen asleep, it seemed to Swipes, Shorts was pulling him out of bed, and the room was full of smoke. Spuddy was sleeping in the next chamber, and the first sound came to him in a haze-like dream. He thought he heard a roar of thunder, and rain descending upon the roof. Never mind. He was safe in bed, and had just escaped expulsion from his fraternity. As he rubbed his aching head, a dazed resolution took form in his brain. He would never get drunk again — never — never! Then the fumes of the wine brought visions of bright-colored dresses, of pretty faces and tender loving arms, such as his father had told him to beware of. He would toss such joys from him, if it brought him — Spuddy groaned, turned in bed, and tried to wake up. But to wake up was to realize his disgrace. He groaned again, a sharp pain ripping through his head. He heard the sound of voices — he was dreaming, of course; the wine floated fantastic visions again through his misty brain, relieving it of the effort of thinking. Then Shorts' voice rang in his ear.

"For the love of God, Spud, get up! The house is on fire, and we're boxed in this cupola like rats in a trap."

Spuddy sprang out of bed. The thunder he had

dreamed of was the roar of the fire in the walls of the great house. The rain descending on the roof was the water being thrown from the long fire-hose. A strong stream of ice-cold water suddenly broke the window, driving Swipes against the wall. He whimpered drunkenly.

"Plagued fire! 'Course the house had to burn down on a night like this!"

Screams and cries from the crazed mob below came up to the boys through the broken pane. The water ceased its flow, and Shorts, the most sober of the three, crept to the opening. Spuddy had crawled back to bed. Far beneath him, Shorts could see his fraternity brothers running wildly to and fro, frantically waving their arms to him. He could hear orders given in loud tones, and recognized the voices of Frederick Graves and Dan Jordan. It all flashed upon Shorts in a moment how greatly he and his chums were to blame for the disaster, for the fire must have started in the dining-room. He thrust his head through the lurid gleam to attract attention, and saw the men and boys in the yard bringing ladders to rescue them. Now they were splicing them together, to make it possible to reach the great height. Shorts made quick resolves. . . . If he lived. . . . He turned with a groan, and dragged Spuddy from the bed to the open window.

"Stay there, and be ready, if you don't want to die," he commanded curtly.

Shorts saw the ladder rear upward, and a form dart from the shadows. Dan Jordan was coming, hand over hand, toward him, the long ladder creaking under his weight. Jordan's face appeared at the opening.

"Come out here," he commanded Shorts.

Shorts pushed Spuddy forward.

"Take him first, Captain," he said, with a twist in his voice. "He's drunk."

Spuddy hung limp on the window-sill for an instant, and was then gathered into Dan's long arms. Shorts' bleared eyes saw the little chap handed safely to the earth, and the ladder again creaked under the upward steps of the big freshman. Shorts pushed Swipes toward the window as Dan called his name. . . . Now he was alone, and he leaned as far out as he could.

"God! God!" he groaned. "The Captain's face is scorched brown. . . . God! dear God, bless him!"

The crowds below were sending up cheer after cheer; myriads of sparks shot rocket-like high into the air, dying in the snow as they fell. Streams of water poured into the flaming windows. Jordan was coming up again.

"Come out, Shorts," he heard Dan say, and he clambered over the sill.

"Slip into my arms, old man," the deep voice persuaded. "Come, now; let go. . . . There, hang limper. . . . You're heavier than the others."

He felt Dan take a downward step, and his head whirled around and around. They passed window after window, Shorts being carefully held under Dan's arm. Flames licked at them greedily, touching and shriveling their flesh. Smoke choked their nostrils cruelly. Shorts could feel the trembling of Dan's body, as his burned fingers grasped each rung of the ladder. To his mind the figures below looked like goblins dancing in the light.

Suddenly, midway to the ground, the ladder creaked and groaned hideously. Jordan halted.

"The ladder is bending, Shorts," he breathed hoarsely. He did not finish his sentence, but shouted, "Catch him!"

Little Brown shot into the air like a rubber ball. . . . A crashing sound broke over the silent, gaping throng below. Then a giant form turned twice in the air, shooting downward like a stone from a sling. . . . The crowd parted, and Dan Jordan struck the frozen ground. His fraternity brothers lifted up the unconscious boy, and the great roof above, with a sickening din, sank into the fire.

The bitter frost hardened the streams of water pouring from holes in the burning house into ropes of ice. Toward morning, the fire died, leaving the huge frame, like an ice-covered palace, looming darkly against the college hill.

In another fraternity house, Shorts was in bed, face and hands swathed in bandages. Swipes and Spuddy, tear-stained and pale, stood by the door, waiting.

"If only they would come and tell us something!" moaned Spuddy. "Boys, if the Captain goes, I'm done for."

"We'll make it all right with him," came hopefully from Shorts. "He can't die, fellows! He's as strong as a horse. If he hadn't thrown me out into that snow pile, I would have been crushed under him. I'll never forget that in all my life," he finished, with a shudder.

"Gad, but he looked dead when they picked him up," said Swipes in despair. "I'm done for, too, if — if . . . Here comes some one! It's Teddy!"

He stepped aside, and Manchester, entering deliberately, closed the door. Then he sat down dazedly.

"He's gone, boys. The Captain's gone." The words came in a stammer through pressed lips.

"I wish it had been I," muttered Swipes brokenly, when they were alone again. "It was all my fault." He burst into a wild sobbing. "I'd give my very life to have heard — the Captain — say he had forgiven me."

"I was more to blame than you were," replied Spuddy. "My mother. . . . God! look at that sun!"

Bright rays slanted golden through the window upon the three woful little freshmen who had ruined the "Cranium" Society.

## CHAPTER XXVII

ONE day in the following July, Tessibel was going to Mrs. Longman's hut, with a list of Bible words she did not understand. She stopped at the edge of the forest, and listened to a curious sobbing sound she thought issued from beyond the gorge. Then, thinking herself mistaken, she ran nimbly on, avoiding the long thorns that lay in her path. The noise came more distinctly through the clear air, making the squatter girl lift her head and pause again. There was no mistake this time.

"It ain't no pup," she said aloud, "'cause a pup don't snivel like that."

Raising the red head, she tore long threads of hair loose from the briars, and, drawing the masses of curls about her shoulders, broke into the opening of the forest. Some one was crying, and any sign of suffering brought an immediate response from Tess. It might be Myra, or it might be some little lost child. Spurred on by sympathy, she bounded over a bed of dead chestnut burrs, waded through the water to the other side of the creek, and struggled up the rocks.

Teola Graves, crouched in an attitude of suffering and despair, was seated on the gnarled root of a huge tree. Tessibel watched her for an instant. Here was a holy personage to the squatter, touched with the finger of the mysterious God the student worshiped. And was she not the sister of Frederick, and had not Teola given her coffee from her own cup that winter night? Tessibel had not spoken to the minister's daughter since her father had been taken away to Auburn, and some of the intensity Tess had felt upon that one great day of her life came back to her as she stood hesitant, watching the student's sister.

Perhaps the girl was weeping for some pleasure denied her — perhaps for a jewel to wear about her neck. She went forward impulsively, and laid her hand upon the rounded shoulder.

"What be ye blattin' over?" she stammered, with a tinge of awe in her voice.

Teola struggled to her feet, suppressing her grief. The question stopped the flow of tears, and the two girls, so differently situated, the one the daughter of an eminent minister, and the other a squatter, wonderingly eyed each other.

"I thought I was alone," was Teola's answer.

"So ye was," replied Tess. "I heard ye cryin' from the lower ledge of the rocks. What air the matter?"

Infinite pity and tenderness in the coarse words, spoken in a sweet, persuasive voice, brought a fresh burst of tears from Teola.

"I'm — I'm ill to-day."

"Ye'll be all right to-morry. . . . 'T'ain't much, air it?"

"It is very much to me," whispered Teola. "I'm so lonely, and so afraid!"

Tessibel sat silently down beside the other girl, twining one arm about the twisted root of the tree. She was used to sorrow, used to watching the agony of human souls without hope. A bird in the top of the tree above them sent a plaintive note into the hot air. Another answered from the forest, and Tessibel raised her head and saw a scarlet bird take wing and disappear into the branches of the wood trees.

She waited for Teola to speak, but at last, seeing there was no cessation of tears, she leaned over and touched her.

"Be ye lonely for yer ma?" she murmured.

Teola shook her head in the negative.

"Then for yer pa?"

"No!"

Ah! Tess had forgotten. Had she not seen Frederick go away weeks before, in a boat filled with pots and kettles and food for a camping expedition? Had he not smiled at her brightly as she passed him on her way to the fish line? She could remember the tense feeling in her throat, and felt again the hot blood rushing madly into her face. Of course, the girl was weeping for her brother!

"Then air ye blattin' for the student?"

She could scarcely utter the last word, scarcely let Teola hear her voice use that beloved name.

"Yes, I was crying for him," replied Teola. "He is dead, you know."

For one instant Tess thought the world had lost its sun. Her face creased into lines, which tightened rope-like under the tanned skin. How could Frederick have died, and she not have known? She rose unsteadily to her feet, uttering one grunt significant of her suffering.

"Were he drowned?" she asked, in a voice so pained that Teola raised her head and looked at her. She did not understand the meaning of the whitened lips nor of the tense drawing-down of the long red-brown eyes.

"No," she replied slowly, "he was killed in the fire on the hill last winter."

The muscles relaxed in the squatter's face. Her legs refused to bear the slender body, and Tessibel dropped again at Teola's side. The kiss she had cherished burned hot upon her lips. Her student lived. The minister's daughter cried for the other one, for him who had called her Miss Skinner, and who afterward helped her smuggle Frederick into the opera-house.

"Why! he air been dead a long time, ain't he?"

"Yes; six months."

"And ye air a-lovin' him yet?"

"Yes."

"But he air dead," philosophized Tess. "He ain't with no other girl."

Teola shivered violently.

"Oh, I know that; I know that. But I — I need him. I want him so!"

"But he air dead," said Tess again steadily.

For many minutes neither spoke. For Teola's new burst of agony settled a solemnity upon Tess which she could not throw off. Forgetting her squatter position, she slipped her hand between the white fingers of the weeper. Teola did not care if the girl's finger-nails were filled with black soot, did not care if the squatter were covered with a dirty, ragged dress, or if her bare feet were calloused from the rocks. Tess was a human being who sympathized with her, and sympathy was as necessary to Teola's soul at that moment as breath was to her body. In the spasmodic whitening of the other girl's face Tess realized a desperate heart agony.

"Ye air sick," she said at last, an enlightened expres-

"THEN YE AIR COMIN' HOM,
WITH ME TO THE SHANTY."

sion widening her lids. "A woman's kind of sick, ain't it? Eh?"

"Yes," answered Teola, flushing deeply; "yes."

"Then ye air a-comin' home with me to the shanty." Tess muttered this in a sly voice, almost in a whisper.

Teola raised her glance, and read in the eyes bent upon her that her whole secret was known. Tessibel Skinner, her father's foe, the daughter of a murderer, was helping her to her feet.

"I'm too sick to walk," she wept, in a barely audible voice. "I tried to throw myself from the rocks, over there, but the water was so silent, blue and terrible, that I couldn't."

"Ye be comin' with me," insisted Tess stolidly.

She was urging her forward, holding Teola by both arms.

"I can't! I can't! Leave me here — I am so ill! I am going to die!"

"Ye air to come," commanded Tess. "And, if ye will, I'll lug ye when ye can't walk. Women like ye don't die, and Mother Moll will come to the hut to-day."

"Mother Moll!" echoed Teola. "Mother Moll! Oh, you mean the witch? And will she — oh, will she help me so they will never know?"

"Yep. And now shut up. Ye air a woman, and was borned for things like this. If ye walks a spell, then I lugs ye across the gully."

"And my father and mother —"

"Shut up, I says," ordered Tess. "It ain't no time to think of fathers and mothers. They don't know nothin' about it, does they?"

"No," said Teola. "They have been in Europe with

my little sister for nearly four months. I've been alone all summer, with Rebecca, our maid, and Frederick, my brother—"

Her lips closed over a moan of pain, and she did not continue her sentence.

Through the forest, over the gullies, and down toward the Skinner hut the two girls went slowly, Teola whimpering in her agony of soul, and Tess carrying her when she could not walk. Only once did Tessibel stop.

"Hold a minute," she said gruffly, releasing Teola. "One of the dum thorns went clean through my toe. . . . It air out now. . . . Come along! What does I care, if it does bleed!"

Teola drew a sigh of relief when they crept under the willow tree. The hut was in its usual dirty condition, the Bible in the accustomed place on the stool. The suffering girl did not notice that the table was littered with the remains of the dinner, and Tess put her in Daddy's bed, and said, with a compelling, forceful glance:

"Ye air to stay there till I gets back. . . . And remember we air a woman, and women, when they loves men, keep their mouths shet. . . . Even if their man air dead. . . . Ye won't let anyone hear ye a-yelpin' while I air gone, will ye?"

"No, no! Go quickly, Tessibel," murmured Teola. "Go quickly!"

This time the briars and thorns pierced the squatter's bare feet without avail. Tess was rushing away upon an errand of love. Was she not perhaps saving the sister of the student from death — keeping from him a knowledge that would rend his heart? Since that night when Daddy Skinner had been taken to prison, Tess had but once visited Mother Moll. In her impatience, she did not wait to reach the hut.

"Mother Moll!" she shouted, bounding across the gully. "Come out! Tess air here!"

"Come in," commanded a cracked voice.

Tessibel entered the shanty, finding Mother Moll stretched out on the bed, with a corn-cob pipe between her shriveled lips.

"Get up from there, Ma Moll," ordered Tess, "and come to my hut. I wants ye."

"It air too hot," muttered the witch. "I ain't a-movin' from the bed to-day."

Tessibel bent over the wrinkled face, and looked determinedly into the blood-shot eyes.

"I got someone what air sick," she exclaimed, grasping the hag's arm forcibly. "Ye air to come with me. . . . See? And if ye does come, I gives ye a mess of eels every week for a year — and more'n that. I'll pick yer berries from yer own patch, if ye can't pick them yerself."

"Who air a-ailin'?" asked the old woman, crawling out of bed.

"Never mind. Come along."

It was a strange couple, forging the gorges and gullies, pushing aside the brambles to the lane almost opposite Minister Graves' home. In the summer's quietude, the squatter girl could mark the long chairs on the Dominie's front porch, and the hammock sagging from the hooks in the corner. No one saw the witch and Tessibel enter the hut; no one heard the girl slip the night lock into its fastening. Teola, frightened and miserable, raised her head, and looked once at Mother Moll, then dropped it again.

## CHAPTER XXVIII

DUSK had fallen over the lake, closing the shanty within the shadows of the weeping willows. Mother Moll had departed before sunset. Tessibel had four candles streaming their twinkling light upon the bare floor of the hut, and was busying herself at the stove. A voice from the bed faintly whispered:

"Did you tell Rebecca what I told you to? Tell me again what you said to her."

"I telled that ye was to stay to-night with a girl below the ragged rocks, and she didn't give a dum. She air only a workin' girl; she ain't yer own flesh and blood."

"And the baby, Tessibel? May I see my baby?"

"Nope, not to-night."

"Please, Tessibel! Please! Are his eyes grey, and has he dark hair on his head?"

"If ye don't shut up, I takes the brat to Ma Moll. . . . Now, then, drink this tea, and eat this bread. To-morry ye has to go home, ye know."

"But my baby, Tess! What shall I do about my baby?"

The nervous whining in Teola's voice brought Tess over to her. The squatter forced the soiled blanket over the young shoulders.

"If ye sleeps to-night, I tells ye in the mornin' about the brat. . . . Sleep, now."

For more than an hour Tessibel sat with Teola Graves'

baby clasped tightly in her arms, moving back and forth silently in the wooden rocker. A broken board squeaked now and then under the girl's weight, but she slipped the chair into other positions, and rocked on.

She marveled at the child born but that afternoon. The eyes were large and grey. Locks of damp hair fell over a wrinkled, broad brow, giving the infant the expression of an old, old man. In the light Tess could mark every feature. She had never seen a babe so small, and so sickly-looking. She ran her fingers over the right cheek, tenderly, rubbing down a livid mark that extended from the dark hair to the upper part of the breast. It was the birth-mark of fire, red and gleaming crimson as the brightest blood, and it had been because of this mark that Tess had refused the young mother's request to see her child. Perhaps in the morning it would be gone. If not, Teola would be stronger and better able to bear the shock. After wrapping the infant closely in a warm cloth, Tess took it in her arms, and laid herself down beside Teola; and the trio slept as all youth sleeps, until the morning sun had been shining long in the window.

"Be ye better now?" asked Tess, trying to stand Teola on her feet.

"I am dreadfully ill yet," was the whispered answer. "But I want to see my baby. . . . And what shall I do with him? Oh, what shall I do?"

"He air a-sleepin' now," replied the squatter. "And he stays here with me, ye hear? Ye can't take him to yer pa's house, and the hut air good enough for him to live in, if it was good enough for him to be borned in."

"You mean, Tessibel, that you will care for my baby,

until I can arrange something for him? — So that my father and mother may not know —"

"Er the student," broke in Tess.

"My brother! Tess, my brother Frederick! He must not know. It would kill him — and me. You, Tess, — you swear that you won't tell him?"

"I ain't a-tellin' him nothin'. I swears it, ye hear? I swears I won't tell the student nothin' about the little kid."

"Of course you won't," answered Teola weakly. "I trust you, Tessibel."

There was a deep questioning in the squatter girl's eyes as they rested upon the quiet bundle on the foot of the bed. How could a mother leave her child in the care of a stranger? — leave him in a squatter's hut, where the rats scurried hungrily about the floor, and the bats fluttered among the ceiling rafters!

"Don't look like that, Tessibel!" Teola burst in. "You understand, don't you, that I can't tell them? — that I can't take him home? My brother loves me better than any other person in the world, and I love him as much as he does me."

The blood suffused the drawn face to the hair line.

"And I want to see my baby before I go," she pleaded.

Tess shook her shoulders, and hesitated awkwardly.

"He air to sleep. . . . And ye ain't no business a-wakin' him up, nuther."

Suddenly a dread flashed into Teola's mind.

"Tessibel, he is. . . . There is something the matter with him!" She was fully dressed, tremblingly holding the post of the bed for support. "There is something the matter with him!" she gasped again.

"Nothin' that air a-hurtin' him," soothed Tess. "He air marked with the fire what killed his pa, that air all. . . . See, t'ain't much."

She lifted the babe from the bed and held him up. The covering dropped from the shoulder, exposing the brilliant scar.

"Not much," moaned Teola. "Not much! Poor little baby Dan!"

The mark gleamed out on the wizened old face, the deep veins in the thin skin showing darkly. To Tess it looked more horrible than in the night before. But she had to reassure the mother — the little mother who, before that year, had never known one twinge of agony.

"It sure goes away sometime," said Tess.

Teola took the infant in her arms for a moment only. Moving the child caused the large grey eyes to open, the mouth widening into a yawn.

"Take him, Tess!" mourned the mother. "Oh, I — I want to die. Dear God! Dear, good God! Dan! . . . Dan, I want to come to you!"

In the presence of such grief Tessibel was silent.

She covered the infant again, and for some minutes she sat by the bed, with her fingers tightly pressed in those of Teola. It was a tragedy with which Tess could not cope. So she remained there until Teola cried herself into a quietude that left an expression of wonder, knowledge and sorrow. As Tess led her up the hill to the minister's cottage, she saw that tears would come no more; that the mother would never know the emotions of a girl again. Teola resembled the squatter, Myra, with her pain-drawn face.

"She falled from the rocks," glibly lied Tess, as

Rebecca placed the pale girl in a chair. "Better put her in bed. . . . She has a bad ankle. . . . She couldn't walk much."

The frightened maid quickly responded to the advice of the squatter.

"She found me," pleaded Teola, "and you will let her come once in a while to see me?"

Rebecca hesitated.

"Your mother and father —"

"They are not here yet, and I am so lonely and ill. Let Tessibel come once in a while!"

"I have my doubts," said the maid, and she followed Tess down the long stairs, just to see that the fisher-girl did not steal anything. Let that dirty squatter come into a minister's home! No, not again, vowed Rebecca inwardly. It was only the girl's duty to save a human being from a fall over the rocks. Tess turned and faced the woman when they were alone.

"I air a-comin' again," she said slyly, "and I ain't one what tells that ye slides from the house every night to the lake with Deacon Hall's coachman, I ain't. I has a tongue in my head, I has, but it ain't a-waggin' 'bout no coachman and yerself."

Tess saw instantly that her point was gained. That anyone had seen her meet the man by the light of the summer's moon had never entered Rebecca's head for one moment.

"And I don't steal from the minister's house, nuther," assured Tess, with a smile. "I brings ye some berries to-morry, and gives them to ye. And ye can keep the Dominie's money for a rag of a ribbon to light the coachman's eyes with."

She smiled again, and left Rebecca, with wide-open mouth, gaping after the scurrying figure.

In the hut Tessibel lifted the blanket from the scarred face, and contemplated it earnestly. She had forgotten all save the babe and the student. She knew that the Longman brat had sugar rags — she had arranged them herself many a time. Tearing a piece from the cloth that was wrapped about the child, she went to the shore, and washed it clean in the blue lake water. Filling it with bread and a liberal amount of sugar, Tessibel soaked it in some warm milk, and put the sop-rag into the small, gaping mouth. She must make a place for him to sleep during his stay in the shanty. Daddy would not need all the old coats hanging about the wall, and the blankets were longer than was necessary. From the back of the stove the squatter dragged a small box, and turned the splinters of wood into the fire. This, too, she washed in the lake, setting it in the sun to dry. From one of the hooks among the rafters she took a large-sized grape-basket, which also received its cleansing treatment. After a bit of blanket had been cut from those on Skinner's bed, Tess slipped the infant into the basket, to see if it were long enough. The tiny feet did not reach the bottom.

"Ye air to sleep many a day in it," she said aloud, "for yer legs ain't as big as a rabbit's, and yer face ain't any beautifulier than Ma Moll's. . . . But ye air a livin' and that air somethin'."

Hardly had she got the words from her lips and fitted the cover securely before the door opened, and Ezra Longman stepped into the hut. Tessibel's clear hearing could detect an unmistakable smack from the babe.

"What did ye come for, Ezy?" she asked. "Air Myry all right, and yer ma?"

"Yep. I come to see ye to-day. Ben Letts says as how ye air a-goin' to marry him some time. Did ye tell him that?"

"Did he tell yer that?" asked Tess, instead of answering the boy's question.

"Nope. Jake Brewer says as how Ben telled him one night that when yer daddy air dead ye air goin' to his shanty. Ye ain't, air ye, Tess?" The pale eyes of the young squatter boy darkened under the emotion that rose in his breast. He looked at the girl he had loved since she had taken her first step. Every wicked act he had committed he laid fretfully at the door of her refusal to marry him.

Tessibel watched Ezra, waiting for him to speak again. She feared the child would cry out — feared that the dark secret of the improvised cradle would get into the hands of her enemies.

"Daddy ain't a-goin' to die," she said, quietly giving the grape-basket a touch with her foot, and deftly shoving it under the bed. Another smack told her that the infant was awake.

"And, what air more, Ezy, I ain't a-goin' to marry Ben Letts, or nobody else, for a lot of years. . . . I air a-goin' to wait here for Daddy."

"And if yer Daddy goes dead?" inquired Ezra longingly.

"If he goes dead," she interrupted, lifting her unfathomable eyes, "if he air hanged, then I comes to the Longman shanty and marries yer. . . . Now go, dum quick!"

She had quieted one of her enemies with a promise

which she would never be forced to keep. For was not the student's God going to save Daddy Skinner? And wasn't she going to Auburn prison to see him? That clean skirt in the corner, washed and dried in the sun, Tess was going to wear. She was going with the great man from the hill. Suddenly came the thought of the babe. With whom could she leave it? Her face whitened with grief. . . . Of course she could not go now.

She turned again to Ezra, who was loitering at the door.

"Ye go now, Ezy, and tell Myra I ain't a-comin' this evenin', and I hopes her brat won't be yelping too much."

The next day Tess appeared at the back of the minister's cottage, with a basket slung over her arm. Rebecca ushered her up the stairs to the pretty blue room. Teola moved her head languidly, but, recognizing her visitor, brightened a little.

"I am so glad you came. Tell me how he is. . . . I have nearly died to see him."

"He air well. Have ye had a doctor?"

"Yes, and I have told him all about it, for I was so sick. I told him about you, and he ordered Rebecca to let you come and see me. He is a friend of my father's, and will never tell anyone."

Tess walked to the door, and listened; then laid her finger on her lips. She raised the basket from the floor, slipped back the cover, and Teola Graves was peeping in upon a tiny sleeping face.

"He air a-goin' with me wherever I has to go. . . . I ain't a-comin' here again with him, fearin' some one will know. . . . I think ye be happier, now that ye hes seen his bed — eh? Now I air a-goin', and when ye gets well ye can come to the hut to see him. He air gettin' powerful hungry. He can smack louder than a dog can holler. . . . Poor little devil!"

That night, a small figure left the Skinner shanty, bent upon an act of theft. Up through the lane to the tracks, with a small pail in her hand, Tessibel went. The brindle bull capered about her as she slid through the wires. Without the slightest compunction, Tessibel returned to the shanty with the warm milk which she had taken from one of the fine cows at Kennedy's; then by the light of the candle she filled the tin cup, and warmed it over the fire. This, too, would have to be sweetened. Spoonful after spoonful she emptied into the smacking lips, and, when the babe slept, Tess placed it under the blankets, and took up the Bible to read of the promises of the student's God.

## CHAPTER XXIX

DURING the illness of Teola, Tessibel had forgotten that she had promised Professor Young she would come some morning to his office in Morril Hall on the hill. Two weeks after the birth of the baby, Tess filled his small stomach with warm milk, shoved the sugar rag into his mouth, hung the child's bed over her arm, and made off toward the tracks. The sun was far in the heavens before she stopped at the building in which Deforest Young had his office. He was looking from the window, and saw her glance about hastily, settling the cover to her basket a little closer.

"That child will be my ruination," he muttered, seating himself at the desk. "She affects me so strangely that I can't get her out of my mind. To bring her to a place of safety . . . But what can I do? She won't let me help her!"

The thought of Frederick Graves came over him with torture. Was it possible for her to love a lad who could not, and did not aid her? If he could but guide the girl, he would know who her companions were. Tessibel stood in the door, the red curls covering the burden upon her arm — one would have thought it was purposely done, if she had not placed it carefully in the corner. She awkwardly seated herself in the chair Young had placed for her near him.

"I thought you were never coming," said he. "I have been looking for you for many days."

"I were a comin', but I couldn't. . . . And I can't go with ye to see Daddy."

Her eyes filled with tears, but she hastily wiped them away with her sleeve.

"Of course you are going," replied the professor. "I suppose you think you can't go in with bare feet. But I will get you a pair of shoes."

"I could get a pair good 'nough for a squatter," Tess assured him, "but I can't go."

"Why?"

"'Cause I can't! I has somethin' to do."

"Can't you do it after you return? Your father will be so disappointed if you do not go to him when you have promised."

He was gazing at her keenly. Her eyes dropped upon her folded hands in her lap.

"I knows that," she breathed, "but I can't go, just the same."

Young did not persist in the argument.

"It is almost a certainty that your father will get another trial," he went on presently. "I shall act as his lawyer, and, little girl, when the snow flies again, your father will be home in the cabin with you."

She flashed him a radiant smile through the tears which still clung to her lashes. He loved to watch the color coming and going swiftly, and the glints thrown into her eyes by the sun.

"It air the student's God what will bring him." She bent eagerly toward him, with a quick motion. "Be ye one of the prayin' kind what tells God all ye needs? Daddy would have been a-hung by the neck till he was dead, only the student telled me how to pray and he air a-prayin', too."

She finished the sentence in a low tone. Young leaned back in his chair, grasping at the arms to hide his emotion. The girl was so close to him that he could feel her warm, swift-coming breath upon his face. How long would he have to suffer over this primitive child? But he loved her, and the only course left him was to snatch her from young Graves while there was opportunity to see her now and then. Her brown eyes were piercing his very soul. The childish excitement upon the upturned face almost tempted him to force her into his arms, to awaken the soul beneath the soiled jacket, to make the girl into a woman in spite of her environment.

"You are still determined to live in the hut?" he said, after clearing his throat, and overlooking her question.

"Yep, till Daddy comes home. And then I's a-goin' to make him get offen that land, 'cause it ain't his'n. It air Minister Graves'."

"But your father has his squatter's right," put in the lawyer, feeling that he was giving the student less chance if he said this. "No one can take the place from him."

"He ain't got no right there," she insisted again, "'cause I asks the student, and he says as how Daddy can have the ground by the law, but that it air a-belongin' to his pappy."

Her face was perfectly grave and serious, and she spoke slowly.

Would the name of Frederick Graves always be flaunted in his face? Deforest Young believed that he was beginning to hate the boy. Suddenly he leaned over, and touched the bell. It pealed loudly through the building. Tess sat up. The bell disturbed her, and she cast her eye upon the basket, with a shifting, darting glance. The janitor appeared at the door.

"Hyram," said Young, "could you find a vessel which would hold berries or fish? I would like to take some home with me."

"I ain't got no fish nor berries," said Tess, rising with a burning blush.

"Then what have you in your basket?" asked the lawyer, getting up also. "Child, you need not feel badly over the money I give you for the food you sell." He was standing beside her when his eyes fell upon the waiting janitor. "Never mind, Hyram," he exclaimed, "Miss Tessibel says she hasn't anything to sell."

Hyram closed the door before Young spoke again.

"Why won't you let me help you, poor little girl?"

Tess stepped between the professor and the babe, lifting the child's bed in one hand.

"I ain't got nothin' to-day," she muttered sullenly. "And when I says I ain't got nothin', I ain't."

"Then why did you bring that with you?" insisted Young, with a motion of his hand. "It is certainly heavy, or you would not have laid it down so carefully. . . . Child, if you won't let me give you anything, please allow me to buy the food which you work so hard to get."

His hand fell upon the handle of the grape-basket, but Tessibel's remained obstinately on the other side.

"I's a-wantin' ye to help Daddy Skinner," she whispered, with drooping lids. "I don't need no help."

At that moment a wail from the infant startled them both. Professor Young's hand dropped as if it had been struck. Tess only grasped the basket more firmly.

# TESS OF THE STORM COUNTRY

Her secret was out. Without a word, she slipped the cover from the child's face, and pushed the sugar rag into its mouth.

"Ye can see it ain't no fish," she said stolidly.

"A child!" murmured Young. "Where did you get that baby, Tessibel Skinner?"

"He air a little bloke without no one to take care of him, and I has him in the basket — that's all."

It seemed for a long time to the man that his brain would burn from the fire kindled in his heart. The sight of the marked baby horrified him, but he took the basket from her hands, and placed her forcibly in a chair. Tess allowed him to do so without speaking.

Young set his teeth fiercely.

"Tessibel Skinner, do you want to save your father — from hanging?"

"Yep," she answered, her eyes roving toward the babe.

"Then listen to me. Is that child yours?"

Her glance sought his for a twinkling, as if she thought he had lost his mind.

She shook her head.

"Nope."

She was not disloyal to Tess in saying this.

"I have offered you all the help a man can give to another human being." Here his voice broke a little. "All I have offered to do for you, you have refused. Now, if you want me to continue to help your father, you are to tell me whose child it is."

Before the vivid mind of the girl rose the handsome, manly face of the student. Her labor for the child and its mother had been wholly for Frederick's sake — not for anything in the world would she have consented to do what she had done, if it had not been to save him pain.

"Well, 'tain't mine," she drawled after a time, "and it ain't belonging to anyone ye know. It air only a brat what ain't nothin' but a grape-basket to sleep in. And now ye says that if I wants my Daddy saved from the rope, I must tell yer whose it air. I says it ain't mine. And I says as how ye knows a new little bloke when ye sees one. Here it air! And if ye don't know that it ain't mine, then ye air a bigger fool lawyer than I thinks ye air."

She was speaking rapidly, and had again slipped the cover from the babe, lifting it from its bed. The fire scar was uppermost, and the loud smacking of the half-naked child caused the man to sink into his seat. The blood-red cheeks of the squatter denoted perfect health. The eyes were wide, confiding and entreating. Young held out his hands and took it from her. Then, for the second time in her life, Tess noted emotion in a man. Once in Daddy Skinner, in the jail — she had given way before it. And now in the strong friend of her father, who laid his face on the body of the infant, and sobbed.

In an instant Tess was on her knees before him.

"Air ye a-blattin' 'cause ye thinks it air my brat? Aw, ye knows it ain't. Ye knows I air but a-takin' care of it till its ma can. If I swears by the student's God, will ye believe?"

Young rose, white and nervous, from his chair. With tender fingers he placed the little one in the receptacle, set the rag securely between its lips, and turned to Tess.

"I believe you, child," he said wearily. "I thought

at first — oh, it was an awful thought for me . . . because I love you, Tessibel."

Tess blinked her eyes as if she were looking into a powerful sun. The strong form of the lawyer was bending over her. She lifted her face to his, not realizing the greatness of his love. She only knew that he was her friend — Daddy's friend. She grasped his hands in hers, kissed them tearfully, and took up the basket.

"I were a-goin' with ye on Thursday, but I can't now. Thank ye for believin' me, and I'll work as hard as ye says I must, and if I air a bad brat, then I air sorry."

She had gone out, crying bitterly, before he could say another word; but a happier feeling was in his heart than had been for many weeks. She had promised to work, and in that promise had failed, for the first time, to utter the name of Frederick Graves.

"Tess air a-gettin' stylish," said Mrs. Longman, rattling the newspaper one Sunday morning. "Her name air right here, in print."

"What do it say, Mammy?" asked Ezra, lighting his pipe with a piece of burning paper.

"As how Tessie air a-goin' to see her Daddy, with the big man on the hill."

Ben Letts shoved his big boots from one side to the other, plainly disturbed by the news.

"Folks on the hill air a-doin' better if they minds their own business, I air a-sayin'," grumbled he. "There ain't no reason why Orn Skinner can't go dead, like other squatters has before him."

His red bandana handkerchief sought the blurred blue eye. A pair of pale gray ones from above the smoking pipe of Ezra Longman settled upon Ben Lett's face, with a tightening of the thick lids.

"Tessibel air so sure that her father air innocent that I hopes they prove it," Myra Longman said, trundling her babe to and fro, in the huge wooden rocker.

"There be some folks as knows more than they'll tell," put in Ezra, keeping his eyes upon the squatter Ben.

"And there air folks what thinks they knows a dum sight more than they can prove," replied Ben.

The great white eye jerked open, the crossed blue one twisting to bring Ezra Longman within its vision.

An expression of deadening hate flashed for a moment across the red face, and the white eye closed again. Myra had seen the by-play, and sat up with a gasp. What was there between Ben and her brother?

Placing the child upon her mother's lap, she stirred the stew bubbling in the pot on the stove.

"Scoot, and get an armful of wood, Ezy," ordered she; and no sooner had the tall boy disappeared than she slipped after him.

She stood beside him at the wood pile, staring down upon the crouched form.

"Hold a minute, Ezy," commanded she.

Ezra stood up.

"What air the matter with yer and Ben Letts?"

"Nothin' ain't the matter."

"There air," insisted Myra, "and it air Tess what air a-doin' it. Ben Letts air a-lovin' Tessibel. And ye hates him."

"Yep."

"Tess ain't for none of ye! She ain't like other squatters. The man from the hill says as how Tess can read better'n most gals can, and she has done it all herself."

"Don't care," grunted Ezra, stooping again. "Ben Letts can keep his hands offen her, or I tells what I knows."

This was Myra's chance. She grasped the boy's arm, and twisted him about so that he faced her.

"What can ye tell?"

"Somethin'."

"About Skinner?"

"Yep."

"Ye'd hang Ben Letts if ye could. But ye won't, ye see? Ye'd not hang a man what ought to be in yer own fambly, would ye?"

"If I tells Pa Satisfied that ye said that, Myry," muttered the boy, "he wouldn't wait for the law to handle Ben Letts — he'd shoot his dum head offen him quicker than a cat can blink."

"I knows a hull lot about you, Ezy," warned Myra, "and if ye tells on Ben, I tells on yer, too. I loves Ben Letts, I does!"

"Bid him keep from Tess, then," answered Ezra sulkily, filling his arms with wood. Myra looked after him fearfully.

The trouble between her child's father and her brother had come upon her so suddenly that she had given Ezra another hold upon the man she loved, by telling him her secret.

That afternoon she followed Letts a short distance

along the shore toward his cabin. When out of sight of her own home, she ran forward.

"Ben! Ben!" she called.

The fisherman turned impatiently.

"What air ye wantin', Myry?"

"Be you and Ezy hatin' each other?"

"He ain't nothin' but a brat," replied Ben scornfully. "Let him keep out of my way, or I fixes him."

"He air a-sayin' the same thing," cautioned Myra. "Ye air a-seekin' Tess? He says as how ye air to keep from her."

She was walking beside him, her red hands rolled in her gingham apron. The hot sun shone on her colorless hair, which was drawn back from the plain face.

"Ye air a-helpin' him with Tess," Ben grunted presently. "If ye ever wants me to come to yer hut, keep yer mouth shet, and let me and Ezy fight it out. Do ye hear?"

"Yep."

"Then scoot home now."

Myra turned, and then stopped.

"Ben," she called softly again.

"What be ye a-wantin' now?"

"If I keeps Ezy away from Tess, will ye—?"

"Ye air a-wantin' me to do somethin' for ye, Myry?" Ben answered, coming toward her eagerly.

"Yep."

"What?"

"If ye'll kiss the brat when Mammy and Satisfied ain't a-lookin'—"

"Scoot home, I says. Scoot home," shot from Ben's lips.

And home she went, this girl of but eighteen with an

old woman's face, a tired young heart beating lovingly for the brat in the box and — for its father.

Her mother was still spelling from the paper when she returned. Satisfied was stretched on the long wooden bench outside the door. Ezra, with his cap pulled over his nose, sat sulking in the corner. Ben was a powerful enemy. The boy knew that the fisherman would stop at nothing to gain an end. But Tess had told him that she wouldn't marry Ben, and Myra had as good as told him that the squatter was the cause of her trouble. He knew another secret that would bring a halt upon Ben's pursuance of Tessibel Skinner. He had told Myra to warn him. Suddenly he rose from his chair, set his cap far back on his head, and disappeared into the underbrush that lay thick back of the hut.

The cause of the hatred between Ezra Longman and Ben Letts was quietly eating her dinner. Teola's child lay smacking the sugar from the wet rag. The large, knowing gray eyes were directed toward the sunlight upon the wall, the blood-red scar shining more crimson in its rays.

Tess was picking the flesh from the spine of a fish, throwing the bones on the floor. Youthful as she was, she was already beginning to show fatigue from staying awake nights, and caring for her dark secret in the daytime.

With the alertness of an Indian she heard the crackling of twigs in the underbrush. She closed the door, slipped the lock and tucked the babe in the basket, and waited. Somebody was coming from the hill above, breaking the branches as he ran. It was Ben Letts, probably. A light tap came upon the door. To Ben she would not open, but, glancing at the window, she saw Ezra Longman's face pressed against the pane.

Slipping back the lock, she flung open the door.

"Ezy, ye air allers a-comin' when I wants to read the Bible. I tells ye to stay away from the shanty, and ye won't!"

Would the babe remain quiet until the pale squatter boy had departed?

"Ben Letts air a-comin' to see ye to-day," Ezra returned sulkily, "and I comed, too."

"Did he tell ye as how he was a-comin'?"

"Nope; but I knowed."

"He can't come in," replied Tess, crossly. "I ain't no notion for company, nohow. . . . Air the men a-nettin' to-night?"

"Yep."

"Air Ben a-goin' with ye?"

"Yep; Ben has a heavy hand, and nets air hard to haul."

Scarcely had the words fallen from his lips before Letts appeared at the door. Both boy and girl saw him, and Tessibel rose up.

"Sunday ain't a good day for ye to be comin' here, Ben," she said sullenly. "I air a-wishin' to be alone to-day."

In spite of the girl's flashing eyes, Ben stepped in, glared at Ezra, and took the stool, from which he moved the Bible with trembling hands. Tess had never been quite so frightened — never so fearful of her own squatter men-folk. Ben and Ezra had come to stay a long time, for each had dragged off his cap, leaving his dirty head exposed. Still the babe slept on, no tell-tale smack coming from it. Tess lifted the Bible, determined to let the men sit as she read, curled up in the wooden rocker, humming as she swung to and fro. A shadow dropped long upon the shanty floor. In the doorway stood Teola Graves, tall, thin, and distressingly pale. Tessibel had not seen her since the day she had carried the babe to the hill-house. That was three whole weeks ago. Tess moved awkwardly from the chair, motioned for Ezra Longman to get up, and stuttered out an invitation for the girl to be seated.

Teola shook her head, and Tess noted her quick survey of the hut.

"I can't sit down," she said weakly, although she allowed Tess to place her in the chair. "I have been ill for some time, but I could not forget how kind you were to me when you found me on the rocks, with my ankle sprained."

The white eye of Ben followed the blue one in its twisting search for the minister's daughter. Teola Graves had lost her sparkling beauty; had lost the vivid coloring and the shy expression of youth that had rested in the dark eyes until the death of Dan Jordan. From her face Ben's one eye turned to the beautiful squatter, and he settled back with a firmer resolve that she should be his. Tess stood thinking rapidly. She made no attempt to introduce the strange trio.

Then she allowed her fingers to come in contact with Teola's shoulder, pressing into the girl's mind some message.

"Ye be a-goin' to see the sick woman to-day, ain't ye?"

Tess could scarcely utter the words. Would Teola understand what she wanted to impress upon her? Her fingers sought the shoulder again.

"Yes," came the low answer.

"Might I ask ye to take her a bit of fish, what I promised her? I has company now, and can't go. And I thought as how if you was a-goin', ye might do it for me."

She stooped and raised the grape-basket in her hand, tendering it to Teola. The white lips became paler — the young mother understood.

"It air a nice day, and the sun will do ye a heap of good," explained Tess. "If I didn't have company, I wouldn't ask ye."

Ben Letts stared sharply. Ezra Longman stupidly shuffled his feet upon the floor. Teola accepted the basket, and answered Tess with meaning:

"I'll take it for you, if you will wait until I return with the money. The fish are to be paid for, aren't they?"

"Yep; come back when ye can. I allers need the money."

For some minutes Tessibel stood in the door, watching the tall figure of the Dominie's daughter as she struggled through the brambles surrounding the mudcellar creek, until she was lost to view.

Tess took a long breath. Ben and Ezra must go before the babe returned. She set herself to rid the shanty of the two men. Without speaking, she took the Bible, and repeated slowly aloud some of the passages she knew best. Both fishermen stared at her in admiration. To read and not spell out almost every word was more than Ezra's own mother could do, and she was the best-educated person in the settlement.

"'But I know ye that ye have not the love of God in ye,'" read Tess.

Ben Letts broke in upon the girl's voice:

"Tessie, will ye row on the lake after the goin' down of the sun? I'll take my fiddle. . . . Ye like my fiddlin', don't ye, Tess?"

"Nope," she replied, her eyes still upon the book. "'I am come in my Father's name, and ye —'"

Ezra interrupted the unfinished verse.

"Tessibel, will ye go to the meetin' at Haytes'? The man says as how the squatters air welcome."

"Nope. . . . 'receive me not,'" read Tess. "'If another shall come —'"

Ben burst forth with an eager invitation:

"Will ye come to Glenwood for some ice-cream, Tessie? It air gooder'n pie on hot nights; and ye like my fiddlin', don't ye, Tess?"

"Nope. . . . 'In His own name, ye will —'"

"Ye don't like no ice-cream, do ye, Tessie?" put in Ezra Longman.

"And ye don't like no meetin's on the hill, eh, Brat?" chuckled Ben.

Suddenly the Bible flew into the corner, and the girl, with an oath, jumped to her feet. Neither man had ever seen her in such a temper. She grasped the broom.

"Get out of here!" she screamed. "I don't want nothin' but to be let alone! See? Scoot! Or I'll bang hell out'n both of ye."

She virtually swept her callers into the sun, and slammed the door in their faces. With remorse in her heart, she sought the place where she had thrown the beloved Bible. One page was quite torn across — the back badly bent.

"It do beat the devil how I could be such a bad brat as to hurt ye like that," she cogitated, smoothing out the crumpled pages with loving fingers. "That damn Ezy and Ben air worser than fleas. But I air a-believin' that they won't be comin' back just yet."

## CHAPTER XXX

TESS closed the door of her shanty, looked about to see if anyone were watching her movements, then she, too, broke into the high weeds tnat surrounded the running brook under the mud cellar. Her little ruse in giving the child to its mother delighted her. She would find Teola, and bring her and the babe back to the shanty. Softly she parted the branches that hid the spot where she had first seen the Dominie's daughter. Through the maze of brambles she saw the girl, with the child clasped closely in her arms. The cloth in which Tess had wrapped it had fallen from the little shoulders, leaving them white, save for the blood-red mark of fire. Teola lifted the infant, and kissed it passionately, bending her head over it, praying. Tess could not enter upon such a holy scene. She sank down upon the turf. The basket yawned upon a bed of moss, its flannel rags hanging over the edge. Teola was making the babe ready to return to its bed, when Tess slipped under the branches of the short sumac trees, and entered the clearing.

"Come back to the shanty," she said. "Ye be here too long."

"I can't. I must go home, Tessibel. . . . I could hardly get away as it was. Oh, Tess, isn't he beautiful? . . . Don't you think the mark will soon go away? What makes him open his mouth so much? Possibly the sugar rag is too large."

"Nope, 'tain't that. He be tired, and that air what

makes him gape like that. Wait until he gets some bigness. He air little yet."

"I haven't asked you, Tess," and Teola turned troubled eyes upon the squatter, "I haven't been able to ask you how you feed him. And where do you get the milk? . . . Oh, if I only had some money! When mother is home, I do get a little. But Rebecca won't give me a cent. Tessibel, where do you get the milk?"

The babe was still clasped in her arms.

"I crib it from the cows at Kennedy's. They all has too much for their calves, anyhow."

"You mean you steal it, Tess?" asked Teola fearfully. "Oh, Tessibel! Oh! Oh, Tess, Tess, how good you are!"

"I ain't good," Tess retorted. "It ain't good to steal, air it? And squatters ain't never good, they ain't. But the brat's got to eat, ain't he? If I ain't got no milk, then I has to crib it. See?"

Bitter tears were falling upon the head of little Dan. They were the mother's first tears since that day when Tess had led her up the hill to the summer cottage.

"But Kennedy will shut his cows up soon," announced the squatter. "Then I don't know what to do. The brat air too little to eat fish, he air."

Suddenly Teola conceived an idea.

"If I should put out a little milk behind the house, in a pail, could you come after it, Tessibel?"

"Yep," replied Tess eagerly. "I could crib it from your yard, if ye'll let me."

"Yes, yes; that's the way to do," replied Teola, with a faint smile. "If I can't get the milk out, you go into the kitchen. Simply take all you can get. Take all you want. My father and mother will be home soon. They know by this time I am ill. My brother also gets back from camping at the same time. You see how careful I shall have to be, Tessibel. And in September, we go back to the city, for school always takes us home then. If I could only have my own baby! My own precious baby!"

Tessibel grunted. Teola misunderstood her.

"Oh, I am grateful to you, dear! I think that you are the best girl in all the world. So does my brother Frederick. He says —"

She stooped to cover the child, her voice ceasing.

The babe had been carefully tucked in.

"He's a been sayin' what?" The tones of the squatter were eager, her eyes so bright that Teola did not answer for a moment.

"He says that there is no girl as good as you, and that your faith in God is what he would rather have than anything else in the world. . . . Oh, Tess, if I could only believe, and be sure that soon the baby and I could go to — his father!"

"If ye asks, ye can go," replied Tess solemnly. "The student says what ye asks with faith ye'll get. Ain't that enough to prove it?"

This fell reverently from the lips of the girl. Faith in Frederick rather than faith in God had given birth to her believing soul. But neither girl realized it. Both were silent for some minutes. Teola was looking dreamily at the opposite hill, the basket with its precious burden already hanging on the squatter's arm. Tess had learned that such loud smacks as the infant was giving were indicative of hunger. So she made a move to go.

"I takes him back to feed him. He air hungry."

"Oh, Tess, if I could only feed him! If I could only always have him! I wish — I wish I were a squatter. Then I would face the world with my baby. . . . Oh, I am so unhappy and ill!"

True, she was ill, for there came to Tessibel's ears a cough that echoed against the rocks with the familiar sound of death in it. It sounded like that of a fisherwoman she had known in a shanty below the great rocks, who had died and been taken to the Potter's field.

"I air a-prayin' every day," said Tess, with a lump in her throat, "that ye be taken with the brat to the sky — to the brat's pa what ye loves. . . . Air that the prayin' ye wants?"

Teola nodded, and Tess, smiling tenderly, hesitated, and whispered:

"The student's God can do anything He wants to. Asks Him to let ye go 'cause ye be sick, and the brat air sick, too, and — the winter'll be cold for him."

She touched the handle on her arm lightly, turned, and disappeared.

Teola sat for some moments dry-eyed, looking at the high hill across the blue water, thinking of the next few weeks, and of how she and the babe would be called away. If she only had the precious uplifting faith of Tessibel! Something must come to her and the baby. Her stern father, who hated Tessibel Skinner with all his heart, must never know of the little Dan. Her mother, weary and nervous, would go to her grave from the shock; and Frederick —

Teola straightened at the thought of her brother. He would help her in all things, even in the tragedy that now covered her life. Of that Teola felt sure, but the humiliation would be too great. Better die apart from her child. With another racking cough, she turned her face toward home, two hectic spots shining clear and red upon the white cheeks. Rebecca silently helped her to bed.

That night, at ten o'clock, after Tess had silenced the child in her arms and Teola had lost her nervousness in a stupor, three boats shot from different points of the west shore, and quietly oared a path through the moonlit lake toward the netting place.

The occupants of one boat were Satisfied Longman and his son. In another Jake Brewer sat, alone. In the third Ben Letts puffed upon his pipe. His thoughts were upon the one person he desired — Tess. Like most of mankind, he wanted what he could not get; wanted the girl who turned a mocking, beautiful face toward him and used such a bitter tongue. Tess was responsible for the scars upon his face, but he would feel them well carried if he gained the girl — and tamed her. That Tess was a devoted admirer of the student Graves made her none the less desirable. Ben dipped his oars with dexterous aptitude and shot under the shadow of the trees. An instant later, his boat was beside those of the other squatters, and he was standing with his hand upon the north reel. Out into the lake the net was carried by Satisfied Longman and Jake Brewer. Ben could see the tall, thin form of Ezra through the shadows, guiding the ropes as they slipped through his fingers. Here was a boy aspiring to the love of Tessibel Skinner. Ben heard the swish of the net far out in the lake as it took to the silent waters, heard the dipping of the oars, and saw the boats strike for the shore. Then Ezra came toward him, at the command of his father, Satisfied Longman.

During that evening, Deforest Young was calling upon Deacon Hall. He refused the Deacon's invitation to row him to the city.

"Thanks," said he, "but the night is delightful. I think I shall walk. I shall go by the shore and skirt to the tracks at the Hoghole."

He failed to say, however, that his reason for walking was that he desired to catch a glimpse of the redhaired Tess. He had not seen her since the discovery of the new-born babe.

The candle was lighted in the Skinner hut, and he tapped gently. For an instant there was no response. He knew the girl was at home — there had been a sudden discontinuance of a humming when he knocked.

"Miss Skinner, it is I — Professor Young," he called. "If it is too late, I will come again."

The door was promptly thrown open.

"Come in," said Tess with a smile. "I thought as how it were someone else."

"I have been at Deacon Hall's," explained he. "They agree with me that you ought to go and see your father. I did not tell them why you could not. Where is the little child?"

Tess glanced at the babe.

"I keeps him in the basket or the box in the daytime, but nights I takes him to bed with me. The rats be so dum thick that one of them big fellers would chew the little chap's ear offen him afore I could stop it."

She said it so naturally, as if she were speaking of the most ordinary thing, that Young felt a hysterical desire to laugh. It was a dreadful thought, this of the rat in the box with the babe.

"Are the men netting to-night?" he asked, quickly changing the subject.

"Yep, they be."

"I suppose there is no stopping it," sighed Young; "and they run such dreadful risks. But, if there were no laws about it, there would be no fish left in the lake."

Tessibel's brow gathered a thick network of wrinkles. She had heard the subject discussed and argued from her babyhood days. The best fish in the waters must be kept for the gentlemen who came for sport during the season. But the fishermen, who needed bread for their families, were forced by the law to go without.

"There oughtn't to be no laws about fishin'," she frowned, in decision. "It air wicked, when brats air a-wantin' bread and beans."

Young saw danger ahead in the argument, so he switched to the home-coming of the minister's family. From that he again spoke of the infant, who was whimpering a little. Tess took him up, and warmed the milk.

"I shall go now, child," said Young, rising. "You are tired. You ought to go to bed."

"Yep, I air tired, I air," answered Tess, wearily "Good-night."

Once out upon the shore, Young looked back at the hut. It was dark. He saw three boats flit silently by him toward the city, as if phantoms guided them. They crossed the moonbeams, and Young lost them in the dark shadows near the shore.

## CHAPTER XXXI

KEEPING to the water's edge, Professor Young walked rapidly toward Ithaca. He knew that further up the shore the fishermen were drawing their nets; he did not wish to advance upon them. Since knowing Tessibel Skinner, he had become more lenient toward the law-breakers.

He turned into the forest at the side of the Hoghole, but the sound of voices brought him to a standstill.

Ezra Longman was shouting out a threat.

"Ye be a-tryin' to get Tess, and I tells ye to look out."

"Shet up!" responded Ben Letts.

"If ye air a-wishin' to live," came the boy's voice again, "I says for ye to keep away from her."

"I lives 'cause I lives, and I ain't afraid of ye, nohow."

The Professor barely caught the words, for they were gurgled in the deep throat.

"I wants Tess for a woman," Ben broke out, "and for a woman I air a-goin' to have her. She'll care for Mammy and me. I gets her. See?"

The north reel stopped turning, but the south one went on silently. Ben Letts and Ezra Longman were turning over and over on the sand, at grips with each other.

Professor Young uttered no word. Then Ezra's voice came from under Ben's big body.

"I tells what I knows about Skinner if ye don't get up and let me be," said he. "I tells—"

Red fingers closed over his throat, and Ezra Longman spoke no more. As the south reel kept turning around and around, the rope slackened from the north reel in the water; and still Ben Letts held his deadly fingers pressed about the neck of his enemy.

Professor Young saw Ben sit up and bend his head to the heart of the other fisherman. Then, with a furtive glance about, he lifted the boy in his arms, and came toward Young, grunting under his burden. Young drew back into the overhanging branches.

The squatter stumbled up the rocks, dragging the boy after him, and with a mighty effort lifted him high in the air, and tumbled the body into the Hoghole.

In another instant, Ben was back upon the shore at the reel, turning swiftly until silently it caught up with the other, just as the net dragged in the shallow waters, with bushels of flopping fish inside.

Professor Young lowered himself into the Hoghole. It was necessary for him to use the greatest caution. The lad came to the surface directly below him, and the Professor saw him catch at a jagged end of a rock.

"Can you breathe?" asked Young, in a low voice. "And can you help yourself a little?"

"Yep," came back the faint answer.

"Then, when I put out my foot, take hold of it, and make no noise, for your enemy is but a short distance away, and he meant to kill you. Now, come up. . . . There! Don't lean too heavily upon me, for the rocks are slippery."

Without any more conversation, the two men, one wet and weak, with bleeding head, with a gash over his right brow, crossed the forest toward the tracks. By dint of persuasion, Young forced the boy to give his father's name. He had caught enough of the talk between the fishermen to know that Tess was the cause of their quarrel. But what Ezra had threatened to tell about Skinner he did not know. Two miles from Ithaca the boy became light-headed and feeble. His tongue was loosened in his delirium, and Young heard a story that made his heart beat faster and revived hopes he had considered almost dead. Through the moonbeams that slanted to the tracks he imagined he saw a little figure skirting the rays, with flying red hair. Not for anything in the world would he lose sight of the boy. He had the first clue in the case that so interested him. Acquittal for the father of Tessibel Skinner was within his grasp. It was late when he dragged Ezra, laughing and gibbering, into a private hospital. He installed a nurse beside the boy, bidding her keep a record of any delirious mutterings he might make, and to observe silence about them.

Ben Letts wondered what Satisfied Longman would ask about his son. He spoke to the father first, his thick brain trying to avoid trouble.

"Ye air both got a lot of nerve to keep three men at the south reel, when I air the only one here."

"Where's Ezy?" asked Longman.

There was no anxiety in his voice. He was tumbling the fish into the cars.

"I ain't no way a-knowin' where he air. He skipped

away, and said how he wanted to speak to his pappy, and I ain't seed him since. . . . Ezy were a fool when he was born."

"Gone home, like a sneakin' kid," put in Jake Brewer. "He ain't no hankerin' for nettin'. He ain't been right since Orn Skinner shot the gamekeeper."

"He air my brat," replied Longman, "and he air good, if he does do what he oughtn't to sometimes. I air satisfied with him. . . . Let's go home."

And, silently, as a spectral fleet, the boats lapped their way back, edging the shore carefully.

Far into the night Satisfied Longman and the tired mother waited for their boy.

"He'll show up to break'us," soothed the father; but the mother trembled with terror. It was the first evening Ezra had missed the netting, and he had never been from home for a whole night.

As day after day passed, it was noised about the settlement that Ezra Longman had run away, some saying that he had been seen upon a line of canal boats going to Albany. The mother watched each hour for some word from him. Then, with a sorrowful expression in the faded eyes, she said to Myra:

"If Ezy had had any edication, he'd 'a' writ. He'll be a-comin' home some of these days."

After that, the fisherman's hut carried along its usual routine — while a boy in the city was wrestling with fever, and the head of the law school hung upon his muttered words with avidity.

"You think he is very ill, Tess?" Teola asked, early one evening in September, when she and Tessibel were alone in the Skinner hut. Tess came forward to the wooden box, holding in her hand the frying-pan filled with bacon fat, and gazed down upon the baby Dan, contemplating the wee old-man face thoughtfully.

"He air sick! He air a look on him what air on Myry's brat — kind of sickly. That air because he has so many lines in his face, and he air so little," she finished, wrinkling the sun-tanned cheeks and shrugging her shoulders almost disdainfully.

Teola knelt down, and slipped one slender arm under the dark head. These two girls had been drawn together during the past few weeks by a tie stronger than death. It had brought Frederick nearer to the squatter, and little did Teola realize that, had it not been for her handsome brother, her secret would have been discovered long before. It was of him she was thinking as she bent over the fire-scarred babe on this stormy September night in the fisherman's hut.

"I may not be able to come down to-morrow, Tessibel," she said, looking up into the serious face, "because my brother is coming home early in the morning."

The frying-pan fell to the floor; the fat spattered and ran across the broken, tilted boards until it congealed into rounded miniature mountains. Teola turned a puzzled face toward the fisher-maid, but there was nothing about the girl to tell her why the accident had happened, for Tessibel, grappling with a huge cloth, was wiping the floor furiously.

"I was saying, Tess," repeated Teola, "that I may not come down to-morrow. . . . Oh! hear how it rains, and the thunder! . . . Tess, since he died, and the baby came, thunder-storms make me shiver."

"It ain't nothin' that'll hurt ye," grunted Tess from her position on the floor.

"I know it, unless one stands directly in the lightning's path. But I am such a coward, Tessibel! You have so much faith — that's why you're not afraid."

The pathetic face turned suddenly upon Tess with a questioning look.

"My brother, you know, thinks you are such a good girl — and — and — you are a good girl, aren't you, Tess?"

"Squatters ain't never good," answered Tess in a low tone, her eyes dropping under the steady gaze of the other girl. "But I — I love the student's God, I does."

She was standing with rag hanging from her right hand, her face illumined by a deep flush that disappeared only when it met the red hair.

"I believe that you do love Him, Tess," Teola breathed. "And Frederick told me that if he had your faith, he could do anything in the world. You know, the Bible says that if we had faith as large as a mustard seed, we could move a mountain."

Her voice faltered on the last words. Tess grunted significantly.

"Aw! a mustard seed ain't no bigger than a speck of dirt."

"I know it, Tess; I know it. But one only has to have a little faith in God to enable Him to answer every prayer we utter."

She grasped the thin baby to her breast frantically, kissed the crimson mark up an down, until where the frenzied lips had traveled the flesh turned purple. Oh!

to have faith to believe that she might soon have her child with her always — always! Of late there had crept over Teola the shadow of the great beyond, into which her student lover had been so hastily summoned. The shrieking of the wind, and the mournful fluttering of the tiny hands made her shiver, and she coughed slightly.

"A mountain air bigger than that hill with the lookout on it," ruminated Tess, picking up a huge knot of wood from behind the stove.

"I know that, too," replied Teola.

For the space of many minutes only the smacking of the baby lips upon the sugar rag and the roaring of the turbulent wind were heard in the hut. Suddenly the vibrations of a great peal of thunder shook the shanty with violent effect; a streak of lightning shot zigzaggedly through the room like some livid, malicious spirit. Teola screamed in terror.

"It hit some place near here," said Tess.

"Yes, and wasn't it awful? Oh, if the storm would only cease!"

"It air comin' nearer," answered Tess, with the keen instincts of a squatter. "It air got to turn sidewise through the window afore it goes over the hill. What air ye afraid of, if ye believes that ye can move a mountain if ye has the faith? God wouldn't hit the brat with lightnin', would He?"

"Oh, I haven't the faith, Tess!" moaned Teola, rocking to and fro in her keen agony of soul. "Long ago I stopped believing the way I did when I was a child. I prayed that night when Dan was killed, until my head ached and pounded for days. I wanted to see him once more, and God wouldn't let me; and then I prayed again — " Teola buried her face in the breast of the infant, and sobbed, "I prayed that the baby might die when he was born, but God didn't see fit to take him. Somehow, it doesn't do any good to pray any more."

Tess paused in her work, standing with her hands on her hips, a solemn expression in the long eyes.

"Yer faith wasn't as big as a speck of dirt, then, were it?" she queried. "And maybe mine ain't for Daddy. But the student air a-prayin' for him! It air a damn shame ye ain't got him a-prayin' for yerself and the kid. . . . Ye'd a seen yer man before now, and the brat would 'a' died, too."

With a start caused by the squatter's words, Teola laid the child down, crouching back upon her feet. She eyed the fisher-girl critically. What a strange mixture of good and bad — of the holy and the unholy — lived in the tawny, magnificent squatter! She answered hesitatingly:

"But if my brother should know about the baby, it would break my heart, Tessibel. It would kill me — and him, too! Nothing could ever make me tell him. You understand, don't you, Tess?"

"Yep."

It was as Tess had said. The storm was coming nearer, sending vivid shafts of lightning in splendid awfulness across the sky. Torrents of rain descended, thrashing the lake into uneven, towering crests of white foam. The weeping willow tree groaned over the shanty roof, jarring and tearing at the broken bits of tarred tin.

"Tess, Tess, how can you bear that awful noise, constantly through the night? It frightens me to death. It sounds like the spirits of people who are dead."

She shivered again, the cutting rasp from the chimney-place stinging her with fright.

"It air spirits," replied Tess softly. "There air one kind of spirits for the sun when it air a-shinin', and the waves just a-ripplin' over the lake. They air good spirits. But on nights like this there air bad ones — the ghosts of Indians, squaws, and sometimes of the Letts' family — them dead 'uns."

She paused, her low voice trailing into silence on that one word "dead," the luminous eyes burning with superstitious fear. How many times had the squaw and her burnt brat, now long since called to the land of their fathers, moaned through the winter nights, making the shanty ring with their piteous plaints! How many times Tessibel had imagined that she had seen the headless man from Haytes' Corner flit from the shadows of the long lane and lose himself in the overhanging willows on the shore!

Suddenly a foreign sound pierced the storm. Tessibel drew near Teola. Both girls were standing over the wooden box. The violence of the storm impelled them to grasp each other's hands. In through the broken window the strange sound was borne again.

"A boat's a-beatin' agin the shore," said Tess quietly. "Some one air a-comin' in out of the rain."

The words were only formed on her lips when the door opened abruptly. Tessibel turned her head; Teola dropped her hand and uttered a cry. Frederick Graves, with his fingers upon the door, was closing it against the fury of the storm.

## CHAPTER XXXII

"YOU didn't mind my running in, did you, Tessibel?" asked Frederick, turning toward the squatter with a broad, comrade-like smile. Then he noticed his sister, with surprise.

"Ah, Teola! you, too, were caught in the storm? What a blessing to have a shelter like this! Miss Tessibel won't mind if we stay until it is over. I came home before I was expected. I almost wish, now, that I had waited until morning. But I am safe here, though. . . . Whew! it is a terrible night."

The distance between Teola and Tessibel widened perceptibly. Neither girl attempted to speak, and the student smiled at the embarrassment upon his sister's face. He made to go toward her.

"You needn't mind being here, dear," he said in a low tone. "I don't believe as Father and Mother do. I shouldn't ask for you to be in a better place than this hut."

He turned his face toward the roof, letting his eyes sweep the cobwebbed net, the old coats upon the wall; and lastly to the stove, out of the top of which jutted the smoking knot.

"There is here," he continued impressively, " a feeling of rest and contentment to me. . . . I believe, Tessibel Skinner, that your faith permeates every inch of it."

He lifted the lid of the stove, and shoved the smouldering wood from sight. His deep voice came again to Tessibel's ears as if from afar:

"I wish I could impress upon my father what it means to pray and be good and pure under such circumstances as surround you. I mean, you know, Tess"— here he turned squarely upon her — "I mean that, for one so young, you have purity of faith and uplifted confidence in God's goodness."

His voice was silenced by a half-smothered cry dragging itself from the squatter's throat. Then he noted that something was wrong. Teola, pale and wretched, had gradually placed a greater distance between herself and the wooden box. Tess had involuntarily drawn closer to it. She dully comprehended that Teola was ashamed of the rabbit-like body, struggling for a mere existence. Expressions of consternation, of indecision and terror swept over her face. Her eyes dropped for an instant upon the silent infant. The child gave one great yawn, and whiningly dropped the sugar rag. Just at this juncture, lightning flashed through the cracked window and played above the face of the babe until the red of the fire mark from head to shoulder glowed crimson under the blotched skin. The tiny, scrawny arms were bare, the withered mouth opened and shut, gapingly. As the eyes of the boy fell upon it, he went so deadly white that Tess thought he was going to fall. Without a word, he walked to the box, considering the wrinkled baby face like a man in a trance. His gaze took in the flaming brand, the gray eyes fastened upon the candle-light, and the tiny, searching fingers, which constantly sought something they could not find. It seemed an eternity before he gathered himself together, forcing his eyes upward to rest first on Teola, then upon Tess.

He was the first to speak.

"Where — did — that — child — come — from?"

There was imperious inquisition in the dark eyes.

His voice had changed, until the deepness of it was terrifying.

Teola came nearer to him. Tessibel dropped down beside the infant.

"I want to know where — that child — came from?" commanded the boy once more. "Whose child is it?"

Tess swung her body round upon the shanty floor, turning cloudy, rebuking eyes upon Teola. She, Tessibel Skinner, crouching squatter-like over Dan Jordan's baby, had sworn never to tell Frederick his sister's secret, and no thought of doing so entered her mind. The minister's daughter must speak the truth. The mother of the babe would answer the question put by the student.

Quickly Tess turned over her great desire for the freedom of her father, followed by the passionate wish to retain the love and prayers of Frederick Graves. If she denied the child, he would turn upon his sister, and the shivering girl would divulge her trouble. It would be the same as breaking her oath. Yet Frederick must not think the child hers. She turned toward Teola again, and seemed about to open her lips, when the expression upon the other girl's face stayed her tongue. It was a mixture of despair, illness and fright. Tessibel imagined she had discovered beneath the pain-drawn face a desire to claim her own. Ah! Teola would gather her babe, that tiny bit of shriveled flesh, into her arms before the whole world. There rose in the squatter's heart a vast respect for Myra Longman, who had taken her child from the beginning of its tiny life, and defied the babbling tongues of the settlement gossips. Teola Graves, although of a different class, was no less a mother — she would do the same. Tessibel sat up, waiting for the confession. Why was the minister's daughter so silent? — why so deathly looking?

"I will be answered," insisted the student. Then, centering his eyes full upon Tess, he added:

"Tessibel Skinner, *it* is — yours!"

Teola's lips were pressed closely together. Spasms of pain drew them down at the corners, making the girl resemble a woman twice her years. With a sudden inspiration, she turned upon her brother.

"Frederick, Frederick," she stammered. "Don't blame her too much. She is only a girl."

A cry escaped from the lips of Frederick; another followed from those of Tess. The minister's daughter was throwing the motherhood of the babe upon her. Teola had branded her squatter savior with a nameless child — a horror from which the student shrank! She saw unbelief rise quickly in his eyes, and saw him draw aside his long rain-coat as it almost touched the box upon the floor. Shrinking disgust of the wriggling, whimpering thing on the rags made Frederick involuntarily reach out his hand to his sister, but his eyes were bent upon Tess.

"And you're the girl I've trusted!" he gasped, as Teola neared him slowly. "Yours is the faith I've envied! — your life the one standard I wish to gain! . . . God!" he groaned, "you — you — you the mother of that!"

His bitter tones stung her to the quick, whipping her

into immediate action. Fire gold-brown and swift as lightning swept into the flashing eyes. Frederick's sister had thrust the child upon her. The secret was dead between them. Tess remembered her oath — remembered her love for the boy, and Teola's cowardice. Her despair gathered as her false position was forced upon her.

She stooped, and grasped the babe in her hands with a passion that tore the meager clothing from its body. She crushed the infant to her as if indeed Teola's words were true. The small dark head fell limply upon her bosom, the thin legs hung straight and bare over the soiled jacket. One little hand clutched her torn sleeve, as if there lived in the infant-brain a fear of harm. Tess, instinct with potent life and rage, wheeled like a tawny tigress furiously upon Frederick and Teola.

"Air it any of yer damn business," she demanded hotly, "if I wants to have a brat?"

She had silenced the student by the condemning words, which seared his soul like molten lead. A dazed terror gathered in his eyes. He smoothed his forehead with trembling fingers. The lightning forked about the squatter and the babe, illuminating the small head and the bony body of the child. Tess felt it shiver and mechanically she lifted her skirt, wrapping him close within it. Her gaze took in sneeringly the shrinking form of Teola, and the arm of the student encircling his sister's waist. For one instant she hated them both with all the strength of her half-savage nature. Still, no thought came of breaking her promise.

"Ye can both go to hell," she ended distinctly.

A fierce cry from Frederick closed her lips, and the anger within her changed to terror. What was she doing? Blasting his love, his faith, his confidence with words that blackened her soul with perfidy and her life with dishonor. Had she not told the student that long-ago night that she loved him? — that she was his squatter for ever and ever? And was she not now at this moment keeping a secret from him for his own sake? Something in her small, ghastly face brought the lad, in his boyish agony, impulsively forward.

"For God's love — and mine, Tess — tell me, it isn't true! Tell me you are shielding someone else —"

Teola caught her breath painfully, and Frederick ended:

"Some other squatter girl."

"I ain't got no other squatter's brat here," she cried, turning her eyes upon Teola. "It ain't no other squatter's brat, air it?"

"No, no, Frederick," replied Teola, white and wan; "she has told you the truth — it isn't another squatter's child."

Hope died in the boy and outraged feeling leaped into its place. He held Tessibel's eyes with his relentlessly.

"Did you expect to mix prayers for your father with filth like that?" he demanded, pointing to the hidden infant in the fold of her dress. "Did you expect God to hear you, when your life was full of — sin? . . . I am ashamed I ever loved you, ashamed that I took my life from your hands. . . . I wish I were — dead! I wish I were dead!"

Teola gasped in her new understanding. The squatter and her handsome brother loved each other! Never for one moment had it dawned upon her, until she saw the tall boy drop beside the stool and sob out his heart agony upon the open Bible.

If she dared speak the truth, she could assure him of the goodness of the fisher-girl. But her lips sealed themselves with her soul's consent. She raised her face, giving Tess one look of terror. Reaching out, she touched her brother's arm.

"Frederick, come home with me. This is awful — awful!"

"I don't want to go home," sobbed the boy, in pitiful abandon. "I didn't know anything could be so hard to bear. And I loved her faith and her character — and her beautiful face. . . . Oh, I love her, I love her, Teola!"

The squatter listened to every passionate word, listened until her face whitened into a despair that settled there and did not vanish. She had not moved from the wooden box, nor ceased pressing the half-clad infant to her breast. Turning, she shot a soul-cutting glance at the other girl, who owed her very life to her. The glance pleaded for the miserable boy by the stool, for the sick babe held close to her heart, and lastly, for herself, her squatter honor, and the powerful love she had for the student brother. From the depths of her eyes came a demand to Teola that she tell the truth. The answer was but a slight negative shake of the proudly-set head, followed by an embarrassment that Teola covered by leaning over her brother, and raising him from the floor. Frederick allowed his sister to lead him by the wooden box, past Tessibel to the door. His eyes traveled back to the open Bible upon the stool, where but a moment since his own dark head had rested. Then he laughed — laughed until the sharp sting of his tones made the fisher-girl grunt in her characteristic way.

Striding forward, he snatched up the book, tore off the

covers, and in another minute had thrust it through the smoke into the stove.

"There goes your faith — your canting trash about your love for the Saviour! I might have known that one of your kind could not rise above the grossness in you. I hope you will be as miserable and as unhappy as I am. . . . I hope that child will . . ."

Tess stopped him with a cry. She stooped down, and placed the little Dan in his bed without a word. Her anger was gone, and from the waters of bitterness that swept over her a better Tess lived. Her faith in the boy died instantly, and a higher, nobler and greater faith in the crucified Saviour lived instead.

She would never tell Frederick that his sister was mother to the little being he had scorned, nor would she as much as utter the name of Dan Jordan. Covering the child tenderly, she faced Frederick Graves without a touch of the awkward girlishness that had hitherto marked her movements. A glorified expression lightened the white face and shone from her eyes. He had taught her a lesson of independence she could not have learned through any other person. Without one glance at the shivering young mother, she walked to the door, and opened it, as she had done that night when he had come first to the hut.

"Ye can go," she said, "both of ye. Ye burned my Book, ye did, but ye can't take it out of my heart. The God up their ain't all yers. He air mine — and Daddy's — and — the brat's."

## CHAPTER XXXIII

THE rain rushed in through the open door. The wind shook the dust in clouds from the overhanging nets, waving the long cobwebs that hung in fine threads from the ceiling into fantastic figures.

Frederick, still supporting his sister, stepped into the glare of the lightning. Tess closed the door behind them, and stood with her back against it. The high chest lifted and lifted, the white, tightened throat choking down the sobs that tried to force themselves to her lips. "She were a damn sneak," were the first words she said, shudderingly covering her face with her hands.

"Aw, aw, I ain't a-goin' to have it here. . . . I can't have it here."

She was thinking of the child, now twisting and turning for more sugar. A whine from its lips drew Tess slowly toward it. She stood looking down upon it for many minutes. The baby had taken away her all, for Tess realized now the extent of her love for Frederick. Nothing would make the days shorter; there was no looking forward to a kindly nod or a gracious word from him.

"I hates ye," she said out loud, slowly, leaning over the infant with a frown on her face, "but I hates yer ma worse than I hates you. Yer ma air a piker, she air."

The babe whimpered and shivered. Tessibel wrapped its bare shoulders in a piece of the blanket.

"I could throw ye out in the rain, I hates ye so," she burst forth in sudden anger. "Ye ain't no right in this shanty."

Her eyes glittered with rage and humiliation; her head sank nearer and nearer the fire-marked child, her shock of red hair falling like a mantle of gold across its thin body. The twisting fingers entangled themselves in the tawny curls, drawing the squatter down until her face was almost in the box. With a grunt of abhorrence she spread out the wiry little hands, extricating lock after lock.

Once free, she squatted back upon her feet, scrutinizing the child with no sign of sympathy in her eyes. Suddenly she caught a glimpse of the forest and the lake beyond through the window. She could see the rain falling in quantities into the water, and the great pine-tree, in which sat her God of Majesty, whitened under the zig-zag glare of lightning. The superstitious, imaginative girl rose unsteadily to her feet. Pressing her face to the smeared pane, she saw the jagged lightning tearing again toward the tree; then it played about the figure that Tess had grown to love. The old man amid the branches bent toward the squatter, and held out his waving arms. A cry burst from Tessibel's lips. She opened the door, standing in bold relief against the candle-light, and shot her hands far into the dark night.

"Oh, Goddy, Goddy!" she breathed, catching her breath in stifling sobs. "The student air gone, and the Bible air burnt, and Daddy air in a prison cell. Might'n I asks ye —?"

She turned, with heaving bosom, without finishing. Bending over the child, she drew him into her arms. With the same sublime expression of suffering, she went back to the open door and knelt in the beating rain, and tendered the little child toward the God of her dreams.

"Might'n it please ye, Goddy, to bless the brat — and Tess?"

The student was no longer the motive power of her prayer. Tess, the squatter, was struggling with a new faith of her own. Flash after flash brightened the sky, and still she knelt, offering the sick child for her God to bless. One long peal of thunder shook the inky waters, and rumbled reverberatingly into the hills. Tessibel's eyes were riveted upon the pine-tree. The wind dropped the shaking branches for a minute — the arms extended straight toward her. With fast-falling tears she bowed over the wailing baby, and stood up with a long breath.

"Goddy, Goddy, it air hard work for ye to forgive Tessibel, I knows. . . . To-day I loved the student best"— a sob tightened her throat —"to-night I love you best, and . . . and the Man hanging on the Cross."

She closed the hut door, and seated herself at the oven, and warmed the infant with tender solicitude, forcing the warm, sweetened water into the meager body. Then she slipped off her clothes, gathered the little Dan to her breast, and crept into bed.

"I said as how I hated ye, brat," she whispered, "but I don't hate ye now, poor little shiverin' dum devil!"

During the rest of the storm the babe slept, but Tessibel wept out her loss of the only love she had ever known save Daddy Skinner's — wept until, from sheer exhaustion, her head dropped upon the dark one of Dan Jordan's babe, and she slept.

The next morning, Tess rose languidly. Without a smile or a prayer, she arranged the sop for the babe, then sat down beside him to think. Such a radical change in her life brought an influx of indescribable emotions. Her Bible was gone — the one book out of which she was learning the secret of happiness and patience. She remembered how, the night before, the realization of her despair had brought her closer to the Cross. Out of the brightness of the lightning she had received a promise of a blessing. Still, the tender, sensitive heart was bleeding for its own. But Tess had the hidden God to help her — and the child. She sat watching him; she could see that he was growing thinner, growing more emaciated as the days passed. He could eat only the food Tess forced into his mouth. But the sugar rags kept him from whining. At this moment he was eying the window-pane with intelligent intentness.

"Ye air the miserablest little devil I ever seed. No pappy, and a mammy what air afraid to say ye air hers. I hated ye last night, but ye air such a wrinkled little tramp that this mornin' I promises ye to keep ye till ye dies."

She was bending over the babe, watching every expression that flitted over the drawn mouth. In this position she did not hear the door open silently, as Teola stepped in.

The minister's daughter whispered to the crouching squatter:

"Tessibel, can — can you ever forgive me?"

Tess stood up and took a long breath. Teola noted how the night had changed the brilliant coloring to a whiteness that startled her. An agony of remorse broke over her, and, dropping upon her knees, she wept upon the face of little Dan.

"Tess, I've nearly died all through the night. . . . Oh, can you forgive me?"

"I ain't no business to be a-forgivin' ye. It be the brat what ye air to asks forgiveness of."

Teola sprang to her feet.

"Tess!" she cried sharply. Never had the girl appeared in this light.

"It air hard on the little kid," Tessibel said meditatively, "when its ma says what another woman air a-mothering it for good and all."

This remark came forth in even tones. Teola had not thought of the harm she had done the child of Dan Jordan, by throwing the motherhood upon the squatter. She turned her troubled eyes, first upon Tess, then upon the child.

"Tessibel, I do love him, even if I disowned him. But I haven't the courage you have. You looked so beautiful when you said he was yours. . . . And Frederick is ill to-day."

Tessibel's heart thumped loudly.

"I heard him crying all night, Tess," went on Teola, "and, oh! so many times I wanted to go and tell him that you were — a good girl; but I didn't have the courage. But I know that sometime — Tess, will you pray for me?"

"I ain't doin' no prayin' to-day," replied Tess. "To-morry, mebbe. . . . Aw! I wanted the student to pray for Daddy, and to like me — "

Teola never forgot the scene that followed.

The fisher-girl settled in a heap upon the floor, bowed the tired head, and wept.

"Tessibel! Tess," called Teola, touching the girl's shoulder, "listen. I'll tell him! — I'll tell him! He shall come back to you to-night — if it kills me."

Tessibel lifted her white face.

"Ye be goin' to tell him that the brat air yers?" queried she brokenly.

"I'll go and make it all right with him. He shall come to you to-day. . . . Oh, what a wicked girl I was! Kiss me, Tess."

Elias Graves' beautiful daughter sank on the breast of the squatter, and there was a kiss of forgiveness.

The baby whimpered. Teola drew away from Tessibel with a long sigh. She reached for the milk-can.

"There ain't none there," Tess said, with a touch of joy in her tones. "It air all gone. He et all that you brought him."

"And I can't get him any more now," moaned Teola. "Oh, Tess, I'm so ill! I wish I were dead!"

A tall boy had repeated the same words the night before. Tess drew herself up painfully. She pitied Teola from the bottom of her heart, but, in spite of her pity, she could not help the thrill of happiness when she thought of Frederick coming, and knowing all.

"It ain't no use to wish ye were dead," said she, "'cause ye can't allers die if ye wants to. When I thought Daddy was a-goin' to the rope, I say every day I were a-goin' to die. . . . Women ain't a-dyin' so easy."

She was preparing the warm sop for the child, and, taking him from his mother's arm, she sat down in the rocking chair. She did not speak again until she had drained the sweetened water from the bread-crusts, and the child had smacked it down eagerly.

Suddenly she spoke, handing the babe to Teola.

"Can't ye put out a drop more milk evenin's?"

"I took all there was last night, and the night before, too. And this morning Rebecca was furious — she had to go without milk in her coffee. I don't know that I can get any to-night."

"The weather air so cold now," explained Tess, "Kennedy won't let his cows stay in the fields nights. I might crib some more if I could. Every time I steals up to yer house, I thinks yer woman'll see me; and yer Pappy and Mammy comes home to-morry."

Teola nodded.

"If yer Pappy catched me swipin' milk, he'd knock the head offen me. I steals it just the same. . . . I air afraid of yer Pappy, though."

"No wonder," replied Teola, and she lapsed into silence.

Her father hated the squatter girl — hated the fishermen who still plied their unlawful trade under the noses of the gamekeepers.

Teola was crying softly. She felt it was only just to relieve Tess of the stigma she had placed upon her. But to go home and face the proud young brother with the story of her sin — with the lie she had told — were almost unbearable. Then another thought pierced her. Could Tess keep the baby all winter? And would she herself have the courage to live, knowing that he might sometimes be hungry and cold? Frederick would help her. She was glad she had decided to tell him.

As she walked up the long hill, she saw her brother standing on the porch, and noted the pallor of his face, the expression of misery in his eyes. At first the boy did not see her — not until she called his name softly.

Teola sank upon the upper step.

"It takes away my breath to climb that hill," she panted, when she could speak. "It grows harder and harder every day."

"I shall be glad when we leave this old cottage," was the boy's moody reply. "I never knew how much I hated the lake until to-day."

Teola did not answer to this, for she knew that she was to blame for that hatred. Frederick was looking at the hut under the willow wofully.

"If anyone had told me what I saw last night," he blurted out, a moment later, "I believe I would have killed him. . . . I loved her, Teola."

Now she would tell him — send him back to Tessibel with joy in his heart. She sprang up impetuously.

"Frederick," she began quickly, "let me tell —"

But he interrupted her.

"You need not tell me that I have to forgive her for such a thing as this because of ignorance. . . . It's too horrible! . . . I shall never get the sight of that child out of my mind. . . . That streak of awful, lurid red . . . that yapping mouth . . . those clawing hands. . . . God! the disgust I felt. . . . Teola! Teola! You are ill! Rebecca, come here! Come! Come!"

Together they lifted her from the porch where she had fallen, like a man stabbed with a knife. Gurgling from her lips poured the fresh red blood from the diseased lungs. Teola tried to speak, tried to tell Frederick the truth, but the awful tugging in her chest, and her brother's order that she must not speak, closed her lips upon the good resolution. Added to his command came one from the doctor, who arrived later, that she must not speak one word until he came the next day. The hemorrhage had been brought on by Frederick's description of her child. After her brother had gone, she thought of the hour when she could tell him, but with a thankful feeling in her heart that it had been delayed a little time.

Until the great University bells chimed the hour of midnight, Tessibel waited in the hut for Frederick.

"She hes forgot to tell him," she muttered wearily, pulling the sleepy babe into her arms, " and — and he ain't a-comin'."

## CHAPTER XXXIV

TESS saw the minister's family arrive in the small lake steamer, and saw Frederick meet them at the dock. She was watching from between the tatters of the ragged curtain, and noted that Teola had not come down the hill with her brother. This disturbed the squatter, for the baby's mother had looked ill when she left the day before, with the resolution to tell the student her secret. As Minister Graves passed, she saw Frederick looking fondly into his father's face, but he sent no friendly glance toward the hut snuggled under the willow. The watching girl saw that the student's face was haggard, and a thrill swept over her. It was because of his love; he wanted to be with her! But he thought she had been — Tess turned her head from the window, blinded by tears. But for the child in the box! There swept into her mind a text she had learned. "If ye have faith as a grain of mustard-seed, ye shall say unto this mountain, remove hence to yonder place, and it shall remove." Ah! if she could have such faith, only such a little faith, she could bring the boy back — bring back, through God's goodness, the student she loved.

"I air a-lovin' ye, Jesus," she trembled. "I takes care of the brat till he croaks. Give me back — "

Emotion left the prayer unuttered in her breast.

At eight o'clock that evening, Tess, hugging the fence, sneaked up through the rain. She turned into

Graves' orchard, scurrying barefooted toward the house, casting glances at intervals behind her. Through the small garret window she could see Rebecca moving in her room, preparing to go out. The library, facing the lane, was dark. But the streak of light flung long upon the porch told the squatter that the Dominie's family was in the drawing-room. Tess ventured to the back of the house, drawing near the dark kitchen. Here was where Teola had placed the milk for several days. She scraped about in the inky darkness, but her fingers touched nothing. The babe's mother had forgotten to put out the pail! Until the coming of the Dominie and his wife, Tess had had but little fear, but now her breath came spasmodically. There was danger of detection if she crept into the kitchen to obtain the milk. If she could only get into Kennedy's barn! If the cows were only out to pasture! Tess turned the handle of the kitchen door softly, and stepped in. A light streak came from the drawing-room, and she located the ice-safe through the dim shadows. Teola had told her to take the milk from there if she failed to find it outside. She advanced slowly into the kitchen, holding her breath, but her heart thumped so loudly that she feared the family would hear it.

Kneeling down at the refrigerator, she fumbled for the lock. The door slid open silently. A small pail of milk stood behind the butter-plate, and Tessibel, clutching it in her fingers, rose up. As she did so, a light flashed into her face, and she looked up to find Dominie Graves towering over her, his brows caught together with anger.

"So Miss Skinner is the thief who takes our milk! The hymn-singing girl! . . . Ah, it is you!"

Tessibel dropped her eyes, still holding the can of milk.

"I air a-stealin' yer milk," she said presently, lifting her gaze. "Air ye goin' to — let me have it?"

"No, my lady, I am not going to let you have it," he mimicked. "But something else you are going to get."

The Dominie stepped to the kitchen door leading into the yard, and turned the key in the lock. He placed the lamp on the table, the squatter waiting with fear-laden eyes.

"For a long time," went on the Dominie, in slow, measured tones, "I have thought it would be a good thing to give you a sound whipping. The Bible says, 'Spare the rod, and spoil the child.' . . . I am going to do something your father forgot to do, Miss Skinner."

The sneer in his voice and his slur on her father brought a bright flush of anger to Tessibel's face.

"Ye can cowhide me if ye wants to, but don't say nothin' against my Daddy!"

"I'll say what I wish to! Now, then, how many times have you stolen from this house?"

Tess looked about for some way of escape; then pondered.

"I dunno," she replied sullenly.

"I can just about tell," answered Graves. "Rebecca says that for many mornings she has had no milk for her coffee. And I left the kitchen door unlocked to-night purposely to catch the thief. Let me see. . . . I think we've been robbed for ten days? That means ten good stripes for you, Tessibel Skinner. . . . Put down that milk!"

"I won't do it," Tessibel whitened. She had not believed the minister when he had threatened to whip her. He was trying to scare her. He would probably take away the milk, and send her home again. But he had stepped to the wall, and taken a riding-whip from a nail. Tess had seen that whip before, once — the time she had twiggled her fingers. Graves had shaken it at her from his saddle-horse. Then she had not been afraid. . . . The clergyman came toward her.

"Ye hit me with that whip," growled Tess, " and — and — I'll kill ye! "

"Oh! you will, eh? . . . Well, then, there it is!"

A stinging blow fell across her shoulders, and another and another. The slender body writhed silently, turned and twisted to escape the descending whip. Drops of milk spattered upon the floor. Never before had Tess known such physical pain. The minister was counting the blows deliberately as they fell. At the eighth stroke, the girl opened her lips and uttered a long, piercing cry — an intense, vibrating cry. The last blow fell upon Tessibel's shivering back,— and Frederick appeared in the doorway. His father leaning against the wall breathlessly, the whip hanging limply from his hand; Tessibel Skinner, barefooted and weeping, with a pail of milk clasped in her fingers — was what the boy saw. He had no chance to speak before Teola, too, with streaming hair, her nightrobe clutched convulsively in one hand, opened the hall door.

The scene whirled before her like a frightful nightmare.

The fisher-girl turned and faced her.

"Yer Pappy air a-beatin' me . . . I hev a-been stealin' milk."

Her words fell between little, broken gasps. They touched Frederick as he never had been touched before. He stepped forward hastily to speak.

"I air a-needin' the milk," she explained, bowing her head before him. "I has to have it!"

The infant rushed into Frederick's mind . . . the squalid cabin, that twisting thing, with thin, discolored veins. It had been for him that Tess had stolen. Teola staggered toward her father, a cough racking the emaciated frame. Minister Graves threw his arms about her.

"Go back! Go back quickly, child! You should not have ventured out of bed. I will settle with the squatter."

"You whipped her!" breathed Teola.

"Yes, and will again, if I catch her stealing from my kitchen. Now, miss, you can go home. Put down that milk; and, if I find you here in the future, I shall put you behind the bars, with your father."

Frederick counted the beats of his heart through the blank silence. He felt impelled to reach forward to Tessibel,— to say something to relieve the white, tense face. His father was waiting for the squatter to take her departure. But Tess remained with the pail in her hand.

Suddenly she lifted her streaming eyes to the minister's face.

"I has been beaten . . . And I air a-feelin' so — bad! Air I to have the milk? I needs it." Tess sobbed again, and continued, "I ain't a-carin' so awful about the lickin' as I does about havin' the milk."

She came forward close to him, with searching sweetness in her gaze. The Dominie drew back, fearing the soiled dress would touch him. The girl was making the appeal to him alone, and a cloud of color gathered slowly over his face under her steady eyes. He regained himself, and replied,

"No, you can't have the milk, no matter how much you may need it."

"Some one'll die without it," she entreated again, lowering her voice, throwing no glance at the silent boy or shivering girl.

"Then let them die," retorted the clergyman. "I do not believe you — anyway!"

He was weakening a little, the attitude of his son and daughter striking him almost to consent. Frederick's eyes were filled with hauteur unusual to the boy, and Teola was clinging to his neck, weeping wildly. The children had never approved of his persecution of the squatters, but both of them could see that the girl had been caught in open-handed theft.

"Father," Teola implored, "give the girl the milk. She says she needs it —"

"Yes, Father," interrupted Frederick, "give it to her. . . . She won't steal again. . . . You won't, will you — girl?"

This was the first word to her since that night he had lost faith in her. His voice seemed harsh; it fell upon her, numbing her senses. Her body went cold as if a frosty gust had struck it.

"You won't steal again — ever? Will you?" demanded he.

Tessibel struggled to speak. At last there came a fluttered confession, which made Teola Graves shiver like an aspen leaf. If she could only summon courage to tell her arrogant father the truth! She could not bear to look upon her squatter friend, nor upon Frederick's white face.

"I has to steal," said Tess. "I has to have the milk. . . . I can't get it no way else."

"There! There!" exclaimed the Dominie, with a derisive laugh. "If that isn't depravity, I don't know what is. . . . Now, then, miss, put down that pail, and go!"

He strode forward and grasped the handle in his fingers. But Tess held it firmly. Her mind flashed to the child in the hut, smacking fiercely through the long night . . . she thought of the morning, of the hungry gray eyes and the ceaseless baby whimper — and defied the minister.

"I air a-goin' to have it," she insisted. "Take yer hand offen that handle."

Graves gasped for breath, but did not relax his hold upon the pail. With a motion as quick as lightning flashes, Tess lowered her head, and set her teeth into the Dominie's fat white hand. A cry of pain escaped him, and he opened his fingers.

"I said as how I got to have the milk — and — and I air got it! Open that door!"

Tess shrieked out the last words, her eyes, full of hatred, bent upon Graves. Frederick strode forward, turned the key in the lock, and Tess sprang out.

Tessibel ran swiftly through the orchard, out into the lane, her rage dying out in her fear for the babe. She had never left him so long before. Her flesh still tingled from the Dominie's blows, but her admission before Frederick that she was compelled to steal hurt her worse than the blue welts rising upon her shoulders. She regretted, too, that she had bitten the clergyman's hand, but that had been done for the baby — little Dan had to live.

She came to an alert standstill in front of the cabin. She saw the light from a candle flickering out through the window. Tess was sure she had left the hut dark — she had extinguished the light just before going out for the milk. Who was in the hut? Or had she made a mistake, and left the candle there? For the sake of the child she had to enter. She set down the pail, lifted her skirt, wiped away the traces of tears. Then, flinging wide the door, she came upon Ben Letts.

## CHAPTER XXXV

BEN was standing beside the bed, with the open grape-basket in his hand, looking down intently upon the child. His one eye flashed past Tess in its blindness, while the watery one with the red veins running through it distorted itself into a squint, and brought its evil gaze upon her. The fat chin, covered with a stubby growth of hair, shook with malicious pleasure, the dark teeth set grimly through the brown, tobacco-stained lips.

"It air a brat!" he said at last, Tess standing paralyzed. "Air its Pappy the —"

He did not finish. Tess snatched the basket from his hand, and covered the whining babe.

"Ye be allers snoopin' yer nose in some one's else's business," she said darkly, her fear of him growing with each minute. "Ye can't keep from my hut any day, and ye ain't no right here nuther."

"I telled ye and the student that the time'd come when I'd get even with ye both — and it air here! . . . It air here, I say!"

"The student ain't nothin' to do with this here brat," retorted Tess. "Ye thinks as how ye knows a heap. . . . Well, ye don't. . . . And it air time for ye to be a-goin' now, Ben Letts!"

"I air a-goin' to stay," said he, "Daddy's" stool creaking under his weight.

From a tree near the forest Tess could hear the screech of a night-owl die away in smothered laughter. The scraping of the willow on the tin roof came dimly to her in the silence. If some other squatter would only come along! God had always saved her from Ben Letts. — Dared she pray? Her eyes sought the window. If she could only see the pine-tree God! — send Him a little petition — He would forgive and save her. Dominie Graves had gone completely from her mind; only a wish, a desperate wish, came to escape the man who had constantly thrown his menacing shadow across the path of her life. Suddenly her bosom heaved. A verse was thrown bomb-like into her mind. Tess opened her lips and muttered, keeping her eyes upon the fisherman,

"If ye have faith as the grain of mustard-seed, ye shall say unto this mountain — "

The time between the present and that night the student had left her in bitter sorrow faded. In her imagination she was alone in the rain, with the child upon her hands, offering it up to the dark God for a blessing. The same uplifting faith was upon her. The Crucified Savior would protect her.

"I believe! I believe!" she ejaculated. No soul-desiring thought of Frederick interrupted her uprising faith. She needed him no more to pray for her.

"A mustard-seed air — a — a mighty little thing, ain't it, Ben Letts?"

Tess stood up, looking beyond him like one in a dream.

"Yep," grunted the fisherman, staring.

He had never understood the moods of Tess. She was as incomprehensible to him as the myriads of stars that strung themselves through the sky.

But his inability to understand her made him desire the girl the more. He had come at an hour when he was sure Tess would be alone. He would force her to come to his cabin, to marry him even before her father was hanged. Ben's eyes settled again upon the basket. Through his heavy senses sifted a wave of hatred for the miserable child, whining for the milk Tess had stolen. Ben moved his great feet, tearing up a long splinter from a broken board with his worn-down heel. It startled Tess from her reverie. In upon her faith came the sickening thought of Frederick, his confidence in her blasted and gone; it choked a prayer that lingered upon her lips. Ben rose to his feet, an oath belching from his ugly mouth.

"Put down that basket. Put it down, I says!"

Never had it entered her mind before to conciliate the dark-browed fisherman who had pestered her with his attentions, but her frightened womanhood caught at the idea.

"Wait till I gives him somethin' to eat," she said stolidly. "If he yaps, someone'll hear him."

Ben sat down and watched her narrowly. Tessibel had grown so beautiful in the last few months that the brute force in the man rose in his desire to possess her. There was one way to bring the girl on her knees to him, one way to bow the proud red head — the little child made no difference to him. And some day he would get even with the student, too. The small bare feet of the squatter girl noiselessly plied their way from the smoking stove to the sugar-bowl, thence to the basket. Tess held the warm, sweet milk to the infant's lips, lifting the withered chin that the child might drink the better. Her mind was working rapidly. How should she escape and rescue the babe? She went back for more milk, wetting the corner of the cloth and wiping little Dan's face. Then she gazed straight at Ben Letts, and said,

"How air yer mammy?"

It seemed the most natural thing that she should ask this of him.

"She air well," answered Ben, thrown off his guard. He took out his pipe, and continued:

"When ye comes to the shanty, ye can't bring that brat."

"Nope; I ain't a-goin' to bring him," Tess replied, whispering a prayer for aid.

"What be ye goin' to do with it?"

"I don't know yet." A muttered petition fell over the baby's face, but she said aloud: "I think it air a-goin' to croak."

"I's a-thinkin' so, too," Ben said thoughtfully. "He hes the look of death on his mug, Tessibel. . . . Air it yer brat?"

"He air mine now," she answered slowly, raising her head, "and I stays here with him till he dies."

"Nope; ye be a-comin' to my shanty to-morry. Mammy air expectin' ye. . . . And ye'll be glad to come — afore I gets done with ye!"

Tess shivered. She remembered Myra's broken wrist, and heard again the woful cry from the other squatter girl as she told of the harm done her. If she could get out of the shanty, she could run from him, but that would leave the child to his mercy. She glanced toward the door. Whatever came to her, she must protect the babe. Lifting him from his bed, she sat down at the oven, and extended the blue legs toward the heat.

"He air so damn thin," she said in excuse, "that he

allers yaps if he air cold. . . . Have ye seen **Myry's** kid lately?"

"Yep; to-day. He air a-growin' a little more pert."

"Glad for Myry," was Tessibel's comment.

"Ye ain't heard nothin' from yer Daddy, have ye?" asked Ben, presently.

"Yep. I had a letter from him. He air a-comin' to the shanty as soon as he air out."

"He ain't a-goin' to get out!"

"Yep, he air; sure he air."

"Air he a-knowin' of yer brat?" Ben was staring at the child.

Tess stared back at him. She had forgotten that she had intimated that the baby was hers.

"I ain't tellin' Daddy nothin'. . . . His troubles be enough for *him*."

Her tone was low and bitter. She turned the babe with its back to the heat to gain time. She had almost decided to run away — she could not face Myra's fate.

"This dum stove ain't got no fire in it," she said, laying Baby Dan in the box. "I's a-goin' for a stick of wood!"

As Tessibel walked past him, Ben did not stop her — squatters never saved steps for their women. The girl flung open the door, but hesitated on the threshold. During the instant of her indecision, a silent panorama of night passed before her. Heavy rain clouds dipped almost to the dark water, obscuring the city and the University hill beyond. A great steamer attached to a number of canal boats lay as a thin black line in the center of the lake. An owl left the branches of the hut tree and circled into the safety of the shore willows, and a stealthy barn cat, with thread-like legs, crept from the water's edge toward the lane with a trailing dead fish in his jaws. He turned glistening green eyes upon Tess, and leapt away with his treasure.

Oh! to be out once more in the darkness with the child — out among God's creatures, her creatures, there she would be safe — safe from Myra's terror.

Glancing back at little Dan, she saw his large gray eyes fixed gravely upon the candlelight. To leave him there was like sending him into the jaws of death. To take him was impossible. She turned back, closed the door with a gasp, and faced Ben Letts.

He was at her side in a moment.

"I air got ye now," sounded in her ear like the roar of the sea. She felt the man crush her in his arms, felt the thick lips upon her face.

"Ye think ye be such a smart kid that ye needn't never mind what a man says to ye. I knows that brat don't belong to yerself. I ain't seed ye all summer for nothin'. Tell me, whose air he?"

Tess wrenched herself free, and sent forth scream after scream. A horny hand left a red mark across the fair face. It was the right of the fisherman to beat the woman he loved. . . . Tessibel Skinner was feeling for the first time the aggressiveness of the male.

"Ben, Ben, I tells ye the truth if ye wait a minute."

Ben relaxed his hold a little, and the girl continued:

"The brat ain't mine — it air a woman's on the hill. She didn't like it, and gave it to me, with a little money, till Daddy comes back."

"Whose brat air it?"

"A woman's I says, a-livin' on the hill."

The words struggled through the fishy hand.

"Ye'll take it back to her to-night, ye does; then ye

comes with me to the shanty. Yer Daddy ain't a-comin' here no more."

Suddenly Tess heard footsteps crushing the pebbles near the hut. She could be saved, if she — She wrenched her face upward, and screamed,

"Rescue ther perishin'!"

The words were sent out in such a strain of agony that Ben Letts thrust his fingers to her throat. With an oath he closed them together.

"I loves ye, ye hussy; that air why I chokes ye!"

The room whirled around before Tessibel's gaze. She tried to draw her breath beneath the tightening grasp. The door burst open, and Frederick Graves received a desperate look of entreaty from the squatter-girl.

## CHAPTER XXXVI

THE babe smacked loudly. The September wind whirled its rain and dead willow leaves over the hut floor. A rasping sound, like the filing of a saw, came from the tin roof.

Frederick Graves took in the scene with one sharp glance. He saw the fisherman, in ugly doggedness, towering over the small figure of the squatter-girl. Then he flung himself upon Ben Letts. He tore Ben's fingers from Tessibel's neck, leaving the skin reddened and scratched by the nails. Tess sank to the floor. The student's fist came down with a stunning blow upon the partly upturned face of the squatter Ben, and the fellow tumbled over.

"Stand up," said Frederick to Tessibel, lifting her gently to her feet. Her hand fluttered to her eyes, then to her throat. Still dizzy from the choking, she sank into the rocking-chair.

"What were you two fighting over?" demanded Frederick impetuously.

Tess gathered her senses at the sound of his voice.

"He were a-tryin' to make me come to his shanty with him — to be his'n — and I ain't a-goin'!"

She whimpered a little, but choked back the tears, and raged:

"A squatter-girl can't live a minute without some damn bloke wants to take her from her Daddy's shanty. . . . I ain't a-goin', I says!"

How brave she felt, with the student near! for there

was an expression upon his face that gave her courage. He looked so strong, so brave — and he had come when she had prayed. Something took from her the terror of the night when she had proclaimed her motherhood to him. Perhaps Teola had told him the truth. When he had turned from her in the agony of the confession, he had scorned her with his proud, dark eyes. Now he threw her the same protective glance that she had received before the tragedy.

The silence in the room became oppressive.

"I ain't a-goin'," she said again, to break it.

Ben was upon the floor. He feared to rise, for Frederick stood threateningly over him.

"She goes to my shanty," insisted Ben, screwing his face to peep through the swollen lids. "She and the brat goes to my hut. . . . I air its pappy!"

Frederick staggered back against the door with a groan, Tess catching her breath in a sob. She could not exonerate herself because of Teola; she knew from Frederick's emotion at Ben's assertion that his sister had not told him. But he should not believe the lie that Letts had uttered.

She saw the fine face of the student fall into his hands, and shudder after shudder run over the giant frame. Ben Letts leered at him with his twisted face, as a demon might at a soul in torment. The boy suffered for her — that was enough. The front portion of her skirt had been almost torn away in her struggle, and unconsciously she lifted it, and pinned a thorn more closely in its place. But for an instant she held back the words ready upon her tongue, and with one long step she reached Frederick, placing her hand upon his arm.

"Don't touch me, please," he shuddered. "It's awful — awful! And I — I loved you so!"

"Haw!" chuckled Ben, settling back against the child's box. "I says as how the gal comes to my shanty. She brings the brat to its pa."

Frederick moodily considered the ugly face. The sneer that accompanied the declaration roused his rage; the brute had sealed the doom of Tessibel Skinner. Again the student was oblivious of his love for the profession he had chosen; forgot that the one book he had studied more than any other taught him that the God he worshiped would avenge all wrong. In one step he was upon the fisherman. He lifted Orn Skinner's stool, and brought it down with a crash upon Ben's head.

Tess uttered a sharp, frightened cry, speeding to interrupt another blow.

"Get out of the way," cried the student, pushing her from him. "I am going to kill him!"

With no ungentle touch she grasped Frederick's arm, holding the stool in the air.

"Ye air to wait," she said, in low, swift tones, her gaze dominating his flashing eyes. "Ye'll kill him if ye hit him again. . . . Wait till I says what I's a-goin' to . . . I loves my Daddy, that ye knows — better'n anything in the hull world — better'n God — better'n — better'n — "

"Better than the child?" demanded Frederick, placing his foot upon Ben.

A grunt issued from the girl's lips.

"Yep, a hundred times better than the brat! And I says this: that I hopes my daddy's neck'll be twisted by the rope, I hopes that I never sees him again"— her voice was raised high above the whistling wind and dashing rain —"I hopes," she finished, "that his soul'll shrivel in hell —"

"Stop! stop!" muttered Frederick. "Why are you saying such things?"

"I hopes it all," insisted Tess, bending her head nearer, "and I swears that I hopes it if Ben Letts ain't a liar!"

Frederick's foot slipped from the round, fat body. He took a long breath, brushing a damp lock from his brow.

"I believe you," he surrendered slowly. "Oh, God! Tessibel, I believe you — and I love you, in spite of that!"

His glance swept over Ben's prostrate body to the deathlike child. Letts sat up with an oath, rubbing the inflicted bruises. Frederick helped him to his feet.

"You go home," he said, piercing the fisherman with his burning eyes. "And let me warn you against fastening any of your lies upon this girl, for whatever she is, or whatever she has done, I know that you lied to-night. . . . Now go!" Frederick pointed toward the door.

Letts, muttering threats and curses against the student and the squatter-girl, stumbled out into the storm. Ben's head was splitting with pain. A gash on his nose bled until his torn sleeve was thickened with blood. He staggered out of the rays of the candle, and took the path to the hill. The sound of footsteps caused him to sink down beside the way and wait. Was the student —? No, the person was coming from the other direction.

In the dim light he saw a man dripping with water totter toward him. Ben peered out upon the wobbling legs, and in another instant had fallen back, shivering with fright and superstitious fear. Ezra Longman, his face haggard and ghastly white, stood directly in front of him.

Frederick closed the door upon Ben, and Tess turned upon him sharply.

"It were a lie he told ye," said she, "and he weren't worth killin'."

"I don't want to speak of him," stammered Frederick. "I came to talk to you. It nearly killed me to-night, when my father whipped you, and I want to save you from such things in the future. . . . My father gives me an allowance — I want to buy the milk for the little child. Will you let me, Tess?" His face had grown scarlet, his eyes fell before hers. The girl seemed glued to the spot. "It will save you from stealing," resumed the boy. "I can't bear to have you steal."

The tragic tone stung Tessibel. Teola had promised to tell him. She herself would; it was only right that he should know. She took two impetuous steps forward, opened her lips — but again remembered her oath.

"I air a-thankin' ye for the milk," was all she said.

With an embarrassed air, Frederick tendered her a silver dollar. Tessibel stepped back, hesitant.

"It will make me happier, if you will take it," he urged.

Tess extended her fingers, blushing crimson, but took the coin from his hand. A sob choked the utterance of further gratitude.

"Professor Young says," broke in Frederick, after

a painful silence, " that he is going to bring your father back here before the winter. . . . But, Tess, I don't want you to live in this shanty. I want you to be a better girl, Tess. Will you? Will you?"

His eyes rested upon the child. The darkness of the night, the ghostly sound of the wind, the swish of the thousands of wet leaves over the roof, roused the romance in the girl until she felt an impulse to tell him the whole painful story; to feel his kisses warm upon her face, to have his arms about her, to kneel with him again, and hear his earnest voice interceding for Daddy Skinner. . . . But her oath! It was Teola's secret, not hers.

"Ye couldn't go on a-trustin' me the same as before ye knowed of him?" Her head inclined toward the infant in a large-eyed question.

Frederick shook his head.

"No," he ejaculated; "no! Nevertheless, I would save you from — worse. The more I think of it, the more I believe that you were honest in your desire to know God and the truth. He will forgive you your sin, Tessibel, if you ask Him."

"If God air forgivin'— then couldn't ye forgive, too?"

It took a desperate effort to utter the words. Nothing but her love for him could have forced them from her.

"That's different," reddened the boy. "I wanted — I wanted to marry you some day."

To marry her! She drew a great, heaving breath, more strongly tempted to tell him than before. But, as she struggled with her desire, her face grew paler, and the drooping mouth gathered sad lines.

She did not reply, and the student continued,

"You have one of the most beautiful voices I have ever heard, Tess. It is a God-given gift, and He will hold you responsible for it if you neglect it."

"I air only a squatter," she moaned forlornly, shaking the red curls. "Daddy air a squatter, too, and if he air a-comin' home, then I stays with him. If he says as how we stay in the shanty, then we stays, even if it air yer Daddy's. I asks Daddy Skinner to give it back, but a brat can't boss her Pappy, can she? . . . Ye sees, don't ye?"

"Yes, Tess, I see," slowly replied Frederick. "But it's not because of my father I want you to go. You have the squatter's rights, and may remain if you wish. . . . It is for your own sake. You are sixteen . . . But, of course, the — child — has changed your life."

"It ain't changed my lovin' you!"

This was the first open confession of her love. She made it emphatically, almost sullenly. Frederick whitened, and turned his face away. In the terror of the thought that she would lose him again, Tess sank upon her knees beside him. This time he did not thrust her aside. The strong young hands pressed upon his shoulders, and the sensitive chin trembled. Tess turned her face up to his.

"Don't!" he breathed hard. "Don't, Tess!"

But the girl heeded him not. Of a sudden, Frederick raised his eyes and looked directly into hers. The jealousy that had risen tiger-like in his breast, forcing him from her, and demanding that he should never look upon her face again, yielded precedence to a nobler and stronger thought. He would help the girl with her living secret — help her, and make her better. Long and fixedly he studied the beautiful face, until he had read to the finish the tale of passion and longing. The auburn head bent nearer and nearer, the panting lips imparting the sweet breath of youth. Then they both forgot the whistling wind and the falling rain . . . forgot even the wriggling, fire-branded babe in its bed.

Frederick's lips closed down upon the girl's, and the dark hair of the student mingled with the red curls of the squatter.

"I shall never let you go again," murmured Frederick, his lips roving in sweet freedom over the flushed cheeks.

"And I ain't a-goin' ter let yer go, nuther," whispered Tess. "I works, fishes and berries the years through — but I air yer squatter."

The child, as if in pain, cried sharply. The student's arms slipped limply from Tessibel, and he stood up.

"I had forgotten it for a moment, Tess. The infant has changed your life and mine. . . . I have loved you dearly — I love you still. But the child is between us, and always will be . . . I must remember it. . . . Ah! I have forgotten one thing I came for. Here!"

He was holding a small Bible out to her.

"In my temper I burned yours. I'm sorry. I was bringing you this when I heard you cry."

Tess took the book in her hand mechanically, and the hope rekindled in her heart died. Frederick bent over her for one short moment, looking into her eyes.

"Forgive me if you can, Tess — and — and be a good girl!"

He opened the door, and was gone before she could

stop him. With chattering teeth, she flung herself upon the stool, resting her head in her arms on the table, heeding not the second whining command from the infant.

Suddenly, with flashing eyes, she bounded up. She would tell him. Teola had promised that he should know. Why not be happy, and make him happy? She would call him back, and —

The door opened under her impulsive hand. She faced the storm — and the tall, gaunt, emaciated form of Ezra Longman.

## CHAPTER XXXVII

EZRA looked so like a wandering night-shade, so tall, wet and thin, that Tess uttered a shriek.

The lad pushed his way into the cabin, and dropped on the floor. All thought of the student was driven from Tessibel's mind by her superstition at the sight of the boy.

"Ezy, Ezy, air it yerself, or air it yer shade what air here? It air yer own self, ain't it, Ezy?"

"Yep."

"Where air yer been?"

"I dunno. I air sick unto death, I air."

"Have ye seen yer mammy?"

"Nope."

"Nor Satisfied?"

"Nope."

"Then ye be a-goin' there now, ain't ye?"

"Yep."

"Was ye to Albany?"

"Nope. I were sick in a house, and the big man from the hill were a-takin' care of me. I weren't a-goin' to stay no longer, so I runned away. I air a-goin' home to Mammy."

"Yep, that air right," rejoined Tess with conviction, "for yer mammy air a-grievin' every day for ye, and Satisfied air a-gettin' older and older-lookin'. They thought as how ye might be in Albany."

Another loud cry caused Ezy to turn his head toward the infant.

"Ye air the same as Myry," he said slowly; but before he could say another word, the girl interposed hastily:

"It ain't my brat. . . . It belongs to a woman on the hill. I gets paid for it."

To every other man save to the one she loved was Tess able to deny the motherhood that had been thrust upon her. To the student she stood condemned of a sin he could not forgive. But to Ezra, Ben, and Professor Young she had told the truth.

The weakness of the squatter as he sat on the floor, panting for breath, aroused Tessibel's sympathy, and she proffered him a cup of little Dan's milk.

"Drink it," she commanded, "and then scoot to yer mammy. And — and ye needn't say as how I air a-carin' for another woman's brat, will ye, Ezy?"

"Nope; I ain't a-sayin' nothin' . . . I goes home to my mammy."

If Tess had never seen the hue of death upon a human face, she saw it now. The boy rose totteringly, and Tessibel, with a tender expression in her eyes, opened the door.

"Ezy, I's sorry for ye! I's sorry that I slicked the dirty dish-rag in yer face. Ye forgives me, don't ye, Ezy?"

"Yep." And Ezra stumbled away.

Tess watched him stagger along the shore through the rain, the shadows of the weeping-willow trees at last swallowing him up.

She turned back into the hut, barred the door, and fed the child with sweetened milk, forcing particles of bread into the yawning throat. Teola had sent the student from her, never to return, yet she fed the child tenderly, tucking it, with its sugar rag, in the warm blanket.

She snuffed the end from the candle, that it might burn brighter, took the little Bible, and sat down to read.

"Who shall deliver me from the body of this death?" she haltingly spelled.

Her eyes sought the small outline of Dan Jordan's babe in the bed. She hardly understood Paul's figurative words, but vaguely imagined that the apostle was afflicted with something like the wizened child which had been thrust upon herself.

Loud, impatient noises issued from the blanket. Tess rose, settled the baby more comfortably, and sat down again. Her eyes sought another verse.

"If ye have the faith of a grain of mustard-seed—"

The passage brought a vivid blush to her face. She rose silently, and knelt by the window.

"Take this here body of my death," she prayed, "and give the poor brat to the Christ! Make its ma tell the student, and give Tessibel faith like a mustard-seed." Thus ended her prayer.

Ezra Longman, sick unto death, as he had said, floundered his way along the wet path. The long walk through the storm from Ithaca had so weakened him that he could hardly stand upright. He wanted to see his mother once more, to be with Satisfied, and to warn Myra of the coming evil. A conversation he had heard between the nurse and Professor Young had decided him to go home if he could, for Ezra knew that his sister loved the ugly fisherman who had tried to put him to death in the Hoghole.

As he neared his cabin home, he saw the candle streaming its flickering ray upon the path that led to the rocks. He saw his mother snuff the flame and Satisfied take Myra's child up from the floor, but he did not see his sister. As if in answer to this thought as to her whereabouts, Myra appeared directly in front of him, carrying a pail of water from the spring. She did not notice him until he pronounced her name in an undertone. The pail dropped from her hand, splashing its contents over her garments, and she uttered a little frightened cry. He whispered her name again and Myra timidly put out her hand.

"Air it yerself, Ezy?" she implored.

"Yep, I air here. I comed to see Mammy and Satisfied, and to tell ye that it air time for ye to be savin' Ben Letts if ye loves him. Ben throwed me in the Hoghole, he did, but I know that ye loved him, and I comed."

The boy staggered with weakness, and his sister threw an arm around him.

"Ye air to come to Mammy," she urged. "Mammy loves ye, Ezy dear."

"Wait," whispered the boy. "Ben Letts air to be arrested."

"What?"

The cry was sharp — the words hurt.

"Ben Letts air to be tooked to jail. It were him what killed the gamekeeper. It weren't Orn Skinner."

"Who were a-sayin' it were Ben?" demanded Myra, her mouth hard and lined.

"I says it," replied Ezy. "I seed him when he done it, and I comed to tell ye, and to see Mammy and Satisfied."

"Then come in, and go to bed, for ye be sick."

A change gradually came over Myra: cunning grew in the faded eyes and determination straightened the thin shoulders, as she led her brother into the hut.

"Mammy," she called softly, opening the door, "here air Ezy!"

"Fetch him in," cried Satisfied.

Mrs. Longman sank weakly into a chair. The sight of her son, her only son, white and emaciated, and the appearance of the livid scar on his brow drew a painful cry from her lips.

"He air sick," continued Myra, "put him to bed."

"Where air ye been all this time, Ezy?" asked Longman, assisting him into the small back room. But Ezra was too ill to tell the story, and the mother hushed him to sleep just as she had in those childhood days when he had been good, and always at home.

Meantime, Myra, pale and thoughtful, moved about the shanty. Her mind was upon one subject — she must save Ben Letts from the dreaded rope. She did not question the verity of her brother's statement, for she realized that Ben was not only capable of killing the inspector, but also of placing the guilt upon an innocent man. It did not, however, change her squatter love. The more she thought of Ben's danger, the more she loved and wanted to save him, the more determined she grew to take him away to some place where the officers could not find him.

"Goin' to bed, Myry?" asked Longman, taking the candle and climbing the ladder to the loft.

"Yep, but I air a-goin' to rock the brat a little while. Ye and Mammy go to bed. I locks the door."

She settled herself in the wooden rocking-chair, trundling the child to and fro, and murmuring a doleful tune. Her son was now almost two years old, and beginning to toddle about upon a pair of crooked, thin legs. As often as Ben had visited the hut he had never deigned to look at the child, but Myra had a dull hope that, if she saved the fisherman, he would show some affection for the little boy.

An hour later, the regular breathing of her father and mother told Myra that they both slept. Ezra, too, was sleeping, for she had bent over him but a little time before. The clock on the mantel pointed to midnight. The girl rose, and fed the baby, dropping some paregoric into his milk to keep him asleep, and then drew a large shawl about the little one, rolling him gently in the warm folds. Finally, she took a piece of paper and a pencil from the shelf.

"Mammy," she wrote, "I's a-goin' to save Ben Letts. Ezy tells ye about it, as how Ben Letts killed the gamekeeper it werent Orn Skinner. I takes the brat cause it air Bens I luves yer and Satisfied."

She pinned the note to the handle of the copper kettle upon the stove, and, lifting the child in her arms, slipped through the door without a sound.

The rain still fell steadily, the turbulent roll of the lake lost only in thunder's roar. Once on the ragged rocks, Myra walked swiftly, afraid of the shadowy objects and ghostly sounds that spectered her path. She threw despairing glances about her, and shrank from the imaginary sneaking figures haunting the dismal night. Almost running, she reached the Letts' shanty.

How soon would the officers come for Ben? They

might have been there before her. The cabin was dark, and she tapped timidly upon the kitchen door. Only a great snore from the sleeping Ben inside answered her. Trying the latch, it lifted in her fingers, and she crept stealthily through the narrow aperture, encircling the child with her left arm.

"Ben!" she whispered. "Ben!"

The squatter turned, muttering sleepily.

"Mammy! What be the matter, Mammy?" The fresh night air startled him.

"Who air it?" he demanded hoarsely.

"Myry," breathed the woman again. "Get up. . . . They air a-comin' to take ye to prison for the killin' of the gamekeeper. I comed to help ye, Ben Letts."

The words soaked slowly into the sluggish brain. Tired from the beating Frederick had given him, and lazy by temperament, Ben did not at first realize that Myra's message meant the hangman's rope for him. He turned again in bed, and sat up. Were the officers of the law waiting for him?

"Ezy air home," resumed Myra rapidly, leaning tensely toward him. "He walked through the rain from Ithacy. He says as how ye air goin' to be tooked to prison. I has the brat here with me . . . we air a-goin' away. . . . Get up, Ben. Hustle yer bones!"

The blue-jeans breeches, streaked with the blood of many a fish, were drawn on in a twinkling. The great squatter boots quickly covered the horny feet, and trembling, Ben waited for Myra to lead him from the cabin.

"Where be we a-goin'?" he asked in a whisper.

"I takes ye 'cross the lake to Ludlowville, and then

we goes into the hills. A awful storm air a-scootin' along from the north, but we can't wait, for ye'll be took."

By this time they were nearing the shore. The autumn lightning shot out from the sky, veering to the north and unmasking the black, raging lake and the distant city. A heavy roll of awe-inspiring thunder followed the flash. The man and woman did not speak until the flat boat topped the breaking waves.

"The storm air a-goin' to be worse," shouted Ben, scanning the dark clouds. "It air foolhardy to try it, ain't it, Myry?"

"Yep; but we go, all the same. I stays with ye, Ben!"

He did not answer to this, nor did he ask a question then about the return of Ezra. He was satisfied that what he had supposed was the boy's wraith — the disembodied spirit of the lad he had thrown into the Hoghole — was the living Ezra Longman. On his way home from the Skinner hut, Ben had planned a terrible revenge upon the student and Tessibel, but the advent of this unforeseen discovery had placed his enemies beyond his reach. The thought of Tess brought a rasp from his throat.

The creaking oars, under his experienced fingers, carried the boat far from the shadowy shore. Through the frequent lightning he could plainly see Myra in the stern, holding to the child. It was all ending differently from what he had hoped. That he had killed the gamekeeper he knew well, but, when Ezra Longman had disappeared into the Hoghole, Ben thought it took from the earth the only witness of his deed.

On and on through the night sped the boat, until Myra

and Ben could see the lights on the college hill. Here and there in the valley beyond, the lightning revealed a farmhouse, the inmates of which were quietly sleeping.

Presently Ben spoke:

"What hes Ezy been a-sayin'?"

"Nothin' but that ye throwed him in the Hoghole, and tried to kill him, and that ye killed the gamekeeper."

"Where hes he been all this time?"

"I dunno. He air awful sick, and Ma put him to bed."

Their voices rose high above the shrieking of the wind. Myra's last words were screamed out. The boat tossed like a bit of tinder, but it was in the hands of a fisherman: Ben knew how to keep it in and out of the troughs of the waves. Once the boat lurched mightily, and Myra gave a frightened cry, wedging the child between her knees. Higher and higher rolled the waves.

"We hev got to bail the water out," yelled Ben. "Bail, Myry, while I rows."

The mother grasped the sleeping child tighter between her knees, and began to throw the water into the lake. Suddenly a great wave half filled the boat.

"Ye can't do it, Ben," Myra screamed. "Ye can't keep the boat top up, and we'll all die to once. . . . Does ye love yer brat, Ben Letts?"

The voice, prophetic and high-pitched, struck terror to the heart of the fisherman. He stopped rowing, and shouted out over the waves for help. The lightning made day of the inky night for an instant, and the squatter Ben saw the woman, holding the child under one arm and clinging to the side of the boat with the other, creep toward him.

"Keep away!" he bellowed. "Keep the boat top up!"

Another flash. . . . She was closer, her white face and her staring eyes frightening him. He raised one great boot to ward her off, but she was at his side before it touched her. A large wave lifted one oar from the lock and bore it away on its crest. The boat, without pilot power, tipped dangerously. Loosening her hand from the side of the boat, Myra wound one arm about the knees of the squatter.

"Ben Letts," she cried, shrieking the words into his ear, "kiss yer brat afore he dies with ye, will ye? Ye ain't so much as ever touched him."

A dark storm-cloud broke directly over their head — one brilliant sheet flared the sky from the north to the south. The child, sleeping heavily under the drug, was close to the squatter's face. A revulsion of feeling overwhelmed Ben — approaching death aided the ghosts of his past bad deeds in their attack upon his wretched, over-wrought soul. . . . With a sob, he laid his lips upon the slumbering babe. A long kiss followed the first; another, and then another.

Myra gasped, and drew the boy back to her. The boat reared high in the boiling, seething waves, and the next whitecap wrenched the child from her hands, snatching it into the water.

"Ben Letts, our brat air gone! . . . There he be! . . . God! . . . There! There!"

Through a sudden, resplendent flood of light, they saw the babe poised for one brief instant on a huge, foaming shoulder of the lake. In her frenzy the squatter woman was murmuring over and over strange, inarticulate words which Ben did not heed. Their arms were locked tightly about each other. Ben Letts slowly fixed his cold, shivering lips on those of the girl, drawing her closer and closer into his embrace. The majesty of death was upon them, this squatter father and mother. Another glare of light showed them still clinging together, but the one following failed to reveal either man, woman or boat.

## CHAPTER XXXVIII

PROFESSOR Young knocked at the Skinner hut. Tess smiled at him from between the tatters of the curtain, and unlocked the door, standing, as her friend took the wooden rocker.

"Daddy air a-comin' home," she breathed timidly.

"Soon. Sit down, child. I have much to say to you. . . . We have discovered the murderer of the gamekeeper. We have positive proof that it was not your father."

Tess squatted on the floor, crossed her legs, and waited.

"Who were it?" she asked presently, as if afraid to speak.

"Ben Letts."

"The damn bloke!" she ejaculated, a dangerous light gathering in her eyes. "And he were a-lettin' Daddy be hung for his own dirty work! He air a wicked cuss, he air!"

"Ezra Longman saw him when he committed the murder," Young told her, watching the interest gather in the eager face. "Letts used your father's gun. That accounts for his having been accused."

Tess nodded her head.

"Ezy were here last night," she commented quietly. "He were sick."

"He was under my care for a long time," explained Young, "and last night escaped and walked home through the rain. . . . He is dead."

"Dead!" gasped Tess. "Dead!"

Impetuously she bent toward him, and finished:

"Ezy Longman ain't dead!"

"Yes, he is," replied Young. "He died in his father's hut, last night. I have just left there, and I feel heartily sorry for them both."

"Myry? . . . Did ye see Myry?"

"She's gone with Ben Letts."

"Gone where?"

"We don't know, but the officers are looking for them. I think the boy heard me tell the nurse that he would be held as a witness in your father's next trial. He must have warned Letts upon his arrival home, for —"

"He knowed Myry loved Ben," broke in Tess.

"That's what I thought," Young answered. "I found Longman and the mother mourning over the boy. They hope to hear from the girl soon."

"If Myry and Ben was in the storm last night —" began Tess.

"They may be dead," ended Young gravely. "Myra took her child with her. I found this note on the dead boy's bed, and brought it away with me. I would have liked to have put the boy on the witness-stand. Nevertheless, I hope to release your father on the evidence I have, without a trial."

For several moments silence reigned in the hut. The sun streamed through the window, and a steamer sent a shrill whistle over the lake, the sound echoing among the rocks. Tessibel was thinking of Ezra Longman; Professor Young was thinking of her.

Presently she leaned over, and took the letter from the man's hand, spelling out Myra's written message.

"Myry air a-writin' so dum well," she observed, handing it back, "that I can't make it out. What air she a-sayin'? You read it."

Young read the badly-spelled note.

"I knowed the brat was Ben Letts'," she said, after the man's voice had died away. "He were a cute kid."

"We hope to find them all," interposed Young thoughtfully. "But, if we don't, the evidence I already have — this note, and the fact that the fisherman is a fugitive — will liberate your father. I shall go to Albany to-morrow to see the Governor. I am sure he will consider the evidence I have. Then we shall know."

"You think the man at Albany will give him to me?"

"Yes, indeed, I do! I would not raise your hopes if I did not. If you persuade your father to leave here — " He stopped and looked at her with a questioning glance.

"I tells him that the hut ain't his'n," she asserted abruptly.

"If you do go away, I shall try to get your father steady work in the city. Would you like that?"

"Yep," replied Tess, in a thick voice. "He wouldn't have to net no more. And he wouldn't have no more froze toes."

"Neither would you, Tess," answered Young.

Suddenly Tess saw the man staring at her arm, where several blue stripes, mingling with red, ran long from her shoulder.

"Heavens! child, what's the matter with your arm?"

The brown eyes clouded. Tess swept her jacket over the marks, and muttered,

"It ain't nothin'. I scratched it on some thorns."

Professor Young leaned forward, and tilted the little chin upward. Still the eyes remained upon the floor.

"Tess!" he pleaded. "Tess! Are you telling me the truth?"

"Nope; I's lyin' to ye."

She tossed her head up angrily.

"I had a damn good lickin'," she finished.

Young sprang forward, and grasped her arm.

"Who dared to mark you like that?" he exclaimed, standing her on her feet. "Wait. I want to see it. Who did it?"

He pushed back the sleeve, and stood analyzing the bruised shoulder and arm.

"Who did it?" he persisted, drawing a quick, sharp breath.

"Dominie Graves," muttered the girl.

"What!" Two deep creases marked the fine brow.

"He licked me," reiterated Tess, with an indifferent droop to her lids. "He had a right. I were a-stealin'."

"Tessibel! Tessibel! Look at me."

She swept him with a glance of truth.

"Are you —? Tess, I demand to know it all — all! Please, tell me about it!"

"There ain't much to tell," she returned; "only that I were a-stealin' from the Dominie's kitchen, and he licked me for it."

"What did you — steal?"

"Milk for the brat. . . . He can't starve, can he?"

Slowly Professor Young dropped her arm, gazing at her mutely.

"Ye ain't mad at me?" she ventured, watching him narrowly.

"No! I'm only sorry — infinitely sorry for you."

The tender tone in his voice, the mist rising in his eyes, brought Tess to his side.

"I thanks ye for all ye been a-doin' for Daddy and me," she said brokenly. "I does thank ye. . . . Don't look at me like that — it air a-hurtin' me."

The low voice, filled with unshed tears, rang with emotion.

A sudden inspiration seized Young.

"Child, if I bring your father back to you, will you — marry me?"

The unexpected question sent Tess staggering back; a tearful smile spread the red lips.

"Ye'r' batty," she said presently, with a dissenting shake of the red curls. "Ye'r' gone plumb crazy. . . . I's a squatter, nothin' but a squatter. I stays here with Daddy. I marries no man. See?"

The proud face of Frederick Graves rose before her. She turned away with a groan.

Young misinterpreted her expression.

"Circumstances have made you a squatter. . . . Sit down. I want to say more to you, Tess. Don't say you won't marry me, just yet. When your father comes home, we will talk to him about it. . . . I love you, child."

"My Daddy air a-wantin' me with him," faltered Tess. "He said oncet as how he wouldn't give me to nobody. Ezy Longman wanted me to marry him, but I hated him. . . . I don't now, though, 'cause he air dead."

"Tessibel, will you let me give you some money to buy milk for the strange little boy?"

"Somebody gived me some money after my lickin' last night, so I don't need none now."

A jealous feeling rose instantly in Young's heart.

"Who gave you money last night?"

"The student," replied Tess. "He said as how I shouldn't steal no more milk for the brat. I takes the student's money, I does."

A faint suspicion flashed over the lawyer.

"You told me the truth about the child belonging to a woman on the hill?"

Without answering his question, Tess stammered,

"Ye said as how ye trusted me, and I were happy because ye did. . . . Ain't ye trustin' me now?"

"Yes, child; but I am so bitterly unhappy over you, and my love for you makes me jealous —"

"Of the student?" queried Tess.

"Yes."

"Well, ye needn't care no more about him, 'cause he don't like me no more. He ain't never carin'—" She cut the words off with a snap. "I were a-goin' to lie then," she went on slowly. "He air a-carin', but — but —"

She dashed a loose curl from her eyes, and flung herself headlong upon the bed, with a burst of sobs that drew Young quickly to her.

"Tessibel Skinner, you love Frederick Graves?"

Tess straightened, and looked at him fearfully.

"Yep, I air a-lovin' him," she wailed.

"And he doesn't love you?"

"He be a-lovin' me, too." She was hardly able to utter the words.

"Then why do you weep, if you love him and he loves you?"

Tessibel's eyes settled upon the babe, yawning in the sun. Young followed her gaze.

"The child has separated you?" he said slowly.

"Yep."

"Why?"

"'Cause —'cause — "

All Teola's perfidy rushed over her in a twinkling. All the student's suffering stung her as if she had been struck in the face. She bounded from the bed, possessed of a dark spirit.

"A damn bloke air a-doin' it. It were a oath I took. . . . Will you go now? — Please!"

"Yes," assented Young. "But it is all a mystery to me. I cannot understand it."

And Tessibel, thinking of Teola, the child, and its dead father, muttered:

"I ain't understandin' it, nuther. . . . Goodbye."

Transfixed, Tess stood for many minutes where Young had left her. A shadow dropped upon the path. Teola, pale and ill, came toward her, and she did not move.

"My father and brother have gone to Ithaca, and I — Tessibel! Tess, don't look at me that way! Don't! don't!"

"You forgot to tell him," dropped from the squatter's lips.

"No, I didn't forget. Tessibel, I've tried, and I can't tell him. . . . I haven't the courage," she ejaculated, waiting long for a reply from the rigid girl. Her lips trembled as she faltered:

"My father was cruel to you, Tess!"

"I were a-stealin'," Tess muttered. "He wouldn't a whipped me if he — had knowed about it, would he?"

"No, no! He would have died first. . . . Tessibel, why didn't you tell him?"

"Didn't ye say it would kill the student if he knowed it? And I swored, didn't I? when the brat was borned, that I wouldn't tell — and I ain't no liar — leastwise about no brats. If it air told, the brat's ma's got to tell it," she finished.

Teola dropped beside her infant.

"I'm afraid to tell it. My father and brother have such confidence in me!" She shifted about, and looked at Tessibel. "We are going to move to the city, Saturday. . . . I have been thinking about the baby's milk — "

"I has money now," broke in Tess. "I don't have to steal no more. Daddy air a-comin' home soon, too."

"I know it. Father heard from Professor Young all about it. I am so glad for you, Tess. What will you say to him about the baby?"

"I dunno," grunted the squatter.

She answered no more of Teola's questions, but for a long time remained moodily looking, with narrowed eyes and burning heart, at the minister's daughter.

## CHAPTER XXXIX

TWO days later, on Friday evening, Teola slipped quietly from her home, and the Skinner hut opened to her timid knock. Tess had no more fear when visitors came. Ben Letts had gone with Myra, and Ezra Longman was dead.

The girls eyed each other for one embarrassed moment. The day for separation was at hand: Tess would face the lean winter, Teola the burden of a conscience in torment.

"Come in," muttered Tess.

"Tessibel," Teola burst out spontaneously, "we are going away to-morrow. I wish I were going to stay with you and the baby!"

Gloomily Tess scrutinized the young mother, checking an ejaculation that rose to her lips.

"I don't understand what you are going to do," said Teola. "Tess, do you think he is very ill? You do! I can see it in your face. Look how he yawns, and screws his mouth, and shuts his eyes! Oh, he is suffering, Tessibel!"

"Yep, he air sick," replied Tess, turning her back. She had grown to love the hapless thing, and knew that he suffered as all human beings suffer when they go slowly away to the mystery of mysteries.

Teola's next words brought her about sharply.

"Tessibel, do you — hate me?"

"Nope."

"Oh, what a coward I am! Frederick has forbidden me to come here."

"That air 'cause he air a good bloke," snorted Tess. "But if he knowed—"

"I can't get my breath when I think of telling him, Tess."

"He ain't to know never, then?" bounded from Tessibel's lips, the passion in the tones lowering the voice almost to a whisper.

"No," replied the young mother; "I can't tell him."

The squatter just caught the next words, "But I am going to die, too, Tess."

The conviction in the statement made Tess spring back.

"Ye ain't yet. Ye ain't goin' yet!"

"The doctor says I am very ill here." Teola placed her hand upon her chest. "I've had three hemorrhages. People ill like I am never get well. I don't want to— either," she ended brokenly.

She looked so forlorn, so thin and ill that Tess went awkwardly to her.

"I takes care of the brat if ye goes before him," said she.

"Thank you, dear," drifted from the depths of the child's box. "And forgive me all the sorrow I have caused you."

"I has forgivin' ye," assured Tess, seating herself. "I were — sorry about the student, though."

"I know, I know; and perhaps God won't forgive me, for I've been so wicked! I make up my mind every night, when I can't sleep, that I will tell; then in the daylight I am afraid."

Tess did not answer.

"I shall think every moment of the day about you

two here. Oh, my precious baby! If I could only take him with me! That mark will never disappear," she concluded, rubbing the tiny red forehead with her fingers. "If he only goes when I do! God couldn't be so cruel as to let him live, with his face like that, and have neither father nor mother."

"Nope," replied Tess with decision. "He'll take the brat, too."

"Will he die soon, Tess?"

"Yep."

"Why do you think so? Why?"

"He air too thin to hold out much longer. He don't eat, nuther. He don't do nothin' but smack all day long on them sugar rags, like a suckin' calf. And there ain't no makin' him eat."

"But he doesn't cry much," argued Teola.

"That air 'cause he air so weak. Ma Moll were here with the hoss doctor, and they says he air to croak dum quick."

Teola raised her head, startled.

"Oh, I didn't know you had had a doctor. I was going to speak about it to-night." She dropped her eyes, reddened, and then added, "But the horse doctor, Tessibel?"

"Squatters allers has the hoss doctor — they air cheaper."

"But he can't die!" Teola moaned. "Not now — not yet! He has never been baptized. If he died now, he wouldn't go to Heaven!"

"Aw! shut up. He air a-goin' in faster'n any of them. Don't you worry yer head over that. God ain't that kind of a bloke that He wouldn't take in a sick brat what ain't never done no harm."

Tess had risen, and was standing over the child, Teola having placed him back in the bed.

"But you don't understand, Tess dear! You see, it's this way: the Bible says that if a child isn't baptized, he will go to a place where he must stay always. He won't go to Heaven. You understand?"

"Air the Bible a-sayin' that?"

"Yes."

"Won't he go to a place where God'll find him, if he ain't sprinkled?"

"No."

"That air strange. The poor brat air so blue, so shiverin'— he air so sick! Aw! Christ'll love him, 'cause he ain't got no friends."

Her eyes spread wide with infinite compassion as she contemplated the grave-shadowed child.

"Did the student tell ye that the Bible were a-sayin' that?" she asked peremptorily.

"Yes; and my father has often preached upon it. I know that it is true," insisted Teola. "A child must be cleansed of its original sin in the church. . . . You see? You see, Tess?"

"I don't see — I don't know, nuther. But what the student says air right. If the little kid ain't to see God's face 'less he air slapped on the head with water in the church, then the brat air got to be tooked there."

"But — but, Tess, is it possible?"

Again the squatter bent her head to gather the words.

"He air a-goin' to die," she replied with conviction, "and he has to be hit with the water, if he air a-goin' to die, don't he? Air that what ye means?"

Teola, dropping her face upon the babe, bowed her head in assent, and wept silently, until the cough that had fastened itself upon the slender chest since the coming of the child, dried the tears.

Tess remained quiet until the paroxysm had passed.

"Air yer pappy a good sprinkler of brats?"

Teola nodded.

"Air it likely he would sprinkle this 'un'?"

"I don't think my father would turn away a dying babe that needed cleansing of its sin by the Holy Ghost."

"The Hully what? The student were a-talkin' 'bout him once."

"The Holy Ghost," explained Teola. "He lives in the church, and when a baby is baptized He comes and stands by the font, and when the water falls upon it, He takes away all the sin that it is born with."

Tess grunted disbelievingly.

"Can ye sees him?"

"No; He is a spirit."

"Ye mean that he air like the headless man from Haytes, and the squaw with her burnt brat?"

They were both down beside the babe again, Tess eying the mother eagerly.

"Oh, no, Tess! Those are but superstitions. This is the truth. No matter how little the child is, he won't go to a holy place if he isn't baptized."

"Air the Huly Ghost livin' only in the church?"

"Yes, He doesn't stay anywhere else."

"Who says it air true?"

"God."

"Your brother's God?"

"Yes."

"Then, of course, it air so. Why didn't ye say so before? Could the brat be sprinkled this comin' Sunday?"

"Yes; yes, it is baptismal Sunday. Deacon Hall's new baby is to be baptized, and lots of others, too!"

"Then yer brat air goin' to be sprinkled with 'em," decided Tessibel.

"Tess!" gasped Teola. "How? How? . . . I should die if I had to take him to the church."

"I takes him," replied Tess grimly. "I takes him, and I says to yer pappy, 'Dominie, I knows that ye don't like me nor my Daddy, but here air a brat what air sick to death. . . . He can't find God by hisself 'cause he air too little, and God won't try and find him if he ain't sprinkled. Will ye do it?'"

Teola shifted her position, and looked into the squatter's face. It was gleaming with heavenly resolve and uplifted faith.

"Tess, would you dare?" gasped she.

"Yep! The little brat has to go. I takes him."

The fisher-girl clambered to her feet, and shoved another log into the stove.

"It air a chilly night," she commented, "and the ghosts air a-howling like mad, 'cause Ma Moll's been here. She can raise spirits any time of night."

Teola evidently did not hear. Her eyes were fixed upon the face of the babe, her mouth twitching nervously at the corners. She wondered silently what her father would say when Tess presented the child for baptism on Sunday morning. She could imagine her own happiness after it was all over. She thought she would get better for a time. She remembered how her mother had worried over her cough, how her father had advised with the best doctors of the city; but they had gravely shaken their heads, saying that the girl might grow out of it; they hoped she would. But day by day she had seen herself growing more and more slender, more and more fragile-looking. And, as Teola knelt over the child in the flickering candlelight, Tess shivered superstitiously. The young mother was so white that the squatter could almost have imagined her one of Ma Moll's ghosts.

"They be a-callin' ye from yer house," remarked Tess, after a long stillness.

"Yes, I hear them. . . . It is my father. But I am so tired that it seems as if I could never climb the hill. I'll see you a minute to-morrow, Tess. . . . If I can't, will you bring the baby to the church Sunday, at eleven o'clock? . . . Thank you, dear; thank you. . . . Good-bye, precious little Dan. . . . And — and forgive me, Tessibel!"

## CHAPTER XL

MINISTER Graves watched his child painfully climb the front steps. He could see, even through the dim shadows, how thin she had become, how she panted for breath over the slight exertion of walking up the hill. A thought that stung him like a whip seized him, convulsing his heart and shaking his powerful frame as if he had been attacked by sudden ague. Was his daughter going to die? She could not die — God would not take her from him! He remembered Teola's birth, with a groan of pain: remembered how he had taken the dark-haired babe, so tiny and helpless, into his study alone, and had uttered the sincerest prayer of a father's life, that the blessings of Heaven would cover his new-found treasure and would guide the little footsteps during the whole bright future — her future must be bright, with his love to shield her. He could remember each succeeding day — his pride and ambitions for her — and now —

Teola paused on the top step, clinging to the veranda pillar. He came hastily to her, the darkness covering the emotions that had paled his face, and bent over the exhausted girl, kissing her lips tenderly.

"Teola, darling! My darling, why will you persist in being out at night? . . . See, now, how you are coughing. . . . Child, what would become of me, if anything should happen to you?"

Teola knew the heart of her father. He had sternly preached orthodox doctrine, had persecuted the squatters according to his beliefs; but he loved his children, and especially had he idolized her. The thought of the babe in the fisherman's hut sped through her mind, her father's consternation and horror if she should be compelled to tell her secret. But Tessibel stood in her place as mother to the little boy, and had taken an oath that nothing could force her to break. The squatter had been the scapegoat upon which had been heaped the sins of a girl no one had thought capable of doing wrong. Teola, resting in her father's arms, struggled with her conscience, trying to press down the moral weakness that had compelled her to keep the tragedy in the cabin quiet. The minister helped her to her chamber, and, after she had retired, went in and prayed with and for her. His voice, low and tender, with the exquisite tones of an orator, was strangely moved.

"Child," he groaned, "I would give much to see you in good health again."

"I shall never be better, dearest; never. I know now that I cannot — that I sha'n't — "

His hand covered her lips.

"If you want to break my heart, Teola," he cried, unnerved, "then say what you were going to. I can't, and won't, bear it! You are not yet eighteen. You've always been well until these past few weeks. . . . Oh! I wish your mother and I had never gone abroad — or that you had gone with us. . . . But you begged so hard to stay at home!"

Teola had coveted the chance to tell him of the little human link betwen Dan Jordan's life and hers. She raised herself on her pillow, the long hair mantling her shoulders and aureoling the death-like face.

"Father," she gasped. "Father! Let me tell you

something about Tessibel Skinner. No! Don't put your fingers over my lips! Don't! Don't! Listen."

"Teola," interjected Graves gravely, "if you want to displease me —"

"She's so lonely," broke in the girl, her courage ebbing away under the bent brows of her father. "I thought — you — might help her."

"Go to sleep," replied the minister, "there's a good girl! . . . Good-night."

For a moment, Teola lay panting nervously. She had been so near the confession, so near telling her father about the little babe in the shanty. She slipped out of bed to the window. The wind still flung the dead leaves, whirling them to and fro in the orchard like willful spirits. The night had darkened until, to Teola, shivering and ill, it seemed alive with shadowy goblins which mocked at her.

She could just make out the dark line of the hut under the willow branches. A candlelight flickered a moment in the window, and was gone. Teola moaned long, muttering loving messages to the child cuddled in Tessibel's arms. She loved it, but could not bring it home — yet! At last sleep, a deep, fatigued sleep, enveloped her. She was too tired to dream.

After Tess was alone, she made ready for bed. The child whimpered drowsily. The squatter lifted it up with infinite tenderness, binding the rags more closely about the scrawny body.

"Ye don't amount to as much as the tuft on Kennedy's mare's tail," she said aloud. "Eat now, I says, or I opens yer mouth and pours it full."

The words, gathered from the vocabulary of the squatter, were harsh, but the emotion in the tones softened them.

"Ye air a-dyin' 'cause ye won't eat, kid, and ye have the smell of a dead rat, too. Yer lips be that blue — and yer mouth air like a baby-bird's. . . . Eat, I says, damn ye. . . . Will ye swallow that?"

She held the withered lips open, and filled the cavity with warm milk.

"Eat, I says," crooned the girl; "eat, and Tess takes ye tight — like this — and the rats can't bite ye, or the ghosts get ye till ye air dead. Tess loves ye, ye poor little brat."

The child, strangling for breath, gulped down a mouthful of milk, but the jaws set again, and the lips settled into a blue line. Tess prepared the sugar rag, putting in a large amount of sweet, and dipped it in the tea-pan in which she had warmed the milk. Then she allowed a little of the syrup to fall upon the lips. The mouth snapped upon it, and long after Tess had gathered the infant into her arms the smacking went on and on, until both slept. Neither heard the wind that rattled the hut boards, that rasped its endless sawing on the tin roof; neither heard the willow branches brushing to and fro against the rickety chimney. The child slept the sleep of a human creature moving silently toward death; and Tess the sleep of the exhausted.

The next morning she stood in the doorway, grimly watching the cottagers' boats, loaded with household goods, one by one as they passed. This time of year was prophetic of the coming winter, and told Tess a few more weeks would see the snow piled up about the hut and the lake covered with ice. Deacon Hall's private launch steamed by, with huge piles of bedding heaped up on the bow. One after another of the summer residents disappeared in the inlet, and Tess was waiting for the hillhouse people also to leave.

She heard Frederick's voice in the lane, and closed the door, pressing her face to the window. She saw him climb into his father's little yacht to make it ready for the summer's stock from the cottage. Teola, too, was on the shore, and Tess saw the girl turn longing eyes toward the hut. Then, with a boyish tug at his belt, Frederick started up the hill. His face in profile showed the squatter that he had changed — he was thinner, paler, and looked years older. Closer pressed the sweet face to the dirty pane, brighter grew the brown eyes. Drawn by his own desire, the student turned and looked at her. First an expression of eagerness leaped into his face; then one of sorrow settled upon it. He went on to the cottage without even nodding his head. He would soon come down with his father, mother and sister Babe, and Tess would see him no more.

She sank down upon the bed beside the sucking child, and did not hear the hut door open softly.

"Tess, Tess! It's Teola, dear. What is the matter?"

The squatter choked back her tears, and sat up.

"There ain't nothin' the matter," she replied sulkily. "I can cry if I wants to, can't I?"

"But, Tessibel, I have never seen you cry like that before, never! Is it money? Here, dear; here is a dollar. Father gave it to me. It will buy some milk, until I can send more. Oh, let me see my baby again. Darling little man! Your mother does love you, even if she must leave you. Tess, he looks worse than he did when I went home last night. You — you will bring him to the church to-morrow?"

"Yep."

"And, Tess, I left a lot of white cloths on the pear-tree near the barn. I could not bring them to you before, for Mother only sorted them out to throw away this morning. Oh, the baby looks so thin and ill, Tess!"

Tears trickled down upon the infant. Teola pressed her lips again and again to the thin mouth. The vivid mark was offering its crimson tinge sharply against the dead blue of the rest of the baby face.

"And, Tess," burst forth Teola, "how gladly I would give you a dress for yourself if I could, and a dress for him! You can't bring him like this to the church. You don't mind coming as you are?"

"Nope," came the bitter interruption from the squatter. "I don't need no clothes to have a brat sprinkled. I air a squatter, and squatters don't give — a hell about nothin'."

Her looks belied the words. With the dignity of a queen, the fine young head had settled back upon the broad shoulders sloping bare at the arms. The sweet face gave the lie to the hardened speech uttered from the grief she had just spent upon the bed.

"Don't speak like that, Tess! Don't! don't!" gasped Teola. "Some day, after the babe and I are dead — "

Teola had come close to the fisher-girl, her pale face thrust beseechingly forward. Tess hesitated; then flung out her arms and drew the minister's daughter into them. Her eyes were filled with awe indescribable.

"I's a mean brat to make ye say that," she faltered. "I brings the kid to-morry to the church. And, yes, I gets him a dress, too. See? And I buys milk for him, and makes him eat, and he sleeps here," Tess pounded her own strong breast, and ended, "till his dead pappy and his ma come after him, poor little cuss."

Both girls cried softly, till Frederick's voice on the hill rang out sharply in answer to a question from his father. Teola kissed her babe over and over, drawing a small shawl about her shoulders, and picked a path out through the fish-bones on the floor. When Frederick returned to the boat, she was listlessly throwing small stones into the water.

## CHAPTER XLI

TESSIBEL watched Minister Graves' yacht steam by the Hoghole, across the head of the lake and into the inlet. With it went the hopes of reconciliation with the student; the Dominie and his glowering glances of hatred; and Teola with her illness, leaving her the helpless babe.

She suddenly decided to share her secret with Mrs. Longman. She would beg a dress for little Dan to wear to the church for his baptism. She had stubbornly kept the presence of the child in her hut from her squatter friend, although Myra had usually had a way of worming into her innermost confidence. But Tess had given her oath and loyalty to Teola, and feared to tell the other girl the parentage of the child, lest Myra, who loved Ben Letts, should blab the truth to him.

During the weeks the babe had been with her, Tess had sent endless excuses about her absence to the Longman hut. She had to read the Bible; was waiting for someone to bring her a message from Daddy; fishing; getting ready for the winter; anything to keep Myra in ignorance of the tragedy being enacted in Skinner's hut. But now Myra was gone with Ben; Ezra was dead; and Mrs. Longman would not be curious about the little child.

She prepared the basket with the clean clothes that Teola had left on the tree, and, with the easy grace of a barefooted squatter, set out for the ragged rocks with bounding steps.

Across the lake the patches of forest, shaded with the scarlet and green of dying leaves, relieved the bareness of the harvested wheat-fields. Tessibel had a passion for the tumbling waves, they seemed to speak an unknown language to her, but to-day the lake was smooth like polished, clear, blue glass, and the birds were racing in flocks over it from the north toward the south. Their flight was so rapid that the squatter paused and followed them with her eyes. One flock after another disappeared behind the college hill so quickly that Tess could scarcely bid them farewell. They were her summer friends, had filled the day with brilliant song, and the night with love-twitterings.

Tessibel's forest solitude and rambles, her communion with night things had passed, gone with the coming of Teola, gone with the care of the babe. A longing for her old free life came back to her. She stooped down and placed the basket upon the rocks, and, with her arms flung over her head, tossed her face up to the sun. Her soul was dreaming, and the dream changed the half-closed eyes from brown to black.

She stood silently, her gaze roving after the fleet-winged birds. They were leaving her to the winter — and the sick child.

But Daddy, dear old Daddy, was coming back home! She caught her breath. At that moment her father was the panacæa for all that she had suffered during the last few weeks. Tears welled into her eyes. Just then another great flock of black birds, huddling together, skimmed by through the clear air. Tess threw out her hands.

"Good-bye, good-bye!" she shouted, with conflicting emotions. "Come back again soon. It air lonely in the winter without ye."

As if the birds understood the longing in a kindred soul, the flock halted an instant, seemingly loath to go, circled their mass of black toward the sky, swept to the water's edge, poised for the fraction of a second, then shot towards the University hill, and disappeared.

With the light-heartedness of youth, Tess reached the Longman cabin. A silence reigned within which at first astonished her. The door was closed, and Satisfied was nowhere in sight. She paused before rapping, and looked to the shore for the boat. Disappointment shot through her: Satisfied and Mrs. Longman had gone to the city. Nevertheless, Tess tapped lightly, and then again. But no voice ordered her in. She lifted the latch, felt the door yield to her touch, and stepped inside. Four lean rats scurried cornerward, sinking from sight into dark holes; numbers of lizards tailed silently backward from the sunbeam slanting across the shanty door. But the sight was so usual to Tess that she merely turned her head slightly, and smiled as if to departing friends, and closed the door behind her. A long object stretched out upon a board arrested her steps. It was covered with a sheet, and the breathless gloom of the shanty caused Tess almost to drop the basket as she set it down. The silent, white thing on the board brought an exclamation of fear from her. With horror settling deep in her eyes she backed against the door. Did the sheet cover death? No; for Ezra had been carried to his grave the day before. The thought freed her from a terror that had gripped her senses at first. She took two steps forward, bent down and looked under the board. Little streams of water had made dark tracks across the hut floor. The corners of the sheet were drenched through. This sent Tess back once more to the door. Would she dare lift the sheet? Controlling her fear by an effort, Tess gathered her courage together and crept again to the long board. With shaking fingers, she lifted the cloth, and drew it back gently. Then a horrified cry fell sharply from her lips, and she dropped it. Ben Letts and Myra Longman, hugged in each other's arms, lay dead before her.

Fascinated and trembling, she stood considering the livid squatters, no sound, after the first cry, issuing from her pale lips. The dead faces were so close to each other that a human hand could not pass between them. Upon the plain face of Myra rested a peaceful expression, as if she possessed a quietude she had never known before. Her eyes were closed, and one arm was tightly clasped about Ben's neck — the other about his waist. The storm had loosened the meager hair, had flung it in disorder over the fisher-girl's shoulders. Ben's brown teeth gleamed dark; the drawn lips were stretched wide, as if a pain, dreadful and torturing, had opened them never to be closed again. His two huge arms, twisted about the frail frame of the girl, were locked together by the horny fingers. To Tessibel it seemed that Myra smiled faintly in the possession of her longed-for happiness. She had Ben Letts at last, and forever — he was her gift of the storm, the eternal gift of a wild night. Myra had sought, and had found him.

The shanty door pushed open. Like one in a dream, Tess was still looking down upon the dead. Lifting her gaze, she saw Satisfied watching her, his eyes glowing with subdued pain.

"Myry air dead," he said, in a low voice, coming forward.

"Ben Letts, too," added the squatter girl.

"And the brat," finished Longman.

Tess, startled, lifted up her head.

"The brat! I had forgot him," she muttered. "He air dead, too?"

"Yep. He air here."

Longman drew down the sheet still further, exposing the lifeless baby. The thin little body lay between the father and mother.

For many minutes they surveyed the dead trio in rapt attention.

"Where air Myry's ma?" asked Tessibel presently.

"Back there, in Ezy's bed. She air sick, and so air Mammy Letts."

"Ezy were buried yesterday," ruminated Tess.

"Yep, and Myry be a-goin' to the same place. Ma and me air — alone."

There was something strangely pathetic in the quiet words, in the stolid, ugly face with its hard lines, in the mouth twitching at the corners as he spoke. Tess sprang toward him, and wound her strong young arms about him.

"Myry air happy," she burst forth; "happier than when she were livin' with you. She air with Ben Letts."

Satisfied, towering over her, blinked confusedly at her words. Puzzling, he drew his heavy brows down darkly.

"Myry were a-seekin' Ben," Tess went on hurriedly,

"and the brat couldn't stay without its pa and ma. I says as how Myry air happy, Satisfied."

"She were a-lovin' Ben Letts?" The pain in his clouded blue eyes stung Tess to the heart. The grief of this lonely old man, bereft of his all, seemed the most tragic spectacle she had ever faced.

"Yep," she replied, trying to smile through her tears; "she were a-lovin' him, and were a-seekin' his lovin's all the time. It were only in the storm — she found what she were a-seekin'."

She turned her head sharply toward the dead.

"Ye can see she air a-smilin', Satisfied, can't ye? And Ben air a-huggin' her up to him. That air somethin' Myry wanted. And ye air a-goin' to leave them like that, ain't ye? Don't tear Ben's arms loose, 'cause Myry won't be happy if ye does. Can't ye put 'em in a box, just like they air?"

Longman made a protesting motion. Some fishermen had picked the two dead ones up, locked in each other's arms. And he himself had covered them with a sheet, without making an effort to part them. He had not thought of putting them in the squatters' cemetery together.

"And let the brat stay with 'em, too," Tess broke in on his reverie.

"Yep," he replied; "I lets 'em all stay together. What Myry seeked for and found, she can have for all of me."

The listening girl knew there was hatred in the father's tones for Ben Letts. Well, she had hated Ben too, but he was all Myra's now, and there was no more hatred for the ugly squatter in the heart of Tessibel.

"She air a-smilin', Satisfied," Tess said again.

Longman loosened Tessibel's arms, and, walking slowly forward, looked down upon his daughter.

"I hain't seed before that she were a-smilin'," he said, taking a long breath. "Ye says as how she air happy, Tess?"

"Yep; she air with Ben Letts."

"I air a-goin' in to tell her ma that Myry air happy," asserted Longman, with relief in his voice. "I thank ye, Tess, for tellin' me that she were. I weren't thinkin' of nothin' but the storm, the water, and the time that ma and me were a-sleepin' when Myry were a-dyin'. She air happy, ye air sure, Tess?"

"Yep, for she were a-seekin' Ben Letts. She told me as how——" Tessibel choked back the words.

"She told ye what?"

Tess was going to tell him of the night on the ragged rocks and of Myra's broken wrist, but, with a flashing glance at the dead woman, changed her mind. In her vivid imagination she thought that Myra was silently entreating her not to speak ill of the dead man in her arms.

"She told me that Ben were the brat's pa, and that——" her eyes gladdened as she finished——" she were a-lovin' him; and, Satisfied, when we air a-lovin', and lovin' damn hard, then ain't we happy when we air with them what we loves?"

She had come close to him, standing near the dead man and woman. The girl slipped her hand into Longman's reassuringly, as she asked the last question.

"Yep," replied Satisfied, disappearing into the back room.

Tessibel had forgotten the child in the basket. She turned her eyes toward it, and a movement of the cover told her that the little Dan was awake. She was bending over it when Longman appeared at her side.

"Mammy says as how ye air to come in, Tess," he said, his eyes falling upon the child. "Whose brat air it?" he asked, with no shadowing suspicion in his glance. "Where did ye get it, Tessibel?"

"I air a-carin' for it for a while. I comed, Satisfied —"

Could she ask these people in sore grief for a dress that the dead child on the board had worn?

"Ye comed for what?" asked the man.

"I air a-wantin' to take him to the church, and I ain't got no dress for him. Would Mammy Longman let me take one?"

"Yep. Go in, and tell her. She air in bed."

Tess covered the babe's face, and placed the basket on the table.

"I can't leave him in the hut," she explained; "the rats air too thick."

"Yes," was all Longman said, and he fell to thinking deeply.

Tess crept away to the back room.

"I comed to see ye, Mammy Longman, and —"

"Sit down on the bed," interrupted the tired voice. "Myry and Ezy air both gone. Satisfied says as how Myry air a-smilin' and as how ye said she were happy. Satisfied and me feels better, we does."

Tessibel choked back the welling tears.

The gray head resting upon a soiled pillow, the pale face turned toward the wall, which had not turned to her, struck Tess deeper than Satisfied's stolid grief.

"Ye be sure Myry air happy?" came the tired voice again.

"Yep."

Mrs. Longman threw her eyes on Tessibel.

"If she air happy, what air ye cryin' for?"

"'Cause it air lonely for ye and Satisfied without her and the brat. I knows, 'cause I ain't had Daddy in such a long time."

"We was lookin' for Myry back, but not like —"

Tess broke in upon her words.

"Mammy Longman, I air a-carin' for a little chap what ain't goin' to live, and I wants a dress to take him to the church. Will ye let me have one?"

Mrs. Longman sat up, a new interest dawning in her faded eyes.

"To a church? Why to a church? He ain't dead yet, air he?"

"Nope; but his ma wants him took to the church where the Huly Ghost air, to have the water put on him. . . . Can I take the dress?"

"Yep, Tess; take one from Myry's box. They ain't good, but our little brat wored them."

Aimlessly, she lay down again and ceased speaking, but whimpered until Tess left the room. The girl made her choice from the small stock of dresses that had been worn by the Longman family, and had at last descended to the little dead boy.

On her way home to the hut once more, Tess paused on the rocks. The spectacle at Longman's had filled her eyes with the shadow of longing. She had seen Myra clasped in the arms of the man she loved. Tessibel's thoughts flew to the student. She could imagine her own happiness if she had been in the storm, and

Frederick had taken her in his arms, and they should have —

"I wish almost I was Myry," she moaned, "and the student was Ben Letts. . . . No, no! not that! not that!"

She sank under the burden of a new thought. Myra had sought, and had found — had searched for Ben in the storm, and had found him. Myra had had more faith than she had.

"Faith the size of a mustard-seed," flashed into her mind. Her own past unbelief pressed upon her, and the color fled from her cheeks, leaving them pale.

She opened the basket, and put her wistful face close to the sleeping child, her mental tension gone in her uprising faith.

"I thought as how ye were a-keepin' the student from me, but ye ain't. God ain't ready to let me have him. But he air a-goin' to let me have him some time. I air glad I got ye, and I hopes that ye live, too. Myry air got Ben Letts, and I air a-goin' to have — Frederick." She walked home in a reverie deep and sweet.

## CHAPTER XLII

SUNDAY morning, Tessibel was out upon the tracks, walking swiftly toward the city. She could hear the church bell at Haytes Corner ringing out a welcome to the country folk; she could hear the tolling of the chapel bell from the University hill. Clothed in the clean skirt she had washed at the time she had thought of going to Auburn prison, and a worn but clean jacket, Tess felt fit to face the best-dressed in Ithaca. Of course she was barefooted, for Daddy's boots were too big to wear into the house of the student's God. Earlier in the morning Tessibel had sat for a long time upon the small fishing dock, swinging her feet in the clear water. They, too, like the skirt and jacket, were clean.

In the basket, snuggling in the nest of white clothes, lay little Dan. He was robed, in the much-worn garment of the Longman child, and Tessibel had looked at him with pride as she settled him in his bed preparatory to her trip.

She passed swiftly through the city, and crossed Dewitt Park. How vividly she remembered the many midnights she had taken the same way, turning toward the jail to visit "Daddy"!

Tessibel paused before Minister Graves' church, and heard him read in deep tones from the Scriptures: "Suffer little children to come unto me, for of such is the kingdom of Heaven." The harmonious voice floated through the window to the fisher-girl, now crouched in the sun. Every word fell distinctly upon her ear.

She lifted the basket cover, and peeped in upon the babe. He looked bluer and thinner than Tess had ever seen him; his lips rested upon the rag with no indrawing movement. Unblinkingly stared the wide gray eyes when the sunbeams flashed upon his face. The vivid birth-mark grew fainter in the yellow light. Tess drew him into the shade, and waited.

The tones rolled out like thunder when Dominie Graves bade the members of his flock bring their children to the Holy Font, that they might receive the blessing of God, and everlasting life. Tess heard him say that the Father in Heaven demanded that all children should be baptized in the name of the crucified Saviour — that to put off such a duty might prove dangerous to their eternal welfare. Many of the long words the squatter did not understand, but she gathered enough to know how necessary it was to obey the minister's commands. She glanced again at the babe, with a worried pucker between her eyes. There was the same stare, the same unmoving lips. But he was quiet, and Tessibel let him lie.

"Come unto me all ye that labor and are heavy-laden —" rang forth the powerful voice. It fell upon the red-haired girl and soothed her.

Tess knew that Teola would be expecting her, and that Frederick would turn his face away when she presented the child for baptism, but no cloud gathered into the downcast eyes, for Tessibel's faith had grown since she knew that Myra's prayers had been answered. Had she not seen the girl clasped in the arms of the fisherman, who had once said that he hated her? Had she not seen the smile upon the dead lips which dripped with lake water? Tessibel had never before been so confident in prayer, and upon this beautiful Sunday morning, in the white light of day, kneeling under the church window, she believed that God would give her back the student — some time. She thought of the pain that would rest in the proud dark eyes of the boy when he saw her; but she smiled, because she knew that God lived, heard and answered the prayers of the heavy-laden.

An anthem rolled up from the church choir, chanting out the love of Christ, chanting His crucifixion and death for a dying world.

"Come unto me, come unto me," it sang, and "Come unto me," rose from the lips of the squatter waiting to take the little human thing, with its burden of sickness and death, to Dominie Graves, that he might petition the Holy Ghost to take away its sin.

"Come unto me," again sang the choir. Then silence. Tess leaned nearer the window. Dominie Graves read out the names of the babies to be baptized that day.

A carriage rolled rapidly to the church door, and Deacon Hall, accompanied by his wife, stepped to the pavement. The Deacon held a bundle with long white draperies hanging from it. It was their new baby, with lace upon its frock, going in to receive a blessing at the altar of God. Tess peered down upon the little Dan, and pulled the coarse dress closer about his chin. A violent wish born of the love she had for him came into her heart. Oh, that she had one bit of lace, to make his skin look less blue and the mouth less drawn! The wide eyes were still fixed upon her, immovable and unblinking. Once only had she seen the lids fall slowly downward, to rise again over the unseeing eyes.

"He knows he air a-goin' to church," she muttered lovingly. "I wonder if that air why he air so good. . . . Mebbe the spirit of his pappy air here."

She heard the names fall from the lips of the clergyman, as he took the infants, one by one, and placed his hand upon them with the water.

"I baptize thee, John Richard," Graves said slowly, "in the name of the Father, and of the Son, and of the Holy Ghost."

"Of the Holy Ghost. . . . He was the Spirit of God Who stood by the children, to take away the sin with which they had been born. Teola had told Tess so. The Holy Ghost would take away the sin of little Dan.

"I baptize thee," broke the silence, time after time, amid the tiny splashes of falling water. The last must have gone up to the altar, for Tess heard the minister telling the fathers and mothers the duty they owed their children.

"I finish my service to-day," said he, "by praying God to bless you all, and calling down the good-will of Heaven upon your children just baptized in His name."

Tessibel did not wait to hear the rest. She raised the child from the basket, shielding him from the sun with her body, stretched him out reverently upon her hands, and tiptoed up the long flight of steps into the church. A sea of heads rose before her startled vision. Transfixed, she paused in the door, waiting for Graves to cease speaking. Her eye caught the pew of the minister. Teola sat next to Frederick on the end, Mrs. Graves between her and her younger daughter. Tess

"BE YE GOIN' TO LET HIM GO A PLACE WHERE GOD CAN'T FIND HIM?"

noticed the tense expression upon the sharp profile of the babe's mother. How glad Teola would be when the baby was baptized! How happy in the new-found Heaven for her child!

The minister's voice had fallen into a prayer. And still Tess waited with the dying infant, staring wide-eyed upward at the great church dome. Every head was bowed: no one saw the strange girl, with hair flung wide about her shoulders, nor the tiny human being resting upon her hands.

Silence fell upon the congregation, and Tessibel commenced her walk down through the sea of faces to the pulpit. She gave no glance toward Teola as she passed, but kept her eyes fixed upon Dominie Graves, who, without noticing her, had turned to the little flight of steps that led to his pulpit. When he reached the Bible stand, and opened his lips to speak, his gaze dropped upon the squatter. At first he thought he was dreaming. He looked again — looked at her — at the child — and paled to his ears. Tessibel was holding the infant up toward him, with a beseeching expression in her eyes that staggered him.

Teola had seen Tess pass, and had caught a glimpse of the thin child upon her hands. The pursed baby lips, from which hung the useless sugar rag, made her lower her head to the prayer cushion, shuddering violently. Frederick had also seen the squatter — everyone in the church had seen her, and the silence grew wider and wider, until even breathing was hushed to catch her words.

Her low, sweet voice began to speak; it thrilled through the congregation like the song of angels.

"I has brought ye a dyin' brat, Dominie Graves,"

began Tess with shaking voice, " who has got to be sprinkled, or he can't go to Heaven."

The vast silence of the edifice echoed her petition.

The gaping minister never once took his eyes from her face, and made no move to answer her.

" It air a-dyin', I say," she went on, " and I wants ye to put the water on it."

So deadly in earnest was the girl that a sob broke out in the back of the church. The lithe, barefooted squatter, and the feeble, dying child offered a living picture of pathos, which with its tragedy slowly dawned upon the more sensitive minds, silently telling its tale of human suffering. Minister Graves refused to answer her. He wore the same expression of scorn Tess had seen in the student when she had acknowledged the child as hers.

" Be ye goin' to sprinkle him? " she demanded steadfastly, her voice growing stronger with her emotions. " Be ye? "

" No, I'm not." Graves' voice fell like the sound of a deep-toned bell.

" Be ye goin' to let him go to a place where God can't find him? Be ye? " Tess entreated.

Anger and revolt glinted through the golden-brown of her eyes; she swayed back a little from the font, still holding out the babe.

" He air so little," she pleaded with a choke, " and so awful sick. Mebbe he won't live till mornin'. He can't hurt the others, now they air done with the water, can he? "

She peeped into the marble basin, and lifted her eyes to his face.

"There air lots of water left. Be there other babies wantin' it worse than this one?"

She turned half-way round, and faced the wall of white faces, sending the question out in high-pitched tones.

Then Graves spoke with austerity and strength, riding down his anger with a mighty effort.

"You will please take the child from the church. You have your own squatter mission for such as that."

He had forgotten his members — forgotten that he was a man of God. As he bent toward her, he remembered only that she was the girl who had thwarted him, who had won in the squatter fight against his own influence. Tessibel heard the words "squatter" and "mission." It had not occurred to her to take the child there. She looked down upon the little fire-marked face. Would baby Dan live until she could get him there? He might be dead before she could carry him to the inlet and cross the tracks to the young rector's house. Teola had said that the baby would never be with his father without baptism, that even she, his mother, could not see him when she, too, went away. Little Dan, uncleansed, would live far from the bright angels. Her anger rose in a twinkling. She took another backward step, threw the red curls into a mass over her shoulder, and spoke again.

"Air I to take him from the church without the water?"

"Yes."

"I'll be damned if I's a-goin' to take him away," she flung back, panting. "He air so near dead, he air blind — look at his eyes! I says, he air to be sprinkled, he air! If ye won't give the Huly Ghost a chance at him — " Here she stepped forward to the font, flashed a look of hatred at Graves, and suddenly dipped her hand into the water.

"I sprinkles him myself," she ended.

The drops fell upon the livid baby face, dripping down upon the bare feet of the squatter.

"I baptize —" Tess wavered for lack of words. She had thought she could not forget the benediction.

A voice from the back of the church broke in abruptly upon her hesitation.

"I baptize thee, child," it rang, "in the name of the Father, and of the Son, and of the Holy Ghost."

Bill Hopkins was in the middle aisle, coming toward her. Tess snatched one glimpse of his face, still holding her wet hand upon the dark-haired babe.

"Say it, girl," Hopkins commanded. "Say it, quick. The child is dying."

"I baptize thee, child, in the name —" gasped Tess.

She stepped back again, throwing an entreating, silent appeal to the huge, bald-headed man.

"Of the Father, and of the Son," repeated Bill.

"Of the Father, and of the Son," echoed Tess.

"And of the Holy Ghost," ended Hopkins.

"And of the Huly Ghost," whispered Tess.

"Amen" rolled from a hundred tear-choked throats, like the distant murmuring of the sea. Hopkins sat down, saying no more.

Minister Graves had sunk into his chair, and on the girl's last words the congregation drew a long, gasping breath. The eyes of the babe gazed steadily on into the shadows of eternal silence; the water seemingly unfelt upon its head. The small boy was slipping away to that place of mystery where his father, Myra and Ben Letts had gone. The long days of suffering with the child in the hut rushed over Tess. She dropped on her knees, facing the pulpit, and hugged him to her breast, and whispered,

"Suffer little children to come unto me — "

Then another voice, shrill, sobbing and terrible, hushed her prayer. The squatter instinctively shifted her position toward the Dominie's pew. Teola Graves was standing up, tall and pale, and was looking directly at the minister.

"Father," she cried, "Father, if you don't take the baby and baptize him in the name of the Saviour, you will consign to everlasting darkness — " She lost her breath, caught it again, and finished, " your own flesh and blood. God! dear God, take us both to Dan! . . . Tessibel, Tessibel, give me my baby!"

She wrenched herself loose from Frederick's detaining fingers, and was in the aisle before her brother realized what had happened.

"He's my baby," she cried, between the spasmodic pressures upon her chest. "Tess! Tess, is he dead?"

"Yep, he air dead," fell from Tessibel; for she had seen the large, glazed eyes draw in at the corners and the little face blanch. The tiny spirit fled as the frantic girl-mother clasped her babe to her breast.

"But he air gone to his pappy," consoled the squatter.

For one awful moment, Dominie Graves looked into the accusing eyes of his congregation. Bill Hopkins was seated, with his face in his hands, but Augusta Hall, with her new baby folded tightly in her arms, was looking at him in dark-eyed disdain.

Graves swayed dizzily, . . . caught at the pulpit table for support.

"Jesus," he appealed dizzily, "Christ Jesus."

Frederick pressed his way to his sister's side. The squatter threw up her head before him: for the first time since that last dreadful night, she looked directly into his eyes, her dishonor slipping from her like a loosened garment. Frederick's soul shone forth in the glance he sent her. God in His own time had given her back the student.

Tessibel turned, and passed up through the mute gathering. Bill Hopkins put out his hand, and touched her.

"Child," he said brokenly, "you are the one bright spirit in this generation."

But Tessibel did not understand. She went down the long flight of steps, and into the sun-lit street, with but a backward glance at the rag-draped basket she had left under the church window.

## CHAPTER XI

TESSIBEL was a child again, a happy, freehearted child. The body of her death had fallen away as Christian's burden had slipped from his shoulders at the foot of the cross. The babe had gone to its father with the blessing of the Holy Ghost!

Then Tess thought of Teola, and stopped on the tracks, the Dominie's last words rushing into her mind. She had understood the import of them. It had been carried to her by the awful expression upon Graves' face. He was sorry, this minister who had persecuted her father and herself — sorry for Teola, sorry for the brat!

"The Dominie ain't likin' Daddy and me, though," she murmured. "But the student air a-likin' me!"

For the next two miles she sang lustily, childishly, with the complete abandon of a girl without a burden. Daddy Skinner was coming home, and God had given her back the student. The remembrance of his eyes thrilled her from head to foot.

Tess passed down the lane, glad for Myra, glad for Teola and her child — glad for everyone. She was still singing when she crossed the wide plank that spanned the mud-cellar creek. She saw Professor Young leaning against the shanty door, and the memory of their last conversation, when he had asked her to marry him, made her pause awkwardly, the color flying in rich waves from the red forehead ringlets to the shapely neck.

Young took her hand, looking searchingly into her face.

"Where is the child?" he demanded in low tones.

"I took it back to its ma — she wanted it," was all Tess replied. "Air ye comin' in and tell me about Daddy?"

"Your father will —"

Tessibel halted, with her hand on the door, waiting for him to finish.

"Go in, child. I will tell you — in there."

He spoke slowly, deliberately. . . . Tess gazed at him, trying to read his thoughts. Nevertheless she obeyed him, pressing open the door with an impatient movement of her head. She had waited so long for just this moment. To know when the big, hump-backed father was coming home seemed more precious to Tessibel than all the uplifting joy she had experienced that day. Her eyes swept the hut; then they rested in a frightened glance upon Daddy Skinner seated on his own stool. He was smiling at her with misty, shaggy-browed eyes, his lips showing his dark teeth with each incoming breath.

Deforest Young saw the girl bound forward, and the red curls shroud the huge fisherman's face. Tears blurred his sight. He turned into the day to regain his control.

"Ye be here to stay!" gasped Tess, sitting up presently, and holding the thick neck with her curved arm. "Ye ain't never goin' back to Auburn?"

"Nope; I's here to stay with my pretty brat. . . . Air ye glad to see yer Daddy?"

"Glad! glad! Daddy, daddy! I air a-goin' to be your brat till we dies!" She had nestled, as in the old days, completely under his chin hair, crying silently, deeply, with low-caught sobs.

For a long time they sat thus, until the man outside entered and spoke to them.

Tess jubilantly cooked the fish for dinner, spattering the bacon fat upon the floor. She smiled alternately at her father and Professor Young; she caroled like a spring bird with bursts of happy song. Then they three sat down to the table to eat the homely squatter fare.

A sickening longing swept over Deforest Young. To have the love of this girl he would be willing to live in the shanty — to eat just such food for the rest of his life. But during the few days past, he had fully realized that he could not make Tess love him. He would never speak of love to her again.

Yet it pleased him to remain with them through the long afternoon, with Tess near him to watch the sun sink behind the western hill.

He had drawn on his coat preparatory to leaving, and stood with Tessibel's hand in his. A sharp, quick knock on the door stayed his farewell. Orn Skinner lifted the latch, and Frederick Graves entered at the fisherman's bidding. His face was drawn and pale, his eyes red from weeping. Tessibel's heart bounded in sympathy, but she remained backed against the shanty wall until his eyes searched hers for a welcome. He spoke first.

"My sister is dead," he said slowly, his voice breaking as the tears came into the dark eyes; "and my father sent you this."

Daddy Skinner was seated blinkingly on his stool;

Professor Young, hat in hand, waited for the girl to take the extended paper. But for several seconds she stood staring at Frederick, with wide-eyed wonderment. He had said that his beautiful sister was dead, that she had gone with the thin babe to her loved one, even as Myra Longman had gone with Ben Letts. To Tess it was but another answered prayer, showered from Heaven. She felt no thrill of grief; she was only glad that the pale, sick mother had had her wish.

She took the paper awkwardly, and scanned it with painful embarrassment.

"I can't read the writin'," she said, handing it back. "Will ye tell me what it says?"

"Oh, I can't, I can't, Tessibel! I am so ashamed, so miserable!"

Tess silently handed the paper to Professor Young; then she slipped forward and stood close to Frederick, rapidly considering his face with forgiving eyes.

Young turned to the student.

"Shall I?"

An acquiescent nod gave him permission to lift the note and read:

"DEAR CHILD:

My daughter is dead. Frederick will tell you. If you can forgive me for all I have done against you and your father, will you come here to us, and tell Mrs. Graves and myself of the past few weeks. Frederick has told me that he loves you, and of your sacrifice for Teola. I can only say at present that we thank you.

Yours in grief and gratitude,
ELIAS GRAVES.

**P. S.**—When your father comes back, I shall ask you to give him the title of the ground upon which your house stands."

Professor Young read it slowly, word by word; each breath taken by the four people could be plainly heard in the silence that followed.

Frederick broke it.

"Tess, will you come to our home, and tell Father and Mother about — Teola?"

The name slipped into a whisper from his lips, and, leaning against the hut door, he burst into boyish, bitter tears.

"Forgive me, please," he murmured; "but it was so awful! And what she must have suffered! . . . And I didn't know — we none of us knew." He lifted his face, swept them with a heartrending glance, and finished. "She died in the church to-day with the baby."

"She air happy to be with the man what she loves, ain't she?" said Tess, softly.

Frederick grasped her hands, her brilliant smile easing the pain that like a knife stabbed his heart.

"You think she was happy to die, Tess? . . . Tell me all she said. . . . Did she know she was going away?"

For an instant the rapid rush of questions daunted Tessibel. But she sorted them out, commencing from the first one to answer them.

"Yep, she air happy," she said positively; "awful happy. She wanted to go to her man in the sky. . . . He were a-waitin' for her every day, and she knowed she were a-goin' to die, 'cause —'cause she prayed every night that God'd take her and the brat."

"Prayed? She prayed to die, when we all loved her so?" stammered Frederick.

"Yep. She were a-lovin' the burnt student better'n anything else. And, when women air a-lovin' like that—"

She ceased abruptly, and her own love for him attacked her as lightning attacks an oak in the autumn. Teola Graves had gone willingly to the burnt student, and Myra Longman had loved the ugly fisherman with a love that hurt like hers.

No one asked the short-skirted, barefooted girl to finish her sentence. The three men understood that her last passionate statement rang from the depths of her woman's heart. Frederick lifted his head.

"Tess — Tessibel, I can only say with my father that we all love you for what you have done for her."

His voice broke.

"And for myself, I say again, as I have said many times, that I — I love you — with my whole soul!"

His fingers closed over hers in an intense, desperate clasp. How long she had waited for him to tell her this once more! And he had confessed his great love in the presence of Daddy Skinner and the big man from the hill.

Her father watched her, this child whom but a year before he had left almost a baby. She was a woman now, with a woman's voice and a woman's love. The fisherman passed his hand over his face with a forlorn gesture. Had he found his darling again but to lose her?

Impetuously Tess turned toward him, and met his misty gaze with her tear-dimmed eyes. The student was still clinging to her hand.

"I air Daddy's brat," she whispered. "But I says," and she flashed Frederick a lightning-like glance through the red lashes before she dropped her eyes, and murmured, "but I says, as how I said before, that I air yer squatter."

THE END

# TITLES SELECTED FROM
# GROSSET & DUNLAP'S LIST

**May be had wherever books are sold.    Ask for Grosset & Dunlap's list.**

HIS HOUR. By Elinor Glyn. Illustrated.

A beautiful blonde Englishwoman visits Russia, and is violently made love to by a young Russian aristocrat. A most unique situation complicates the romance.

THE GAMBLERS.    By Charles Klein and Arthur Hornblow.
Illustrated by C. E. Chambers.

A big, vital treatment of a present day situation wherein men play for big financial stakes and women flourish on the profits—or repudiate the methods.

CHEERFUL AMERICANS.  By Charles Battell Loomis.  Illustrated by Florence Scovel Shinn and others.

A good, wholesome, laughable presentation of some Americans at home and abroad, on their vacations, and during their hours of relaxation.

THE WOMAN OF THE WORLD. By Ella Wheeler Wilcox.

Clever, original presentations of present day social problems and the best solutions of them. A book every girl and woman should possess.

THE LIGHT THAT LURES. By Percy Brebner.

Illustrated.  Handsomely colored wrapper.

A young Southerner who loved Lafayette, goes to France to aid him during the days of terror, and is lured in a certain direction by the lovely eyes of a Frenchwoman.

THE RAMRODDERS.    By Holman Day.    Frontispiece by
Harold Matthews Brett.

A clever, timely story that will make politicians think and will make women realize the part that politics play—even in their romances.

*Ask for complete free list of G. & D. Popular Copyrighted Fiction*

GROSSET & DUNLAP, 526 WEST 26th ST., NEW YORK

# TITLES SELECTED FROM
# GROSSET & DUNLAP'S LIST

May be had wherever books are sold.   Ask for Grosset & Dunlap's list

**A CERTAIN RICH MAN.** By William Allen White.

A vivid, startling portrayal of one man's financial greed, its wide spreading power, its action in Wall Street, and its effect on the three women most intimately in his life. A splendid, entertaining American novel.

**IN OUR TOWN.** By William Allen White. Illustrated by F. R. Gruger and W. Glackens.

Made up of the observations of a keen newspaper editor, involving the town millionaire, the smart set, the literary set, the bohemian set, and many others. All humorously related and sure to hold the attention.

**NATHAN BURKE.** By Mary S. Watts.

The story of an ambitious, backwoods Ohio boy who rose to prominence. Everyday humor of American rustic life permeates the book.

**THE HIGH HAND.** By Jacques Futrelle. Illustrated by Will Grefe.

A splendid story of the political game, with a son of the soil on the one side, and a "kid glove" politician on the other. A pretty girl, interested in both men, is the chief figure.

**THE BACKWOODSMEN.** By Charles G. D. Roberts. Illustrated.

Realistic stories of men and women living midst the savage beauty of the wilderness. Human nature at its best and worst is well protrayed.

**YELLOWSTONE NIGHTS.** By Herbert Quick.

A jolly company of six artists, writers and other clever folks take a trip through the National Park, and tell stories around camp fire at night. Brilliantly clever and original.

**THE PROFESSOR'S MYSTERY.** By Wells Hastings and Brian Hooker. Illustrated by Hanson Booth.

A young college professor, missing his steamer for Europe, has a romantic meeting with a pretty girl, escorts her home, and is enveloped in a big mystery.

---

*Ask for complete free list of G. & D. Popular Copyrighted Fiction*

GROSSET & DUNLAP, 526 WEST 26th ST., NEW YORK

# TITLES SELECTED FROM
# GROSSET & DUNLAP'S LIST

May be had wherever books are sold.   Ask for Grosset & Dunlap's list.

THE SECOND WIFE. By Thompson Buchanan. Illustrated by W. W. Fawcett. Harrison Fisher wrapper printed in four colors and gold.

An intensely interesting story of a marital complication in a wealthy New York family involving the happiness of a beautiful young girl.

TESS OF THE STORM COUNTRY. By Grace Miller White.

Illustrated by Howard Chandler Christy.

An amazingly vivid picture of low class life in a New York college town, with a heroine beautiful and noble, who makes a great sacrifice for love.

FROM THE VALLEY OF THE MISSING. By Grace Miller White.

Frontispiece and wrapper in colors by Penrhyn Stanlaws.

Another story of "the storm country." Two beautiful children are kidnapped from a wealthy home and appear many years after showing the effects of a deep, malicious scheme behind their disappearance.

THE LIGHTED MATCH. By Charles Neville Buck. Illustrated by R. F. Schabelitz.

A lovely princess travels incognito through the States and falls in love with an American man. There are ties that bind her to someone in her own home, and the great plot revolves round her efforts to work her way out.

MAUD BAXTER. By C. C. Hotchkiss. Illustrated by Will Grefe.

A romance both daring and delightful, involving an American girl and a young man who had been impressed into English service during the Revolution.

THE HIGHWAYMAN. By Guy Rawlence. Illustrated by Will Grefe.

A French beauty of mysterious antecedents wins the love of an Englishman of title. Devolopments of a startling character, and a clever untangling of affairs hold the reader's iuterest.

THE PURPLE STOCKINGS. By Edward Salisbury Field.

Illustrated in colors; marginal illustrations.

A young New York business man, his pretty sweetheart, his sentimental stenographer, and his fashionable sister are all mixed up in a misunderstanding that surpasses anything in the way of comedy in years. A story with a laugh on every page.

*Ask for complete free list of G. & D. Popular Copyrighted Fiction*

GROSSET & DUNLAP, 526 WEST 26th ST., NEW YORK

# GROSSET & DUNLAP'S DRAMATIZED NOVELS

Original, sincere and courageous—often amusing—the kind that are making theatrical history.

**MADAME X.** By Alexandre Bisson and J. W. McConaughy. Illustrated with scenes from the play.

A beautiful Parisienne became an outcast because her husband would not forgive an error of her youth. Her love for her son is the great final influence in her career. A tremendous dramatic success.

**THE GARDEN OF ALLAH.** By Robert Hichens.

An unconventional English woman and an inscrutable stranger meet and love in an oasis of the Sahara. Staged this season with magnificent cast and gorgeous properties.

**THE PRINCE OF INDIA.** By Lew. Wallace.

A glowing romance of the Byzantine Empire, presenting with extraordinary power the siege of Constantinople, and lighting its tragedy with the warm underglow of an Oriental romance. As a play it is a great dramatic spectacle.

**TESS OF THE STORM COUNTRY.** By Grace Miller White. Illust. by Howard Chandler Christy.

A girl from the dregs of society, loves a young Cornell University student, and it works startling changes in her life and the lives of those about her. The dramatic version is one of the sensations of the season.

**YOUNG WALLINGFORD.** By George Randolph Chester. Illust. by F. R. Gruger and Henry Raleigh.

A series of clever swindles conducted by a cheerful young man, each of which is just on the safe side of a State's prison offence. As "Get-Rich-Quick Wallingford," it is probably the most amusing expose of money manipulation ever seen on the stage.

**THE INTRUSION OF JIMMY.** By P. G. Wodehouse. Illustrations by Will Grefe.

Social and club life in London and New York, an amateur burglary adventure and a love story. Dramatized under the title of "A Gentleman of Leisure," it furnishes hours of laughter to the play-goers.

GROSSET & DUNLAP, 526 WEST 26th ST., NEW YORK

## TITLES SELECTED FROM
# GROSSET & DUNLAP'S LIST
### REALISTIC, ENGAGING PICTURES OF LIFE.

**THE GARDEN OF FATE.** By Roy Norton. Illustrated by Joseph Clement Coll.

The colorful romance of an American girl in Morocco, and of a beautiful garden, whose beauty and traditions of strange subtle happenings were closed to the world by a Sultan's seal.

**THE MAN HIGHER UP.** By Henry Russell Miller. Full page vignette illustrations by M Leone Bracker.

The story of a tenement waif who rose by his own ingenuity to the office of mayor of his native city. His experiences while "climbing," make a most interesting example of the possibilities of human nature to rise above circumstances.

**THE KEY TO YESTERDAY.** By Charles Neville Buck. Illustrated by R. Schabelitz.

Robert Saxon, a prominent artist, has an accident, while in Paris, which obliterates his memory, and the only clue he has to his former life is a rusty key. What door in Paris will it unlock? He must know that before he woos the girl he loves.

**THE DANGER TRAIL.** By James Oliver Curwood. Illustrated by Charles Livingston Bull.

The danger trail is over the snow-smothered North. A young Chicago engineer, who is building a road through the Hudson Bay region, is involved in mystery, and is led into ambush by a young woman.

**THE GAY LORD WARING.** By Houghton Townley. Illustrated by Will Grefe.

A story of the smart hunting set in England. A gay young lord wins in love against his selfish and cowardly brother and apparently against fate itself.

**BY INHERITANCE.** By Octave Thanet. Illustrated by Thomas Fogarty. Elaborate wrapper in colors.

A wealthy New England spinster with the most elaborate plans for the education of the negro goes to visit her nephew in Arkansas, where she learns the needs of the colored race first hand and begins to lose her theories.

GROSSET & DUNLAP, 526 WEST 26th ST., NEW YORK

# A FEW OF
# GROSSET & DUNLAP'S
# Great Books at Little Prices

**HAPPY HAWKINS.** By Robert Alexander Wason. Illustrated by Howard Giles.

A ranch and cowboy novel. Happy Hawkins tells his own story with such a fine capacity for knowing how to do it and with so much humor that the reader's interest is held in surprise, then admiration, and at last in positive affection.

**COMRADES.** By Thomas Dixon, Jr. Illustrated by C. D. Williams.

The locale of this story is in California, where a few socialists establish a little community.

The author leads the little band along the path of disillusionment, and gives some brilliant flashes of light on one side of an important question.

**TONO-BUNGAY.** By Herbert George Wells.

The hero of this novel is a young man who, through hard work, earns a scholarship and goes to London.

Written with a frankness verging on Rousseau's, Mr. Wells still uses rare discrimination and the border line of propriety is never crossed. An entertaining book with both a story and a moral, and without a dull page—Mr. Wells's most notable achievement.

**A HUSBAND BY PROXY.** By Jack Steele.

A young criminologist, but recently arrived in New York city, is drawn into a mystery, partly through financial need and partly through his interest in a beautiful woman, who seems at times the simplest child and again a perfect mistress of intrigue. A baffling detective story.

**LIKE ANOTHER HELEN.** By George Horton. Illustrated by C. M. Relyea.

Mr. Horton's powerful romance stands in a new field and brings an almost unknown world in reality before the reader—the world of conflict between Greek and Turk on the Island of Crete. The "Helen" of the story is a Greek, beautiful, desolate, defiant—pure as snow.

There is a certain new force about the story, a kind of master-craftsmanship and mental dominance that holds the reader.

**THE MASTER OF APPLEBY.** By Francis Lynde. Illustrated by T. de Thulstrup.

"A novel tale concerning itself in part with the great struggle in the two Carolinas, but chiefly with the adventures therein of two gentlemen who loved one and the same lady.

A strong, masculine and persuasive story.

**A MODERN MADONNA.** By Caroline Abbot Stanley.

A story of American life, founded on facts as they existed some years ago in the District of Columbia. The theme is the maternal love and splendid courage of a woman.

GROSSET & DUNLAP, 526 WEST 26th ST., NEW YORK

# THE NOVELS OF
# GEORGE BARR McCUTCHEON

**GRAUSTARK.**
  A story of love behind a throne, telling how a young American met a lovely girl and followed her to a new and strange country. A thrilling, dashing narrative.

**BEVERLY OF GRAUSTARK.**
  Beverly is a bewitching American girl who has gone to that stirring little principality—Graustark—to visit her friend the princess, and there has a romantic affair of her own.

**BREWSTER'S MILLIONS.**
  A young man is required to spend *one* million dollars in one year in order to inherit *seven*. How he does it forms the basis of a lively story.

**CASTLE CRANEYCROW.**
  The story revolves round the abduction of a young American woman, her imprisonment in an old castle and the adventures created through her rescue.

**COWARDICE COURT.**
  An amusing social feud in the Adirondacks in which an English girl is tempted into being a traitor by a romantic young American, forms the plot.

**THE DAUGHTER OF ANDERSON CROW.**
  The story centers about the adopted daughter of the town marshal in a western village. Her parentage is shrouded in mystery, and the story concerns the secret that deviously works to the surface.

**THE MAN FROM BRODNEY'S.**
  The hero meets a princess in a far-away island among fanatically hostile Musselmen. Romantic love making amid amusing situations and exciting adventures.

**NEDRA.**
  A young couple elope from Chicago to go to London traveling as brother and sister. They are shipwrecked and a strange mix-up occurs on account of it.

**THE SHERRODS.**
  The scene is the Middle West and centers around a man who leads a double life. A most enthralling novel.

**TRUXTON KING.**
  A handsome good natured young fellow ranges on the earth looking for romantic adventures and is finally enmeshed in most complicated intrigues in Graustark.

GROSSET & DUNLAP, 526 WEST 26th ST., NEW YORK

# THE NOVELS OF
# STEWART EDWARD WHITE

**THE RULES OF THE GAME.** Illustrated by Lajaren A. Hiller

The romance of the son of "The Riverman." The young college hero goes into the lumber camp, is antagonized by "graft" and comes into the romance of his life.

**ARIZONA NIGHTS.** Illus. and cover inlay by N. C. Wyeth.

A series of spirited tales emphasizing some phases of the life of the ranch, plains and desert. A masterpiece.

**THE BLAZED TRAIL.** With illustrations by Thomas Fogarty.

A wholesome story with gleams of humor, telling of a young man who blazed his way to fortune through the heart of the Michigan pines.

**THE CLAIM JUMPERS.** A Romance.

The tenderfoot manager of a mine in a lonesome gulch of the Black Hills has a hard time of it, but "wins out" in more ways than one.

**CONJUROR'S HOUSE.** Illustrated Theatrical Edition.

Dramatized under the title of "The Call of the North."

"Conjuror's House is a Hudson Bay trading post where the head factor is the absolute lord. A young fellow risked his life and won a bride on this forbidden land.

**THE MAGIC FOREST.** A Modern Fairy Tale. Illustrated.

The sympathetic way in which the children of the wild and their life is treated could only belong to one who is in love with the forest and open air. Based on fact.

**THE RIVERMAN.** Illus. by N. C. Wyeth and C. Underwood.

The story of a man's fight against a river and of a struggle between honesty and grit on the one side, and dishonesty and shrewdness on the other.

**THE SILENT PLACES.** Illustrations by Philip R. Goodwin.

The wonders of the northern forests, the heights of feminine devotion, and masculine power, the intelligence of the Caucasian and the instinct of the Indian, are all finely drawn in this story.

**THE WESTERNERS.**

A story of the Black Hills that is justly placed among the best American novels. It portrays the life of the new West as no other book has done in recent years.

**THE MYSTERY.** In collaboration with Samuel Hopkins Adams

With illustrations by Will Crawford.

The disappearance of three successive crews from the stout ship "Laughing Lass" in mid-Pacific, is a mystery weird and inscrutable. In the solution, there is a story of the most exciting voyage that man ever undertook.

GROSSET & DUNLAP, 526 WEST 26th ST., NEW YORK

# LOUIS TRACY'S
## CAPTIVATING AND EXHILARATING ROMANCES

May be had wherever books are sold.    Ask for Grosset & Dunlap's list

CYNTHIA'S CHAUFFEUR. Illustrated by Howard Chandler Christy.

A pretty American girl in London is touring in a car with a chauffeur whose identity puzzles her. An amusing mystery.

THE STOWAWAY GIRL. Illustrated by Nesbitt Benson.

A shipwreck, a lovely girl stowaway, a rascally captain, a fascinating officer, and thrilling adventures in South Seas.

THE CAPTAIN OF THE KANSAS.

Love and the salt sea, a helpless ship whirled into the hands of cannibals, desperate fighting and a tender romance.

THE MESSAGE. Illustrated by Joseph Cummings Chase.

A bit of parchment found in the figurehead of an old vessel tells of a buried treasure. A thrilling mystery develops.

THE PILLAR OF LIGHT.

The pillar thus designated was a lighthouse, and the author tells with exciting detail the terrible dilemma of its cut-off inhabitants.

THE WHEEL O'FORTUNE. With illustrations by James Montgomery Flagg.

The story deals with the finding of a papyrus containing the particulars of some of the treasures of the Queen of Sheba.

A SON OF THE IMMORTALS. Illustrated by Howard Chandler Christy.

A young American is proclaimed king of a little Balkan Kingdom, and a pretty Parisian art student is the power behind the throne.

THE WINGS OF THE MORNING.

A sort of Robinson Crusoe *redivivus* with modern settings and a very pretty love story added. The hero and heroine, are the only survivors of a wreck, and have many thrilling adventures on their desert island.

*Ask for complete free list of G. & D. Popular Copyrighted Fiction*

GROSSET & DUNLAP, 526 WEST 26th ST., NEW YORK

# THE NOVELS OF
# WINSTON CHURCHILL

Skillful in plot, dramatic in episode, powerful and original in climax.

MR. CREWE'S CAREER. Illus. by A.I. Keller and Kinneys.

A New England state is under the political domination of a railway and Mr. Crewe, a millionaire, seizes the moment when the cause of the people against corporation greed is being espoused by an ardent young attorney, to further his own interest in a political way, by taking up this cause.

The daughter of the railway president, with the sunny humor and shrewd common sense of the New England girl, plays no small part in the situation as well as in the life of the young attorney who stands so unflinchingly for clean politics.

THE CROSSING. Illus. by S. Adamson and L. Baylis.

Describing the battle of Fort Moultrie and the British fleet in the harbor of Charleston, the blazing of the Kentucky wilderness, the expedition of Clark and his handful of dauntless followers in Illinois, the beginning of civilization along the Ohio and Mississippi, and the treasonable schemes builded against Washington and the Federal Government.

CONISTON. Illustrated by Florence Scovel Shinn.

A deft blending of love and politics distinguishes this book. The author has taken for his hero a New Englander, a crude man of the tannery, who rose to political prominence by his own powers, and then surrendered all for the love of a woman.

It is a sermon on civic righteousness, and a love story of a deep motive.

THE CELEBRITY. An Episode.

An inimitable bit of comedy describing an interchange of personalities between a celebrated author and a bicycle salesman of the most blatant type. The story is adorned with some character sketches more living than pen work. It is the purest, keenest fun—no such piece of humor has appeared for years: it is American to the core.

THE CRISIS. Illus. by Howard Chandler Christy.

A book that presents the great crisis in our national life with splendid power and with a sympathy, a sincerity, and a patriotism that are inspiring. The several scenes in the book in which Abraham Lincoln figures must be read in their entirety for they give a picture of that great, magnetic, lovable man, which has been drawn with evident affection and exceptional success.

GROSSET & DUNLAP, 526 WEST 26TH ST., NEW YORK